# The Brothers McKay

*By Craig Johnson*

*The Longmire Series*

The Cold Dish
Death Without Company
Kindness Goes Unpunished
Another Man's Moccasins
The Dark Horse
Junkyard Dogs
Hell Is Empty
As the Crow Flies
A Serpent's Tooth
Any Other Name
Dry Bones
An Obvious Fact
The Western Star
Depth of Winter
Land of Wolves
Next to Last Stand
Daughter of the Morning Star
Hell and Back
The Longmire Defense
First Frost
Return to Sender

*Also by Craig Johnson*

Spirit of Steamboat (a novella)
Wait for Signs (short stories)
The Highwayman (a novella)
Tooth and Claw (a novella)

*Stand-alone E-stories*

(Also available in *Wait for Signs*)
Christmas in Absaroka County
Divorce Horse
Messenger

Craig Johnson

# The Brothers McKay

Viking

VIKING
An imprint of Penguin Random House LLC
1745 Broadway, New York, NY 10019
penguinrandomhouse.com



Set in Dante MT Std

Library of Congress Cataloging-in-Publication Data

Names: Johnson, Craig, 1961- author
Title: The brothers McKay / Craig Johnson.
Description: New York, NY: Viking, 2026. | Series: Longmire series
Identifiers: LCCN 2026001686 (print) | LCCN 2026001687 (ebook) |
ISBN 9780593830734 hardcover | ISBN 9780593830741 ebook
Subjects: LCGFT: Fiction | Detective and mystery fiction | Novels
Classification: LCC PS3610.O325 B76 2026 (print) | LCC PS3610.O325(ebook)
LC record available at https://lccn.loc.gov/2026001686
LC ebook record available at https://lccn.loc.gov/2026001687

Printed in the United States of America
1st Printing

The authorized representative in the EU for product safety and compliance is Penguin Random House Ireland, Morrison Chambers, 32 Nassau Street, Dublin D02 YH68, Ireland, https://eu-contact.penguin.ie.

*For my wife, Judy*

When reason fails, the devil helps!

—Fyodor Dostoyevsky

People speak sometimes about the bestial cruelty of man, but that is terribly unjust and offensive to beasts, no animal could ever be so cruel as a man, so artfully, so artistically cruel.

—Fyodor Dostoyevsky

# Acknowledgments

An institution in the Johnson family was to always give books on Christmas Eve, which I'm to understand is a long-held tradition in Iceland—*Jolabokaflod*, or the Christmas flood of books. My parents were both voracious readers and I came to it naturally, although my precociousness might've been something of a trial to them—like when I threw a copy of *The Grapes of Wrath* onto our kitchen table and, with all the world-weariness that a thirteen-year-old can muster, informed my mother that she needed to read this book.

I still remember her looking at me and saying, "Honey, I've lived through two world wars and a stock market crash, and don't need to read depressing things."

Evidently, I was still at it a couple of years later when my father dropped a copy of Dostoyevsky's *The Brothers Karamazov* on me for Christmas Eve, all one thousand and fifty-six pages of it. I read it that evening, I read it all that night and the next morning, and the next two days when I finally finished it.

I still remember sitting in his den and him asking me, "What do you think?"

"I think it's one of the most epic theological dramas I've ever read, dealing with free will, morality, spirituality, societal justice, humanity, authority, power, and patricide."

The last part being a dig at him.

Filling up his pipe, he lit it and took a few puffs. "Do you think you understood it?"

"Mostly, but I also think it's one of the worst murder mysteries ever written."

"How so?"

"If you don't know who killed the old man, Fyodor Pavlovich Karamazov, by book eight you're an idiot."

Taking the pipe from his mouth, he considered me. "Did you know that the novel was the first of three, and that Dostoyevsky died four months after finishing it, so he never got the chance to write the other two?"

"No."

Taking the book from me, he leafed through the pages. "Do you remember the courtroom scene in chapter twelve?"

"Yep."

"Do you remember the title?"

"No."

He held it out to me. "The Court Makes a Mistake." "Do you think that Dostoyevsky was trying to tell the reader something, like the character you think did it really didn't do it?"

I took the book from him, staring at the chapter. "Then who did?"

He raised his hands. "We'll never know, will we?"

This conversation has haunted me my whole literary life, so when I heard recently that an eminent Dostoyevsky scholar had undertaken a stab at trying to figure out who really had murdered the patriarch, I knew I had to read it.

Once I had, I knew I had to use it in a Walt Longmire novel.

Restricting myself to the basic plot to avoid writing my own thousand-page novel, I knew it had all the makings of a traditional, red-blooded mystery novel, hence *The Brothers McKay*.

It takes a village to publish a book, and *The Brothers McKay* is no different. First and foremost is my little Gail "Grushenka" Hochman and her righthand woman, Marianne "Katerina" Merola. Over on the other side of the Volga would be head boatman Brian "Pavlovich" Tart and the newly appointed Camille "Alexandrovna" LeBlanc. Next would be the carriage drivers Sara "Ivanovna" DeLozier and Magdalena "Svetlova" Deniz. Posting bills on the St. Basil's Cathedral walls would be Michael "Igor" Brown and Chantal "Verhovtseva" Canales. And where would I be without the dynamic duo of Eric "Fyodorovich" Wechter and Francesca "Agrafena" Drago?

But most of all, thank you to Judy "Lisichka" Johnson, my own little fox.

# The Brothers McKay

# 1

It wasn't so much of a surprise that Pepper McKay was dead as much as it was an amazement to everyone in the county that it had taken so long for him to die, or for somebody to kill him.

My undersheriff, Victoria Moretti, held one of the new two-way radios she'd ordered for the department in an attempt to sell me on the things. "Eight hundred megahertz, which is what the highway patrol, fire departments, and rescue squads are using. It's got the extended battery system so it'll last longer than those pieces of single-band crap we've been using from back when Marconi patched 'em together."

The patriarch of the extended McKay family was not a complicated man but had led a somewhat complex life with business interests that spanned the globe, including but not restricted to the O-Kay Ranch at the mouth of Crazy Woman Canyon in Absaroka County, Wyoming. The original name of the ranch had been the O-Slash-Y outfit and had belonged to the Harris family, who were the first non-Natives born in the county when the territory had become a state.

"It's got an extended tac button, dual speakers, and can have an RSM, not that you'll ever be wearing a microphone on your lapel, you dinosaur."

The O-Slash-Y had been a working cattle ranch during my youth, but as times had changed in the sixties, it had transmogrified into a guest, or dude, ranch where well-heeled left and right coasters had flocked to experience the *authentic* ranch lifestyle. That was how Pepper McKay had been introduced to the O-Slash-Y, or more important, to the heir of its family fortune, Miss BeeBee Harris. Pepper had been married twice before, once annulled and once divorced with a child, whereas BeeBee, to say the most, had not.

"It's got Bluetooth and GPS."

I looked at her. "Did you just say that newfangled radio has blue teeth?"

She stared at me as we sat there in the long line of vehicles, waiting for the WYDOT crew and construction workers to give us our turn at heading south on the Old Highway 87 that ran alongside the interstate, partially closed because of a grass fire. "Something like that." She fiddled with the device some more. "See these two knobs here on top?"

"Yep."

"You twist the one on the right to turn it on."

"That's all I need to know?"

"We're going to start slow on your training." She slumped back in her seat, staring at the long line of cars ahead of us. "So, this Pepper McKay basically screwed BeeBee to get the ranch?"

"Well, I don't think that was the official policy . . ."

"So, he's not from here?"

"No."

"Children?"

"Three sons, and maybe a half."

"A half?"

"I'll get to that." I inched my truck forward. "The eldest is David at about forty. He's probably the most like the old man and is from the previous wife. Both Pepper and David are or were given to carousing, gambling, and drinking as a career. David did a stint in the army and even got corralled by the CIA from what I'm to understand, but got the boot when his indiscretions caught up with him. I think he was working as a security consultant down in Texas, but I'm not sure."

Victoria Moretti placed the new radio on the seat between us, rolled the window down, and leaned her head out to check on our progress. "You can smell the smoke." Pulling her head back in, she added, "And the other two?"

"BeeBee's two sons, Ian in his late thirties and Alan in his early thirties. Ian's an interesting young man, a journalist who works for the *High Plains Bulletin*."

"The newspaper blog thing?"

"I guess. Ruby prints out articles she thinks might interest me, and Cady quotes from it sometimes."

"And Alan?"

"He's a monk."

"Excuse me." She stared at me with her tarnished gold eyes. "Did you just say a monk?"

"I did, the Saint Benedict's Monastery here in Wyoming."

"Get out of here."

I smiled. "Over near Meeteetse; it's a beautiful place and they're building a Gothic cathedral."

"In Meeteetse, Wyoming?"

The cars in the opposite lane passed, and as the pilot car circled around in front of us, we started moving forward and I joined the pack. "You might want to close that window unless you want the smell of burned grass and sagebrush filling up the truck."

"It would be better than the smell of Dog." She did as I said, leaning back and scratching the beast's head just to make sure he understood there were no odiferous bad feelings. "A monastery, honestly?"

"Started at the turn of the century, the most recent one, through the Cheyenne diocese. They grow and grind their own coffee and even have a cattle herd."

"That's weird."

I shrugged. "Why? It's an atmosphere of natural solitude, a wild and remote environment of geological enclosure that's separated from the world, providing a secluded life of contemplation and prayer."

"Is that from the brochure?" She laughed. "You sound like a convert."

"I thought about it."

She looked at me. "The hell you say?"

"Yep, after Martha died, I went over and met with the Elder bishop, Elder Zebrowski, and we discussed it."

We watched out the window as the big bulldozers and graders pushed some of the still smoldering brush into a pile. "But speaking as a lapsed Catholic, you're not."

"Not what?"

"Catholic."

"Yep, that came up. That, and the fact that the bishop thought that I might've seen and done a little too much to be satisfied by a simple life of contemplative prayer."

"I have a hard time seeing you as a monk with the whole hermit, poverty, and chastity thing . . . Especially the chastity part."

"Thanks."

"So what is Alan doing out here in the real world?"

"The same elder within the monastery, Father Zebrowski, decided he needed a little sabbatical seasoning in the world and couldn't think of a more seasoned group than Alan's own family."

Driving around the waiting vehicles, I drew alongside, recognizing the commander of the National Interagency Fire Center. "Wow, this must be one heck of a grass fire for them to send down the head muckety-muck."

The blond-haired man with a beard and green hard hat covered in stickers ambled over and leaned his elbows on the door of my truck. "Just waiting to get through, the same as you."

I gestured toward Vic. "J. R. Rose, meet my second-in-command, Victoria Moretti."

Rose reached across me and shook hands with my undersheriff before glancing down between us. "Is that one of those new APXs?"

I interrupted. "Where are you headed?"

He looked over the top of my truck toward the mountain. "You've got a red flag up there."

"First I've heard of it."

"Started last night with a lightning strike: two of 'em. We've got a bunch of smoke jumpers, fire engine crews, fire managers, and aerial observers coming in, but right now we're locating the exact position of the two fires, measuring the rate of spread, assessing their futures, and ranking them against the other forty-seven fires we've got going in the district."

"Busy time of year."

"You can say that again."

"Why didn't anybody call me?"

Leaning back at arm's length, he peered again over the roof of my truck. "We were waiting to see what the terrain looked like, both sites are near Highway 16, but it gets kind of rugged in there."

"Did you say you had smoke jumpers?"

"On standby over in Greybull, but they aren't too keen on jumping into forested areas where there are a lot of cliffs."

"I can understand that." Putting the truck back into gear, I gave him a salute. "Keep me informed, Commander."

He saluted back. "Will do."

Moving back onto the road, I headed south, taking a right at Crazy Woman Canyon Road.

"And?"

"And what?"

"The half son?"

"Oh, that. Well, a lot of it is rumor but, according to Henry, the young man who's the head wrangler at the ranch, Manx Henenoka, is Pepper's illegitimate son, the product of a tryst with a Shoshone cook who used to work there before she died. Pepper never took responsibility for the kid, and he grew up half wild, except for the guidance of the ranch foreman, Gary Lyman, and his wife, Lynn, who basically raised him to be one of the best trackers in the state."

"What do you think?"

Driving on the gravel road that meandered beside the North Fork of Crazy Woman Creek, I pointed past the corrals toward the mouth of the canyon that led into the Bighorn Mountains and the elaborate structure perched on the right. "There it is, the historic O-Kay Lodge."

"Wow."

It was impressive. A log structure that had been built at the turn of the century, the previous one, it had a lone tower offset by a great hall and porches and balconies aplenty. I don't think there was a log in the thing that was any less than thirty inches in circumference, and the river-rock work was so abundant that I was surprised there were any left in Crazy Woman Creek.

"The Harris family were some of the first whites in the county and established a logging concern that eventually provided lumber for everyone along the front range of the Rocky Mountains. Then they expanded into mineral rights and became even richer, moving the majority of their operations into Idaho, but they always kept this place as their original home. I knew the granddaughter, BeeBee, who was the one who transformed it into a resort, or dude ranch; I think mostly for tax purposes."

"Then got swept off her feet by Pepper?"

We wound our way up the mountain road, popping a few elk from the brush and watching them disappear into the surrounding forest. Turning a corner, we stopped before crossing an ancient log bridge and found a Wyoming Highway Patrol unit.

We parked and got out and headed over to where two men stood near the banks of Crazy Woman Creek. "And now Pepper McKay's dead?" Vic asked.

"So they say, but I'm sure there will be more than a few folks who'll want to stick a needle into him to make sure." I looked down the bank where a body was covered with a plastic tarp.

A young HP, whom I didn't know, was standing to the side talking with Gary Lyman, who was openly weeping. "I honestly didn't know what to do, I mean, the body was going to wash away and I just couldn't let that happen."

The patrolman turned to look at me. "They moved the body."

I placed a hand on the older man's shoulder. "It's okay, Gary, just tell me what happened?"

Taking out a bandanna, he wiped his face and then blew his broad nose loudly before speaking. "He was fishing. Lynn made him sandwiches and a lunch early this morning before breakfast, but in the afternoon, I was getting a little worried and couldn't see him at any of his favorite holes, and thought I should go check on him." He gestured toward the stream. "I went up but didn't see any tracks, so I came down this way. He sometimes liked to sit on the bridge and eat his lunch . . ." The emotion began overtaking him again and he swallowed. "I looked down and there he was, floating face down."

"What'd you do?"

"I wasn't thinking, I just dragged him on the bank, where he is now, and called you."

I patted his shoulder again. "Why don't you go to the house and call 911 requesting a medical transport of the body to Durant Memorial. Can you do that for me?"

"Sure, sure . . . I just can't believe he's dead."

I watched the older man start up the road to a four-by-four before asking the HP with an extended goatee, "How'd you get here, Troop?"

The young man shrugged. "I was working the fire down below and heard the radio call and figured you'd get slowed down and thought I'd lend a hand." He stuck his out. "Shane Wilson, I took Wes Roger's post."

We shook. "Good to meet you, Officer Wilson. I'm Walt Longmire."

"I figured, just make it Shane."

Vic breezed past us and began descending the bank toward the body. "That officer that so cavalierly walked past is my undersheriff, Victoria Moretti."

He called after her. "Pleased to meet you."

We both looked down at the body as Vic knelt and uncovered it, peeling back a lid to expose one of Pepper's trademark jade-colored eyes. "He's dead."

"Well, if he's not he's doing a hell of an impression." I turned back to the HP. "Anything suspicious?"

"He'd been drinking."

"Did you know Pepper McKay?"

"Some."

"Well, in the forty years I've known him, he's always been drinking." We started down the embankment to the shelf that led to the concrete abutment of the bridge. "How could you tell?"

"The smell, but then I saw a flattened flask in his vest pocket."

"Anything else?"

"There was a Hardy 5-weight rod broke in half, maybe that's what killed him. I know if I broke one it would kill me."

Vic rolled the body on its side and examined the back of the head with a more than passing interest. "TBI, if I was making a guess."

The young officer glanced at me.

"Traumatic brain injury." I studied the discolored portion at the base of the man's skull. "Diffused?"

She laid him back on the ground. "Yep."

"A rock?"

"Most likely or maybe a tree branch. Hell, I don't know, maybe a trout jumped up and smacked him in the back of the head." She resumed studying the man. "Handsome booger, wasn't he?"

"Yep, or so the ladies tell me."

"Pepper McKay, he cut a pretty wide swath around these parts," said the patrolman. "I had to get him out of a little jam down near Powder Junction about a week ago."

"What was that?"

"Oh, there was a young woman he took a shine to and was helping her with a flat tire when Boris Agirra happened by."

"The one that owns Powder River Auto Repair?"

"Yeah, she had called him, but then Pepper got there and they got into it."

"Boris have his son, Charlie, with him?"

"The sick one, yeah—as far as I know he never goes anywhere without him. How do you know about little Charlie?"

"There was a leukemia fundraiser for him . . . How is he doing?"

"Okay, from what I hear. Not great, but okay," said the patrolman. "Pepper had a gun out when I pulled up, and it's probably a good thing he did because I'm pretty sure that if I hadn't stumbled upon them, that old Basquo would've stuffed him into a culvert."

Vic lifted the edge of the dead man's vest. "He's got a Sig 9 millimeter on him now."

I nodded. "I think he went armed pretty much everywhere." I gazed over at the HP. "How old was the girl he was making the moves on?"

"Eighteen."

I studied the body. "Yep, that's Pepper's MO all right."

"Multiple abrasions and contusions, but those could've been received postmortem." Vic pulled on his shoulder again. "He's heavy."

"Meaning?"

"His lungs are full of water."

"He drowned?"

"Possibly he was still breathing when he went in or rolled over in the water. Diffuse injuries to the brain are tricky and sometimes lead to coma or a vegetative state."

Gary Lyman reappeared at the bridge with a young man at his side, who I recognized as Manx Henenoka. "He dead?"

I stood, looking at the twentysomething in hiking boots, jeans, a flannel shirt, battered cowboy hat, mirrored sunglasses, and at what seemed to be a holstered S&W M&P .45 caliber. "It would appear."

He took a sip from the battered Kum & Go travel mug he was holding. "Hmm."

"You don't seem too torn up about it."

"I'm not." He took a few steps, sliding down to join us. "He was loaded this morning, and I reminded him that he'd dunked himself yesterday." He looked at the stream, tossing his dark hair back from his print-model face and taking off the glasses to reveal startling green eyes. "Even with the minimal water flow, there's a lot of moss, and he never watched where he was going."

"Any idea where it might've happened?"

He gazed upstream again. "That way, somewhere . . . Bodies don't generally swim upstream."

"Have a lot of experience with bodies?"

"A little."

"Maybe you could show me a few of his favorite spots?"

He stared at me. "I'm kind of busy."

"So am I."

Without another word, he turned and began working his way along the bank.

Glancing back at Vic, I started after the young man. "You two stay here and wait for the transport; I'll be back in a bit."

Following Manx, I watched as he rounded a corner in the babbling brook and then stopped, pointing a finger toward the other side of the stream where a large patch of moss had been scraped away.

I caught up with him and studied the spot. "Might've been where the body rubbed against it before continuing on down to the bridge."

He took a sip from the travel mug. "I'm just pointing out anything unusual."

"I appreciate that, but there's nothing disturbed adjacent to that spot, and if he fell, he would've had to have gotten over there."

"He was wearing waders."

"Yep, but do you see anything disturbed under the water surface?"

He said nothing and shrugged, continuing on.

We'd worked our way another fifty yards when we came to a grassy area that led down from the massive lodge, where a couple of Adirondack chairs sat on either side of a rustic table with several empty bottles and beer cans lying about.

Catching me noticing, Manx called back. "Breakfast."

Continuing to shadow, I caught up with him as we traced our way along the bank. "Any idea why he drank so much?"

The young man shrugged. "Because he was a prick?"

I had to smile. "You two didn't get along very well, did you?"

After a moment, he stopped, staring into the fast-moving water. "Does it show?"

"A bit." I stood there for a moment, letting him have a little time. "How long have you worked here, Manx?"

"My whole life."

"How old were you when Maya Noota died?"

"You remember my mother?"

"I do."

"I don't." He let out a deep sigh. "In answer to your question, I was four."

"You didn't have any other family?"

"She came from an extended family, but they were religious, and their religion didn't extend to forgiving their daughter for being raped by him."

"Pepper."

"She was seventeen and he was forty-four." He turned to face me. "If it wasn't for Gary and Lynn, I probably would've been raised by wolves, which wouldn't have been that much different from being raised by Pepper."

"David, Ian, and Alan seem to be all right."

"You think?"

"Well, I can't say I know them very well."

He didn't say anything.

I joined him, looking across the banks toward a road that connected to a barn and corrals and finally the main road that led into Crazy Woman Canyon, the water spilling from the glaciers above, on its way to the Powder River. "I guess they'll be coming in, after all this."

"They're already here."

I turned to look at him. "All three?"

"Yeah, they had some kind of big family meeting last night. Ian was the latest, drove in from Denver yesterday. David came in from Idaho and he's been here a week, and Alan came in a few days ago."

"Do they know?"

"About what?"

"About their father being dead?"

"I don't know, I haven't told them."

He headed up the bank as I stood there, a little surprised when he stopped again, raising a finger to indicate a large rock at the center of the stream. Moving closer, I could see where the moss was scoured off the downstream side and where a number of the smaller rocks surrounding it had been disturbed.

Manx knelt to look at the area. "Yeah, he could've fallen here and hit the back of his head on the same rock." He looked downstream. "If he was unconscious, he could've rolled over down in that big tub at the bend and drowned."

"You heard Vic talking?"

"I did." He stood. "There's only one problem."

"What's that?"

"There's two sets of boot prints in there."

---

My second-in-command gave me a sideways squint. "You think somebody actually killed him?"

"I don't know, but we're going to have to get the Division of Criminal Investigation's mobile crime lab here and find out."

"Woody Woodson and the Mystery Mobile?"

I thought about the DCI director's propensity toward anything to do with fish. "Well, the crime involves fly-fishing, so it'll probably pique his interest."

"So, we're doing the notification of kin, I presume?" We watched as they loaded Pepper McKay's waterlogged body in the van. "That and the first series of interviews when the brothers get back."

"No, I figured we'd go ahead and interview Manx, Gary, and Lynn."

I watched as a smile crept upon Vic's lips. "Where are the brothers?"

"According to Gary, David is visiting a lady friend in Sheridan and Ian and Alan are at the library in Durant."

"So, we're just waiting around for them until they show up?"

"For now." As the van drove away her smile broadened. "Do you mind if I ask why you're smiling?"

"Do you suppose there's a study, where we can interview the suspects?"

"They're not really suspects."

"The hell they're not. We've got a dead guy and two sets of prints." She moved over to the bridge railing, turned, and leaned back, tipping her head to catch a few rays. "I've always wanted to have an investigation that was one of those murder mysteries dealing with an eccentric family, a Gothic background . . ."

I glanced up at the lodge. "I'm not sure I would call the place Gothic."

"Sure it is, logs and stone, and I bet there's a study. Can we interview the suspects in the study?"

"Colonel Mustard in the library with the wrench?" I took out my pocket watch and checked the time. "Well, let's go see if we can find one, huh?"

"Colonel Mustard or the wrench?"

Slipping my watch back in the pocket of my jeans, I headed for the main house. "Anthony E. Pratt."

Catching up with me, she shook her head. "Who is Anthony E. Pratt?"

"The guy who invented the game."

"This is when you tell me the history of the board game Clue."

"Nope."

She seemed genuinely disappointed. "Why not?"

I stopped, turning to look at her. "The game's original name was Murder! and then Cluedo."

"What the hell does that mean?"

"A combination of words, *clue* and the Latin *ludo*, for *I play*." As we continued along the slope and around the bend toward the house, I held forth. "Pratt and his wife are the ones that came up with the idea while hiding in his house during the air raids of World War II. They thought a board game based on all those parlor murder games might be entertaining and applied for a patent in 1944. A company called Waddingtons bought it, and so did Parker Brothers in the US, which shortened the name to Clue."

"So, the original was British?"

"Imagine that?" I kept walking as she caught me. "There was a rage there for cozies and other types of murder mysteries, mostly based on the popularity of Agatha Christie's novels and plays."

"We had the board game when I was growing up back in Philadelphia, but then I remember playing it again on a lark while I was at the academy, and I think it was slightly different?"

"It's essentially unchanged, but it's gone through a lot of versions with characters, rooms, and weapons being added." We stopped at the path that led to the lodge. "But the original was six characters, six weapons, and nine rooms, enabling three hundred and twenty-four permutations."

Vic studied the massive lodge. "I'm betting this place has more than nine rooms."

"It does, but the debut game was said to be based on the Tudor Close Hotel in Sussex."

She barked a laugh.

"What?"

Shaking her head, she moved on. "The shit in your head . . ."

I followed her up the walk and onto the expansive porch with more twig, willow, and Adirondack furniture, where a handsome older woman sat, with a newspaper folded on her lap, sipping what looked to be tea. "Lynn, I'm sorry to interrupt your down-time."

She turned to look at us with a sad but beatific smile. "Hello, Walt."

I pulled out a seat for Vic and myself. "How have you been?"

"Better." She sighed, sniffing the air. "Seems like the world is on fire, and now this."

"Do you mind if we ask you a few questions?"

She sat her cup in the saucer on the craft table. "I would imagine you have to."

"This is my undersheriff, Victoria Moretti." They shook hands and I explained. "It's just preliminary interviews to establish a timeline on Pepper's death."

She cringed at the word. "So, he is dead?"

"Yep, I don't think there's any question about that." I sat back in the chair, listening to it squeal in protest. "When was the first time you saw Pepper this morning?"

She sat still for a moment, generally something most people don't do when they're being spoken to by law enforcement, unless they want a lawyer. "He had told me he wanted a lunch for his fishing this morning and I know how picky he can be about it, so rather than make it last night, I just got up at around five. I heard him stumbling around in the mudroom in the back, where we keep the private fishing gear, and brought his lunch to him. He was talking to himself."

"You're sure he was alone?"

"Well, he talks to himself all the time."

"You mentioned stumbling around?"

She grew silent again, but then finally spoke. "He'd been drinking."

Vic shook her head. "At five in the morning?"

"I think he was drunk from last night and I can't be sure that he'd slept at all; he certainly didn't look it."

"Was that the last time you saw him?"

She turned back toward me. "Yes."

"Did you see anybody else this morning?"

"My husband, Gary, and then Manx."

"And when was that?"

"About a half hour later in the kitchen, I fixed breakfast for both of them."

"So, five-thirty?"

"I think so."

"When they left where did they go?"

She studied me, quiet again. "Walt, surely you don't think . . . ?"

"I'm just trying to get an accountability for everyone, for their protection as well as everyone else's."

She studied me for a bit longer. "Gary went to our office and then Manx went out the back."

"Toward Crazy Woman Creek?"

She sighed. "Yes."

I leaned forward in my chair, speaking quietly. "Have Pepper and Manx been having any difficulties lately?"

"Lately?" She laughed and then covered her mouth with a hand as if to capture the sound. "You mean beyond the last twenty-two years?"

"Manx didn't seem very torn up about Pepper's passing."

"Do you honestly think anybody in the county will be?"

I glanced at Vic, silent for a moment before asking the next question. "Lynn, would you mind if I ask what your and Gary's relationship was like with the man?"

"Pepper?"

"Yep."

"He pays us, and we worked for him."

"You originally worked for the Harris family, didn't you?"

For the first time she genuinely smiled. "Are you asking me that question, Walt Longmire?"

I smiled back, just glad to have something the two of us could smile about. "I seem to remember a New Year's Eve party a number of years ago . . ."

"That's the only time I ever remember seeing you drunk."

I could feel the color rushing into my face. "I've been told that I was pretty inebriated that particular night."

Lynn smiled at Vic. "He tried to wrestle Bart, the taxidermy grizzly bear in the study."

My undersheriff guffawed. "Tell me more."

"Then he wrestled with the suit of armor in the main hall, claiming it was . . . let me see if I've got this right . . . Sir Simon?"

Peeking through my fingers, I gave out with a half-hearted explanation. "The Canterville Ghost, from a novella by Oscar Wilde."

Vic shook her head in newfound admiration. "Wrestling both a bear and a ghost in one night; that must've been one hell of a drunk."

Lynn laid a hand on my undersheriff's arm. "Martha had to drive him home."

Attempting to change the subject, I asked again. "This working relationship with Pepper . . ."

The smile faded but she was quick to answer. "We disliked him in the extreme."

The smile on Vic's lips lingered. "But not enough to kill him, I'm assuming?"

"There have been moments." Lynn's voice wavered a bit before continuing. "I'm just trying to be honest here. You can't live with someone like that for as long as we have and not want to kill them."

"Then why did you stay?"

The older woman looked at her. "Oh, young woman, you don't understand how life can be when you find yourself in a rut, a rut that becomes your life. Gary and I were so happy here when the Harris family owned the place, and we've always held to the thought that we'd be happy again." She cleared her throat. "It's not as bad as I'm making it sound. He's not been here all that often, but when he was, it's just been a living hell."

"In what way?"

"The carousing, drinking, and financial situation has always been precarious to say the least, but lately it's been worse, and he's threatened to sell the place every time he's here."

"How's the business been?"

"Wonderful, hasn't ever been better. We had a profile piece in *The Wall Street Journal* and the *Los Angeles Times* two years ago and the people have just flocked here. We've got a waiting list that's over five pages long."

Vic looked around. "But you're closed now?"

"I'm sorry, I keep forgetting that you're not from here." The hand on the arm, again. The dude ranch season generally runs from Memorial Day through Labor Day, especially in places as remote and with the altitude of this one."

"What happens in the offseason?"

"Not a great deal, we're in the process of winding down now, shipping the horses south to winter pasture and keeping at the general maintenance, which is quite a job in itself for a place this large."

"Don't you run a sizable herd of cattle too?"

Turning to me, she nodded her head. "We do, always have. Pepper hated the cattle business, but with the irrigated pastureland we have, it was either lease it out or use it. Besides, it gave Manx something to do year-round."

"Hard work."

"You'd know, wouldn't you?"

I waved her off. "Oh, I've kind of let my grandfather's place go to seed."

"I heard you were fixing it up."

Amazing how quickly word got around in open spaces. I eased back in my chair. "Slow going on a municipal salary, but I guess the guilt finally got to me."

"Us too." She gazed around at the idyllic surroundings. "No one seems to appreciate the place as much as Gary and me, so I guess we've always felt obliged."

"How about the sons?"

"David loves the place, but it's awfully remote, and it's kind of the same situation with Ian working down in Denver, and then there's Alan . . ."

"What about Alan?"

She started to speak, stopped, and then began again. "He's not really of this world."

Vic smiled. "Sounds like a monk."

"It's more than that, he's always been like that—the peacemaker."

"Is there a lot of trouble between the brothers?"

"No, but a great deal between them and their father."

"Were any of the McKay brothers here last night?"

"All of them."

"And were any of their whereabouts accounted for this morning?"

"If you're asking if any of them were awake at that hour, the answer is only one. Alan always rises early when he visits, and he has a schedule of prayer and meditation on the back deck, beginning at six when the weather allows."

"Then what?"

"He usually has breakfast with me after the men have gone their way."

"Just the two of you?"

She shrugged. "He's the baby and has always been a favorite."

"What about the other two?"

"Ian was up by seven and had coffee with us before the two of them left for Durant and the library."

Vic interrupted. "Why the library?"

"Ian needed to do some research for an article he's writing for the *High Plains Bulletin*, and he seemed to think that what he was looking for wouldn't be in the library here or on the internet."

"And when did they leave?"

"Around nine o'clock. I think Ian wanted to be there when they opened."

"What about David?"

"I don't think Master David has seen the close side of revelry since he was discharged from the army three years ago. I'm not sure when he roused himself, but he usually wanders down and fixes himself something—that is, if he's alone."

"Meaning?"

"David is very popular with the local female gentry."

"Was there anyone else here?"

"Not that I'm aware of, but one never knows."

I broke eye contact with her and looked out at the gentle slope leading out and into the Powder River Country. "Lynn, I seem to recall that Manx has had a few run-ins with my deputy down in Powder Junction, Double-Tough?"

"He's high-spirited, Walt. There have been a few instances, but I don't think anything of any consequence."

"I hate to disagree with you, but I think there might've been an aggravated assault charge and criminal battery, two of them that I know of offhand."

"There was an instance at the rodeo in Powder Junction, but you know how these things are, Walt. Somebody says something about an Indian, somebody says something back and things escalate pretty quick, and then once the dust settles, it's always the Indian who ends up in trouble."

"That doesn't particularly sound like Double-Tough."

"Well, I'd imagine that the damage had already been done by the time he arrived." She hugged herself and shuddered. "You should've seen him when they let him out and he got home. It's a wonder to me that he survived a beating like that at all."

"And you don't think an instance such as that was of any consequence?"

She lifted her teacup, taking a sip and avoiding my eye. "I've felt as though they're my boys, Walt, all of them. Ever since they were children, I've been the only mother they've ever had. Maybe not so much with David since he was a little older when we got him, but Gary has taken him under his wing and he's a fine young man. They're all fine young men, and none of them a murderer."

"Lynn, I'm not sure if I've been clear but so far—there hasn't been a murder. Whenever someone like Pepper dies there are going to be a lot of questions, and we just want to make sure we've got the answers." I stood and walked toward the porch railing to our right, looking out at the moving water of Crazy Woman Creek that had taken Pepper McKay's life. "I'm going to need to speak with all of those quasi sons of yours, but I think I can still catch Alan and Ian at the library. Would you make sure that when David returns he knows that I need to speak with him?"

She stood as Vic joined me. "I will."

"And at the risk of sounding overly dramatic, I'll need you, Gary, and Manx to not leave the ranch here."

"Surely you're joking."

"I'm afraid not. Until I get a preliminary autopsy from DCI on the condition of Pepper's body, I'll still need to treat this as a potential homicide."

"Good Lord."

"It's just standard procedure. Everything was simple until we found that second set of prints where the incident might've happened, but now we'll have to look into it. Needless to say, we don't want anybody going near that area or any other area that Pepper might've been in until the DCI investigators have a look around."

She walked toward me. "Manx has the horses all loaded in the trailer and is supposed to leave today for Patagonia, Arizona."

"That can't happen."

"I don't know what we can do to keep that from happening."

"You better, because if you leave it to me, I'll be sending out an APB with the Wyoming Highway Patrol for his arrest on sight, and I guarantee he'll never make it out of the state."

She cocked her head in surprise. "You wouldn't do that."

"Yes, ma'am, I will."

She stood there for a moment more and then went over and collected her teacup, saucer, and newspaper, starting for the door but then stopping to look back at me. "You know, I can't help but think that more than just a little of this is personal, Walt."

We watched as she continued inside, the slapping of one of the screen doors a final punctuation to her statement.

Vic took a few steps after her and then looked at me. "Wow, way to finesse her." She leaned to one side, peeking through the screen. "Now I'm never going to get to see the study or the grizzly bear you wrestled."

I stepped off the porch and headed toward my truck back at the bridge, making it to the walkway before she caught up.

"So?"

"So what?"

"C'mon." She stopped there on the walkway as I kept going. "Walt!"

I turned to look at her. "What?"

"What's all this about the situation with Pepper being personal?"

Stuffing my hands in the pockets of my jeans, I stood there huffing a sigh and thinking about a New Year's Eve many, many years ago. "It might have something to do with him trying to rape my wife."

# 2

"Pepper McKay raped your wife?"

"He tried." I inched forward with the rest of traffic, waiting to get past the remains of the fire and finally reaching down to move my seat belt far enough aside to pull out my pocket watch. "Shouldn't this work crew be finishing by now?"

"Tried?"

I studied the long line of cars ahead of us and then the mountains, smelling the smoke and gauging how much light there was left in the day. "I didn't find out about it until much later, and Martha made me swear that I wouldn't do anything."

"So, is this a confession?"

I stared at the blackened vegetation by the road.

"C'mon, that was funny."

Re-pocketing my watch, I inched ahead some more. "There was a friend of ours who advised her not to tell me because I'd likely kill him."

"Sound advice. Who was that?"

"Lucian."

"Wait, the voice of discretion, ex-Absaroka County Sheriff Lucian "Shoot 'em All and Let God Sort 'em Out" Connally?"

"Hard to believe, huh?" I let out a deep sigh, hoping that the cask-strength, double-distilled vintage anger wouldn't overtake me. "Like any ambush predator, Pepper picked his time carefully, or maybe it was just an unlucky coincidence."

"Was this before or after wrestling the bear?"

I had to smile, in that it actually was funny. "I wasn't conscious, but they tell me it took four of them to carry me out to my truck. I guess Martha needed to go to the bathroom and Pepper told her about some redecorating they'd done on the second floor and that she could use the bathroom there and give him her opinion on the decor."

"Come up and see my etchings?"

"Something like that." The pilot car circled in front of us and we started off and around the resurfacing. As we pulled out, I could see the young HP, Shane Wilson, sitting in his unit talking to the flag woman.

I pulled to the side and called him over to my window with a wave. "Hey, what's the word on the two fires up the mountain?"

He squinted in that direction. "There's a fire on Sisters Hill, and the spotters say they're seeing smoke down the draw from Poison Creek. I guess it started after that lightning storm the other night."

"That's what J. R. Rose said . . . anything I need to worry about?"

"I don't think so, supposedly they've got it under control, but you know what they say—where there's smoke . . ."

"There's smoke. Well, I hope they're right." Rolling the window back up, I smiled at him. "Be careful out there."

"Roger that."

Pulling away, I flicked my fingers at him, and he waved back. "In answer to your question, I guess Lucian was the first one to notice that Pepper and Martha were taking an awfully long time and climbed the stairs to check on her."

"And?"

"He found them in a bedroom adjacent to the master bathroom." As the pilot car drove back in the other direction, I headed north. "Lucian never has come forward with the details, but Martha's dress was torn at the shoulder and Pepper had a bloody nose."

"Good for him."

"Her."

She shrugged. "Even better."

"I guess Lucian ushered her out and had her stay at the top of the stairs while he went and got her coat, but when he got back, she and Pepper were having a continuation of the argument on the landing. Lucian helped Martha get her coat on and then brought her downstairs, walking her out to the truck and helping her in before driving us home."

"And?"

"I woke up in the bed of my truck the next morning, about to freeze to death. I saw Lucian's unit parked there in front of the rented house we had and stumbled in to find him and her drinking coffee and talking quietly at the kitchen table—they stopped when I came in and sat down."

"They didn't tell you?"

"Not for twelve years."

"How did you find out?"

Driving past the new high school, I headed for the new library and considered how much my little part of the world was changing, or maybe it was the lack of change in me. "Martha finally told me, and only under the condition that I do nothing."

"Did you?"

Driving down Main, I took a left and passed our offices in the old Carnegie building behind the courthouse and then took a right past the bank and into the parking lot of the library, slipping in beside a Dodge three-quarter ton with the O-Kay brand painted on the doors. "Did I what?"

"Do nothing?"

I cut the motor and climbed out. "Define *nothing.*"

The new library was a thing to behold, with rows and rows of books, a special collection room where I'd donated the original county jail logbook, a children's section, an event room, and a front desk that would've looked more at home in a Hyatt Regency hotel.

Walking through the sliding glass doors with Vic in hot pursuit, I cut off the would-be conversation by waving at the library director, Lindsay Belliveau. "Hey, Lin, have you got any McKays in the place?"

She smiled. "Two of them in the special collections room right now. You want me to go in and flush 'em out?"

I leaned against the counter as she smiled at my second-in-command. "Hi, Vic."

"Hi, Lin."

"Anybody else in there with them?"

She turned back to me. "No, why?"

"I just think the conversation I'm about to have with them might be better if it was somewhat private."

"Close the door and flip the sign and I'll tell everyone it's not available at the moment."

I waved again and walked toward the inner sanctum, passing the counter and moving toward the glass door to the right. Allowing Vic to go first, I nodded at the two young men at one of the library tables surrounded by stacks of books.

Vic moved to one side as I closed the door behind me and flipped the sign that read PRIVATE. "Ian, Alan, how are you?"

The one in the corduroy jacket and wavy hair stood, smiling and extending a hand, the green eyes on high-bright behind thick glasses. "Walt Longmire, how the hell are you?"

"I'm good." I gestured toward Vic, still standing by the door. "This is my undersheriff, Victoria Moretti."

They both smiled.

"How goes the revolution, Ian?"

We shook. "Better if you were on our side."

"But I am."

He continued to smile. "Maybe it's our fault then."

I glanced down at the other young man with the same green eyes, and the shaved head of the novice—I couldn't remember what the hairstyle was called—and the robed cassock as he stood and took my hand with less vigor but the same amount of conviviality. "Alan, how are you?"

"Doing very well, Sheriff. How's your daughter, Cady?"

I'd forgotten that the two of them knew each other rather than just gone to school together—Cady would've been older. "She's fine, she's back here in Wyoming."

"Really?"

"Yep, living in Cheyenne at the present."

Ian, not one to miss much, studied the closed door. "Something up?"

I gave Vic a quick look and then pulled out a chair. "Fellows, you might want to sit down."

They did as I asked and glanced at each other and then back at me as I took off my hat and sat it on one of the stacks of books. "I've got some bad news . . ."

"Dad's dead."

I looked at Alan. "Um, yes, he is. Do you mind telling me how you knew that?"

"I spoke with him this morning and he was just acting kind of strange, and I was thinking that maybe I should stay with him."

"You spoke with your father this morning?"

"Yes, briefly, out on the deck, where I do my morning meditation and prayers."

"He seemed strange, how?"

"Just sad. You know, depressed, but I didn't think he was suicidal."

I stared at him. "Suicidal?"

"Is that what it was, did he commit suicide?"

I leaned forward in my chair. "He drowned, as near as we can tell. There's a traumatic blow to the back of the head and we're thinking he might've slipped and hit his head on a rock, knocked himself unconscious, and then drowned."

I turned to Ian. "Did you see your father this morning?"

"No, I didn't but I saw him late last night."

"And what kind of condition was he in?"

"Drunk."

"Did he seem depressed?"

"No, but then he was always less likely to confide in me the way he does with the father confessor here."

Alan shook his head. "You're sure he's dead?"

I raised an eyebrow. "You're the second person to ask that."

"Who was the first?"

"Gary Lyman."

"Are he and Lynn all right?"

"Upset, but I think so."

"What about Manx?"

I touched the brim of my hat, watching it spin on the point of the crown like a carousel. "He doesn't appear to be very upset at all."

Alan's lips curled into a sad smile. "Don't let him fool you, he's much more sensitive than he appears."

"Did you see him this morning, Alan?"

"No."

"What about you, Ian?"

"No."

"How about David, do either of you think he saw your father this morning?"

"Doubtful, but he saw him last night the same as us."

"There was supposedly some kind of family meeting last night?"

Ian glanced at his brother and then back at me. "More business than family . . ."

"You want to tell me about it?"

"Not really."

"Even if it might give us some indication as to his mental state and why it is he might've killed himself?"

"It's a personal matter and I don't think it has anything to do with anything we're discussing here. Besides, it has to do with David, and I wouldn't feel comfortable discussing it without his permission."

"I thought you said it was business?"

"It's a bit of both, requiring some delicacy."

I studied Ian for a moment and then let it slide, figuring I'd get the answers eventually. "I'm assuming you two are spending the night back at the lodge along with David, perhaps we can discuss it then?"

Ian fidgeted. "I was actually heading back to Denver later today."

"I'd prefer you stay here, at least until we get some answers."

He made a face. "Answers to what?"

"Your father's death."

He threw up his hands. "You just said it was a suicide."

"No, your brother did. We've got a DCI crew coming in from Cheyenne to examine what we think is the location of the incident along with your father's body, and I'd appreciate it if you stuck around here until they finish their work."

Ian ran his fingers through his hair and then gestured toward all the books on the table. "You have got to be kidding; I've got a deadline on this story I'm working on."

Saying nothing, I put on my hat.

He threw his hands up again, but with a bit less enthusiasm. "I suppose I'll make do. The resources are a little primitive, but I guess I'll have to make it work."

I stood. "Sorry for the inconvenience, Ian."

The two of them also came to their feet, and Ian came around the table to pat me on the shoulder. "Not as sorry as I am for being such an asshole." He shook his head. "Maybe the old man's passing is having more of an effect on me than I thought."

"Well, I'm sorry to be the one bringing you the news." I shook hands with them both and started for the door. "Just one more thing, was Manx at this meeting last night?"

They gave a fleeting glance at each other again before answering. "No."

"Okay." I flipped the sign and swung open the door. "Well, I'll see you tonight with the DCI folks."

"Attorney general for the State of Wyoming on line one."

"Joe Meyer?" I called back into the main office. "Isn't he retired?"

"Don't ask me." Ruby, my dispatcher, came and hung in the doorway of my office with Dog as Vic sat in my visitor chair. "Line one."

Slipping off my jacket, I tossed it onto my chair and punched the little red button, snarling, "What do you want?"

There was a pause and then a voice I knew very well. "Is that any way to speak to the freshly minted attorney general for the State of Wyoming?"

"I'm sorry, Ruby said that Joe Meyer . . ." I sat in my chair. "Wait a minute, has something happened?"

"Yeah, the Right Honorable Robert Lang came to his senses and appointed your daughter the most powerful law-enforcement agent in the state."

I shook my head at the second and third most powerful law-enforcement agents in the state as they grinned like collective Cheshire cats at me from across my desk. "Oh, punk, I am so proud of you."

"Don't tell anybody, the public announcement doesn't come out until tomorrow."

I watched as Saizarbitoria joined Ruby in the doorway, also grinning. "Evidently everybody else in my office knew, but I'll keep your secret at least until tomorrow. Then I'm putting up billboards and planning on doing a little skywriting."

"When are we celebrating?"

"How fast can you and my granddaughter get here?"

"Maybe over the weekend."

"I'll plan a dinner." I glanced at my dispatcher. "Or Ruby will."

"How's the election going?"

"What election?" I laughed. "I think it's on Tuesday of next week."

"Anybody running against you?"

"Nobody I know of."

"Well, I'm going to need a favor from you, and I wanted to make sure you were still gainfully employed."

"What's that?"

"You know that guy who was in with Mike Regis in that incident out at great-grandpa's place?"

"Which guy?"

"The Russian they got to turn state's witness."

"Maxim Sidorov?" Vic leaned forward with a questioning look on her face.

"That's the one, he's filed for relocation."

Dog came around the desk and lay down by my chair. "What's that got to do with me?"

"He's wanting to move to Durant and because there is no parole officer in situ, the responsibility falls to the local constabulary, which means . . ."

I adjusted the phone in my ear. "Me."

"Yep."

"Do they, meaning your department now, know he tried to kill me?"

"I think they're aware of that, but he's been an extraordinarily valuable state witness, and he actually mentioned you as being one of the main reasons for the relocation."

"I bet."

There was a pause. "Is he really that dangerous?"

"He's a genuinely licensed spook with the SVR, FSB, FSO, or GUSP. I can't remember which, but he lost an eye courtesy of me and is wearing an ankle monitor, so I think he's come down a notch. Besides, he's supposedly helping me try to track down your great-aunt, Ruth One Heart."

"Then you have to take him?"

"Like they say, keep your friends close and your enemies closer—only for you, oh great General of All Attorneys." I smiled. "So do you get flags to stick on your Jeep for parades?"

She laughed back. "We'll see you this weekend."

The phone went dead in my hand, and I hung it up, looking at the rebel scum on the other side of my desk. "All right, how long have you turdbirds known?"

Ruby smiled, hugging herself in happiness. "Just this morning. I texted Vic; see what you miss by not having a phone?"

"Maybe, but we've got these great new radios . . ." I glanced at Sancho. "Hey, call the Board of Parole down in Cheyenne and get all the information on Maxim Sidorov that they've got, then find out if he already has an address. I know he has a cell phone and a motorcycle, so see if you can track him down. I'm going to want to talk to him before I agree to this."

He saluted. "Got it, Boss."

He disappeared and I sat back in my chair.

Vic cocked her head at me. "You all right?"

I thought about it. "I remember her first day of school."

"I bet you do."

"She lost her Bionic Woman lunchbox."

"And now she is the Bionic Woman." She stood. "C'mon, I think this calls for a celebratory drink."

I studied the old Seth Thomas clock on the wall. "Are you forgetting, we have to meet with Woody and the DCI folks back at the O-Kay Ranch."

"Are you really going to commit to this? He slipped and fell, Walt, and as many people as there are that wanted him dead, it looks like Crazy Woman Creek finally got him first."

"Maybe."

"What is it?"

"The second set of prints."

"In the creek bed, who knows how old those are if everybody in the place is out there walking around."

"Manx said they were fishing-wader treads."

"So?"

"It means somebody else was fishing with him . . . Or."

"Or what?"

"It was premeditated." I stood. "And there's something else."

"What?"

"His flask was crushed."

"Again, so?"

"It was in the front of his vest, and to have the blunt trauma we saw, Pepper would've had to have fallen backward."

"So he bobbed down the stream and flattened it on a rock. What's the big deal?"

"Only one way to find out." I grabbed my jacket from my chair. "C'mon, they've got a study and a library, maybe they have a bar."

"This is a blue-ribbon stream, my friend."

Leaning on the railing of the bridge, we watched as Woody Woodson, the director of Wyoming's Division of Criminal Investigation, cast across the rocks and into an overgrown portion of the bank, his fly landing expertly on the surface of the water like a feather coming to rest on a pillow.

The strike was sudden and ferocious, a big brown a good fourteen inches in length. "Aren't you supposed to be working?"

"You know, Sheriff." He reeled the trout in, careful to keep the tip of his rod up, arching the 5-weight perfectly. "You need to get your priorities straight."

Snatching the net from a magnetic connector at his back, he lifted the magnificent specimen, carefully unhooking him and gently lowering him back into the stream and letting him go. The brown stayed there for a moment and then, with a flip of his tail, disappeared back into the darkish water on the far side.

"That could've been dinner."

Straightening his equipment, Woody looked at us. "Wouldn't be sporting, besides I've already caught twelve of them."

Sitting on the railing, I watched the sun, close to slipping behind the mountains. "How's the investigation going?"

"Oh, that . . ." He struggled up the bank and then stretched his back with a hand at the lower portion. "You know, if my back keeps giving me trouble, I may actually have to work for a living."

"Did you get a look at all the locations I mapped for you?"

"I didn't, but my second-in-command did."

"You have a second-in-command?"

"Yes, you're not the only one." He joined us at the road. "I think they're finishing up, but we got lots of castings and photographs." We fell in behind him as he started toward the house, where I could see the black Tahoe and the large van parked.

"What's the story on the second set of prints?"

"I don't know, so we'll find out together." Woodson chuckled. "I got bored when they decided to block off part of the stream and do plaster castings of the prints."

As we skirted the house, I could see where the majority of their labor had commenced. There were about a half dozen of them in the stream, where they had, indeed, rechanneled Crazy Woman to reveal the portion of the creek bed at which Manx had pointed out the second set of fishing-wader prints.

There was a younger blond-haired woman with an extremely short haircut in waders and a flannel shirt and fleece top with the letters *DCI* stitched on the zippered pocket. She was struggling with a plaster cast, carefully removing it from the mud. "Tammy Payson, meet Walt Longmire and Victoria Moretti."

She squinted at us and spoke with a slight accent. "Just a minute."

Woody moved past her, looking at the undisturbed stream to the west. "I'll be right back."

Watching him go, she wiped off some of the mud and then waded toward us. "Yeah, right."

I offered her a hand and pulled her up the bank. "He retired now?"

"Might as well be." She leaned to the side to address my undersheriff. "Hi, how you doin'?"

Vic stared at her for a good thirty seconds. "Delco, South Lancaster . . . Maybe Chester?"

The woman laughed. "Good. North Wilmington, Delaware, actually."

I glanced between the two of them. "Are you two speaking some language I'm not familiar with?"

Vic gestured toward the woman as the DCI tech put the cast down and wiped off her hands. "She's from west of the city."

They shook hands as the blonde looked at her questioningly. "And what city is that?"

"Right."

Payson turned to me. "How did you get the Pennamite out here, Sheriff?"

"We used cheesesteaks, Yuengling, and nets. That, and I promised her I'd get a look at the study in the big house here."

She handled the cast and flipped it over. "She had her shots?"

"No." We waited as she studied the indented surface of the plaster. "What have we got here?"

"Simms Flyweight fishing boot in a size 12."

"I neglected to notice, is that what Pepper McKay was wearing?"

"Yes."

Vic leaned in, studying the cast. "And the other set of prints?"

"Simms Flyweight fishing boot in a size 12."

"Same boot?"

"Possibly, but one set is more worn than the other. But that could just mean that that set of prints were made previously. At this point it's difficult to tell."

"I'm assuming there are more waders in the back mudroom?"

Handing the cast to Vic, she stretched her back and swiped some of the blond hair from her face, and even though it was getting cool, I could see she was sweating. "Don't know, this is as far as I've gotten in parting the Red Sea."

I peered up at the sky again. "Well, it looks to me like you've only got an hour's worth of daylight left."

"Oh, that's okay, we'll work through the night if need be."

"Really?"

"Yeah, then we'll get together with the mortem guys at the hospital and see what they found in the autopsy."

"Dave Nickerson?"

"Not Bloomfield?"

"I'm afraid he retired."

"What was he, a hundred years old?"

"Actually, I think he was. Anything we can do?"

"Go check the fishing equipment and see how many pairs of Simms Flyweight fishing boots there are in a size 12."

I saluted. "Roger that."

She stuck out a hand to my second-in-command. "Jawn."

Vic nodded. "Jawn."

I followed my undersheriff up the lawn past the tagged and labeled bottles and cans in a cardboard evidence box. "What's *jawn* mean?"

"Nobody really knows."

The mudroom occupied most of the floor level of the back of the lodge, a long, narrow room with paned windows looking out at the green hardwood floors, scattered with ancient Navajo runners and weathered bench seats with lifting lids. The seat benches practically had tons of hunting and fishing equipment stored within them. An assortment of fishing vests, hunting jackets, shooting vests, and waders hung off pegs driven into the heavy and highly lacquered log walls.

Vic studied a mule deer mount at the end of the long room with some sort of Native artifact hung in the antlers. "I could live here."

"Kind of over the top for a mudroom, huh?"

"I can't wait to see what the rest of the place looks like."

I lifted one of the bench lids and poked around inside, finding mostly hunting equipment with gaiters, shell bags, and such. "I'm sure we can arrange a tour." I moved down to where the waders were hung, figuring that the rest of the fishing equipment might be there.

"What the hell, I mean, really?"

I turned to see her reaching up and trailing her fingers in the buckskin fringe of a vintage Cheyenne war club, probably a hundred and fifty years old.

She glanced at me. "You think this thing is real?"

"Probably, they used to call them skull-crackers."

"The fringe is stiff, should you oil something like this?"

"If you cared, I suppose."

She studied it with more interest, finally unable to resist the temptation and took it down. "What's something like this worth?"

"I have no idea, three or four thousand dollars at auction for a good one, I'd imagine—and that's a good one."

"And it's just lodged in the antlers of a deer mount in the mudroom?"

I shrugged, opening another bench seat but finding only more wading boots and no antiquities. "Southern Cheyenne from the looks of it; maybe they don't care about stuff from outside the state."

Balancing the thing in her hands, she slapped the business end of the river stone held in place by the beaded rawhide. "So, not Henry Standing Bear's tribe?"

"The southern extension: the ones that didn't make a break for it, trying to get back to Montana."

Unable to just dump the museum piece back in a cabinet, she carefully cradled it in the mule deer's antlers.

Having discovered the other wading boots, I began pulling pairs out only to discover the first pair I came upon were Simms Flyweight fishing boots in a size 12. Setting them on the adjacent bench, I motioned to her. "C'mere."

She walked over. "Let me guess, slightly worn, Simms Flyweight fishing boots in a size 12?"

"Feel inside them."

She did as I said and drew her hand out. "They're wet."

"Yep. They are."

After pulling all the boots from the cubbies and confirming that none of the other eighteen pairs were either Simms Flyweight, size 12, or in any way wet, we carried them out to where Tammy Payson and Woody Woodson were having a confab, creekside.

"Bingo?"

Vic handed the boots to the young woman. "Wet on the inside."

We watched as she felt them. "They certainly are."

Vic looked at the three of us. "Is it me, or is the killer monumentally fucking stupid or what?"

Woody was the first to answer, running his fingers through his beard. "Well, first we have to find out if it really is a murder. Second, Pepper could've tried that pair and decided that he didn't like them and switched."

"How long would they stay wet like that?"

He took a boot from Tammy and squeezed his fingers into the lining. "Whoa, those are really wet—I'd say those had to be used within the last twenty-four hours."

"That's because they were."

The four of us turned to see a tall, handsome young man walking down from the house, and when I say handsome, I mean Hollywood handsome, like a younger version of the Marlboro Man, with a perfect tan and five o'clock shadow. David McKay extended a hand to me, shaking vigorously. "Look at you, Walt Longmire. I don't think I've seen you in, what, twelve years?"

"It's been about that long at least. How are you, David?"

He nodded at the others with a lopsided grin that only enhanced his good looks. "As well as can be expected, considering the circumstances."

"I'm sorry about your father."

"You'd be the only one." He glanced at the others. "I'm sorry, did I just make the suspect list?" When no one laughed his head dropped and he stood there for a moment before raising his face and having reset. "I'm sorry to report that my father was a monumental prick, and if you're responsible for finding his murderer, you might want to hold a raffle."

"Be that as it may . . . David, this is my undersheriff, Victoria Moretti, and Woody Woodson and Tammy Payson with the Division of Criminal Investigation."

"I apologize for my candor." He took off his pristine cowboy hat, revealing startling green eyes, and shook hands all around.

"Good to meet all of you." He then pivoted back to me. "So, you think it honestly was a murder?"

"David, we don't know but we're covering all the bases." I gestured toward the Adirondack chairs and table farther up the lawn. "Do you mind if we ask you a few questions?"

"No problem. I was just going to head in and have a drink, perhaps you'd all like to join me?"

Vic looked at the house. "In the study?"

"There's liquor in there but there's liquor in practically every room in the house—it belonged to Pepper McKay, after all." Without another word, he turned and started up the hill.

Woody slapped my shoulder. "We're going to pass since we've got business at Durant Memorial, but do let me know about the wet wading boots."

Payson added to Vic. "And the study."

"Jawn." Vic and I trailed after David McKay. "Jeez, does this guy have a girlfriend?"

"Quite a few, from what I'm to understand." Opening the mudroom door, we filed past the pantry into the kitchen, with its small, black-and-white tiled floors and walls. I couldn't help but wonder if the place had been built around the same time as my grandfather's ranch.

Through the swinging doors we entered the main hall, which connected to the front entryway and practically every other room in the lodge, and was dominated by the dark burl wood stairs at the center that led to the second floor.

The sense of a hunting lodge permeated the place, with its taxidermy mounts, Native rugs, and old-world crests on shields that came from who knew where.

Vic twirled, looking around, her eyes finally settling on the suit of armor beside the stairs. "Sir Simon, I presume?"

"Does he have a dent in the right side of his breastplate?"

Walking over to the thing, she examined the metal. "He does." She turned to look at me. "You punched him?"

"No, that would be what my head did when he fell over, on top of me."

"The fateful night?"

I walked over and gave the old ghost a salute. "I think . . . I'm not sure I was all there."

A whistle sounded from behind the stairs and to the right, accompanied by David's voice. "Abandon all hope ye who enter here."

Following the voice, we could see an open door in the corner where the younger McKay had opened a large globe, accessing the hidden bar inside. "What'll it be?"

Vic checked her wristwatch. "Sun's over the yardarm, I'll take a dirty martini, if you would."

"And you, Sheriff?"

"Nothing for me."

"I've got Rainier in the refrigerator in the kitchen?"

"No, I'm good." I studied the gun cases, which held the most extravagant collection I'd ever seen outside of the Buffalo Bill Center of the West over in Cody.

Vic, of course, focused immediately on the massive grizzly mount dominating an entire corner of the study, where a large fringe-carved table and club chairs stood. "This the one you fought?"

"I think so, I fight so many bears it's hard to keep track."

She studied the behemoth. "Unlike Sir Simon, it doesn't appear to have sustained any damage."

"Oh, it did." David stood by the globe-bar, shaking the mixture. "From what I'm to understand, they had to do a little repair work to him after the two of you were done going twelve rounds."

"I'm sorry."

"I'm sorry if I keep staring at you, but you have to keep in mind that you are a legend around here, bigger than life."

Vic joined him at the libation globe. "Tell me more."

He poured the contents into a glass and added the brine and an olive on a toothpick before handing it over to the Terror, the dirty martini in full dress. "Oh, I could tell you a bunch of stories, but the one that comes to mind the quickest was the time we were at the Sinclair service station on the south side of Durant. I think I was about seven years old, and Gary and I were filling up one of the ranch trucks, and there was a hubbub going on where this guy was slapping his wife in their car. So they must've called it in, and pretty soon this little Bronco pulls in and the biggest man I've ever seen gets out and goes over to have a word with this guy. Well, by that time, the couple was out of the car and still going at it, but paused for a moment when the sheriff—"

I interrupted. "Deputy, at the time."

David went on. "When the deputy here arrived, and that's when Gary leaned over to me and said, 'You be a good boy, or you'll find out what happens to you.' The guy was still screaming, but the woman put out a hand to calm him down and then he backhanded her across the face."

Vic looked up at me.

David glanced at me and then back at Vic. "I have never seen anything happen so fast in my life: One second the guy was standing there and the next, this one had him by the throat, lifting him off the ground and slamming him onto the hood of his car with a finger in his face and a conversation so low, I'm pretty sure that they were the only two to hear it."

My undersheriff smirked. "Mister restraint."

David handled two snifters. "What did you say to him, Walt? I've always wondered."

I stuffed my hands in my jacket pockets and stared at the carpet. "We had a wide-ranging conversation about the use of force in a public and/or private setting."

He shook his head at me, continuing to smile. "Walt, I'm having an Armagnac if you'll join me?"

"Nope, I'm good, honest."

"Ever had any? C'mon, it's from a small distillery I know of in Gascony, just south of Bordeaux."

"Three Musketeers region."

He pulled out an ancient-looking bottle, with the label ready to fall off, and poured some into one of the snifters. He held it out to me. "It's a '65 Dartigalongue that I kept hidden from Pepper."

"I'm afraid it would be lost on me."

"At least once."

I took the snifter and held it to my nose, breathing in what I figured to be about 50-percent alcohol. "Strong."

Pouring himself one, he held it up to the chandelier light. "Not as smooth as a cognac, but just as enjoyable, I think you'll find."

Vic raised her martini. "All for one, and one for all?" We all took a sip, and then she asked him, more than point-blank, "So what's the story on the wading boots?"

David, caught a little off guard, smiled at Vic. "Just for the record, I'm the only other size 12 in the family." He smiled the winning grin. "I went out very early this morning to try to get him to go to bed, but he ignored me and was out there stumbling around at sunup."

"He was drunk?"

"Was he ever." He came over and sat on the corner of the table. "I didn't want to soak my Luccheses, so I just slipped the wading boots on and tried to get him to come back in before he broke his damn neck . . . A lot of good it did in that he ended up breaking his damn neck anyway."

"Head, actually."

Vic broke from her expoloration of a bookshelf long enough to ask a pertinent question. "Was he upset or emotionally unstable?"

David made a face. "For about sixty years now."

"I understand there was a big family meeting last night?"

The young man laughed. "There was that."

"And what was that about?"

He sighed. "It's a long story, and not a very pleasant one."

"You aren't the first person we've seen who doesn't appear to be broken up about the passing of your father." I sat in one of the overstuffed club chairs as Vic moved around the room some more, taking it all in.

"Who else have you been talking to?"

"Well, Manx, for one."

"Yeah, there's no love lost there, that's for sure—it's bad enough being the legitimate son of a son of a bitch, try being his half-breed bastard." He sipped his drink and laughed. "I assumed that after hearing from Ian and Alan that none of us were going anywhere—including Manx."

"Yep."

"Well, that didn't work out so well, huh?"

I sat forward. "What are you talking about?"

"Uh . . ." His eyes scanned the open door and front of the lodge, where the road led to the outside world. "Manx left for Arizona about forty minutes ago."

# 3

Newly minted Major Jim Thomas was kind enough to not laugh in my ear. "A white Chevrolet dually one-ton diesel with an eight-stall horse trailer is the getaway vehicle?"

I was standing in the entryway, where the honest to goodness phone table—or gossip bench, as my predecessor and previous sheriff of Absaroka County used to refer to it—still sat. Stretching the cord, I looked back into the house where Lynn pushed a cart with coffee and sandwiches into the study. "Yep, so not exactly a high-speed chase."

"He got horses in there?"

"Yep."

Number four in the Wyoming Highway Patrol hierarchy assured me. "We'll get him, but when we do, what do you want us to do with him?"

"Send him home."

"Think he'll follow orders?"

I thought about sitting on the delicate piece of furniture but then had second and third thoughts. "Debatable."

"Well, rather than chase him down again, maybe we'll just give him an escort."

"Sounds good." I listened as Jim rustled some papers and could almost hear him calculating the speed, topography, and distance of a one-ton diesel truck hauling eight thousand pounds of horseflesh on I-25, southbound. "Just so you're aware, he's armed."

"I've got just the man for the job."

"Shane Wilson?"

"You met him?"

"He was the attending officer in the discovery of the body, good kid."

"Take it easy on him. He's brand new and we don't want to lose him."

"I figured."

"We'll get this fellow before he gets to Casper, Walt."

"That a promise?"

"Anything for the daddy of the attorney general."

I rolled my eyes. "Is that going to be my official title for the next four years?"

"Oh, probably longer than that." The line went dead in my hand, and I gently placed the trusty Bakelite device back in the heavy cradle, thinking about how the younger generation would never know the satisfaction of slamming one of the heavy-duty monsters down in somebody's ear.

It was an odd device but had the usual rotary dial, gold filigree decals, a brass handle that folded down, and a small medallion with the letters *RTT* on it. At the center of the dial, instead of a phone number, was Room 37 in typewritten print.

I lifted it, confirming my belief that the damn thing weighed a ton and would make a considerable weapon if need be.

"Thinking about stealing it?" I turned to find Lynn handing me a cup of coffee. "Black, as I remember."

"Yes, ma'am."

She glanced at the phone. "Everything in this house has a story, if we could just get them to talk."

"Lynn, not to interrupt, but did you relay my message to Manx about not leaving?"

She made a face. "I did, but he didn't seem to take it all that seriously. He said it sounded like a bad movie, you know, don't leave town and all."

"Well, the HPs are going to be bringing him back here in a bit."

"That may cause some trouble."

"Not for the HPs."

She shrugged and started off. "Ian and Alan are in the study with David and your deputy."

"That why you brought in the coffee and sandwiches?"

She turned back. "I thought you guys might need it."

"Thank you."

I sipped from my cup and studied the phone. "Imported?"

"Belgian. Pepper was staying in a hotel in Antwerp and stole it."

"The towels weren't good enough?"

"I suppose not. He just cut the wire and stuffed it in his suitcase, appropriating it like he did with a lot of things."

She headed off toward the kitchen as I stood there taking another sip of the really good coffee. Then I started toward the study to find Vic holding court with the brothers McKay. Hanging in the doorway, I listened as they peppered her with friendly questions. I couldn't blame them: With her ball cap off and seated in the club chair with the martini glass in her hand, she looked at home, as if she were leading the "round table" in the Algonquin Hotel.

I cleared my throat.

They all turned to look at me, Alan the first to speak. "You're getting married?"

"I don't know. She hasn't said yes, yet."

They all studied her as she sipped her drink. "I like to keep my options open."

I entered and stood at the center of the room, glancing around. "Would you gentlemen like to talk, or would you rather wait on Manx?"

Ian shook his head. "They caught him?"

"They will."

Alan, seated on the Turkish carpet with his legs folded up in his cassock, smiled at me. "It's getting a little late for me, so I'd just as soon we got started."

"You're an early riser, Alan?"

"I am. Morning meditations and prayers are usually at six."

"And you were up early this morning?"

"I was."

"And you spoke with your father, you said."

"I did, briefly."

"You said he was behaving strangely?"

"Well, sad . . . He seemed depressed."

"Any idea why?"

The young monk turned and looked at his half-sibling, David.

David freshened his drink, grabbed one of the small sandwiches from the cart, and then reseated himself in a campaign chair by the gun cases that looked like they might've been owned by Teddy Roosevelt and probably had been. "It's likely going to come out anyway, but he and I are, were, um . . . having relations with the same woman."

Vic took another sip of her drink. "Oh, my fuck."

"Exactly." He ate a bit of the sandwich and glanced at his brothers as we all stood around the cart helping ourselves. "We kind of had it out last night."

Ian extricated himself from the other club chair and poured himself a cup of coffee. "It wasn't pleasant, to say the least." He flicked his eyes at David, who continued to eat his sandwich and waved his hand for his brother to go on, which Ian did. "It's been going on for quite awhile now, the situation."

"Who is the woman?"

David suddenly found his voice again. "Is that really necessary?"

"You can't really expect us to not check on your stories—I mean, your father is dead."

"Paetra Agirra."

I raised both eyebrows in response. "As in the somewhat legendary Boris Agirra?"

"Not quite as legendary as he used to be, but that's the one. Her uncle."

"The highway patrolman, Wilson, said your father had a little dustup with Boris on the side of the road a week ago."

David smiled, shaking his head. "That sounds about right, he's threatened to kill Pepper about a dozen times now for fooling around with his niece." He glanced at us. "Not that I think he'd do it."

"Wouldn't be the first time he killed someone."

Vic interrupted. "Am I missing a key part of local history here?"

"Boris got into a little argument over some tire chains up the mountain one time and ended it killing three men."

"No shit."

Taking my own sandwich, I moved over and looked at the stuffed bear. "Yep, he was elk hunting and after he got through dressing out the elk, it was snowing pretty heavy, and when he got to his truck, he discovered the chains he'd laid out were gone. He saw lights from some fellows who were camping not too far away and saw them putting *his* chains on *their* truck. He asked them about it, and they cussed him out and one went for his gun. Boris shot him and then the other two went for theirs and he shot them too."

"He got off?"

"Boris's defense was that without those chains he would've been a dead man, which was a relatively valid point."

"And the jury let him off?"

"They did."

"Sounds like a tough old bird."

"He's got a lot of hard bark on him, yep." I turned to David. "And how's your relationship with him?"

"*Nonexistent* is the word I'd use."

"Well, I'm going to have to go talk with him."

"And mention my name?"

"Possibly."

"I wish you wouldn't."

"David, it seems I remember reading an article in the *Durant Courant* about you getting married?"

He cleared his throat, looking a little embarrassed. "I was engaged, but it didn't work out."

"And what was her name?"

"Katherine Verkhov, from over in Jackson. I helped her father out with a financial situation, and we thought we were in love, but you know how things go."

Saying nothing more about David's overly complicated love life, I moved around the room, looking at the artwork. "Ian, you said that a portion of the conversation last night was business oriented—is that something I should be concerned with?"

The newspaperman gazed at his brothers and then ran his hands through his thick hair and adjusted his glasses. "Not unless having close to sixty-three million dollars is reason enough to commit suicide."

"Excuse me?"

"It would appear the old man was holding out on us to a great degree."

David shook his head. "After crying poverty his whole life."

"That's a more than substantial amount of money. Do you mind if I ask how it is you found out about all this?"

Ian raised a hand. "It was me. I was doing research on the Cowboy Cocktail for this article for the *High Plains Bulletin*."

"The tax shelter?"

He smiled. "Yeah, remember when everybody used to make jokes about offshore tax sheltering in the Caymans and places like that? Well, the hot place to hide your money is Wyoming with trusts and multiple private companies that conceal ownership, protected by the strongest privacy laws in the country that allow some of the wealthiest people in the world to move funds here in absolute secrecy."

"And you stumbled onto your father's wealth?"

"I did, through this thing called the Pandora Papers that was given to *The Washington Post*. At first, I tried to ignore it, but my curiosity got the better of me, and we confronted him with the information last night."

"And how did that go?"

Alan answered this time, once again glancing at David. "Not well."

Then David admitted, "He's been holding my inheritance for years and saying he didn't have the money. I've basically been surviving off a remittance from my mother."

"You realize that none of this looks good for you, David."

"I'm aware of that, but I'm also aware that I didn't kill him."

"Ian, you said you didn't see your father this morning?"

"No, I had some more research to do, and after I got up and grabbed a cup of coffee in the kitchen, I headed out for the library." He gestured toward his youngest brother. "Alan was heading up the stairs as I was leaving and he asked if he could come along, so I got the truck and pulled it around front."

"And Lynn and Gary?"

"I saw Lynn in the kitchen for a moment, but I never saw Gary. He was probably long gone and out working; he's always working."

"And that's everyone who was here this morning?"

Ian glanced at his brothers and then back to me. "Here at the lodge, yes."

"So in summation, Alan, you saw your father for a few moments on the lawn before his death; Ian didn't see him at all; David spoke with him out in the stream; and Manx didn't have any interaction with him but was the one who pointed out the second set of prints in the creek bed where we think Pepper might've fallen."

Alan raised a hand. "There was that water purification guy and the FedEx driver, but both of them were here for only a few minutes."

"Well, hopefully this is all for naught and we can move on with making preparations for the burial of your father." They all looked at me blankly. "I assume someone is doing that?"

"I am." We turned to find Lynn in the doorway. "Can I take the cart away?"

"Well, there are enough suspects around."

I pulled into town, slowing as we drove up Main Street, the traffic lights blinking yellow. "Not if it isn't a murder."

"Aw, c'mon, can't we pretend like it is? We haven't had one in a while, and I think I'm losing my edge."

"Well, it's agreed that everyone on the North American continent hated the man."

"Oh, I don't know. He could be hated around the world by all accounts." She considered it. "Alan doesn't hate him."

"I don't think monks are allowed to hate people."

"He's the last one we suspect, so he's obviously the killer."

"You mean if this was a murder-mystery?"

"Yeah, if it was a thriller, we'd know who it was in chapter two and then have five hundred pages of chase."

"You've put a lot of thought into this."

"I have." She sat forward, looking into our parking area beside the old Carnegie library. "Is that a motorcycle parked in our lot?"

Turning the corner, I pulled in behind the BMW dual sport with all its snazzy outer-space accessories and DC diplomatic plates, a helmet hanging from the handlebars.

Vic looked at me. "Well, he didn't waste any time getting here, did he?"

Cutting the lights and ignition, I cracked open the door and walked toward the thing, but then stopped when I saw a lump on the front steps at the foot of our doors in a sleeping bag and covered with a leather jacket, vociferously snoring.

Continuing, I mounted the steps with Vic and then nudged the body with my boot. "Hey."

He continued snoring, and I nudged him again.

"Hey?"

He grunted in his blown-out voice. "*Ukhodit . . .*"

Vic sat and jostled his shoulder. "*Privet, Komissar . . .*"

Peeling the collar of his jacket back, he peeked at her from the one eye not covered with a patch. "Little Italian Mother, how are you—more of the importance, are you of the armed?"

"Always."

I sat on the concrete steps beside his legs as he sat up, one of his heavily tattooed hands pulling away the sleeping bag. "Sheriff, I wait for you but is very cold this early in season."

"So, you decided to establish a bivouac on my doorstep?"

"Out of the money and I have nowhere to go, so am surrendering myself of the incarceration."

"You want to be arrested?"

"Da, but only of the night."

"You need someplace to sleep."

He looked a little sheepish as he shrugged himself up, rubbing his face and Dizzy Gillespie cookie duster before patting down his wild hair. "Da."

"Sidorov, you realize being arrested will be in direct violation of your parole?"

Scrunching the rest of the way out of the bag, he yawned. "Then we perhaps forgo arrest, and you invite me to cell of temporary usage for night?"

"That means one of us has to stay here with you."

The Russian peeked at Vic. "Does not sound so bad."

"I'm afraid it'd be me." I glanced at Vic. "You'd have to go home in that Ruby dropped Dog off there."

She frowned. "Why don't we just buy him a motel room?"

Pulling his legs from the bag, he searched for his socks, found them, and pulled them on with his motorcycle boots. "I'm not buying him a motel room."

"We can use a voucher, and it'll be seventy-five bucks."

"I like idea, nice lady."

"Shut the fuck up."

He began lacing his boots with a broad smile. "Yes, please."

She stood, looking down, first at him, then me. "Your loss."

"Agreed."

I removed the truck key and tossed it to her, watching her saunter off with my heart, turning only briefly to blow me a kiss before slamming the driver's side door and whipping out of the parking lot like one of the Blue Angels late for formation.

I hoped my truck survived it.

Looking down at Maxim, I took the remaining keys and unlocked the front door as he gathered his things and followed after me. "You do not have security system?"

I closed the door and locked it behind him. "No."

"Even with jail?"

"This building is over a hundred years old, and there's somebody here at night when we have a lodger."

"Lodger." We both stopped at the landing. "I like this, is funny."

"This is where you make a choice; there are cells downstairs and then there are two holding cells upstairs."

"Which has better of view?"

"The downstairs ones don't have any windows."

"I will go up the stairs." We climbed the remaining steps to arrive at the main office and Ruby's desk as he glanced about. "Marble floors, pressed tin ceiling, and fireplace—does work?"

"It does, but we hardly ever use it."

"May I use, if sleep on floor in this room?"

"You can, but you won't be able to sleep in; the staff will be here early."

He stopped at the counter and looked longingly at the small marble fireplace. "How early?"

"Early."

"I will sleep in holding cell?"

"Follow me."

Walking down the hall and past the open doors of all the offices, I watched as he glanced in each one. "Where are you to sleep?"

"Probably in the other holding cell. I've tried sleeping in my chair, but I usually wake up like a human pretzel." Pushing open the heavy metal door, I ushered him through and pointed to the one on the left. "The one on the right is usually mine, so you get the other."

I watched as he headed in that direction and then scanned around and entered the eight-foot-by-six-foot space, unrolling his sleeping bag on the bunk and fluffing the one, very flat pillow.

I quietly closed the door and used the key to turn the lock as he paused to look at me. "You are arrest me?"

"Nope, just securing you." I pulled the visitors chair from the wall and sat facing him. "Well?"

Taking off his well-worn boots, Sidorov placed them on the floor beneath the cot and made himself comfortable, adjusting his eye patch, then looking back at me with his one good eye. "What?"

I sat there looking at him, conveying the importance of my next statement. "Ruth One Heart."

"Ah, yes . . . I was hoping to postpone conversation until tomorrow."

"Nope, we'll have it now."

He leaned his back against the concrete-block wall. "What leads of the belief that I have of information?"

"Why else on earth would you want to move here?"

He crossed his arms and considered me. "To be closer to you if obtain information?"

"Well, I'd be disappointed if that was the answer."

He laughed and then stretched out on the sleeping bag on the cot. "Then I better of come up with different answer."

"As long as it's the truth."

He waited a moment and then responded. "You still do not trust me."

"No farther than I can throw you."

He grinned at the ceiling, and I had to admit that it was an open and seemingly honest response. "As can throw me . . . This is very good." His face turned toward me. "You have cost me eye, but yet it is I that must solicit trust, yes?"

"Yes."

Reaching into the breast pocket of his leather jacket, he produced a folded piece of paper, holding it out to me between the bars.

I stared at his hand for a moment and then stretched forward, taking the piece of paper and unfolding it to reveal a printer-sized photocopy of a black and white, grainy in nature, as if taken by a low-grade security camera.

It might as well have been a chute in a slaughterhouse for livestock. There was a concrete floor with drains, and what appeared to be twelve-foot concrete walls topped with bulletproof glass, with armed guards wearing BDUs and holding automatic weapons.

The photo was clandestine, with part of the aperture covered by what must've been the photographer's hand and coat. And there, in the center, was a dark-haired woman pushing one of those carts you get at the airport to assist with your bags.

Ruth One Heart.

"Where is this?"

"It is airport, she is going somewhere."

"Where?"

He rolled over, leaning forward to reach through the bars and tap the edge of the paper I held. "Best to ask two men whose feet of we see behind her."

"Where would she be going to from there?"

Taking the paper from me, he studied the photograph. "The

tactical boots of which these two of men wearing are the ones I myself wore in my time in Spetsnaz of special forces."

"Meaning?"

"They are professionals."

I grunted a laugh. "At what?"

"Intelligence community."

I looked back at the photo and tried to make out more details but simply couldn't. "Why would they want Ruth?"

He handed me back the photo. "My supposition is that Regis family outsources situation with you through business partners not connected of official Russian Federation."

"Mercenaries?"

"Yes, is term used, but of connection to oligarchs, so more of powerful." He stared at me. "One thing is of sure, rich of peoples stick together."

"What leads you to believe this is a commercial line she's on?"

"On closer of the examination, barcode on bag reads VVO, Vladivostok, gateway to Far Eastern Federal District of Russia."

"And what's there?"

He shrugged. "Difficult of say, but have operatives still in community, which is of how I receive photograph—very dangerous of the business."

"But she's still alive."

"Yes, value is of her living."

"Why?"

His head dropped and he smiled silently to himself. "Of you."

"I'm that important to them, really?"

"You kill their son."

"Actually, she did."

"Truly?" He shrugged again and I was getting the idea that it was his favorite expression in response to everything. "Does not matter. They consider you of responsibility."

"So, what do we do now?"

"We wait; they will be of in touch when they are of ready."

"Ready for what?"

His response was predictable.

"Stop shrugging at me, she's an American citizen and a part of the law enforcement community. What's to keep me from just handing this photograph over to the federal government?"

"Federal government of you?"

"Yes."

"They will say all is very interesting but there is nothing of they do. Possibly treat her as traitor."

"So, you're my only hope of getting her back?"

"Da."

"You'll forgive me if I'm less than enthusiastic."

He stood, coming over to the bars and draping his hands, covered with prison tattoos, near the lock mechanism. "They will be of contacting me when they discover I am in proximity of you, assuming that I am seeking retribution."

"Why wouldn't they just have you kill me?"

"They want of something far more than simple death. I would say are want to make suffer you for the loss of their son. I know there was talk through channels of daughter you have, yes?"

I stood, towering over him.

His eyes widened a bit as he stepped back. "Only talk, but with appointment of new position, it is thought that this be too much of high-profile action." The crooked smile crept onto his face. "Ah, this is man I see at grandfather ranch, the man they fear." He came close to the bars again, looking at me with the singular hazel eye. "Man who half blind me."

"I didn't pull the trigger on the weapon that blew up in your face, you did."

The smile held. "What is biblical saying of eye for eye?"

Thrusting my arms through the bars, I gripped the front of his shirt, pulling him toward me with a jerk powerful enough to bounce his face off the bars, and held him there. "You better be playing me straight, Sidorov."

Straining, he grunted the words through the bars, his head pressed sideways from the force I was exerting in holding him there. "Sheriff, if I am to want you dead, you would been of dead in hotel in Cheyenne."

After a moment I released him and he stepped back, straightening the collar of his black Henley shirt and staring at the floor. "In Perm region of Northern Ural Mountains, the first time I was of incarcerated, sitting in KPZ . . ." He began taking off his shirt, sliding it over his head, revealing the mass of crude tattoos that covered his body with crucifixes, daggers, women's faces, numbers, stars, scorpions, and spiders, along with other designs and Cyrillic writing I couldn't decipher. "Preliminary detention of cell of fifty convicts or smaller pretrial detention center, or SIZO, with perhaps half of dozen. These inform others of who is to be on trial or of sentencing."

He ran a hand over his chest as if smoothing the pages on a book. "The first thing they do is ask you to remove of clothing." He sat, looking at me. "They can be of very persuasive." He pointed to some writing at his neck. "You see this?"

"I do."

"Tri Muzhchiny, you know what means?"

"No."

"I kill man in SIZO, first day of the captivity. I spend next year in solitary confinement and when I get out, am attacked by deputy enforcer who I kill." He shrugged. "Another year in solitude, but when am released am confronted by Pakhan, or man-in-charge-of, informs me that I work for him now. I work for next nine weeks, but then he is of dead by unnatural causes." He sighed, staring at the floor. "Tri Muzhchiny—three men—is prison name of me from point on."

"And the reason for telling me all of this?"

He lay back on the cot, covering his eyes with a heavily inked arm. "Do not underestimated me, Sheriff."

"Oh, I don't think there's much of a chance of that. It's trusting you I have a problem with." I started around the corner, reaching for the switch. "Lights on or off?"

"Off please, but could trouble you for glass of water?"

"I'll see what I can do." Switching off the light, I went down the hallway toward my office. Spotting a few of Ruby's Post-its on the door facing, I plucked them off and went in, sitting in my chair, leafing through them.

The first was a reminder to sign the stack of payroll checks that sat in a neat pile at the center of my blotter. The next was a request for interviews with the Cheyenne and Casper papers and *Cowboy Daily* about the appointment of my daughter as attorney general. The next was simply the cell phone number for Woody Woodson, which was a little ominous.

I glanced up at the Seth Thomas, which I seemed to be consulting more than usual lately, and immediately dismissed the idea of calling the head of DCI, who was probably in his motel room tying flies in his sleep.

I thought about what Sidorov had said and wondered if I could trust the Russian mercenary any, if at all. I also tried to think of what other options I had, which were exceedingly limited. I was out of my depth in all this cloak and dagger stuff, and there wasn't anybody I could think of who could help me, except for one man.

The phone in the main office rang and I walked into the outside area and snatched the receiver before it forwarded to whoever had the rock tonight. Putting the handset to my ear, I suppressed a yawn and spoke. "Absaroka County Sheriff's Department, Walt Longmire, Absaroka County sheriff, speaking."

"Lock the fucker up."

I tucked the receiver into the crook of my neck, studying Ruby's other notes on the entry notebook lying on her blotter. "Hi."

"I'm not kidding, lock Sputnik up. I don't trust that greasy pudknocker."

"I already did."

There was a pause. "You actually did?"

"Yep, and I think I might be losing my charming Western naivete."

I listened as she settled in and wondered what I was doing here at the office. "It was never that charming."

"How is Dog?"

"Commandeering three-quarters of the bed, but I told him it was okay since the spot is vacant." She yawned herself, and I listened to her stretch. "He say anything about One Heart?"

"A lot. He actually has a photo of her in some airport in Russia."

"You're kidding."

"I'm not. She was being escorted by some goons through Vladivostok, headed for some place in the far-eastern Russian Federation."

"Where and why in the hell . . . ?"

"I have no idea, but you know the old saying."

"Yeah, yeah, keep your friends close, but your enemies closer?"

"Exactly." I listened to her breathe.

She laughed. "All right, I'll see you in the morning and I'll bring doughnuts."

"I don't like doughnuts."

"Yeah, but I do."

The phone went dead in my hand, and I returned it to the cradle thinking about breaking the cardinal rule of incarceration, leaving a prisoner unsupervised, when I heard noises coming from down in the jail. There was no one in the office but Sidorov and me, and he was locked up tight in the holding cell behind me. It was a strange sound, familiar and almost rhythmical.

Rising, I moved around the counter and toward the stairs that led to the front door and the landing, which descended left to the basement jail proper. Standing at the top of the steps, I listened but heard nothing more. I'd just decided to go grab some sleep in the opposite holding cell, when I swore I heard the strange, almost liquid and burbling sound again.

Drawing my sidearm, I started down the steps, past all the 8 × 10s of the previous sheriffs of Absaroka County, noting the most recent before me, Lucian Connally, and reminded myself that it was Tuesday, and I was due a chess match over at the Durant Home for Assisted Living this evening.

Turning the corner, I eased down the steps and into the commissary portion of the partially subterranean jail, which housed an abbreviated kitchen and a full bathroom, including a shower. I listened again and could make out the noise.

The coffee maker.

Walking over to the thing on the commissary counter, I considered it, never having paid that much attention to it before, preferring to use the one upstairs by Ruby's desk, which was so complicated that no one let me touch it. This one was simpler, with a clock and some other stuff built in, and I figured someone must've put on the timer so that coffee would be ready when they came in.

Probably Saizarbitoria, he was our go-to guy for tech services and usually the one here the earliest, unless I was sleeping in the holding cell, which I seemed to be doing less and less these days, and nights.

Studying the area, I noticed the Basquo had even set his Euskadi mug out for early morning duty.

Shaking my head at myself, I holstered my .45 and began mounting the steps, continuing back and into the main office. I'd just made the landing when I heard a faint scraping noise coming from the holding cell area down the hall.

So I slipped past the offices of my staff and through the heavy metal door at the end and peered into the locked holding cell with the Russian spook inside. He lay there on the cot, with one leg drawn up and crossed over the other, staring at the ceiling and smoking a handmade cigarette.

"There's no smoking in here."

After a moment, he sucked in another covert drag and then took the butt from his lips. "This is of why?"

"Fire hazard."

"You are of kidding."

"Nope."

Taking the butt between his fingers, he put it out on his tongue and then stuffed it in the breast pocket of his shirt. "There, all of the tidy," he said as I was leaving, then called after me. "Please to make sure am told when coffee is ready."

I stopped, turned, and looked at him. "Excuse me?"

"Do you have of cream?" He looked back to the ceiling and closed his eyes. "When coffee is ready, please to be told."

I pulled on the bars of the door, but they didn't move. I started to speak again, but the phone began ringing in the outer office. I figured it was Vic and started in that direction. "We'll be continuing this conversation in just a minute."

I made it down the hall just in time to catch the phone before it was transferred. Snatching the receiver, I panted. "He's locked up . . . At least I think he is."

Woody Woodson's, the director of the Division of Criminal Investigation's, voice sounded in my ear. "That's good, because I think we have a murder here."

# 4

It's always a unique situation, discussing the more professional aspects of what you do for a living in a public setting, especially when you're in a profession like mine in which the details can be more than a little off-putting to customers who are trying to eat. Fortunately, this was not the first time I'd found myself in this situation, and when Dorothy saw the director of the Division of Criminal Investigation, she was kind enough to seat us on the other side of the lobby of the Virginian Hotel, in the saloon—the ancillary seating for the Busy Bee Café.

Nursing our coffee, we discussed the latest findings in the privacy of the crown jewel of Western drinking establishments.

"Something like eighty percent of children who die from abuse die from abusive head trauma and, tragically, that's where we get the majority of our research on the pathology of inflicted head trauma."

Vic sipped her coffee and studied Woodson. "That's horrifying."

"Yeah." He placed his mug down on the long table where we sat. "In children hospitalized for inflicted head injuries, the mortality rate is about twenty percent."

I tasted my coffee. "So you're sure about this?"

He nodded.

"How so?"

Tammy Payson, Vic's countryman, flipped through the autopsy with photographs, and slid it toward me. "Subdural hemorrhage, or SDH, which is found in about ninety-five percent of such cases. It's a lot easier in our line of work when the victim is generally dead."

Vic sat her own mug down. "Lucky them, huh?"

"Fortunately, the inflicted head trauma where SDH is detectable on CT imaging reveals very thin layers of subdural blood over the cerebral convexities, which may not be visible by CT, but can be observed at autopsy."

I pretended like I knew what all that meant.

"The most typical form of SDH at autopsy in an inflicted head injury is a thin layer of SD blood over the cerebral convexities—one or both, more commonly both—and the amount of blood often less than ten milliliters and there's usually SDH in one or more of the cranial fossae."

I glanced at my second-in-command and slid the file back over to her. "Are you getting all of this?"

She studied the photos. "Yeah."

Payson reached over, pointing out a detail in the gruesome photo of Pepper McKay's exposed brain. "This type of SDH is the result of inertial brain rotational motion within the cranial cavity, in which bridging veins are torn and bleeding occurs into the cleaved subdural space; pretty much always an indication of abusive brain trauma."

I leaned over a bit, glancing toward the bottom of one of the grim photos. "Are those his eyes?"

She nodded, picking up her coffee and drinking. "Retinal hemorrhage, another leading indicator of SDH."

I leaned back in my chair as Dorothy approached with all our breakfasts expertly balanced on a single tray. "One round of the Usual?"

"Huevos rancheros with homemade chorizo."

"La usual?"

"Exactamundo." She swiped the plates from the tray one by one, setting them in front of us before holding up a couple of small bottles. "Hot sauce?"

"Knowing your cooking, I'll refrain."

The others followed suit as Vic forked a bite. "These retinal hemorrhages, are they usually present in only one or both eyes?"

Payson, caught in mid-bite, chewed and then answered. "Both, and other findings that indicate severe inflicted head trauma include retinal folds and retinoschisis, or separation of the retinal layers to produce a cavity filled with blood. At autopsy, folds may occur artifactually in the retina, and these are usually circumferential and linear while the folds associated with fissures are along the margins and around the cavity. RHs may occur in accidental head trauma, although usually they're found in fewer cases with inflicted head injury and that particular type of accidental trauma tends to be very severe, such as motor vehicle accidents."

Scooping up some of my huevos with the available tortilla, I chewed and asked, "So, what did the deed?"

The young woman looked at me. "If I was guessing—and we always are in our line of work—I'd say a rock."

"A rock?"

"That or a baseball." She shrugged. "My bet is a baseball-sized rock."

"So, Bob Gibson is the killer?"

Woody volunteered between bites. "I think he's dead."

I spoke out of the side of my mouth to Vic. "Take him off the list."

She forked in another bite. "Right."

"Well, if that's correct, and it certainly sounds as if it is, then that changes the demeanor of the killing."

"How is that?"

I turned, surprised to find that Dorothy was still there. "Usually if someone is intending a premeditated attack on someone, they don't grab whatever happens to be handy, and Crazy Woman Creek is chock-full of rocks."

"So, unpremeditated?" Dorothy asked.

"Possibly." I kept eating as she swept away, unimpressed with my rudimentary deductions. "I can keep this copy of the autopsy?"

Payson nodded, as did Woody.

"So, you guys are done?"

"Unless you've got something else for us." Woodson finished off his breakfast, tossing his napkin onto his plate in surrender. "Hey, do you think it'd be unprofessional to ask if I could spend a couple of hours on that private portion of Crazy Woman Creek?"

His partner, Tammy Payson, was quick to respond. "Yes."

He made a face. "I don't believe I was addressing you, technician."

"I know, that's why I answered." She looked at me. "Don't let him, he has things to do in Cheyenne."

Caught between a rock and a baseball, I answered. "You could always ask the McKay family."

He smiled through the beard. "I was kind of hoping you would."

"Basque deputy is of wonderful teacher." I watched as Sidorov reached through the bars and moved his queen, perplexing the Basquo. "I feel as if English of mine is improving of the dramatically."

"Uh-huh." I hung an arm on the locked gate. "How was your coffee?"

Without taking his eyes off the board, he lifted the mug from the floor and held it out to me through the food-tray opening, or bean slot, as it was historically called. "I would take of more, if you are going."

"Sancho, would you excuse us for a moment?"

He studied me questioningly, and then stood, vacating the guest chair and heading out the door, but pausing to take Maxim's empty mug, twirling it like a gunfighter as he went.

I sat in the chair Sancho had vacated. "Okay, we need to establish some rules here."

He did his best to look contrite. "I am sorry if I am of upset you . . . Basque deputy says I am of using word *of* too much in sentence structure?"

"You do."

"No one is of tell me these things?"

"You just did it again."

"You see? I need of . . . I need instruction?"

"Very good."

He glanced around. "I like this place, but I think I . . . I think I have found apartment."

"From this cell you found an apartment?"

"Yes."

"Where, and with whom?"

"Nice lady in front office? She say she has extra room over garage in her house place."

I stared at him. "Ruby?"

"Yes, she is one."

I held up a finger. "I'll be right back."

Leaving him, I moved down the hall and confronted my dispatcher, who sat in her chair reading the paper. "You offered your guest apartment to Maxim Sidorov?"

Setting her cup of tea aside, she studied me right back. "He seems like a nice man."

"He's a professional killer."

Laying her forearms on her counter, she threaded her fingers together. "In the greater scheme of things, I'm the only one in the building who isn't a killer, Walter. Besides, the two of you appear to have become bosom buddies."

"And what gave you that idea?"

"You gave him a place to stay."

"Behind bars."

"He *still* seems like a nice man."

"He's a Russian Spetsnaz special forces and a member of their Federal Security Service, or FSS, part of their espionage community, and he spent who knows how much time in their gulag for who knows what and killed three men that I know of—not to mention he tried to kill me."

Ruby got up and went over to the commissary table, where she poured more hot water into her cup before re-adding the tea bag. "Everybody's always trying to kill you, Walter. If we held that against people, we wouldn't be able to transact business with anybody. Besides, you're now his parole officer as I'm to understand it, so I thought you'd like to keep track of his whereabouts."

"I don't trust him, Ruby."

"Well, I don't trust him any further than paying his rent once a month." She returned and sat at her counter. "If it makes you feel any better, I'll lock my doors."

"A lot of good that'll do." I leaned on the counter, trying my best to change her mind. "You know he doesn't have any money?"

"He paid me six months' rent in advance." She sipped her tea. "I took him to the ATM machine this morning."

"You what?"

"While you were having breakfast. He needed some money, Walter."

I looked around for someone to witness this insanity, but evidently everyone was hiding like they always did whenever she was on a crusade. "Ruby, he's an assassin."

"Everybody deserves a second chance."

"No, they don't. That's why we're still in business."

"Well, I've made up my mind."

"No."

"Excuse me?"

"I said no, I'm not going to let you do this."

She removed her cat-eye glasses with the pearl lanyard, getting down to business. "Walter, the last time I looked, your name wasn't on either the deed for my house or my marriage license, so you really don't have much say in this."

"Ruby, I will arrest him and keep him in jail for the rest of his unnatural life rather than let him take your garage apartment— I'm not kidding."

"You wouldn't dare."

"You watch me."

We stood there nose to nose and then she dropped the bomb. "I'm calling the attorney general."

I couldn't speak for the next moment, but then found my voice, straightening and looking down at her with all the righteous indignation I could muster. "Oh, so that's what I've got to look forward to for the next four years?"

"If you don't behave yourself, yes."

"Behave myself." I started to turn but then whipped back around. "Behave myself?"

She sat on her stool, looking at me as she picked up the receiver. "I'm not bluffing."

I found my head nodding in a taut gesture as my finger rose, pointing at her. "You do that, call her." I stormed off to my office, almost tripping over Dog as I threw myself into my chair.

The beast's claws clicked on the marble floor and he stood there in the doorway, deciding if he was staying or seeking refuge elsewhere.

I patted my leg. "C'mere."

He seemed undecided.

I patted my leg again. "C'mon, I need all the friends I can get."

He eased his bulk over and rested his head on my knee. I ruffled his ears. "We're about to get a phone call that will determine our collective fates for the next four years because I don't think there's a doghouse big enough for the two of us."

My archnemesis, the little red light on my phone, began blinking and then went steady as I stared at it. A few moments later it began blinking again as my dispatcher squalled from the outer office. "Walter, line one."

With a deep sigh, I gave Dog one last pet and then snatched the receiver. "Walt Longmire speaking."

"Has she lost her mind?"

"Now, wait just a minute—" I stopped and then swallowed, beginning again. "You're on my side?"

"Dad, it's not a question of sides, but I don't think it's a good idea for Ruby to use her rental as a halfway house for international assassins."

"Excuse me for asking, but who is this and what have you done with my daughter, Cady Longmire, the Greatest Legal Mind of Our Time?"

"Ha, ha . . ."

"How's the new job?"

"Very intimidating."

"You'll get the hang of it; I've got faith in you."

"I'm glad somebody does." There was some rustling of papers. "You know, I can deny his request of relocation on the grounds that there's no actual probation officer in Durant."

"Then where would he go?"

"I don't know, Sheridan probably; there or Gillette."

I sat there, thinking.

"Don't like those options?"

I shrugged. "I was just getting used to the idea that he was going to be around and if he's really working on finding Ruth One Heart . . ."

"Do you think he actually is, or is this just another ploy and he's actually working for the people that have her?"

"That possibility had crossed my mind."

"So you're wanting to keep him close but not too close."

"Exactly."

"I can always pull the jurisdiction card and tell the Rubster that as the attending parole officer, you have final say in every aspect of Maxim's day-to-day life, especially where he lives, so long as he reports to you within seventy-two hours and notifies you of his relocation within ten days."

I lowered my voice. "Can we use that, say that there's a probation period of ten days before he can actually establish residence?"

"We can try. It's not legal so I can't sign off on it, but we can try to bluff her."

"So, you're not going to go to bat for me completely, huh?"

"Hey, that's my go-to babysitter for your granddaughter when I'm up there."

"She'll threaten to quit."

"Tell her to call me and I'll explain that we really don't have any choice in the ten days."

"Okay." I settled in my chair as Dog, determining the crisis was abated, coiled on the floor beside my desk. "By the way, how is my granddaughter?"

"Talking up a storm."

"So, the Second Greatest Legal Mind of Our Time?"

She laughed. "Actually, I think she's got more of a sheriffing temperament."

"God help you."

"I better call Ruby back, or you can just transfer me back to her?"

I stared at the myriad buttons and lights on my twenty-year-old phone. "I don't know how to do that."

"I didn't figure." She laughed again. "Bye, Dad. I love you."

"Love you too, punk."

The phone went dead in my hand as I noticed Maxim Sidorov standing in my doorway, Dog's growl rumbling deep in his throat.

"I do not think dog likes me."

"He's a shrewd judge of character." I hung up the phone. "What are you doing out of your cell?"

He revealed a towel and Dopp kit from behind his back. "Am taking shower in facility in basement, if is okay?"

I gestured toward my guest chair. "Maxim, have a seat."

He did as I suggested. "My friends refer to me as Max. You may call me Max."

"Maxim, there's a problem with your relocation. A notification of ten days is needed before relocation within the state."

"Seriously?"

"Yep."

"A probation period within probation period?"

"I'm afraid so. I just got off the phone with the Wyoming attorney general . . ."

"Daughter of yours."

I cleared my throat. "Nevertheless, yes, you're required to give ten days' notice."

He adjusted his eye patch and stared at me with the one eye. "You are sure of this?"

"Yep."

He shrugged. "May I have to stay in jail for ten days? Seems of wasteful to live in motel for ten days after giving nice lady damage deposit and six-month rent." He shook his head as if to clear it. "I have permission?"

"Yep, you can even move downstairs where there's a commissary and private bathroom."

"I think I like up here better, gives me opportunity to interact with staff and populace."

"That, you can't do. I can't have you interfering with the day-to-day operations of the department."

Resting the towel and kit in his lap, he raised his hands. "Not to interrupt, I am to understand."

"Good."

He stood, gathering his things and looking at me questioningly. "Probation within probation, never to have heard of such bureaucracy outside of my country."

"It's in the books."

He cleared his throat. "So long as you do not disapprove of my presence in office."

"So long as you do not become a problem here in the office."

"I will do best to become asset to working community and assist in any way possible."

Getting up from my chair, I raised a hand like a traffic cop, half warning and half pleading. "Please don't."

He started to go but then turned. "We play more chess?"

I thought about my game date tonight with the previous sheriff of Absaroka County. "Possibly with me, and maybe someone else . . ."

"Murder." He paused, sitting on the porch steps of the lodge as his legs refused to support him. "You can't be serious."

"Sorry, but I'm afraid I am." I sat beside him and watched as his eyes brimmed. "You know, Gary, you may be the only one who genuinely liked Pepper."

He half sobbed and half guffawed. "I suppose that's true."

"You and Lynn have been here since he took it over?"

"1963." He wiped his eyes. "Were you here?"

"Nope, finishing up college in California and then Vietnam."

"Oh."

He gazed off into the fading evening, the sun just beginning to hide behind the Bighorn Mountains, casting long, smoky shadows across the Powder River Country. "Do you remember our son, Peter?"

I thought of the thin, bookish young man in the obituary who wore the Buddy Holly glasses that framed his intelligent green eyes. "Vaguely, was he quite a few years behind me?"

"Yes." There was a long pause as he rose and walked out into the dry grass. "You know he drowned?"

"I remember hearing about it, in Lake De Smet, wasn't it?"

"Yes." He stood there for a while, unmoving. "It was a bet; some of the other boys said he couldn't swim all the way across the reservoir. He was a good swimmer, but I guess he got a cramp or something." He took a few more steps, toeing the grass with a boot and studying the ground for a long time. "Do you think about life and death much, Walt? I mean really think about it?"

"As an occupational hazard I have to say yep, I do."

"I know you had a wife who passed away, but you never lost any children, did you?"

"I actually did. Martha had a miscarriage when we were young, and we lost a boy."

"Oh." He turned to look at me. "I'm so sorry."

I stood, stuffing my hands in my jeans. "It was a long time ago."

"There's no such thing as a long time ago when you're talking about losing a child. There's not a day goes by that I don't think of Peter."

I nodded. "At least I was spared the pain of meeting and getting to know mine."

His eyes stayed on me. "I guess that's why we bonded so closely with Manx. Pepper never wanted him, and when his mother died, he just gravitated toward us or we gravitated to him, I'm not sure which. He was four when his mother died and the rest of his family up in Hardin didn't want him . . . How do you discard a four-year-old? How do you do that?"

"I don't know."

He stared at the grass between us. "So we took him in, maybe as a replacement for Peter. I don't know."

"Maybe because it was the right thing to do, and you were in a position to do it."

He sighed. "Is it as simple as that?"

"Sometimes." I walked over to him and placed a hand on his shoulder. "I get the feeling that you're trying to tell me something here, Gary. And generally when people are trying to tell me something that's important to them, they talk about everything else, but I think you slipped up."

"That obvious, huh?"

"Well, you should probably know that I haven't even started formulating a list of suspects as to who killed Pepper."

"I'm glad to hear that. Look, I know it seems fishy that Manx tried to get out of here but he's just, well . . . kind of a free spirit."

"I understand."

"He didn't kill Pepper, Walt."

"If you know anything that would support that supposition, I'd appreciate any evidence you might have."

"I'm not sure what you mean?"

Looking at the dry grass, I thought about the fires that had sprung up along the east face. "Were you with him yesterday morning?"

"Who?"

"Manx."

"No."

I didn't move. "You're sure?"

"Yes."

"Gary, let me give you a little piece of advice? Whenever law enforcement asks you a question, they generally already know the answer. So, I'll ask you again, did you see Manx yesterday morning?"

He licked his lips and rubbed the lower part of his face with a calloused hand as if to prime the pump. "I did."

"And when was that?"

"I'm not sure . . . early. I had breakfast with him and Lynn."

"And then what?"

"I went up to my office, so I don't know where he went."

"You're sure about that? You're sure he didn't head out the back toward Crazy Woman Creek?"

He made an agonized face. "He might've."

"Around five-thirty?"

"Closer to six." He turned to look at me. "I'm not a very good criminal, am I?"

"Not something to be ashamed of, Gary." I started to go but then called back. "Are they down at the lower corral, near the barn?"

"Yep, just take the first cutoff to the left that leads to the main road heading up the canyon."

"Thanks." Thinking of something else, I spoke to him again. "Hey Gary, do you remember Woody Woodson, the director of DCI who was here yesterday?"

"The fisher fellow?"

"That's him. Would you mind if he came down tomorrow and wet a line in Crazy Woman?"

"Will that work better for Manx?"

I smiled at him, just to be clear that I wasn't taking him seriously. "Nope, won't make any difference at all."

"You can't blame a fella for trying. Sure, does he need a place to stay?"

"I don't think so, but you can ask him when you see him." I climbed into my truck and started it before driving down the curvy road that crossed the bridge where we'd found the body of Pepper McKay. Vic had gotten bored listening to Gary and me, and had joined the highway patrolman, Shane, down below.

The big pines crowded out the sky and I had to lurch to a stop to keep from missing the cutoff to the barn and lower corrals, as opposed to the upper ones that were used on the ranch's expansive trails that led through Crazy Woman Canyon.

Wilson's highway patrol cruiser was parked near the main

corral, and he and Vic were draped on the fence watching Manx work a very large, dusky john mule with a light muzzle and three stockings.

"Been here long?"

"Long enough to know I don't know shit about mules." My undersheriff disentangled herself from the fence and glanced up at me. "But he sure as hell does."

I nodded to the HP. "Hey, Shane."

"Sheriff." He pulled his sunglasses down to look at me. "This guy is good. I've never seen a mule work like that."

"Putting him through the paces, huh?"

"Yeah."

Manx gently heeled the mule to the right, keeping him centered but crabbing in that direction with all four feet. We watched Manx lay the reins to one side and pitch the big animal around to face us then lay the reins gently against the other side of the mule's withers and swivel him back, stopping in the exact same position as before. "I can put my jacket over a four-pole fence and convince him what it is I want him to do, and he'll jump it from a standing start."

"You've got to be kidding."

"Not one bit."

I raised my voice. "He got a name?"

"Borax."

I smiled to myself. "Looks like he's coming along."

"Yeah, he just has to reach the conclusion on his own that he can do this, that he doesn't have to be upset, and that nobody's going to hurt him, but when I block him, I want his weight to go back and across, just the way it would if he were working cattle. I'm just looking for him to get a feel for what we're doing here."

"Had him long?"

"Long enough." Manx turned the roan and then backed him away. "A bridle animal really needs to bridle up, and he hasn't learned to do that with the speed I know he can muster."

"I'd imagine they're happy to be out of the trailer."

"None of them like that. This one tends to stomp his hooves all the way to the pass in Raton, but then he gets quiet."

Wilson laughed. "Only nine hours to calm down, huh?"

"I'm pretty much the same way." Manx smiled toward the HP. "This one . . . I had the music on and wasn't paying any attention, and he comes whipping in front of me and slows down. I almost crashed into the back of him, but then got the trailer slowed down and pulled over. I jumped out and this guy pulls his gun on me . . ."

"I told you to stay in your truck."

"Didn't hear that, my man."

The patrolman shrugged. "Doesn't matter."

"Doesn't, huh?" Manx spun Borax again and then began getting the mule's weight on the rear legs as he gently nudged him, resulting in the big guy pivoting a step to the right and then a step to the left. "Right, left, right, left . . ." After a moment, he stopped, raising his face and looking at the HP. "Would you really have shot me?"

"Yeah, I guess I would've; you were a suspect at large, and you were approaching me in an aggressive manner."

"An aggressive manner?" His head cocked to one side. "You been on the job long, Mister Aggressive Manner?"

Figuring it was time to step in, I raised my voice. "Hey, I'm the one who asked you not to leave."

Manx looked down at me with the disdain that a man on horseback reserves for a man afoot. "Yeah, but I didn't take you seriously."

Climbing the fence, I sat on the top rail, about even with him. "Your father was killed, so I need you to start taking everything I say seriously."

He stared at the horn of his well-worn saddle. "He was killed."

"It would appear."

He continued to stare at the saddle. "So, I'm suspect number one."

"There isn't any real order, but everybody's on the list, so far."

"Even the legitimate ones?"

"Everybody."

He barely touched the john mule's flanks, and it leaped forward, its great nose only inches from my face.

Vic was the first to respond. "Hey, motherfucker!"

Bridling up, I watched as he raised Borax's head above mine, the heavy breath of the thousand-pound animal heating my face as I watched Wilson pull his sidearm and direct it at both mule and rider.

I just sat there looking at Manx, a thin smile playing on my face.

Laying the reins over hard, he and his mount spun with the speed of a great deal of mule muscle, bunching like steel springs and flashing around with great clumps of hard earth flying through the air as he pivoted a full circle before stopping with Borax's nose, once again, only inches from my face.

Vic pulled her own sidearm and pointed it at him. "Hey, you need to stand the fuck down!"

"You know, my father was a blacksmith."

Manx's eyes came back to me. "Z'at so?"

"Yep."

"He teach you anything?"

"Will is to grace as the horse is to the rider."

"What's that supposed to mean?"

"I think the original quote is from Sigmund Freud." The mule he sat on, growing curious as they are wont to do, stretched his nose out and sniffed at the brim of my hat. "You think on it for a while, and maybe it'll come to you."

Moving slowly, I brushed the back of my hand on the velvety nose in the few inches left between us.

"Don't touch his chin." Manx breathed a response and then backed Borax away, giving a momentary look to both Shane and Vic. "Easy there, T. J. Hooker, easy there . . ."

Turning the big mule, he moved toward the gate and expertly opened it while still in the saddle, skirting the animal through and then continuing into a narrow chute and the darkness of the barn.

I looked at my two comrades. "Well, I'm glad we didn't have to shoot anybody."

My undersheriff holstered her 9 mm. "Let's go arrest that son of a bitch."

"Nah, just give me a few minutes alone with him." I turned to the highway patrolman who was also holstering his weapon. "You okay?"

"That's the second time I've had to draw down on him today. Can I have a say as to where he goes on the list?" He snapped his safety strap. "What the hell is a Borax?"

"Death Valley and the Twenty Mule Team."

"Never heard of it."

"I guess you never did laundry." I laughed and moved across the corral, through the gate, and into the darkened barn. I let my eyes adjust to the floating motes in the shafts of light streaming through the cracks in the slats. I heard Manx working with the tack, down the lane of stalls.

"Down here." Seeking out the voice, I continued on and found him lifting the saddle and placing it on a stand, wiping off the bridle, and then brushing Borax down with a wooden-handled brush.

Placing a hand on the mule's hindquarters, I asked, "So, why couldn't I touch his chin?"

Manx smiled with a mischievous grin and reached under Borax's muzzle, scratching his chin, and in an instant, a rear hoof larger than a coffee can shot out right beside me like a strike of lightning. The mule glanced back at me and then settled again as if nothing had happened. "He had a bad trainer when he was young, some horse's ass who used to pinch under his chin to get his attention." He stopped brushing the mule and regarded me. "Don't ever insult a mule—because they never forget."

I smiled at him but said nothing.

"Think that trooper would've shot me?"

I closed the lid on a large trunk full of saddle blankets. "I don't know, he had two chances."

"What about her?"

"My undersheriff? Oh yeah, in a heartbeat, or a Philadelphia minute; whichever came first."

"What about you?"

"Me, nah." I reached up and massaged Borax's withers. "I watched you handle this big guy so I knew you wouldn't hit me unless you meant to."

"And what if I meant to?"

"I would've been knocked off the fence, but I've been knocked off fences before."

He lifted his signature Kum & Go travel mug and took a sip, then carefully replaced it on a nearby shelf that held a collection of brushes and a holstered Smith & Wesson. "You don't ruffle easy, do you?"

"Nope."

"You get that from your dad too?"

"Some."

"Yeah, well, I never knew mine." He wiped more of the lathered sweat from the mule. "What was that quote again?"

"Will is to grace as the horse is to the rider."

"Right." He stood there with his arms trailing over the mule's back, the brush still in his hands as he waxed philosophical. "I think it has something to do with your life being controlled by your will or your emotions, drive and primitive power, while grace is the consciousness of reason and rationalization, the focus of your life—the part that gives it meaning."

"The rider without grace will ride for a fall—grace could also be seen as God's grace."

"Was your father religious?"

"More than me." I picked up another brush from the shelf behind me and began rubbing down my side of Borax and enjoying the smell. "Was Pepper religious?"

Manx resumed working on his side. "Oh, he had religion, if you want to call it that. The highest sacrament being 'I got mine; now screw you, go get your own.'"

"What about your brothers?"

He paused for a moment. "Half brothers and they won't even half claim me. You'll have to ask them; they were raised different from me."

"In what way?"

"If you ask me a question, I'm going to give you an answer. Now, you may not like it, but you can take it to the bank as the truth."

"Are you saying that one of them lied to me?"

"No."

I worked on the mule some more. "Good."

Reaching out, he tapped the brim of my hat with the wooden-handled brush to get my attention. "I'm saying all of them lied to you."

# 5

"So, you're saying there were other people here the night before last?"

"Yes." Manx led Borax through the main opening and removed his halter, turning him loose in a paddock to our left.

"More than one?"

Pulling his long, dark hair from his face, he thought about the answer before delivering it. "Yes."

"Who?"

"With all due respect, you'll have to ask them about that. I've got work to do and I'm behind because you brought me back here." He draped the halter over his shoulder as Vic and Shane appeared from around the corner of the barn. Reaching over, he plucked the Kum & Go travel mug from the shelf and took another sip. "Any idea how long before I can head to Arizona?"

"Not really. Now that it's a homicide investigation, there are a lot of variables."

"Variables?"

"Yep."

He glanced at the HP and the Terror. "You'll let me know when I can head south? I don't like keeping the riding stock around here with all the fires."

"Sure."

He took another sip from the travel mug and Vic, of course, had to ask: "So what's in the mug?"

He lifted it. "This? Only the finest Himalayan loose-leaf black tea." He held it out to her in an attempt at making amends. "Care to try?"

She took a sip and handed it back. "Say, not bad."

He smiled and disappeared into the darkness without saying anything more.

I walked over to the gate where my two brethren in blue awaited me. Vic opened the latch and let me out. "So I say we shoot him but not the mule."

I studied the big john as he lowered himself to the ground to roll over on his back; first one heroic effort, then another, and rolling over to the other side. "Thousand-dollar mule."

"Excuse me?"

"The old saying goes that if he only rolls halfway, he's a five-hundred-dollar mule, but if he goes all the way over . . ."

"Well, that's scientific."

"Very."

Wilson threw a hand up. "You need me?"

"Not particularly, but thanks for being here. Something up?"

"The fire."

"I thought they were pretty much out?"

"Pole Creek. It's getting ready to jump Highway 16."

"Pole Creek, is that a new one?"

He shrugged as we walked the length of the barn and toward his unit, still parked at the corral by the road leading into the canyon. "It is."

"How many is that?"

"Three in the immediate vicinity. Sisters Hill, Poison Creek—both of which are pretty much out—and now Pole Creek."

"Did they get that grass fire down on Old Highway 87 put out?"

"Yes."

"Well, we're three for four."

Unlocking his unit with the key fob, he paused, taking off his Smokey Bear hat and tossing it inside. "And that's the way I'm headed."

"Be careful."

He peered past me and toward the barn. "I think you're the one who needs to be careful, Sheriff."

We watched as Wilson backed out and flipped on his emergency lights, the blue flashes chasing him up the gravel road of the mountain, the smell of smoke once again drifting in our nostrils. "You smell that?"

She turned, looking at the mountain range as if she might be able to see the flames. "Yeah, where is Pole Creek?"

I paused at the other side of the hood of my truck, pointing due west. "About ten miles, that way."

"Sisters Hill?"

I repointed slightly north. "About fourteen miles that way."

"Poison Creek?"

I adjusted my finger south. "About sixteen miles the other way."

"I'm glad they're pretty much out, but what would happen if they were to join up?"

"Catastrophe of the first order." I started for my truck. "Fortunately, the winds have died down, so they're not spreading as fast as they were, but that Pole Creek fire is disturbing because it's the one that could connect them all."

"And it's jumping the highway?"

Opening the door, I climbed in. "I guess we'll find out."

Climbing in the other side, she continued to peer at the mountains through the top of the windshield. "Why so many fires this season?"

"You remember how dry it was this past summer from the lack of snow last winter?"

"Yeah?"

"My father used to call the snow 'money in the bank' because of the water it provided to the reservoir system. With it being as dry as it was, we haven't had as much moisture and the forest has gotten dry, hence the lightning storm the other night and subsequent fires."

As we drove up the hill toward the lodge, she looked out the glass, even going so far as to lower her window to feel the air. "Shouldn't we have had a snow by now?"

"Yep, we should've."

"It rained about a month ago, didn't it?"

"A little." I pulled in and parked in the front lot near the lodge. "But not enough."

"Where to now?"

"I think I'm going to let the McKay brothers stew a little and come back in the morning. Besides, I've got a chess game to officiate."

Dumping some more chili from the illegal slow cooker in room 32 of the Durant Home for Assisted Living, I dolloped in some sour cream and a little cheese before snagging another Rainier from the mini fridge and joining Vic on the sofa.

Not since Kasparov vs Topalov, Byrne vs Fischer, Tal vs Larsen, or Fischer vs Spassky had there been such a monumental battle of the chessboard. Maxim Sidorov had taken an early lead by winning the first two games, but then Lucian began learning his adversary's moves and was about to pass him.

The games had slowed as they'd developed strategies and tactics, and read tendencies, but they were both aggressive players and generally reaped the rewards and paid the price for their passionate play.

Commanding black, Lucian had opened with the Sicilian Defense and Maxim had responded by moving a white pawn to d4. The old sheriff took the pawn, only to have the Russian move another pawn to c3, which the old Doolittle Raider then took. "We just gonna pawn ourselves to death?"

Sidorov moved a knight out, taking the pawn. "You are happy now?"

"Two pawns for one, I'll play that all night."

"Smith–Morra Gambit in response to the Sicilian Defense. You do not know this move, old man?" We shared a glance as I recognized the move as the one he'd used on me the night we'd met.

"If you're waiting on an e5 with that knight of mine, you can forget it."

Moving the next pawn to e6, Lucian sat back in his overstuffed leather chair and took a sip of his Pappy Van Winkle 23 Years Old Family Reserve bourbon whiskey. "Take that instead."

He watched as Sidorov brought out a bishop to c4.

Lucian moved a pawn out to b6, effectively slowing the quick attack, and I was proud of him. There were a few other moves and then I thought the old sheriff had made a mistake when he brought his knight out to d5.

Sidorov studied him and took the knight with another pawn. Lucian took that pawn, clearing the way to the black king with a rook e1. "Check."

The Russian stared at the board, considering moving a piece to block the rook, but if he did, there was a pawn perfectly placed to remove it. As near as I could tell, there was nowhere for Maxim to go. He could move a knight and forestall the inevitable, but sooner or later the rook was going to get him.

The old Raider turned toward me, sitting on the far end of his horsehide sofa. "I ever tell you about Bob Emmens?"

"Who?"

"Fella that worked for JCPenney? He got canceled for the raid, but then they had to ferry one of the B-25s to California and he got the duty. And when he got there, he lobbied the old man into including him, even though he didn't have any training on the short takeoff we were gonna be using on the USS *Hornet* for the raid." He glanced at Sidorov. "You figure it out there yet?"

Maxim chewed a fingernail. "No."

"Well, you let me know." Setting the tumbler down, Lucian stared out the window. "Flight eight, they couldn't find their primary target and circled around till they found a cluster of factories, power plants, and a railyard where they dropped their ordnance. It was about then that they took a look at their fuel gauges and knew there was no way they were going to make it to the crash site in China, so they set off for Vladivostok, in the Soviet Union."

Finishing my chili, I plucked the bottle of very expensive bourbon from the side table and poured Vic a bit more into her outstretched tumbler.

"Bob and the crew spent thirteen months under house arrest, with a side of malnutrition and dysentery, before deciding that maybe they didn't want to spend the rest of the war in a shitty gulag."

Vic took a sip. "I thought the Russians were on our side in that one?"

"They were eventually, but at that point they'd signed a nonaggression pact with the Japanese. So anyway, with two hundred fifty dollars' worth of poker winnings and some shady character from Turkmenistan, they got across the border into Iran and made contact with the nearby British consulate, which shipped 'em off to India, where they got back to the US by 1943."

"Wow."

"Bob learned fluent Russian in those thirteen months, which served him in good stead till he retired in Oregon around '64." He turned back to Sidorov, gesturing toward the board. "Just so you know, there ain't no way out there, Baryshnikov."

I shook my head, glancing at Vic. "You've got him doing it?"

She sipped her drink and smiled, the elongated canine tooth on display. "Doing what?"

Maxim flicked the king face down on the board, reached over, and took a sip of his own drink. "I have had the bourbon before, but this one is good, yes?"

"The best there is." He lifted his glass. "Here's to Pepper McKay. God help the world if he'd been born twins."

"How come you never told me, Lucian?"

He took a sip, taking his time in answering. "Told you what?"

"About Pepper and Martha."

"Because she asked me not to, that's why." He studied me. "I'm surprised she finally told you."

"I guess she figured enough time had gone by that I'd be over it."

The old sheriff breathed a laugh. "That was a mistake."

Vic leaned in. "So?"

I sipped my beer. "So what?"

"What'd you do?"

"Well, I didn't go looking for him, if that's what you mean."

"Both of you in this county for that length of time, you had to see each other again."

"We did." Figuring I wasn't going to get out of it, I gave them the *Reader's Digest* version. "Pepper was out at one of those bars on the Powder River, harassing some woman, and the call came in and I happened to be in the area . . . I remember walking in there and seeing him, knowing who he was. I took him by the arm and escorted him outside, and when I spun him around, a pistol fell out of his pants."

I sipped my drink.

"And?"

I turned to her. "I think he knew that if I wanted to kill him, that would've been the time to do it, but I didn't. I just stooped down and picked up his pistol and threw it into the weeds at the end of the parking lot and told him to go home."

"And what'd he do?"

"He went and got in his car and started off, but then pulled to a stop out there and rolled the window down. I think he'd planned on something to say, and I couldn't help but think he was going to be foolish enough to ask about Martha, but I could tell he knew that I knew. I guess he lost his nerve at that point because he just rolled the window back up and drove away."

"That's it?"

"Yep, I saw him at the grocery store one time when Martha was with me, but she didn't speak to him, so I didn't either."

We all sat there in silence when Maxim began speaking. "A Romanian and a Bulgarian are driving through Russia when policeman stops them and says, 'I stopped you because I am looking for two rapists.' The Romanian and the Bulgarian look at each other and then back at policeman and say, 'We'll do it!'"

We all sat there, looking at him.

He shrugged. "Perhaps joke is better in Russian."

Vic ignored him. "So you never had it out?"

"Uh . . . What was I going to do, bloody his nose again?"

She slumped back into her side of the sofa. "Yeah."

"It seemed disrespectful. Martha had taken care of him all

those years ago, so what would I be doing, exercising my ego?" I could see Sidorov studying me as he began resetting the chess pieces. "What do you think, Maxim?"

He reached over, picking up his glass and sipping the bourbon of choice.

"I think you are very dangerous man."

I laughed. "How so?"

He smiled at the others and then back to me. "A man who can control the emotions to this extent is measured and capable of anything—calculating and truly dangerous." He sipped his drink again, looking out the sliding glass windows. "When anger and revenge are married, their daughter is called cruelty."

Vic smiled. "Nice."

He turned to me. "This is man who is dead?"

"Yep."

"And you think is murder?"

"Pretty sure, yep."

"Why?"

"The medical examiner and the experts from Cheyenne are pretty sure, and they're rarely wrong."

"Hmm . . . Maybe, maybe not."

Vic shook her head, pushing her dark hair from one eye. "And what do you know about it, Vladimir?"

"I was MUR officer, Moscovite Murder Division."

I leaned forward. "You were a homicide investigator in Moscow?"

"Yes."

Vic snorted. "You were a cop?"

He smiled. "You find this hard to believe, little mother?"

"A little."

I stood and took my empty bowl and spoon back to the kitchenette, placing them in the sink before returning. "What happened?"

He watched as Lucian finished resetting the chess pieces. "Unfortunate investigation."

I sat. "Concerning?"

"The body of a young woman . . . Girl student found in Neskuchny Garden, near the pavilion, was stabbed eighteen times."

My undersheriff shrugged. "That is unfortunate."

He took a sip of his drink and stared out the windows and into the dark. "That was not unfortunate part."

"What was?"

"I was convicted of this crime."

After locking Maxim in his cell, for whatever it was worth, I moved away but then sat in the guest chair. "We're going to have to have an agreement concerning this door here."

"And is?"

"That you resist the temptation to open it."

"What if need drink of water or to go to bathroom, or to investigate of strange noises?" He gazed up and around in a bemused manner, finally settling the one eye on me. "I believe old library is haunted."

"It is . . . by me."

He laughed and then sat on the edge of his cot and spread his hands, all smiles. "May have other cup of coffee?"

I reached out and took the mug but didn't move.

"What can I do for you, Sheriff?"

"Stay put." Leaning back in the chair, I sat the mug on the floor and then pushed my hat back on my head. "Look, I don't mind if you go to the bathroom or get a glass of water, but you can't be wandering around out here even when nobody else is around, and maybe most importantly not then."

"Da, I see."

"It's state law that a person cannot be incarcerated without twenty-four-hour supervision, but for the first time in a long time, I'd really like to go home and sleep in my own bed."

"Yes, I have seen her, and I would want to go home and sleep in bed too."

I stared at him.

"Sorry, she is beautiful woman, intelligent, humorous and . . . What is word?" He snapped his fingers. "Feisty! Yes, is feisty?"

"I think she blew past feisty when she was eight years old. Anyway, you see my point—that I'm breaking the law by leaving you here alone—mitigated by the fact that with your illicit skills you can come and go as you please and you're not technically under arrest."

"Yes."

"Just don't abuse the privilege."

"The promise is mine."

"All right." I started to get up when he spoke again.

"I thought you would ask me about girl student found killed in Neskuchny Garden when I was with MUR's Murder Division in Moscow."

I sighed, staring at the concrete floor between us. "I think you've done a lot of truly despicable things in your life, but I prefer to think you wouldn't do something like that. Stabbing a woman eighteen times in a park reeks of a random and violent act, and I don't think you've ever done anything random in your life—truly extreme and calculated for sure, but never random."

"Thank you."

"I'm not sure for what."

"For small measure of the trust." He started to reach for the eye patch but then stopped. "Do you mind if I take off patch? Is tiring to wear constantly."

"Feel free."

I watched as he lowered his face and slipped the thing off, stuffing it into his shirt pocket. Sidarov's face slowly rose, and I could now see the damage that the exploding rifle had done that night at my grandfather's ranch.

The flesh around the eye socket looked like shattered glass, as if his visage had been a single pane until the rifle had broken the surface. Caught in that spider's web of scars hung the orb of his eye, slightly extended. It looked as though a wayward albino arachnid had buried itself in his face.

It was odd because his remaining eye was a late-summer-in-the-high-plains hazel, but paled in comparison with the bleached-out sphere in the damaged socket. You had to look closely to see any difference between the white of his eye and the iris at all.

It was as if the one eye had witnessed something so shocking and fitfully true that the color had blanched and simply couldn't remain.

"Thank you." His voice broke the spell.

"For what?"

"For not turning away." He smiled, revealing the gold tooth, and in combination with the eye, it was ghastly. "You are being gracious, yes?"

"Possibly, but that eye of yours is my work and my responsibility—it would be disingenuous for me to not look at it."

The smile broadened as both eyes blinked, the damaged one just a bit slower. "I have you pegged correct, yes, Sheriff?"

"Meaning?"

"You are man of principle; you have code that you live by. Do you have any idea how rare this is in world?" He stared at me, even going so far as to cock his head so that the pale moon of an orb gazed at me unseeing. "You know why I have not had the plastic surgery or replacement of eye inserted?"

"You said it was because you didn't think it would be honest."

"That was about eye patch but is true. You think is true, that at age fifty everyone has face they deserve?"

"Orwell, but I think the Abraham Lincoln quote is better: Every man over forty is responsible for his face."

"Ah, this I did not know." I glanced up at the clock above the door and began to stand. "I would like to tell you of story concerning girl student found in Neskuchny Garden when I was police officer."

I stopped, half standing. "It's getting kind of late . . ."

"Please, to humor me."

I sat back down and waited, watching that washed-out and damaged eye peer backward into his head and into its past, and summon the ghosts that still haunted the man.

"I was thirty years old and still idealistic, even after of military service. I was assigned a case where young woman was supposedly offered ride in man's car to American embassy. My partner at the time was of Inspector Sergei Yashina, who had been on the force so long, had pigeon shit on shoulders from being monument."

He took a breath.

"As mentioned, body was found behind of pavilion: very large outdoor structure, which hold over thousand people. Had been concert night before and there was much of trash. One of park workers was first to find body and report it to Moscovite Metro Police, who, after observing of body, call us.

"We arrive and identify body as girl student, but I cannot help but feel that Sergei is reluctant to be involved with investigation, especially after ascertaining cause of death. He explain to me that this method of death was same as of three other women who had been murdered and that he personally capture culprit and help to achieve of death sentence that was carried out two years before."

"Eighteen knife wounds."

"Yes." He stood and approached the bars. "Perhaps is not so of random? Eighteen: six, six, and six."

I unzipped my jacket and leaned forward, resting my elbows on my knees. "Some sort of satanic numerology?"

"Crime was referred to as Whore of Babylon Murders, very high-profile case. Sergei is of great concern that only did he capture and execute of wrong man, but what will do to his standing in department because so close to retirement and of pension. He is very upset and produce knife, which he says was similar to used in other murders, asking me to stab body of girl one more time so that details are not of same." Sidarov sat back on the cot, his back making a thump against the concrete block wall. "At first, I tell him no, but he plead with me to help him, and I finally stab girl again, figuring of what is harm?"

"A lot."

He nodded. "I discover this, yes."

"What happened?"

"Two weeks later I am taken into custody, my fingerprints on supposed murder weapon, doctored security footage with time of stamp placing me in park night of girl's killing, and they find planted notebooks and photographs in apartment condemning me of being kopirovat' kota, or copy the cat killer."

"All that to protect his pension?"

"No."

I didn't think about it for long. "He knew the murderer, the real murderer."

"Yes. While in prison I am making of contact with man who is soldier for crime syndicate in Moscow, very powerful and rich family, well respected with many of connections worldwide—vor v zakone, or thief in law. Name of family is one of Anatoly

Mogilevich and that he has son, Mikhail, who has extreme tastes with women. Please to remember that I have lot of time on hands . . . Limited resource, da, but lot of time and entire mind trust of those in Zone."

"Zone?"

"Maximum security prison."

"Ah."

"Day I am released, nineteen years later, I immediately go to apartment of Inspector Sergei Yashina, but he is long dead, shooting self in parked car in suspicious suicide. Wife is nice woman and explain that before death Sergei say that I would come looking for him when released, and that when I did, she was to give me of package."

Plumping a thin pillow, he placed it in his lap. "This is nice jail; you have no lice."

"What was in the package?"

"Wrapped in wax and newspaper, like fish, I find falsified documents, altered security tape, and signed affidavit of Sergei, stating how he was pressured by Mogilevich family to falsify of information on first murders and on subsequent one of which I was convicted." His eyes rose to mine. "There is also complete dossier on Mikhail, uncooked file of true investigation, making it clear he is murderer not only of these women but numerous others."

"What did you do?"

He breathed a laugh. "Mikhail was now head of family, moving of enterprise in more respectable endeavors, more rich and more powerful."

"How about going to the authorities?"

He stared at me.

"Okay, I'm not so sure I want to hear the rest of this."

"I did not kill him."

"Well, good."

"Anatoly, father did." Straightening the pillow, he smoothed the surface with his hands. "I held gun to father's head and made him choose to either shoot son or I would shoot father. Can you imagine man that would shoot of own child rather than be shot? I cannot, but I have witnessed hand of first."

I cleared my throat. "And you killed Mikhail for the women, or for your nineteen years?"

He looked at me, surprised. "But both."

I nodded. "And why is it you felt compelled to tell me this story?"

"You are fighting same battle with oligarchy; these people believe they are untouchable, that they move in societies doing as they wish and that there will be no repercussions of their actions. You and I, we realize there is no such thing as safety. The only thing can do is make the repercussions of such actions so terrible that to even consider them is of insufferable."

"And you think our situations are similar?"

"No, but adversaries are, and this is why I help you."

"Hmm."

"You have seen photographs; they are taking her somewhere where they keep her. She is useless to them if dead—her only of value is you."

"All this because I killed their son."

"Yes."

"Even though Ruth is the one that shot him."

"They have weakness."

"And what's that?"

"Racism, bigotry . . . They are narrow of the mind and do not believe a Native woman could have killed the son, so you have become target of lust of blood."

"I don't suppose I could go get her, wherever she is, and just bring her back?"

"Not likely. They will demand payment for her freedom."

"My life for hers?"

"Likely, yes."

"What's to keep me from going to the authorities?"

He stared at me and then finally spoke. "Layers."

I stood and took the chair, placing it back in the corner for the next visitor, then picked up his mug. "Okay, I'll bite, what layers?"

"There are unwritten rules of types of negotiations. She is only useful to them in bait for you, but if situation becomes more volatile, they may surrender or dispose of person the way old sheriff and I cast aside pawns in game of chess earlier tonight—layers of deniability, as we have discussed before." Threading his fingers together, he stretched his arms above his head and then pointed toward the mug in my hand. "May I have of coffee before you leave?"

I stared at him for a moment more and then twirled the mug like a gunfighter the same as Saizarbitoria had. "Sure."

Filling the mug in the commissary downstairs where Sancho had brewed the pot, I thought about what Sidarov had said and what my next move might be. Far Eastern Russia . . . Where the hell was I going to find Ruth One Heart there?

I didn't even know any Russians.

Well, I knew one and thought about what he'd said.

Finishing the pour, I stood there with his coffee mug in my hand and my head cocked to one side, listening.

There was a noise upstairs, nothing solid, but just a few sounds indicating that someone, or something, was there moving around. I couldn't believe that Maxim hadn't even waited for me to leave before prowling all over the place.

Carrying the mug, I reached the landing and just stood there for a very long time listening but heard nothing more. "Hell, maybe the place *is* haunted." Glancing over at the gallery of sheriffs, I started up the next flight, glancing at the photos of all the men who had had my job. "Is it one of you guys haunting the place? If so, just let me know and you can have your old job back."

On the top landing, I scanned the entire outer office, listening. It wasn't so much that I heard anything more, but there was a feeling that something was out there watching me, a hunter's instinct if you will.

Down the hallway, I could see the lights were still on in the holding cell area.

Sure of my instincts, I stood there a moment more before entering the holding cell area, then handed him his coffee through the bars. "You know, you could've waited for me to get out of here."

He sipped from the mug and looked at me. "You are speaking of what?"

"You, getting out of the cell while I'm still here. You could at least do me the courtesy of waiting until I leave."

He stared at me blankly. "I do not know of which you speak."

"I heard you up here, walking around."

He shook his head. "Was not me."

"You're sure?"

Shrugging, he sipped his coffee. "Perhaps is ghosts."

I let it go and asked the important question that I'd taken the time to carefully formulate downstairs. "So, one of those pawns has been in touch with you?"

He took a deep breath and let it out like a tire going flat on the side of a bad stretch of road. "Yes."

"And what did they say?"

"They say there is of message coming."

"When?"

"Very soon." He took another sip of his coffee. "And when does, we should be ready to be move."

"We?"

He shrugged. "The two of us and whoever else might wish bring along."

"Why would I want to bring anybody along on something like this?"

"We need of all help we get."

"In all honesty, I don't see me bringing you."

He sipped his coffee some more. "Still not trust me?"

"Not completely, no."

"Even after I tell you story?"

"I'm sure you've got all kinds of hellacious stories, but that doesn't mean I trust you."

"Then how do I earn of trust?"

I walked over to the bars, lodging an elbow in between. "You could start by staying put in your cell tonight."

He watched me start to go but caught me again with his words. "You are sure you are not wanting to bring the friends when call?"

I zipped my jacket, making my intentions clear. "No, there isn't anyone I'd want to subject to a situation like this."

"Nobody?" We both turned to find a large, lethal-looking individual leaning in the doorway with arms crossed over his broad chest like bundled steel cables. We watched as the Cheyenne Nation inclined his head slightly, his black curtain of hair slipping aside to reveal an even deadlier looking smile as thin as a paper cut as he toed a leather chukka across the wooden planks. "The only thing haunting this place is old carpentry. These floors are loud."

# 6

"I was driving home from competing with Rick Waters down at the Denver Indian Center and the Native Archery Longbow Invitational Tournament and saw your truck and thought I would stop in and check on you." Henry Standing Bear walked outside with me and sat on the fender of his Baltic Blue '59 Thunderbird, Lola, looking up at the blanket of stars weaving their pattern in the cold, blackened fabric of the night sky.

"Lola's last run for the season?"

"Yes." He sniffed the air. "How are the fires?"

"The grass fire south of town is out, but there are still a few smoldering on the Sisters Hill and Poison Creek areas."

"We are due a real fire."

"It's dry and with all the vegetation from the wet summer and fall, we're looking at a bomb going off."

He glanced back into the building, pointedly grinning. "So, your Russian followed you home?"

"Something like that. I'm his de facto live-in parole officer for the next ten days, whether I like it or not."

"Handy."

"Having him underfoot?"

"Yes."

"You still think I should trust him, huh?"

"That is not what I said. I said you should *use* him."

"My experience with crooked tools is that they can make a mess."

"Worse than the one you are in now?"

I took a few steps into the parking lot. "He says they've been in touch through an intermediary."

"So I heard."

"How long were you standing there?"

"A minute or two."

"I wish you wouldn't do that."

"Why?"

"It's a little unnerving."

He chuckled. "You knew I was there; I watched you checking your intuition. You just did not follow through. Dangerous."

"How so?"

"If you do not trust your instincts, what have you got?"

"Maybe I'm getting rusty."

"Maybe."

I turned to look at my closest friend in the world. "Do you trust him?"

He pursed his lips and pointed at the ground as his voice rumbled from within his chest. "Strangely enough, I do."

"Eastern Russia."

"An airport in Far Eastern Russia."

"Meaning?"

"They are taking Ruth somewhere beyond there."

I laughed. "What's beyond there?"

"The Arctic, Alaska?"

"I don't know if you remember the last time we were in Alaska . . ."

"I have indelible reminders." He reached over his shoulder, scratching a point on his back. "Perhaps the islands in between?"

"Why there?"

"It is the ends of the earth, as we know it. International waters and a perfect place for this type of activity."

"And what kind of activity is that?"

"Killing."

I took some time to think about it, not particularly caring for any of the thoughts. "On both sides?"

"Yes." He hopped off the fender and walked beside me, studying the blinking-yellow late-night traffic lights strung down the street. "We can try to not kill them, but after your meeting with them at your grandfather's, I am afraid I do not see any other way."

"What's to keep them from killing her?"

"Nothing, but as your Russian friend says, she is the only bargaining chip they have—and they do have her." He sighed, his breath just visible in the cool of the night. "There is another option."

"Which is?"

"The Regis family has another son?"

I waited a moment before responding. "They do. I don't recall his name, but he's the one they're not grooming for office—at least they weren't."

He half crossed his arms, the one hand supporting his jaw. "We take him and offer him in trade for Ruth One Heart."

"That makes us as bad as them." I stared at him, incredulous. "What are we then, some kind of criminal element ourselves?" I tapped the star on my chest. "I can't do that kind of thing, Henry."

"Before this is over you may find yourself doing many things you do not wish to."

"Possibly, but those actions will at least have an improvisational aspect to them: a reaction rather than a premeditated act of homicide."

"As you wish."

"You don't approve."

He started back for his car. "There is action and there is reaction, and action will always have the advantage. Reaction by nature is a response and will never be as fast as an act."

"Let me know if you think of some alternatives in the world of physics."

He opened the door of the vintage convertible and climbed in. "Kill them all."

I stared at him and tapped the hardware on my chest yet again. "Something other than that too."

He hit the starter, and the big engine purred to life easily, even after the six-hour drive.

"Hey, do you know Manx Henenoka, the son of the cook Maya Noota, who used to work for Pepper McKay down at the O-Kay Ranch?"

"She died quite awhile ago, did she not?"

"So did he, only not so long ago."

He threw an arm over the two-tone leather seat, not even slightly surprised. "Pepper?"

"Two days ago, in the postmortem flesh; somebody hit him in the head with a rock."

"Hmm . . . Many would say it was long overdue. And you are asking me about Manx because?"

"At the moment he's suspect number one."

This time his eyes widened in disbelief. "Who else made the list?"

"Pepper's three legitimate sons."

"All of them?" He shook his head. "Is there anyone who did not make the list?"

"You, me . . ." I gestured toward the jail. "And I don't think Sidorov did it either because he was locked up, sort of."

"Well, that certainly narrows it down."

He pulled the gear selector into reverse, and I noticed the longbow and quiver of competition arrows peeking out from the wrapped blanket in the back seat. "Who won the archery tournament?"

"Rick, he always wins."

"Better than you?"

"Yes, even better than me. For a confirmed pacifist, he has a frightening ability with the longbow." He started to back out but then looked again at me. "Perhaps I will invite him to go on this trip with us."

"We're going on a trip?"

He studied me for a moment and then backed out, spinning the wheel and blasting down Main Street like a Mercury-Redstone rocket, the two taillights glowing like twin crimson turbines as he jetted north.

Giving Vic a break, I did return and sleep in the jail and didn't hear a peep out of Maxim Sidorov all night. In the morning, Saizarbitoria fetched him breakfast from the Busy Bee Café.

"Can I have breakfast too?"

"Sure." I looked up at my Basque deputy, standing on the top landing as I held the front handle and tried to get out the door before Ruby arrived. "Hey, do me a favor and tell Double-Tough that I'm down in his area and might need some backup before the day is over?"

"You want me to go with you?"

"No, he's already down there and we might as well save the county fuel costs. Besides, I haven't seen him in months."

Sancho chuckled. "He hasn't grown his eye back or anything."

"I didn't figure he had, but maybe I should introduce him to Sidorov."

"Sure, they could start a club."

Pushing the door open, I saw a forest green Subaru covered with bumper stickers slot into one of our parking spots and thought about running for it, but then figured I might as well stand my ground and take my medicine. Descending the steps, I leaned against the railing, remembering an old proverb. "For want of a metaphor, the kingdom was lost."

"Excuse me?" Ruby stood there, re-hitching her purse strap and looking disgruntled as Dog settled in against my leg and sat on my foot.

Reaching down, I scratched the monster's head. "Sorry, I was amusing myself."

My dispatcher continued up the steps. "Well, at least you're amusing somebody."

I called after her. "Hey, how about a truce, here."

She stopped and squared off. "You went over my head."

"Only after you tried to go over mine."

She stuck a finger out at me. "I've served in three long-term administrations of this office and you don't tell me what to do outside our official duties."

I spread my hands in gesture of an obvious fact. "Maxim Sidorov is not outside our official duties."

"You're charging him with something?"

"I don't have to; he's a known killer and I don't trust him."

Unwedging my foot from under Dog's sizable haunches, I began climbing the steps toward her, but she held out a hand to stop me. "Stay."

Both Dog and I stopped.

"I'll probably get over this, but for now I'm not."

"Okay."

She flicked her fingers at Dog. "And you get to take care of your own dog."

"Okay. Do you mean for good, because he loves you probably more than me."

She turned and went up the steps. "Well, that makes two of us."

I'd just about started to scamper away with my tail between my legs when she called after the two of us. "Not for good."

"Not for good, what?"

"I'll start dog sitting again after I get over being mad at you."

I called after her as she slipped through the heavy glass door. "Any idea when that'll be?"

The only response was the door hissing shut on its hydraulics, sounding like an angry Medusa's head.

"Well, you can take comfort in knowing that you're not the only one who lied to me, for whatever consolation that is."

Alan McKay sat in the Adirondack chair with his legs folded in his cassock, his hiking boots lying in the grass. "I honestly didn't think it mattered. He's a friend of mine and he left the night before to go back to the monastery."

"When I asked if anybody else was here, I meant anybody."

He nodded, looking out at the rushing water of Crazy Woman Creek, then reached down and stroked Dog's broad head. "My friend Michael has been having something of a crisis of faith and I've been trying to help him."

"What's his name?"

"Rakin, Michael Rakin."

I wrote the name in my leatherbound notepad, something I

was more likely to do these days, unless I forgot where I'd put it or my pen. "Well, I'm going to have to talk with him."

"Is that necessary?"

"Yes."

"I really don't know how . . . I mean he's already back at Saint Benedict."

"Near Meeteetse."

"Yes, but he's in a bit of trouble there, and if you go over and start asking a lot of questions in an official capacity, I'm afraid that . . ."

"You could have him come back here if you think it's best, but I'm definitely going to need to speak with him."

"I don't know if he can, his sabbatical time may have run out, and I'm not sure that crappy Pinto of his can make it back over here."

"Well, it's either here or there."

"Would a phone call do?"

"No." I stared at him as his head dropped, revealing a small shaved pate at the top, reminding myself how innocent and naive the kid was to the ways of the world. "You have a way of contacting him?"

He continued petting Dog as the monster placed his head on Alan's knee. "I suppose, through Elder Zebrowski."

I laughed. "Zebrowski?"

"Yes, why is that funny?"

"Believe it or not, I spoke with him a great number of years ago when I was considering joining the order."

For the first time, he seemed a bit awestruck. "You were going to join the order?"

Ignoring his question, I posed one of my own. "How old is he now?"

"In his nineties, at least."

"I doubt if he'd remember me, but do give him my regards while getting in touch with Michael Rakin."

"Um, he was here too."

"Excuse me?"

"You wanted to know who else was here the night before my father was killed." He shrugged. "Elder Zebrowski." He made a face. "And the Abbot Deputy Brian Schiffer was here, I think to retrieve Michael."

Responding to his face, I had to ask. "What's the story with Schiffer?"

"Oh, he's an odd duck, one of Elder Zebrowski's reclamation projects with quite the wayward past."

"Did they spend the night?"

"No."

"Good, I'd just as soon not include a ninety-nine-year-old cleric on my suspect list." I cleared my throat, indicating a change in gears. "Um, when are you due to be back at the monastery?"

"With my father . . ." He glanced at the stream as if Pepper's body might still be out there. "I'm on an extended personal leave, for now."

Closing the notebook and stuffing it into the inside pocket of my jacket, I allowed myself the indulgence. "Alan, can I ask you a personal question?"

He looked at me, and the easy smile returned to his boyish face. "Sure."

"How did the son of Pepper McKay ever end up being a novice?"

"It was actually Pepper's idea, of sorts." He chewed a fingernail. "I had a philosophical bent as a child and Dad and I used to talk about a lot of things. I don't think my brothers would disagree that he and I were the closest at his death. I'm not sure why, other than maybe with the tone of our conversations, it was less confrontational." He shrugged. "That, and I never asked him for money. An awful lot of my father's relationships were based on commerce: what was in it for him or what was in it for them. I guess that's not unusual for a businessperson like he was."

"You say you were the closest?"

"Yes."

"And what was his relationship like with David and Ian?"

He stared at me, his eyes finally dropping to his lap. "You're not trying to get me to implicate my brothers in his murder, I hope."

"I'm not, but I'd like to get a clearer idea of the familial dynamic between all of you, and to be honest, until recently, you and your brothers—Manx and Gary and Lynn—were the only ones actually here."

"It couldn't have been any of us."

"Then it won't hurt to talk about it, will it?"

He thought for a moment. "He had certain difficulties with both David and Ian; one with money and the other with politics."

"Which was which?"

"David and Dad never got along, mostly because they were too much alike. David incurred a lot of debts because of his lifestyle, which was remarkably like Dad's, and when he got in trouble, Dad began loaning him money. A few years later David came of age for his inheritance, and that's when Pepper informed him that he'd been loaning the money from his mother's trust and there wasn't much of the inheritance left."

"Yikes."

"Yeah. There were a lot of hard feelings between the two of them, but nothing that would've motivated David to kill our father—that's just crazy. Like I said, they were a lot alike, but I don't think either of them was rash enough to contemplate an act like that."

I thought about my wife, Martha, and what she might have had to say about the moral core of Pepper McKay.

"With Ian it was another story altogether. Dad had always been a rock-ribbed conservative, but with Ian working at the newspaper, he had a more liberal-minded bent about things, and they both liked to argue."

"And how would you describe those arguments?"

Lifting Dog's head, he gazed into the beast's eyes. "Vehement, that's how I would describe them. They would both be drinking, and one would end up saying something to bait the other, which was really easy in that they were both easily provoked."

"Any personal conflicts between the two?"

"Oh, Dad always wanted Ian to come back and run the ranch, but Ian was never interested."

"Did that cause some friction between David and Ian, with David being the elder brother?"

"Not really. I mean, everybody figured that David would be about as good as Dad at running the ranch and that wasn't very good at all. Ian has a fine mind, but he never wanted to come back here and run the place. He's been very happy in Denver, and I don't see him ever coming back. He's gotten . . . how can I say this . . . more metropolitan, and he'd feel trapped in a place like this."

I stood, stretched my back, and walked out onto the lawn toward the water, still smelling the tang of woodsmoke. "That big meeting the night before Pepper was killed, what was that about?"

"Money, I think. Historically, almost all the family meetings have been about money."

"Can you be more detailed?"

"Not really. We talked about a lot of things, and when they got to the financial part, I did what I always do."

"Which is?"

"Leave."

"You left the family meeting?"

"Yeah." He petted Dog one last time and then also stood, slipping on his sandals and walking out to where I was, both of us watching and listening to the water. "I've renounced any monetary goods or anything else attaching me to the avarice of this world, so why should I care what happens to this ranch or any of Dad's money?"

I watched as Dog walked past us, looking at the stream and perhaps farther. "Very noble, considering the amount of money we're talking about."

"Not really. I've just seen what that kind of money can do to people, and I don't want any part of it."

"Very altruistic." I took a deep breath. "How about you get in touch with your friend Michael Rakin over at Saint Benedict's and see how he'd like to proceed?"

"I can do that."

"I'll need you to do it pretty quick."

"I'll call him right away."

"One more question. Who are your father's neighbors? I mean, who has land adjacent to the O-Kay?"

"Well, this is embarrassing . . ." He licked his lips, but it took a few seconds for the words to come out. "I really don't know."

Ian counted off on his fingers. "Bob Erlichman to the north, Con and Kat Ryan and Boris Agirra to the south, and Nick Monsarrat and Wiley Van Slyke to the east—and of course, our friends, the federal government, with the Bighorn National Forest to the west."

"Wow, that's pretty good. Do you walk around with all those folks in your head?"

Ian smiled, lowering his fingers and continuing to tap away on his computer at the dining room table, finishing up a few emails. As I waited for him, Dog lay by my chair, quietly snoring on the vintage Turkish rug. "No, I wrote that article on the Cowboy Cocktail I was telling you about, concerning the conflicts that have arisen here in the New West."

"Such as?"

He laughed, running his fingers through his thick, wavy hair, looking like a young professor in active pursuit of tenure. "Oh God, I have to tell you?"

"Humor me."

Leaning back in the chair, he smiled some more. "Wanting to take advantage of the one resource that seems to be in endless supply here in Wyoming, Bob Erlichman wants to construct a wind farm down on the flat portion of his ranch, which has Con and Kat fit to be tied, in that they're wanting to open up a dude ranch and go into competition with us. Wiley Van Slyke wants us to all go back to dirt roads and no taxes, and Nick Monsarrat is an activist who wants to fence off the whole south end of the Bighorns and leave it to the pronghorn, elk, bear, and mountain lions."

"Who's winning?"

"Nobody." He made a face. "I'm surprised you've never heard of these people. Shakers and movers, I mean, we're still in Absaroka County."

"I've met a few of them through public affairs and fundraisers, but unless they've got specific issues that bring them into contact with the sheriff's office, they're kind of under my radar." I thought about it. "Didn't Monsarrat run for county commissioner?"

"He did and got trounced."

"Where is he from?"

"Louisiana."

"What about Boris Agirra? Pepper and Boris got into it and only the timely arrival of the highway patrolman Shane Wilson saved bloodshed."

"Did it have anything to do with Boris's niece, Paetra Agirra?"

"From what I'm to understand, it had everything to do with Paetra."

Ian suddenly looked uncomfortable and adjusted his blue-tinted glasses. "Yeah, well, you'll have to ask David about that. Just make sure Katherine isn't around when you do."

"And who is Katherine?"

"Katherine Verkhov, his fiancée from over in Jackson."

I nodded and then nudged Dog with my boot because his snoring had grown louder. "He mentioned her when I was talking with him before, but he intimated to me that the relationship was over."

"He'd like for it to be." Ian sat up and rested his elbows on the smooth surface of the table between us. "David helped her father out of a jam, and she feels some kind of obligation, even though he's made it clear that she doesn't owe him anything."

"What was the problem, and how did he solve it for her?"

"Oh, now that's a personal question you're going to have to ask David about, not me."

"All right then, who was your guest the night before your father was killed?"

He started and then stared at me without flinching. "I beg your pardon?"

"You had a guest here, the night before your father was murdered?"

He stood and walked toward the long wall behind him that

held some huge, tastefully framed Audubon prints of owls—originals, I was sure. "Who told you that?"

I took a moment to allow him to become aware that he might've overstepped his bounds and course-correct. "Ian, this isn't a press conference, it's a murder investigation interview, and you need to answer my questions and not come up with those of your own."

"I see, Sheriff Spank?"

"You were about to tell me who your guest was, the other night."

Ian returned to his chair. "If you're going to depend on my discretion, I'm assuming I can rely on yours?"

"Certainly."

"Paetra Agirra."

I sat back in my chair, allowing the air to escape from my lungs like a leaking bellows. "My, that young woman gets around."

"She wanted to talk with me about David."

"In what sense?"

"She says she loves him and that she wanted to know if he loved her."

"And you're in a position to say?"

"I've kind of been a go-between for the two of them after she and I called it quits."

I pinched the bridge of my nose with thumb and forefinger, attempting to pluck away the headache I could feel forming there. "You were having a relationship with her too?"

"Yes."

"Is there anybody down here who isn't having an affair with this young woman?"

He laughed. "I don't think Alan is."

"Alan is a monk."

He smiled a sly grin. "Have you ever met Paetra Agirra?"

"I'm afraid I haven't had the pleasure."

Lacing his fingers together he leaned over the table, looking both ways before whispering, "In full disclosure, I think she could poke the pope if she had a mind to."

I cleared my throat. "And how can I go about getting in touch with Paetra Agirra?"

Reluctantly, he came forth with the information. "I have her cell phone number." Sliding my pad and pen across to him, I watched as he scribbled down the number. "I'd appreciate it if you didn't say where you got the number."

"No problem. From your colorful description, I'm looking forward to making her in-demand acquaintance."

I watched as David tried to track down a short in the wiring of the vintage Land Rover, having rolled up his sleeves and traced the wiring harness from the back of the alternator. Suddenly snatching his hand back from a spark, he cursed, holding the fingers to his mouth to suck on them but then upon seeing the amount of grease and dirt there, having second thoughts. "Son of a bitch."

"I think you found it."

He eyed me, still half sitting in the driver's seat as he'd instructed me, Dog sitting on the concrete pad outside the shop, panting in the streaming sunshine. "You ever work on a Land Rover?"

"Can't say that I have."

"There's probably more than one short in this marvelous Lucas electrical system." He smiled, wiping his hair back from his face with the back of his hand, but still succeeding in smearing dark grease across his forehead. "You know why the British drink warm beer?"

"No."

"They have Lucas refrigerators." When I didn't laugh, he apologized. "Sorry, old car joke."

"What year is this thing?"

"'68 Series IIA 88, to be exact. Pepper was going to junk it, but I took it instead."

"Where do you have to go to get it worked on?"

"Oh, there's a guy in Billings, but usually Manx keeps it running."

I glanced around. "Where's he, lately?"

"Working with that mule of his." He stared into the engine bay and the myriad British mysteries there. "I guess we're all dealing with the loss in our own way."

"So what's going to happen to this place?"

"Your guess is as good as mine. We've got a meeting with the lawyer later in the week, but I'd imagine that even with the trust, some of it'll end up going into probate. Even if one of us brothers wanted to keep it, the one would have to buy out the other two."

"Sounds like Alan would just give his third away to either you or Ian."

"That sounds like Alan all right." Tempting the fates, he reached in and began running his fingers along the wiring near the intake manifold that led to the firewall. "You know, they say 90 percent of Land Rovers are still on the road—the other 10 percent reached their destination." He pulled out of the engine compartment when I didn't respond and frowned. "Just to be clear, Ian and I have discussed it, and no matter what happens, we're going to put Alan's third with Ian and me as cotrustees."

"He'll be the richest monk at Saint Benedict."

"Maybe the world." Pulling a small tool bag from off the top of the front bumper, he sat it on the flat portion of the fender and pulled out electrical tape and a utility knife. "Ian says he doesn't want the money now, but who knows what the future holds? Either way we're not letting him give it away to the Church of the Happy Cup of Coffee or the Dog and Cat Hospital, which is exactly what he would do."

"What can you tell me about this friend and fellow novice of his, Michael Rakin?"

He barked a laugh and then peeked around the open hood at me. "He's an argumentative little prick, I can tell you that much."

"An argumentative monk?"

"Well, therein lies the problem." Peeling up some electrical tape, he cut about four inches off and then again disappeared into the engine compartment. "I guess he thought the order was going to be this endless debate with him, the Elders, and God. Imagine his surprise when he discovered they only wanted him to follow orders." Pulling his head out, he looked at me again. "You know what you call a Land Rover with operating lights and windshield wipers?"

"What?"

"Customized." I still didn't laugh and he said, "Mind if I ask why you're asking about him?"

"From what I'm to understand, he was here the night before your father died."

"That night, yeah, but then he had to scamper back to the monastery."

"Was there anybody else here that particular night?"

"No."

I waited a moment. "You're sure about that?"

Another moment passed and then he withdrew from the front of the vehicle and stood there with his hands on his hips. "You mind hitting the starter?"

I did as he asked, and nothing happened.

"The original anti-theft device: Lucas electronics." He tossed the shop rag onto the fender, literally throwing in the towel. "Well, that's what we get for winning the War of 1812."

"Actually, it kind of ended in a draw, but the British couldn't support their supply lines or the blockades of the East Coast, so we kept the country and got a great overture out of it." Turning the switch off, I stepped out and joined him in studying the aged motor. "So tell me, David, who was visiting you?"

He side-eyed me and then confessed. "Um, Katherine was here, but she left later that night."

"Katherine Verkhov, your ex-fiancée?"

"Yeah." He turned to me. "Look, she left that night, and I don't know why you'd think that . . ."

"Anybody else?"

The answer was a little too quick. "No."

"David . . ."

"You know why Land Rovers are like married women?"

"Nope."

"They moan on long journeys, embarrass you in front of your friends, and you spend more money than you ever expected once you've committed yourself to one." The eldest McKay shook his head, wiping his hands on a red shop rag and sighing. "Ian told you."

"He mentioned that Paetra Agirra had also been here that night."

He whipped off his hat in disgust. "Did he mention anybody else in the wide world of sports?"

"I'm not sure, and I can't say for sure since I wasn't here."

"Well, you're the only one." He sat on the fender, looking at me. "My personal life is, um . . . kind of complicated."

"Sounds like."

"But what does that have to do with anything?"

"Pardon my asking, but did either of the women spend the night?"

"No."

I gave him my best Joe Friday look. "You're sure?"

He made a noise in his throat. "Paetra stayed the night."

I widened my eyes for theatrical effect and then pointedly closed my notebook at this juncture in the interview, indicating we were off the record. "Paetra Agirra?"

"Yeah."

"And she left when?"

"Early."

"Earlier than when Pepper went out fishing?"

"Yeah, I squirreled her out while it was still dark. I didn't want the two of them running into each other, for obvious reasons."

"Boy howdy, David, you live dangerously."

"Yeah, I'm trying to get out of the habit."

"Do you mind if I ask about your relationship with Katherine Verkhov and her father?"

"Why, what does that have to do with all of this?"

"I'm trying to mark people off the list of potential suspects, but I need to understand their motivations for what they've been doing, and since you say she wasn't even here, I'm trying to eliminate her if I can."

"She seems to have this misguided loyalty because I helped her father."

"And how did you do that?"

"Nothing too nefarious. Some West Coast guys over in Jackson were trying to financially maneuver him out of a plot of land he had over there next to the Elk Refuge, and I just stood up to them, that's all."

"It probably helped that at that time you were his future son-in-law?"

"Probably."

"Nobody got hurt?"

"I think I hurt their feelings, but that was about it."

I flipped open my notepad to indicate that the off-the-record portion of the interview was over. "I'm going to need to talk with Katherine Verkhov. Have you got a number for her?"

"I thought you said you were removing her from the list?"

"Possibly, but I'll need to confirm everything you've said with her."

"Why?"

I stood there looking at him for a good, long while. "David, in case it's slipped your mind with all these goings-on, I'm endeavoring to find out who killed your father."

He read the number off and I wrote it down. "If you would be kind enough to leave Paetra Agirra out of the conversation, I'd appreciate it."

"I will do my best to be as tactful as possible." Finishing the number, I raised my face to look at him. "Ian seems to think there's a lot of animosity with your neighbors, one of whom is Boris Agirra?"

"Oh, God . . ."

"Shane Wilson told me about the confrontation Boris had with Pepper on the side of the road near Powder Junction."

"From experience I can tell you that the only interaction Boris has with his fellow man is confrontational." He studied the Land Rover. "I used to have him work on this thing, but he finally gave up the ghost and told me to shoot it."

"He's the only one in question who has a history of killing people, and it would appear that the old Basquo was aware of the relationship between his niece and Pepper."

"There's that."

"Have you seen him around?"

"No, but then I have my own reasons for avoiding Boris's company." David closed the hood, delivering the next line like a benediction. "Alexander Graham Bell invented the telephone, Thomas Edison invented the light bulb, and Joseph Lucas?" He turned to look at me. "He invented the short circuit."

# 7

The Absaroka County Substation in Powder Junction has been described as the most depressing place in the world, mostly by me, and since a fire a few years ago, its charms hadn't intensified.

An aged Quonset hut with a concrete-block bunker attached in the rear with a cot, shower stall, a battered dresser, and a clothes rod attached to the wall was about all there was.

The front office had a metal desk that I think you could've used as an anvil, three mid-century metal chairs, a metal filing cabinet, and a plastic clock that had been ten minutes off since I'd occupied the space in my very limited trial period under Lucian many years ago. "Your clock is ten minutes fast."

Double-Tough glimpsed up with his one good eye, the other a slightly different hue and focusing on something else. "Yeah, it's been that way since I got here."

I sipped the coffee he'd offered me. "You ever try to reset it?"

"Yeah, but it always goes back to being ten minutes fast."

"Rushing headlong toward its inevitable end?"

"Something like that."

I looked at the collection of quad sheets that comprised a mammoth map of the county, a small golden star representing where we now sat in the second largest city in Absaroka. "I've always wondered who put the star on there."

He glanced over his shoulder at the makeshift map, and I noticed the mottled skin on the side of his face where he'd been burned was almost completely gone. "I thought you did."

"Nope, must've been before me."

"The Ferg?"

I thought of the man who had been a deputy with me in those early years, now retired. "Maybe, that would've been his style."

He sipped his coffee, which, I had a suspicion, was at least a day old. "How's he doing?"

I stood and stepped over Dog, who was enjoying the cool concrete floor, and walked to the single window that offered a view of the main street of Powder Junction. "I can't honestly say. After he moved to Laramie, we kind of lost touch with each other."

His voice carried surprise. "Laramie?"

"It's south of here and he heard the weather was nice."

"Compared to what?"

"Nome, Alaska. I think he's not completely retired in that he's working part-time as a security guard for the University of Wyoming." I took in the corrugated interior surface of the hut. "You know, you can fix this place up, if you want to."

He sat his mug down and looked around. "I have."

Holding back a laugh, I bit my lip. "Really nice, what you've done with the place."

"Thanks."

I quickly changed the subject. "Boris Agirra?"

"Oh, God . . ."

"That bad, huh?"

He crossed his boots on the scuffed surface of his desk, saying nothing.

I returned, again stepping over Dog and reseating myself. "What about the niece, Paetra Agirra?"

"She casts a wide net around these parts, I can tell you that much."

"The HP, Wilson, says he stopped Boris from lynching Pepper a few weeks ago."

"Yeah, I backed him up on that one. There's no doubt in my mind Boris would've killed ol' Pepper."

"Think he could've come back later to finish the job?"

"Not with a rock. I don't think that's Boris's style. Besides, if he killed him, he'd want everyone to know about it."

"Well, I want to talk with his niece, so I guess we need to go through him, even though I have her cell number."

"No need to. I know where she is right now."

"Where's that?"

He withdrew his boots from his desk and stood, walking over to me and taking my cold cup of coffee before setting both mugs on his desk and continuing toward the windowed door. The reverse image of the ABSAROKA COUNTY SHERIFF star decal clung to the pane, faded by the sun and partially peeling, the remnants shredded by the wind in a piecemeal escape.

Opening the door, he held it wide, the small bell attached to the top tinkling. "C'mon, I'll buy you a real cup of coffee."

I trailed out after him and then waited as he turned the sign in the window and closed and locked the door. We walked left on Barber Street along the Murphy Ditch, only to hang a right on Nolan Avenue.

We crossed the parking lot of what looked to have been a service station at one time, but now with a sign that read CAFÉ EUSKADI and festooned with those flag-like banners, announcing ESPRESSO, LATTE, MACCHIATO!

"Wow."

He turned to look at me, then waved for me to follow. "C'mon."

Catching the glass door, I brought up the rear, entering a room where a number of French café chairs were scattered about with small tables. There were prints of the Basque Country, posters from the Basque Museum in Bayonne, France, and sayings in Euskara that said, what, I had no idea.

There was an athletic, shapely young woman cleaning a gigantic, multi-handled machine, which I assumed produced some form of coffee, as she swayed and shimmied to a tune barely audible to us in her earbuds.

I watched as Double-Tough raised a hand to try to get her attention, but realizing that she might stop dancing, he froze and simply stood there, focused on the young woman's posterior.

Sights like this in Powder Junction were probably few and far between.

I noticed that there was a pastry cooler with a number of exotic items from Baroja's, the Basque bakery in Durant.

I watched as the woman in her early twenties spun, the front of her sheathed in a denim apron as devastating as the rear. She danced with her eyes closed, raising her arms above her head and slide-stepping back and forth as she popped the rag from one side to the other like a modern-day Salome.

I glanced at Double-Tough, but it was as if the rest of the world wasn't even there.

She had streaked ash-brown hair, which wasn't unusual in the Basques, that in conjunction with her olive-colored skin gave her an earthy quality. Admiring her supple movements, my eyes traced across her from toe to head, only to find her eyes now open and appraising me as she continued to dance.

She took in Double-Tough but then turned and continued to dance, taking a mug from the rack above and busying herself with some kind of caffeine concoction.

After a moment, she slid the mug toward Double-Tough and then pivoted toward me, pulling a bud from an ear and said with a sultry voice, "What'll you have, big man?"

"Um . . ." I looked up at the board on the wall, recognizing nothing. "I guess a cup of coffee."

She stared at me. "Just coffee?"

"Yep." I went for my wallet.

She threw a hand out to stop me. "My treat, but my choice, okay?"

"The Usual?" I shrugged. "You bet."

She flicked her dark-blue eyes toward DT and delivered marching orders. "Take the table by the window and I'll join you guys in a moment."

Turning her back to us, she began working her barista black magic. Double-Tough and I sat at the smallish table, and he sipped his . . . whatever it was. "What is that?"

He studied the mug. "I don't know, it's something different every time."

"Espresso con panna, and here's your espresso macchiato." She placed the mug before me and sat on the open chair, crossing her legs somewhat provocatively. "Careful there, cowboy, it's got three shots and it'll take the enamel off your teeth."

I took a careful sip, and she was right—it was strong.

"Like it?"

I wiped the froth from my upper lip. "Very good."

"Should get you through the day."

"And halfway into the night." I extended a hand. "Paetra Agirra, I'm Walt Longmire."

She nodded and we shook. "I know, we've met, at least momentarily."

I thought about it but couldn't place the incident. "And when was that?"

"About four years ago at the county fair and rodeo when I was crowned rodeo princess. There were two guys fighting over me and a fellow deputy of yours, Saizarbitoria, sent 'em both home."

"Sorry."

"I'm not. They were assholes and yet I was the one who got arrested."

I sat my mug on the tiny table. "I'm here about Pepper McKay . . ."

"Another asshole."

"Please, a little respect for the dead."

She stared at me. "What?"

I paused for a moment, considering that I might've overrun the Powder River grapevine. "You didn't know he was dead?"

"Pepper?"

I sat back in my tiny chair and studied her. "Died yesterday morning or thereabouts."

"No shit?"

"Nope."

She stared out the window in the general direction of the O-Kay Ranch, and I could see her thinking; the eyebrows twitching and then drawing together. "Wow."

"The preliminary properties of the case seem to indicate that he was murdered."

Her eyes came back to me. "Killed?"

"Yep."

"You mean by somebody?"

"Yep."

Her eyes searched the room, and either she was genuinely surprised, or she was a hell of an actress. "Well, it wasn't me."

"But you were there the night before he was killed, weren't you?"

She uncrossed her legs, placing her ankle-high cowboy boots on the floor. "Who told you that?"

"Um . . ." I paused a moment, lowering my face into her line of sight and enabling her a full view of my bemused expression. "Everybody?"

Crossing her arms, she sat back in her chair, the portrait of disgruntled. "I went up there to talk to Ian about David."

"You're in a relationship with David?"

"I am."

"But you were also in a relationship with Ian?"

"I was."

"And what about Pepper?"

"What about him?"

"Were you in a relationship with him?"

She clutched her chest a little tighter. "I don't see what right you've got to ask me these questions about my personal life."

"A murder investigation gives me that right, and you can answer my questions here, or we can haul you back over to the sheriff's substation and have a more formal conversation there."

The eyes flared. "You wouldn't dare."

I stood.

She tried to stay tough, but I could see the tears beginning to well in her submariner eyes. "Do you know who my uncle is?"

"Yep, and I've arrested Boris before too."

Wiping her eyes, she grew tough again. "It wasn't really a relationship."

"Which one?"

She stared at me before enunciating the name very clearly and then stood and scooted her chair in as if the interview were over. "Pepper."

"I'm sorry, were you under the impression that we were done here?" I gestured toward her chair. "I understand there was a little altercation on the side of the road between your uncle and him a week ago."

Sliding the chair back out, she sat. "Since my mother, his sister, died he feels as if he has to look after me—it wasn't anything."

"That's not what Highway Patrolman Wilson and my deputy here had to say." I watched as she gave Double-Tough an accusatory look and thought she might snatch his coffee away. "They pretty much agreed that if Pepper hadn't been armed that day, he'd likely have ended up hung from a tree or found in a shallow grave."

"Oh, Boris was just trying to scare him off. Pepper's been after me for the better part of a year now."

"So there was nothing going on there?"

"Not on my part."

"Is there any other reason why Boris might carry a grudge against Pepper?"

"Hell, everybody west of the Mississippi River has a grudge against Pepper. Like I told you, he was a professional asshole."

"Enough of a grudge to want to see him dead?"

"I don't know. Why don't you ask Boris?"

"I intend to." I lifted the mug and sipped my fancy coffee. "The other night when you were at the O-Kay, when did you leave?"

"I don't know. Sometime that night."

"You're sure?"

"Yeah."

I sat there, waiting. One of my better law enforcement techniques, especially when dealing with the younger generation who seem incapable of enduring any amount of silence longer than twenty seconds.

"What?"

"Not the next morning?"

She barked what would pass as a laugh. "Sure, I was there in the morning, but it was dark, so how the hell would I know what time it was?"

"David was the last one you saw before you left?"

"No."

"Who else?"

"A bunch of people, it was like a genuine FFA Convention."

"Who, exactly, did you see?"

"That witch, Lynn Lyman, for one. She caught David trying to sneak me out the back door and she doesn't miss anything. If you want to know what happened to Pepper, just ask her."

"Who else?"

"That spooky, illegitimate half-breed son of his, Manx what's-his-name . . ."

"Henenoka."

"Yeah, him. Talk about people with a reason to whack Pepper, he'd sure as hell be on my list. The prick treated him like dirt his whole life."

"Any others?"

"Hundreds."

"But no one in your family."

"Like I said, you'd have to ask them." She got up and sauntered away, and this time I let her go in a form of sheriff catch and release.

---

Double-Tough continued petting Dog as we drove along. "She's a pip."

"I'll say." We were headed up the gravel surface of Patch Road toward the Agirra Ranch. "I think I may have lost you your free coffee supplier."

"Ah, she'll get over it. She gets mad all the time, but she doesn't hold a grudge, mostly."

Paetra Agirra had said her uncle and nephews were working with some heavy equipment, replacing a culvert on their property, and that we'd have no problem finding them on Patch Road because their deconstruction was blocking the majority of it.

"Think she was involved with anybody else along with both Pepper and the two sons?"

"Is a trout's ass watertight?"

I shook my head at the turn of phrase the Appalachian was wont to use. "Why, DT, I'm not sure whether it is."

"Well, I am." He pointed ahead. "There they are."

It was a large culvert constructed of a massive, round, corrugated metal pipe you could ride a horse through. Rust had had its way with the aged metal and the thing was falling apart as they struggled to drag it out of the ground.

Stopping in the middle of the road, all three of us climbed out, me enabling Dog to an avenue of escape, figuring he was probably in need of a rest stop.

As the monster moved toward the side of the road, one of the nephews approached, covered in mud and not looking to be in the best of moods. He was tall, much taller than his uncle, whom I remembered being a smaller man built like a fireplug.

"Help you?"

I stuck my hand out, "Walt Longmire. I need to talk with your uncle, Boris."

He ignored my hand and glanced over his shoulder at the backhoe. "He's kind of busy right now."

"We won't take long."

"Uh-huh." He studied me for a moment more, then gave DT and Dog the eye before turning and moving back to where the heavy equipment made an effort to leverage the twisting metal from the mud.

I decided to use the ex-contractor's knowledge. "So, is that a backhoe or an excavator?"

DT glanced at me with his good eye. "Excavator."

"What's the difference?"

"Size, mostly, but that's got tracks and backhoes generally have wheels. The other major difference is that an excavator can pivot 360 degrees, whereas a backhoe is more limited with a house that doesn't turn."

"House?"

He pointed. "House, cabin, cockpit: the part where the operator sits."

The other two nephews were on the opposite side of the road, watching as the first walked over to the edge of the ditch and waved his hand to get Boris's attention.

After a moment, the excavator stalled in its stab at lifting the massive pipe, the majority falling apart and crashing into the running water below like a giant rusted Slinky. The motor of the excavator lowered to an idle as the bucket became disengaged and the house spun around, the long arm reaching out, facing the waving young man.

I could hear some shouting, and then the big piece of equipment backed up on its tracks just a bit and pivoted the rest of the way toward us as Boris Agirra peered out, finally waving for us to come closer.

We moved in as he shut off the motor on the excavator. Leaning over the controls, he studied me with a face like beef jerky. "What the hell do you want?"

"Hi Boris, how are you?"

"Busy."

"You give up working on cars and decided to destroy roads?"

"The county don't got equipment this big handy, so I'm helping out."

"Well, I promise we won't take up too much of your time." I moved closer, standing by the big bucket. "I assume you heard that Pepper McKay is dead."

He stared at me, his eyes like a double-barreled shotgun, much in the same way as his niece's. "Say again?"

"Pepper McKay is dead."

His stare stayed steady as the other two nephews went down into the culvert space, wading through the mud and water and then climbing the hill to join the other one on this side. "Honest to God?"

"Yep."

"Well, that's the best news I've heard all day."

It was easy to see where Paetra inherited her graciousness and sense of decorum. "He was killed."

"This just gets better and better." Sticking a leg out onto the tracks of the excavator, I watched as he took out a half-smoked cigar and pack of matches from his shirt pocket and carefully lit the stogie, taking a deep toke before adding, "I'm assuming you didn't come all this way just to break the happy news. So I guess you think I did it."

"The thought had crossed my mind, seeing as how you almost killed him on the side of the road a week ago."

He nodded, remaining thoughtful as he waved a hand, dismissing the altercation. "How'd he get killed?"

"With a rock."

"You're shitting me."

"Nope."

"Well, that's downright biblical."

"Mind if I ask where you were three nights ago, Boris?"

He took the cigar from his mouth, examining it in his stubby fingers. "Why, picking out rocks, of course."

"I'm serious."

"So am I." He stuffed the cigar back in the corner of his mouth and got down off the tank treads. "Till you figure out who did it, do you mind if I take credit?"

"You didn't do it?"

He got close and I was reminded just how short he was, barely breaking five feet in his steel-toed, high-heeled logging boots. "I didn't say that." Adjusting his glasses, he looked past me at Double-Tough. "How you doin', you one-eyed bastard?"

DT shrugged and waved back, keeping the one eye on the nephews as Dog came over to join me. "Do you know if any of your family have been at the O-Kay recently?"

"Why in the hell would they want to do that?"

"Well, to kill Pepper, of course."

"We drew straws, and I lost, so you got me."

I slapped a hand on the heavy metal and looked down at him. "You know what they say, Boris?"

"What's that?"

"The bigger they are . . ."

"Yeah?"

"The harder they fall on you."

He stood there motionless for a moment and then chuckled as

his family members edged closer, DT positioning himself to stand them off. "You could try."

I stood there motionless as Dog began growling.

He gazed at Dog, over at Double-Tough, and then back at me, finally puffing his cigar and gesturing to the nephews to stay back. "No, there ain't been any of mine over there, that much I can assure you."

"Really?" I hissed at Dog to quiet him down. "I thought maybe your niece might've been there."

He studied me. "Are you saying something about Paetra?"

"Nothing, other than there are reports that she was there the morning Pepper was killed."

"Morning?"

"Yep."

"Indicating that she might've spent the night over there?" He puffed on the cigar a bit more, but his demeanor had shifted, just slightly. "My brother tells me daughters are hard."

"Tell me about it."

For the first time, he smiled. "How's that daughter of yours?"

"The new attorney general of the state."

His stout head jumped back on his shoulders as if he'd been struck. "No way."

"Way."

He reached out, tapping the ash of his cigar onto the leather of my boot toe. "Well, I guess we're never getting rid of you now, are we?"

I looked at the ash on my footwear and then back at him. "Nope."

"Oh, Paetra's been sniffing around over there as of late." He walked around Dog and toward DT before turning and staring at the ground, still puffing the cigar. "I think she's got something for the oldest one. What's his name . . . David?"

"That's what I've heard too."

"She ain't a killer, at least not that way." He glanced at me. "A lot like my wife, she'll break your heart but not your head."

"How *is* Lottie?"

"In a home down in Casper; lost her mind."

"I'm sorry, Boris."

Readjusting the cigar to the other corner of his mouth. "Well, living with me would drive a woman to it, I suppose."

"I doubt that was it."

Looking past me, he yelled at Double-Tough. "Hey, I left you a present back at your office, cyclops!"

DT nodded. "Does it explode?"

"It might, at that." He stood there silent for a moment before walking back over to me, where he took the tread of his logging boot and wiped off the ash from my boot. "Ain't none of the rest of us been over to the O-Kay, Walt."

"I've got your word on that?"

"Yeah, you do."

"All right, then." I started to go, but he stuck out a hand to stop me. "What I just did, is that called cooperating with the authorities?"

"I believe it is. This your first time?"

He rolled the cigar in his fingers, finally jamming it back in the corner of his mouth again. "It is."

"How's it feel?"

"Kinda odd, now that you mention it."

I walked past him with Dog in tow, headed for my truck. "Who knows, Boris, maybe you'll pick it up as a hobby."

"Think he's telling the truth?"

"I don't see why not." I navigated the gravel road on our way back to Powder Junction, feeling the rear end of the big three-quarter-ton swiveling behind us not unlike Paetra Agirra. "He seemed more concerned with his niece's reputation than establishing an alibi for anybody, including himself."

Double-Tough studied the road. "What now?"

"We circle around. I'll drop you off at the substation and head back over to the O-Kay and see if anything has developed."

"You want company?"

"No, I don't want to put you through watching me stumbling around not knowing what I'm doing."

He reached back and scratched the head of Dog as we watched our small portion of the world roll by. "So, who do you really think did it?"

"I really don't know."

He smiled. "Really?"

"Yeah, over the years I've learned from the old-timers, like Lucian, that you can get into trouble trying to figure out who did it too soon. If you do, you're likely to have to unpack that bag just to find out who actually *did* do it."

As we reached the outskirts of the tiny village in the southern portion of my county, we came upon a young man with mop-like hair tucked under a stocking cap and carrying a rucksack. We watched as he made a right and continued north, walking along on the side of the road at a determined pace.

Turning right, I watched as DT looked back. "A little late in the season for the bums, isn't it?"

I glanced in the rearview mirror at the retreating figure on the side of the road. "Can't be a bum."

"Why is that?"

"A hobo is a migrant worker who is willing to travel and work, a tramp travels but avoids work when possible, and bums neither travel nor work."

He shook his head. "Where in the world do you get this stuff?"

"It's in the Absaroka County docket as an arrestable offence under vagrancy, probably since the Dirty Thirties."

He shook his head as we drove along the creek and took the bridge, pulling into the substation, where we were surprised to find a battered and weather-beaten economy car. "My gosh, I haven't seen a Pinto in years."

Parking beside the thing, we climbed out. "I thought they all blew up."

I noticed the Park County plates and escorted Dog around as Double-Tough took a grimy business card from under a dry-rotted windshield wiper. Holding it to his one eye, he read it and chuckled. "It's from Powder River Auto Repair of all things, Boris Agirra. He says a guy dropped it off to get a new timing belt in the thing but then couldn't pay the bill, so he's leaving it with us."

"What the heck are we supposed to do with it?"

He started for the door. "Search me."

"Aren't you going to take the keys?"

Unlocking the door, he went inside. "Who'd steal it?"

Studying the rusted little hulk, I figured he was probably right and entered the Quonset hut after him, where he sat at his desk, ignoring the flashing red light on his phone. "You need to get that?"

"No, it's probably Boris, telling me they just made me a gift of the gold Pinto."

I looked around as Dog settled on the floor. "DT, I'm thinking of hiring a new deputy, and I was wondering if you wanted to make the leap to the big time in Durant. It seems like I've had you here in exile with our version of the Foreign Legion long enough."

"What about your part-time dispatcher, Barrett?"

"With work-study he had enough credits to transfer down to Laramie, so I won't get him back for a year or two."

He thought about it. "No, thanks."

Somewhat surprised, I said, "Honestly?"

"Yeah." He gazed around. "The place has kind of grown on me. I'm not so sure I'd fit in up there in the big office, I'm so used to doing things my own way down here."

"Suit yourself." I watched as he acquiesced and hit the flashing red light on his phone.

"Where the fuck are you?"

We looked at each other like truants.

"I've been sitting here at the fucking O-Kay Ranch waiting for you to get your fucking ass here so that we can act like we're doing some fucking police work. Now, if you don't get your fucking ass in here and save me from cutting my own fucking wrists from boredom, I'm going to fucking kill you." There was a pause. "Fuckety bye-bye."

We both stared at the phone, and he was the first to speak. "You should fucking go."

"I guess." I patted my leg as Dog lumbered back up and headed for the door, waving goodbye to my loyal deputy in exile. "I'll see you before long."

He nodded, hitting the button and erasing Vic's recording. "You know, I don't think I've ever heard anybody use that word that many times in that short of a message."

Shutting the door behind me, I walked over to my truck and ushered the monster into the passenger seat. Climbing in, I thought about the lack of radio frequency in the canyons leading into the mountains and considered calling the Terror now, but then figured I'd just take my beating when I got there.

Starting the Bullet, I backed out and headed north, driving by the Café Euskadi, and thought about getting her a caffeinated drink as a form of atonement, but decided against it—she was wired enough.

Turning right on Old Highway 87, I spotted the same individual with the rucksack on the side of the road. When he heard the motor of my truck, he stuck out a thumb.

Slowing, I pulled up beside him as he swiveled and looked at me, his eyes widening as I stopped. Motioning for Dog to jump in the back, I rolled the passenger-side window down. "Need a lift?"

He slipped off his stocking cap and clutched what appeared to be a prayer shawl around his shoulders. "No, no thank you."

"You had your thumb out."

Unable to make eye contact with me, he looked at the road, and I noticed the shaved bald spot at the top of his head. "Yeah, well, I was just . . ."

"It's not illegal to hitchhike in Wyoming."

"It's not?"

"No."

He looked up and down the desolate highway, weighing his options.

"I can take you as far as Durant."

I watched as he pulled a cell phone from his pack and began punching letters into it. "Where's that?"

"About forty-five minutes that way." I pointed.

"Oh, I'm not going that far." He held the phone up, looking at the screen. "Actually, just down the road here."

"Well then, come on."

Somewhat reluctantly, he climbed in and then stared at the monster in the back, who sniffed at him as he huddled against the door. "Is that a dog?"

"Some say, but I have my doubts." I watched as he sat his pack on the floor and put his stocking cap back on.

"Thanks for the ride."

I pulled out, musing to myself and mumbling. "Tonsure."

Settling in, he glanced over. "Excuse me?"

Accelerating, I got my truck leveled off and hit the cruise control. "Tonsure, the practice of shaving some or all of the hair on the scalp as a sign of devotion or humility. From the Latin, *tonsure*, meaning clipping or shearing. Abandoned by papal order in 1972, it's now only used by certain outlying brotherhoods, including Saint Benedict's Monastery over in Meeteetse."

I smiled at him as he clutched his shawl and played on his phone.

"Michael Rakin, I presume?"

# 8

"We didn't have enough monks, so you had to go picking them off the roadside?"

Victoria Moretti sidled up as we watched the young man climb the steps of the grand old lodge and ring the bell, stand to the side, and wait. After a moment Lynn opened the door and immediately recognized him, swinging the door wide and allowing him ingress.

"So, how did the Spanish Inquisition go?"

"I guess he left that night, but got about as far as Powder Junction before the Pinto began misfiring and the check-engine light came on and the thing started losing power."

Vic turned back to me. "I don't recall them having power in the first place."

"Well, less power." Stepping out of the way, I let Dog jump out and watched as he went about sniffing all of the exact spots he'd sniffed the last time we'd parked here. "I guess he slept in the car there, in front of Powder River Auto Repair, until Boris opened for business. And then he had to get the parts, but by the time they got it fixed, the kid came to the shocking conclusion that he didn't have enough money to pay for it."

"Just for the record, how dumb is he?"

"Let's assume he's just inexperienced in this wicked world—although he does have a cell phone."

"So what'd he do for two nights before hitchhiking back here to the O-Kay?"

"I have no idea."

She glanced back up at the lodge. "Are you giving him a few moments to collect himself before we follow him in there and get the straight dope?"

"Something like that, he seems a little frazzled."

"I know how he feels, my first car was a Pinto."

I considered her. "Wasn't that a little vintage by your time? His is a 1974 model."

"I didn't say it was new." She took a few steps, watching Dog memorize the yard. "How'd it go with the Queen of the Rodeo?"

"I don't think it was her first."

She smiled mischievously. "Thoughts?"

"Her uncle doesn't think she did it."

"Uh-huh."

"Oh, now why do I not like the sound of that?"

She looked at me. "I ran her."

"And?"

"Like you said, it isn't her first rodeo."

"I don't think that's what I was referring to."

"Attacked one of her competitors in that whole 'rodeo princess' competition at the county fair."

"Really?"

"Yeah, and hit her in the head with a rock."

I adjusted my hat and then folded my arms, thinking. "Hmm . . . The weapon of choice, huh?"

She shrugged. "Just thought I'd mention it."

"Think it could be the same rock?"

"You never know, but we can start working our way through all of Crazy Woman Creek." She walked back toward me, the smile still on her lips. "You mentioned big bad Boris—how did that go?"

"Surprisingly well, I didn't have to throw him in the creek."

"He confess?"

"A couple of times—wanted to know if he could take the credit till we figure out who did it."

"Ballsy bastard."

I smiled. "I'd say that's a pretty apt description."

"What are you smiling about?"

"Of all the challenges Boris Agirra has faced in his tumultuous and dramatic life, suddenly raising a niece after his sister died may be the thing that has finally gotten the best of him."

"Think he did it?"

"Not his MO. If he was to have killed Pepper, he'd have done it out on Main Street, at high noon, just so everybody could be sure that he was the one to do it."

"Her brothers, Huey, Dewey, and Louie?"

"You know, I don't know their names, but I don't think they'd try something like that without Boris's say so."

"Put 'em on the back burner?"

"Sure."

"Is there anybody on the front burner?" She choked out a laugh, wrapping her arms around me. "The Queen of the Rodeo? She had opportunity and motive. I mean, she's schtupping everybody in the lodge except the mule, and we can't be sure about that. And she's used a rock to bash somebody's brains in before."

"Doesn't look good, does it?"

"In a word, no."

"Ahem . . ." Lynn appeared at the top of the steps at the edge of the porch. "I've given the young man a cup of tea, but he says he promised to talk with you."

"So you left the ranch at what time?"

He folded the prayer shawl and stuffed it in his sling pack, and I pet Dog, who had stretched out his great girth on the marble floor like a dozing Kodiak. "I'm not really sure, around midnight, I guess."

"That's all right, I can check with Alan too." I sat my own cup of tea down on the kitchen table. "Why so late?"

"Alan and I were talking theology, it's what we novices do, and the conversation got long." He glanced at Vic, standing with her back to the farm sink of the sizable kitchen, her thumbs hitched in her gun belt. "I'm thinking of leaving the order and he's trying to talk me out of it."

"If you don't mind my asking, why?"

"I'm just not sure if I believe anymore and it's having an effect on everything in my life."

He took another sip of his tea. "I think I believe in Alan more than I do in God."

"He's an amazing young man, wise beyond his years."

"Yes, I wish I had his theological certitude."

I leaned back in my chair. "So the car starts breaking down, and then what?"

"I found Powder River Auto Repair on my phone in . . . what's the name of the town?"

"Powder Junction."

Vic shook her head. "You use your phone a lot, for a monk."

"I'd be lost without it, especially the navigational apps." He glanced back at me. "I pulled off the highway and by that time the car was making a real racket, and I think I was lucky to get it to the mechanic shop."

"And that would be about one in the morning?"

"I guess."

"What'd you do?"

"I slept in the car until dawn and then took a walk east out of town as the sun was coming up, and it was beautiful, then I walked back in and by that time the shop was open, so I talked with the grumpy Boris guy about fixing the car. He said they could get the parts from Casper, and the belt was only about thirty bucks, but that it probably wouldn't be finished until today."

"Where did you sleep these past nights?"

"In the park."

"It didn't occur to you to come back here?"

"No, it seemed like they were having enough trouble, and I didn't want to be in the way."

"So you got up and went in and checked on the car this morning?"

He looked sheepish, reaching down and petting Dog again. "I kind of overslept."

"Till?"

"Close to noon, then I went over to the shop, and Boris told me how much it was."

Vic joined the conversation. "How much?"

"Close to four hundred dollars."

She made a show of looking surprised. "From my experience in working for the family auto shop back in Philadelphia, that's actually pretty cheap for that much labor."

"Didn't matter." He shrugged, sipping his tea. "I've only got eighty dollars to my name."

She glanced at me, rolling her eyes. "And that's when you started back for this place?"

"Yes, ma'am."

"Are you in trouble?"

He looked at me. "Excuse me?"

"Are you in trouble for not making it back to the monastery? I mean, is there someone we should call?"

"I hadn't thought of that."

Vic rolled her eyes again, pulling her cell phone from her jacket pocket. "I don't suppose you know the phone number?"

Taking the cell from his pack, Rakin punched a few buttons and then turned it to show the blank screen to me. "It's in my phone but it's dead."

Shaking her head, Vic went through the swinging doors into the dining room to search for the number.

"She doesn't like me much, does she?"

I sipped my tea and nodded toward the snoring beast. "She doesn't like anybody much but Dog, and me, sometimes."

He gave a quick look down at the snoring monster. "What is he, anyway?"

"We're not sure, part wolf, part Saint Bernard, which you should be familiar with."

"Why is that?"

"Saint Bernard?"

He continued to look confused. "I'm sorry."

"You don't know the story of one line of this guy's ancestors from the Great Saint Bernard Pass?"

"No."

"It's a gap in the Alps between Switzerland and Italy. In 57 BC,

Caesar was attempting to conquer the mountain tribes and needed a passage through the mountains during the Gallic Wars. Over the years, the route was improved and given the rank of Imperial Road, and a temple was constructed to honor Jupiter at the top of the gorge, with a small villa to accommodate travelers. When the Roman Empire went its way, the structure was inherited by the Roman Catholic Church in 1177 and placed in papal shelter by Pope Alexander III, thereby given the name Saint Bernard."

"The dog?"

"Not yet, but they had a problem in that travelers were continually hampered by thieves and, worse, the weather. By the 1700s, the monks kept dogs in the monastery for protection but were constantly called upon to rescue people who were crossing the pass. With practice, the monks, and especially the dogs, got very good at it. So good, in fact, that they were sometimes sent out alone in teams of two or three to retrieve victims of storms and avalanches." I glanced down at the beast, looking at his massive paws. "The dogs could dig through snow and ice to find travelers and then one would stay to keep them warm while the other would go back to the monastery to get help. In the two hundred years the dogs worked the route, it's estimated that they saved more than two thousand people."

Interrupting my dissertation, Vic returned with her phone in her ear, talking to someone on the other end. "Well, you can tell him yourself, he's right here."

She handed it to me. "What?"

"Elder Zebrowski, who doesn't particularly sound like a one-hundred-year-old."

I held the device to my ear. "Hello?"

"I have often wondered what had happened to you, my friend;

what path you might've taken." Vic was right in that his voice was strong, sharp, and energetic.

"How are you, Elder Zebrowski?"

"Still pursuing the good works, young man."

"Oh, not so young as I used to be."

"Everyone is young in the eyes of God, and me." He chuckled.

"I'm assuming my undersheriff explained the situation with Michael Rakin."

The old man sighed. "He is a troubled young man."

"Like me?"

"No, you were always singular in your troubles in the brief time we knew each other, whereas his problems stem from a constant acquaintance with that thief of joy, comparison with others."

I glanced at the young man, continually petting Dog.

"He has not learned yet that redemption is not a competition."

"Well, I'd imagine you'd like to speak with him."

"If it's not too much trouble. It has been wonderful talking with you, and perhaps we'll meet sometime in the not-too-distant future?"

"You never know. Nice talking with you too, Elder Zebrowski." I handed the phone to the young man. "He'd like to speak with you."

Rakin hesitated but then took the phone as I stood and patted my leg, Dog immediately standing and accompanying Vic and me into the dining room to give the young man a bit of privacy.

"You know, I think the old fart was flirting with me."

"As I recall, he had a playful side."

She sat at the head of the table. "So, who follows up with Alan and who goes down to Powder River Auto Repair?"

I pulled out my pocket watch and checked the time. "I'll give you the easy one and I'll drive back down to PJ to see if I can deal with Boris again."

"You could have Double-Tough go over and get a statement from him."

I stared at her. "You know, I keep forgetting that I have staff in the far-flung regions of the world."

"Or the county, at least." She nodded toward the kitchen door. "I'll call DT when I get my phone back."

"So?"

I edged forward in the construction traffic as WYDOT worked to repair the damage to the side of the road where the grass fire had burned it bare. "So what?"

She lodged her tactical boots on my dash, the way she always did, as we watched a very large plane thunder overhead. "What the hell is that?"

Turning my head to the side, I peered up at the thundering monstrosity. "I'm not sure, but it's the wrong color."

She ducked down, looking through the top of the windshield. "What do you mean?"

"Ours are generally gray but that guy is yellow."

She slumped back in her seat. "So do you think the monk did it?"

Pulling my head back in the cab, I stared at her. "Which monk?"

"Monk number two with the dead phone."

Continuing to inch north on the old highway that ran parallel to the interstate, I thought about it. "He doesn't have much of a motive, in that as far as we know, he never even met Pepper until the night before he was killed."

She stared out the windshield, presenting a magnificent profile. "And the fact that Alan corroborated his departing at around midnight."

"So, we've cleared one suspect?"

She raised a fist in triumph. "Twelve to go."

"Yep."

After a moment, she spoke again. "Do you find it odd that Elder Zebrowski is being driven all the way over here to pick Rakin up and bring him home?"

"He's probably going to pay the auto shop bill."

"I think he wants to see you."

I had to laugh. "I doubt that; I only met him for an hour or two a very long time ago."

"I think you made an impression on him; you do that with people."

"I do, do I?"

Moving forward again, I saw Shane Wilson's unit parked on the side of the road and hailed the highway patrolman. He waved back and then pulled beside me, facing the other direction, before rolling his window down. "How's the investigation going?"

"In a lot of different directions. We just picked up another monk down in Powder Junction."

He smiled. "Now, I'm not as knowledgeable or experienced as you are in these types of things, but I would think that monks are generally low on the suspect list."

"We are in accordance with that one." I nodded at the mountains as the yellow plane dropped its load of water up topside. "How are the fires?"

"Mandatory fire exclusion zone as of now."

"That's not what I wanted to hear."

"You and everybody else, but that wind that came through last night ignited it all again, and if they meet, it's going to scour the whole east face of the Bighorns and be what they call unmanageable, according to FMO."

"FMO?"

"Fire Management Officer J. R. Rose."

I threw a thumb at the plane. "What's that?"

"Canadian, CL-415, a Super Scooper from our neighbors to the north."

"Super Scooper?"

"Yeah, two of 'em. They skim over on De Smet and pump in 1,620 gallons of water, then fly up there and dump it on the fires."

"No C-130s?"

"Yeah, they've been up there too, dropping fire retardant."

My eyes widened. "How big is this fire?"

He reached down, checking the computer monitor on the center console. "Big, like I said, if it all joins together."

"The area adjacent to Crazy Woman?"

"Right at the top."

I thought about it. "If that fire gets loose in that canyon, then they'll never get it suppressed."

"No, I can't see the planes getting in there, so they'd just have to let it burn itself out."

I shook my head. "One of the most beautiful canyons in the world."

"Uh-huh."

I glanced at Vic. "Have you ever seen it?"

"Once, years ago."

"I wouldn't advise it right now," Wilson said to Vic. "If it's not on fire, they might still drop a thousand gallons of water on top of you."

"Roger that."

A horn sounded behind us, and I noticed that the lineup had moved two car lengths ahead of us. Glancing in the rearview mirror of my truck, I could see an irate driver glowering at my negligence. "I guess he didn't notice I was a sheriff."

Shane blipped his siren and moved past me. "I'll have a little chat with him about that."

Moving forward, I watched as the HP nosed his unit in front of the sedan and got out, walking toward the guy and slapping his ticket book on his thigh.

Vic shifted in her seat and placed her boots in my lap before reaching back to pet Dog. "So what's next?"

"I guess we have to canvas the neighborhood."

"Starting with?"

"Bob Erlichman is right up here to the left, if we can get through the traffic jam."

"That's the windmill guy?"

"Yep, according to which way the wind blows."

"Just got back into town for this mess, so I had no idea." The tall, balding man pulled his cell phone from the pocket of his fleece jacket with the words WIND PROSPECTOR INC scripted on the breast. "I didn't figure anything less than a lightning strike would kill ol' Pepper. That, or getting shot in the back of the head while dressing in a married woman's closet with a pocket full of change in his trousers." He thought about it as he sat on the tailgate of his very expensive GMC crew cab, also with WIND PROSPECTOR INC scripted across the doors in reflective gold. "A rock, you say?"

"Yep."

"Wow, somebody's going to want to bronze that thing."

Vic and I sat on my not-so-fancy tailgate across from him. "There hasn't exactly been a great outpouring of public empathy."

"I bet."

Vic sipped one of the bottles of WIND PROSPECTOR INC water he'd given us. "What'd he do to you?"

"Helped shoot down my wind farm."

"How'd that all happen?"

"I got in touch with a guy at the meteorological society to get me the readings from this area, going back to the fifties, and this channel way at the base of the mountains is perfect for a wind farm."

"I heard Boris Agirra lost his mind?"

"Has he ever found it?" He sat his phone on the surface of the tailgate and lifted his own bottle of water, glancing back at the words on the doors of his truck. "Con and Kat Ryan started calling me a *wind prospector* and, I don't know, the name kind of stuck, and now I've got four fields alone here in Wyoming."

"Is it profitable?"

"After the initial investment is paid off, it can be very profitable, but that first investment can be a little daunting—getting site permits, environmental assessments, and interconnection contracts with the big utility companies that still call all the shots. Fortunately, I hadn't gotten much past the feasibility phase before everybody lost their minds and I had to shut the idea down."

Vic's eyes scanned around at the foothills of the Bighorns. "Nobody wanted to look at it?"

"I'm afraid so. Hell, Pepper even keyed my truck down at the county rodeo this summer. He denied it, but he was caught on one of the security cameras at the bank." He patted the tailgate. "I used to really enjoy driving by him in this truck."

"What do one of those wind turbines cost?"

"Two and a half to four million."

"Yeah, that's out of my reach."

"And about fifty thousand a year in maintenance, but this area had three major advantages: copious amounts of wind, a power substation down here for one of the big coal outfits for transmission, and I own it."

"How much land do you have here, Bob?"

"A little less than three thousand acres."

"That should do it."

"Yeah." He shook his head in disbelief. "The thing is, I wasn't going to put the damn things all along the mountainside. Instead, I was going to put them out there toward that Powder River Country." He laughed. "You'd have thought I was trying to put 'em on the top of the Tetons instead of out there with the sagebrush and juniper trees. I mean, it's not like those open-pit coal mines are things of beauty, you know?"

"Did you have any other interactions with Pepper, other than when he keyed your truck?"

"Oh, we'd see each other around every once in a while, but I guess the only time that was a little spooky was the time he was waiting for me here at the house when I got back from a trip overseas."

Vic sat up. "He was in your home?"

"Yeah, sitting in my living room with a five-gallon gas can. It was late and I came in, and there he was on the sofa. He'd even made a fire in the fireplace and sat there with a Bic lighter, flicking it off and on. I dropped my bags and asked him what the hell he was doing in my house."

"What'd he say?"

"First, he didn't say anything, just sat there flipping that lighter on and off. Then he looked at me, and I could see he was drunk, so I asked him if he wanted me to give him a ride home. He just stared at me and then said—you're away from home a lot, aren't you?"

Vic stared at him. "Uh-oh."

"Yeah, he stood up as best he could and then grabbed the gas can, and I could tell from the weight that it was full. He sat it on the coffee table and told me it was a gift before staggering out the door, still flicking the lighter."

"Subtle."

"Yeah, I thought so too."

"I don't remember you ever reporting that."

"I didn't. I figured they had enough trouble down there, so I just let it go."

I edged off my tailgate and stood there with my hands in my jeans. "You don't sound like you would've killed him."

"Is that why you're here?" He blinked. "I'm a suspect?"

"Not really, but then until we figure out who did it, everybody is."

"Huh, I guess I never thought of it like that."

I shrugged. "Part of the job, keeping our options open."

"You know he was fooling around with Paetra Agirra, right?"

"Allegedly. I already talked with Boris, and he wanted me to give him a certificate of public service until we figured out who really did it."

"That sounds like Boris, but I was talking about Paetra herself."

"We heard she hit one of her competitors in the rodeo princess pageant a few years ago with a rock."

"She did. It was my daughter, Anita, before she and her mother decamped." He climbed off his own tailgate and stood there looking at me. "Got any ideas about who it really is, Walt?"

"You mean besides you?"

"Yeah, besides me. I was in Kuala Lumpur two days ago."

I spoke to Vic out of the side of my mouth. "Take Bob off the list."

She mimed scratching a name off an imaginary notepad. "Right."

"Anybody else get crossed off?"

"Bob Gibson."

"The pitcher?"

"Yep."

"Bob Marley?"

"Nope."

"Bob Dylan?"

"He's not on there either."

Erlichman smiled and adjusted his glasses. "So nobody named Bob then, huh?"

I snapped my fingers and turned back to my undersheriff. "Make a note, no Bobs."

She scribbled on the imaginary notepad. "No Bobs."

Con and Kat Ryan were in their hot tub when we arrived at their log home, which hung over a rock escarpment with gigantic glass walls and extravagant decks that jutted out in all directions.

As we pulled up, Kat, clad in only a bikini and a towel, hung over the railing and called down to us as we got out of my truck. "Cheese it, it's the law."

I called to the attractive blonde in her fifties. "Howdy, Katherine."

"We're having a soak; you bring your swimsuit?"

"No, I'm afraid not."

"C'mon up, you two can go commando."

She disappeared and I turned to my second-in-command as she

joined me. "Life gets a little racy down here in the southern part of the county, huh?"

I started climbing the steps that wound around the corner of the large house as Vic paused. "No Dog?"

"No, because he will, most indubitably, jump in the hot tub."

When we got to the top level, Kat had rejoined her husband, and Conrad waved a hand at me. "It wasn't us who did it."

Vic joined me, standing as I sat on a bench seat connected to the railing. "It wasn't you who did what, Con?"

"Killed Pepper McKay."

"Well, you're the first ones to deny it; everybody else wants a parade in their honor."

He adjusted his sunglasses, muscles rippling from what I assumed was more than an hour regimen in his private weight room. "I just want his ranch."

"Really?"

"Yeah, I don't think any of his sons relish the thought of being in the hospitality business, and from what I heard, the old skinflint left them all a sizable inheritance."

Vic was drawn around the deck, looking up the mountain slope, where a hovering layer of clouds, or smoke, was visible. "What, your place isn't big enough?"

"Sure, it's big enough, but it's not old enough or authentic enough. People like the idea of an actual working ranch that's been here since the old days. You know, a 'Buffalo Bill slept here' kind of thing."

Kat reached behind her husband's head, lifting a highball glass that looked like it had been pretty well emptied. "Excuse us, Walt, how inconsiderate. Would you like a drink?"

"No, thanks."

She glanced at Vic and smiled. "Your friend?"

"I'm sorry, this is my undersheriff, Victoria Moretti."

Kat smiled. "Victoria, would you like something?"

She called over her shoulder as she took in the view. "Got the fixings for a dirty martini?"

"Always." Kat climbed out with the empty glass, eyeing me again. "Sure you won't have something, Sheriff?"

"Well, if you've got a Rainier, I guess I'll take that."

She disappeared through one of the French doors and into the mammoth house.

"This place and the O-Kay, that'd make you a really big landowner here in the county, Con."

"I guess." He moved over in the hot tub, hanging on the side nearer me. "The kids are all gone and Kat's bored, so we've got to find something for her to do."

"Uh-oh."

"Uh-oh is right. Her last hobby was designing yachts and that got expensive."

"I can imagine."

He looked up at me, incredulity writ large on his face. "Did I hear it right that somebody hit Pepper in the head with a rock?"

"That's what the report from DCI says."

"Not much imagination in that."

"I guess it could've been a spur of the moment thing. He was fishing in Crazy Woman Creek when it happened."

He smirked. "Probably Game and Fish."

"They're getting pretty strict about the catch and release thing."

Kat reappeared with the drinks and circled the hot tub. I noticed she hadn't made one for herself. "Nothing for you?"

She settled in on the far side, trailing her arms out and floating. "I imbibed a bit too much last night, so I'm on the proverbial wagon today."

"So, who did it, Walt?"

I turned back to Con. "We don't have a definitive answer to that just yet."

Kat closed her eyes. "You know he was dating . . ."

"Yep, we know."

"Her uncle . . ."

"Yep, we know that too."

Her eyes opened and she looked at me. "What's the son's name, the illegitimate one? The Indian?"

"Manx."

"Yes, him . . ." She studied me.

"He's one of the sons who found him, floating in the stream."

"I bet he was."

Con looked back at his wife and then at me. "You need another deputy?"

"Actually, I do, but I don't think she'd like the pay."

Kat closed her eyes again, like a cat being stroked. "I'm expensive, but I'm worth it."

Ignoring the remark, I sipped my beer. "When's the last time you two saw Pepper?"

They both thought about it and then looked at each other and then back at me, Con starting the story. "Well, in all honesty, it wasn't Pepper . . . It was about six months ago, and we stopped in the Sinclair station down in Powder Junction. I filled the Yukon up and we were pulling out when we saw this guy in a hoodie, sitting out near the sign island with his thumb out."

Kat added. "It was looking like it was going to rain, sleet, or snow—you know, usual Wyoming weather—and I thought we should give him a ride."

Con gazed at her and then shook his head. "She wants to pick up everybody on the side of the road, and one of these days we're going to pick up the wrong guy."

She laughed, splashing over to our side. "I thought we had that day."

"The guy climbed in the back but didn't say a word; just sat there with his face looking out the window."

"I looked at him and asked where he was going, and he said to just drop him off halfway between the Middle Fork and Buffalo Sussex Cutoff, I mean just mile marker 279 out in the middle of nowhere. So I asked him if he knew where he was going and he said yeah, he did."

Kat studied her husband and then brought her eyes back to me. "It was about then that I noticed there was blood dripping down the front of his sweatshirt, and I asked him if he was all right. He said he was fine, but I reached into the glovebox and handed him a package of tissues."

Con sipped his drink. "I was watching him through the rear-view mirror and could only see part of his face, but the part that I could see was pretty messed up. His nose was broken, and one eye was pretty well swollen shut."

Kat stared at my boots. "After a while I could see that he was crying, just silently sobbing, and I reached back and took the wad of used tissues from him and then moved to touch his chin, you know, just to comfort him. He jerked back and the hoodie fell from his face, and he immediately tried to cover again, but I told him that it was all right."

"I asked him if he was sure he didn't want to go to the hospital in Durant, but he said no, that this wasn't the first time his father and he had gotten into it." Con sat his glass down. "Once we got to the mile marker he'd indicated, I pulled over to the side of the road and he started to get out, and I asked him if he really knew where he was going?"

Kat nodded. "He said yes and then cut across the highway and loped up the embankment and climbed over the fence, just disappearing."

"There's only one ranch in that direction, Walt."

Kat bit her lip and finished the story. "It was the illegitimate one."

Con added. "The Indian."

She glanced at him and then at me. "Manx."

# 9

"Always blame the Indian, huh?" The Cheyenne Nation sat on the bench by the stairs of the Sheriff's Department, drinking a glass of fancy European water he kept in Ruby's refrigerator for just such emergencies.

It wasn't really much of an emergency, but I was sitting on my dispatcher's stool and drinking another beer because I figured Vic could drive us the rest of the way home. "The strange thing is, if I was putting money on who could kick whose ass, I'm pretty sure that my money would've been on Manx. I mean Pepper wasn't in bad shape, but the kid is young, big, and muscled."

"Did you ever strike your father?"

I sipped my beer. "No."

"Neither did I."

"We were never provoked to that point."

"No, probably not."

"No one asked me." We both turned to Vic, lying on the marble floor next to Dog, her right hand tracing patterns in the thick fur of his side as he snored contentedly.

I glanced at Henry. "I'm betting yep."

The Bear's smile flattened. "As am I."

She laughed. "Thanks for the vote of confidence."

"You hit everybody."

She patted the beast. "I don't hit Dog."

"I'm talking about people."

"When's the last time I hit you?"

"Three days ago."

She thought about it. "That doesn't count."

"Why?"

"I didn't draw blood."

"There are rules?"

She yawned, stretching her arms across the floor as her uniform shirt rose to alarming reaches. "Sure, the ninth Marquess of Queensberry."

"I don't think he dealt with your kind of fighting."

"Sure he did." She sat up. "What ever happened to him, anyway?"

"He died of syphilis."

"Ooh, low blow."

I turned back to the Cheyenne Nation. "So, you think Manx just took a beating from his dad?"

"Not knowing the details, yes, I would."

"Do you think it was a reoccurring situation?"

"I have heard rumors."

"On the Rez?"

He sipped the last of his water, then set the glass on the floor beside his beaded moccasins. "Wind River Rez, and yes."

"Is can I have of beer?"

We all looked over to find Maxim Sidorov leaning against the opening of the hallway that led to the holding cells. He was clad in a T-shirt, jeans, and no boots, revealing his electronic ankle monitor. "I thought your English was getting better?"

"No one comes back and talks of me. Young deputy is covering for two of you and too of the busy to visit."

Vic barked a command as Dog raised his head to peer at him. "Get back in your cell, Rasputin."

Waving her off, I stood and went over to the small refrigerator in the commissary area and took out a Rainier, handing it to him as I passed and sat back in Ruby's stool. "Don't pay any attention to her. She's never happy unless she's hitting people."

Crossing in front of me, he passed by Henry and then stood there. "May I sit?"

The Bear gestured. "Be my guest."

He sat and offered the Bear a hand. "Maxim Sidorov."

"Henry Standing Bear." The Cheyenne Nation shook the hand. "I have heard a great deal about you."

"All of it bad I am of sure." The Russian cracked open the beer, tasted it, and then made a face. "Is not very good."

I took another swig of my own. "It'll grow on you."

He glanced around at all of us. "You are discussing of case?"

"We are, and you don't have to use the preposition *of* in every statement. It's generally used to express the difference between a part and the whole, or as a function word to indicate belonging or a possessive relationship."

He nodded, studying me. "May I join of conversation?"

"Sure."

"What is case?"

We all looked at one another, and I was the first to give it a try. "Um, there was this fellow, Pepper McKay, who was killed."

"Oh yes, this Pepper . . ." He sipped his beer again, but this time made less of a face. "He was good fellow or was bad?"

Vic piped up. "Well, if you remember, he tried to rape Walt's wife."

Maxim stared at the floor and belched. "Right, right . . . So, is very bad man."

"Evidently he was fishing when someone hit him in the back of the head with a rock."

The Russian made the face again, but not because of the beer. "Rock?"

"Yep, anyway, at first we thought the only people in the lodge were his three . . ."

Henry interrupted. "Four."

"Four sons, three legitimate and one maybe not so much. And the groundskeeper and the housekeeper, Gary and Lynn Lyman."

"Only six suspects and you cannot of suppose who did murder?"

"Well, it turns out there were more people there than at first surmised: the fiancée of one brother, as well as his girlfriend, and the friend and fellow novice of the youngest brother."

"Novice?"

"Yep, members of a religious order here in Wyoming."

He shook his head. "So, is of nine suspects?"

"And two more, an elder and a deputy of the abbey who were in the house either the night or morning of Pepper's murder. And then there are the neighbors in all directions who have their own reasons for wanting McKay dead."

He studied the floor for a moment, reaching down and adjusting the ankle monitor, before finally looking up at me. "Rock?"

"Yep, I was thinking the same thing."

"That act was not of premeditated, more act of impulse."

"Yep."

He gave out with an exaggerated shrug as if to say the answer was obvious. "Which of four sons hate him of most?"

I glanced at Henry and then back to Sidorov. "Probably the illegitimate one."

"And this is primary suspect?"

"With an aggravated assault charge and two charges of criminal battery, and there has been physical violence between him and his father before."

Henry rumbled. "He does not seem the type."

"It is my experience in Moscow Police Department that peoples go against of type." The Russian pursed his lips and bobbed his head. "This son, is of Native delineation?"

The Bear smiled. "Yes."

"How Native?"

The question seemed to be directed at the group as a whole, but I answered. "I'm not sure I understand the question."

"Son is traditional in nature?"

"Not particularly." I glanced at Henry again. "Would you say?"

"No, but he is Native. Why do you ask?"

Sidorov mulled it over for a moment. "There are traditional weapons that the Natives use that incorporate of rocks, yes?"

"The club." We all turned to Vic, who rose from the floor. "The fucking club hanging in the deer antlers of the mudroom we saw in our initial search of the O-Kay Lodge."

"The war club."

"I remember thinking it was strange that it was there." She reached down and took my beer, gulping.

"It was clean."

"The fucker was killed in a stream. Why couldn't the killer have just washed it off?"

"It wasn't wet, was it?"

"No, but the fringe was stiff, remember? So it could have been wet and dried."

She handed me back the empty can as I lumbered to a standing position, glancing at Sidorov. "How in the world did you put those two together?"

He scratched the side of his face where his beard was growing in. "I am negligent to tell you."

"What?"

"During last afternoon, I am to go to small museum across street, Jim Gatchell."

"You left the jail?"

"Was bored and went for walk, is amazing museum and has display of Indian weaponry—has war club you mention."

I plucked my jacket from the back of Ruby's chair and put it on. "Well, I guess we need to go get that club and maybe have a little conversation with Manx." I glanced at the Cheyenne Nation as he stood. "Do you mind coming with us?"

"Meaning you would rather be wrong with a Native friend than just wrong?"

"You still don't think he did it?"

"No."

Holding Vic's duty jacket, I helped her slip it on. "Then you can be the better angel of my nature, 'cause it's looking more and more like it was him."

Sidorov interrupted. "Excuse, but would like to go?"

"Permission denied."

"And why?"

"You're in jail, damn it, even though you seem to have a somewhat cavalier attitude toward institutional incarceration."

"Did I not just help to break case?"

I started toward the steps as Dog and the others scrambled after me. "Yep, but that doesn't mean you joined the force."

"NIFC out of Boise says this fire is turning into doomsday stuff." Trooper Wilson stood beside the road, sipping coffee from his

Stanley travel mug and looking over his shoulder to where the grass fire had enveloped the roadway in the night. "If you're headed for the O-Kay, you're going to have to go back to the Durant Sussex Cutoff and take the highway down to the Middle Fork exit and double back here on Old 87."

"That'll take the better part of an hour."

He leaned forward, past Vic, who had decided to drive. "Mostly, yeah."

Cocking her head, my undersheriff looked into the dense smoke. "What's the NIFC?"

Wilson studied the mountains. "The National Interagency Fire Center is run by the BLM but also hosts five other federal agencies: the Forest Service, National Park Service, Fish and Wildlife Service, Bureau of Indian Affairs, and the National Weather Service."

She pursed her lips. "What if I drive through it?"

"Drive through what?" Following her eyes, he glanced at the smoke covering the road behind him, his mouth dropping open in a comic display. "I'd advise against it." He gestured toward me. "It's my highway but it's his county."

Putting my truck in gear, Vic glanced over at Henry, and then back at me and Dog. "Slow and steady wins the race, right?"

"You're going to have to go by feel, just try to keep it on the pavement."

She smiled her sideways grin, revealing the elongated canine tooth. "Roger that."

Vic started to let off the brake when he spoke again, tapping the pillar of my truck with his Maglite. "You also might want to roll up your windows."

"Roger that too." She did and then closed the vents, driving into the smoke where visibility quickly dropped to zero, even with the headlights on.

Leaning forward, the Bear peered through the windshield. "I can see nothing, you?"

"No, but it still feels like we're on the road." She'd just finished the statement when I felt the front right tire dip over the berm and into the gravel. She straightened the steering wheel, and I felt it as we climbed back onto the pavement.

Vic's voice echoed to the back. "What are the chances of our tires or gas tank catching on fire?"

"Fairly low as long as we keep moving."

She laughed. "Done this shit a lot, have you?"

"Not really."

Henry's voice interrupted the small talk. "Flames."

Veering to the left, she avoided the majority of the plumes and then we felt the front left tire go off the road to the left. She rolled the steering wheel, bringing the big three-quarter-ton back on the road. "There went the paint."

Henry shrugged. "Maybe so."

"Is the smoke getting thinner?"

"I think so."

As we drove south, we all leaned forward and to the side to try to catch a glimpse of the orange glow that seemed to crown the top rim of the Bighorn Mountain Range. Vic was the first to speak. "This is horrible. What are they going to do if it comes down the front slope?"

"*Ready, set, go.*"

"What's that supposed to mean?"

"*Ready* means having all the things you want to save by the door and *ready* to go. *Set* means having everything in your vehicle *set* to go, and *go* means this is your last warning to get the hell out of here—*go.*"

She turned the wheel and began driving up the gravel road,

chasing my headlights toward the O-Kay Ranch. "Have you ever seen a fire like this?"

"Not in this area and not this big."

The place was dark, as I'd assumed it would be. I could've called ahead but figured waking the entire house once was probably enough—that, and whatever element of surprise I had would've been lost.

The dusk to dawn light in the front parking area came on, and I wasn't surprised to see Gary Lyman standing at the door of the lodge in his bathrobe with a Remington shotgun in his hands.

Climbing out, we advanced as he came to the edge of the porch, adjusting his glasses. "Walt?"

"Hey, Gary. Sorry to bother you this time of night, but I was wondering if we could have a peek at that back mudroom again?"

"Huh?"

"I know it's inconvenient, but there was something we found earlier that we'd like to glimpse again."

"Here at the lodge, in the mudroom?"

I propped a boot onto the first step. "Yep, if you would, please?"

"Well, sure. Do you want to come through the house?"

"If it's not too much of an imposition." He gestured for us to enter, and we did, even Dog. "Everybody asleep?"

"This time of night?" He grumbled. "I should hope so . . ."

"Boy, Gary, you're kind of grumpy early in the morning." With no further comment, he ushered us through the great hall, without turning on any lights, and then through the dining room and into the kitchen. We took a right there, into the hallway that connected to the mudroom that held so much of the sporting equipment. "Gary, could we get the lights on in here?"

There was no response, but the lights flicked on, along with the ones on the patio out back.

Studying the mule deer mount at the far end of the narrow room, I turned to Vic. "Didn't you place it on the deer antlers?"

"Yes."

"It's not there now."

She passed me, squeezing by and continuing to where the mule deer mount gazed down haughtily. She stood there for a moment in a face-off.

"You were here, and I'm telling you the damn thing was right there, up in the deer antlers, on open display."

Henry joined us, glancing around the room. "What did it look like?"

I thought about it. "About 1880s, maybe '90s, handle about two feet in length with a dark stone on the head a little larger than a baseball, fringe on the end with two beaded bands on the shaft and a beaded sinew strap over the stone, attaching it to the hide-bound handle."

"Bead color?"

"Cobalt blue, greasy yellow, and chalk white in a square pattern I've only seen in a Southern Cheyenne design."

He smiled at my collective knowledge. "Genuine and in good condition?"

"Missing a few beads, but absolutely."

"So, not the kind of thing you leave lying about."

"No." I called over Henry's shoulder. "Gary, are you still here?"

He appeared in the doorway, clutching his bathrobe and cradling the shotgun in his arms as Dog stood and studied him. "I am."

Moving past Henry, I walked over and gently took the Remington from his hands. "First things first, let's get rid of this, okay?"

He released it. "Sure, anything you say, Walt."

Checking to see if the safety was on, I draped it under my arm.

"Gary, have you ever seen the thing we're looking for, a Southern Cheyenne war club?"

He slowly shook his head. "I don't know, I mean, there's tons of that stuff all over the house. Pepper went through a phase when he collected everything he could get his hands on." He thought about it. "There was an old display in the library with some of that stuff."

"This one was resting on the antlers of that mounted deer head on the morning Pepper was murdered, and we think it might've been the weapon that killed him. Vic and I found it in this mudroom that morning, but now it's gone. Do you know if anyone has been back here going through the things in the cabinets and bench-seat storage, or removing anything that was hanging off that mule deer?"

He glanced past me to where Vic and Henry were examining the rest of the cabinets. "Hanging off the mount?"

"Cradled in the antlers, yep."

"No, I haven't seen it or anybody back here except passing through to get to the rear entrance. I mean, somebody could've been in here getting fishing or hunting equipment, but I don't know who."

"The sons?"

"Possibly."

"Anybody else?"

"Well Walt, I don't know, maybe me and Lynn."

"Where's Manx?"

He stared at me. "Oh, Walt . . ."

"I just want to talk to him."

"I'd imagine he's in his room, out at the barn, so he can be near the horses and that damn mule."

"All right, I'll head there and roust him out." I started back through the house with Dog at my heels, but then stopped and called out, "I'm going to need you to get everyone awake so I can speak with them."

He stood there staring at me and then checked his wristwatch. "At three o'clock in the blooming morning?"

"I don't care if it's the end of time, Gary. I'm going to need to speak with everybody in this house."

Starting through the kitchen, I pushed the doors open and held it for Dog. "C'mon, you're my backup."

Figuring I'd forgo the truck, I started down the hill for the cut-off that led to the corrals and barn. The lights didn't come on in the parking lot, either because they didn't want to disturb the animals or because I wasn't big enough to trip them.

Either way, the only animal I saw in the front corral was the big mule, quietly standing there as if he'd been waiting for me. "Hey, Borax, where's your boss?"

The great ears pivoted toward me but then laid back when he observed Dog.

"No, he's a friend."

The ears immediately returned to their forward and curious position as the mule dipped his head, sniffing at Dog as the beast stretched out his neck, giving Borax a mutual sniff.

It appeared they'd made peace, so I continued toward the barn where a motion-detecting light came on near the stalls. I stood still, unsure if I was close enough to cause the thing to activate. "Manx?" There was no answer, and I advanced, automatically raising the barrel of the shotgun. "Manx?"

There were no horses in any of the stalls, but I noticed the doorway to his small apartment near the middle was closed and no light escaped from under the door and into the breezeway.

I moved in that direction, feeling Dog brush up against my leg and beat me to the door, sniffing at the space between the door and the sill.

"Dog?"

After a moment, his large head rose.

I watched as the motion-detecting light at the other side of the barn flicked on, and I could've sworn I'd seen something move around the corner. "Hello?"

Dog, seeing my reaction, leaped in that direction and disappeared into the darkness outside.

"Oh, hell . . ." Running after Dog, I yelled at the monster, but when I got outside, Dog was nowhere to be seen. There was a smaller area to the right that looked like the place where they parked the heavy equipment used on a ranch the size of the O-Kay.

There was a larger building to the left beyond the open area where Manx and I had talked, connected to the front corral and loading chutes—possibly an indoor arena.

Hearing a bark in that direction, I hustled toward the arena and found one of the doors ajar and stepped through. It was coal-black inside, so I slipped my Maglite from its loop and flicked it on, trailing the beam around the massive area, the floor covered with wood shavings.

Dog was nowhere to be seen, but there was another opening on the far side, about sixty yards away, and that door hung open too.

If this was the direction Dog had taken, then there was no other way he could've gone.

I'd just started to move that way when I felt something behind me—turning quickly with the shotgun at the ready, I was confronted with Borax.

The big mule gazed at me impassively with his soft, brown eyes, as if he'd had shotguns pointed at him his whole life.

Lowering the gun, I shook my head at him. "Hey, you see my dog?"

Without answering, he slowly ambled past me and toward the other doorway on the far side. With nothing else to do, I followed him, and we made the long trek across the arena, shadowing the beam of my flashlight. "Was that you that tripped on the light and sent my Dog off on a wild-goose chase?"

Borax didn't answer.

I continued following the mule until he stopped at the partially closed door, where I reached out to pull it the rest of the way open and he entered in front of me.

To the right, I was relieved to see a light switch and flipped the thing on to bring illumination to a washing stall and some more unused stalls with all sorts of groundskeeping equipment stowed there for lack of anywhere else.

Dog stood at the far end of the arena by a closed door.

"What do you think you're doing?"

He ignored me and kept his attention on the door.

Walking past the mule, I got beside Dog and then turned the knob and swung the door wide, revealing a bathroom. "What, you needed to go?"

Switching the light on, I noticed the window above the toilet was open and there was a fresh scuff mark on the closed toilet seat along with a few wood shavings from the area I'd just walked through.

I took a step back, only to find the way barred by the thousand-pound mule.

"You need to go too?"

He gave out a long sigh and then backed up a step, enabling me to escape with Dog close behind.

Walking toward the arena, I traced the beam of the flashlight across the shavings and could now see where another set of tracks arched to the right but then joined our own when arriving at the doorway. There were two sets of prints: One set obviously made by someone with two legs, and then another that had run over that set with four of its own.

Kneeling down, I examined the prints, but the shavings made them indistinct and there wasn't any way I could tell who or what could've made them—other than it was likely a human being trailed by a dog.

I began walking across the open space, aware that I had an entourage. Glancing back, I was amused to see the big mule and Dog in my wake, like a team, minus eighteen members.

Throwing the shotgun on my shoulder, I walked out into the open area between buildings and peered at the sky, trying to figure out what had happened. It was possible that it was Manx who had tripped the light in the breezeway, but then why would he have run away? Someone had definitely been here in the barn and then had made a hasty exit when Dog and I had shown up.

If it was Manx, then why hadn't he stayed or responded?

Only one way to find out.

Walking into the barn with the motion-activated lights springing on, I made my way to the middle of the breezeway and then raised a fist, banging solidly on the tongue-and-groove surface of a Dutch door. "Manx, if you're in there I need to talk to you."

Turning my head, I could see my associates watching me intently.

I knocked again. "Manx, if you don't open this door, I'm going to have Borax here kick it in."

Silence.

Raising the butt of the twelve-gauge, I thumped it into the door and raised my voice. "Manx?!"

Silence.

"Manx, if you don't answer I'm going to break the door in and I'm not kidding!"

Silence.

Since it didn't appear as if I had any choice, I looked at the heavy two-part door, wondering which part was actually locked. Figuring it had to be the bottom, and unable to overcome my upbringing by harming the Remington, I set it aside and sought a more suitable battering ram.

As luck would have it, there was a metal-post pile driver leaning against a stall separator across the walkway. With handles on both of its sides, it was the perfect tool for either opening the door or breaking my fingers, whichever came first.

Hoisting the thing, I strode across the walkway as Dog and Borax watched. The beast, a little more used to my methods, backed up a bit, but the big mule only stood there continuing to watch from short distance.

Rearing back, I slammed the metal tube into the hard wood as the thing bounced in my hand, ringing through my wrapped fingers like a workingman's bell.

Taking a breath, I examined the dent in the wood and then turned to Borax, who hadn't moved an inch from where he stood there, blinking. "You're sure you don't want to give it a try?"

Getting no response, I slammed the thing into the door again with a great deal of sound and fury, but pretty much with the same effect.

Borax still stood there, unmoving.

"Well, you're bulletproof, I'll give you that."

Taking a step back, I spun around again, this time putting everything I had into it. The door buckled inward with an explosion of wooden splinters and shards. Tapping the broken parts away enough so that I could reach an arm through, I groped around, trying to find the latch that was attached to the lower door.

"Manx?"

Still hearing nothing, I thought about how embarrassing it was going to be, breaking in the door of an empty room.

"Manx!"

Finally finding the catch, I pulled the lever up and released the door, giving it my hip and swinging it wide.

Other than the muted light from the window across the room, the place was completely dark. I fumbled a hand on the wall until I flipped the light switch.

Manx was there in the middle of the room in a T-shirt and underwear, seated in a chair that leaned forward on its two front legs. His hands were cuffed behind his back, and around his neck was a noose, tied off to a hook in the ceiling.

Leaping forward, I grabbed his shoulders and tipped the chair backward to where it landed square on the floor as I struggled with the brass clip, struggling to get the braided horse lead from around his neck—staring at the bulging, sightless eyes and the swollen purple tongue hanging from his open mouth.

# 10

"Autoerotic asphyxia." Tammy Payson seemed surprisingly chipper for a woman whose boss had woken her at four in the morning in Cheyenne to drive five hours to come look at another dead body.

"So, Vic was right?"

The DCI second-in-command jotted down info in her notebook before she stuffed it in her shirt pocket and took more photographs of Manx's body in the bedroom. "We didn't think there was any reason to move him down until you got here."

"Thank you."

"How long?"

"Temperature and rigor indicate approximately nine hours."

"So, late last night?"

"Or thereabouts." She stood and took more photographs. "I'm not saying it couldn't be a suicide, but the arrangement leads me to believe autoerotic death. It's obvious that he meant to hang himself but not necessarily end his life—the act could have taken an unforeseen twist."

Picking up Manx's signature Kum & Go travel mug from the floor, I sat it on the nightstand and seated myself on the edge of the bed, looking at the gray light of morning as it seeped through the windows. "Excuse my ignorance, but how does this work?"

Lowering the camera and examining the viewer on the back of the device, she glanced at me. "Autoerotic asphyxia is a method of increasing sexual excitement by restricting the oxygen supply to the brain, usually by tightening a noose around the neck in the belief that the practice heightens sensation at orgasm."

"Somebody mention my favorite word?" Vic entered from the breezeway and leaned against the wall, reaching down and turning the travel mug to read the logo, the irony not lost on her as she took a sniff and then took a sip of what I assumed was Manx's signature tea. "Mmm . . . still warm." She looked sad. "So you're saying he came and he went?"

Payson folded her arms. "That's the interesting thing, there's none of the usual paraphernalia, pornographic magazines, lube . . ."

Vic nodded, wiping her lip and then placing the mug back in its resting place. "His pecker in his hand."

Payson shrugged. "He was cuffed."

"Is that odd?"

"Define odd."

"Do they usually cuff themselves if they're into this stuff?"

The blond woman sat on a stool by the window, resting the camera in her lap. "If they're into the whole sadomasochistic thing, you know, bondage and stuff, it's entirely possible."

"But then, how do they . . . You know."

Vic interrupted. "What my boss with his delicate sensibilities is trying to say, is that, with the recently departed's hands cuffed, how do they massage the bologna pony?"

"Uh, hands free." Payson cleared her throat. "The tricky part is the vagus nerve located in the neck. The sudden increase in pressure sends a message to the heart to shut down, resulting in sudden cardiac arrest and subsequent death."

"Excuse me, the vagus nerve?"

She paused for a moment. "It can have a large-scale effect in the body, traveling from the brain stem to all the major organs. With the right amount of pressure, it can slow down the heart and eventually stop it completely and in very short order." She went back to examining Manx's body. "It happens a lot more than you can imagine, like a thousand victims a year here in the states alone. Kevin Gilbert, David Carradine . . ."

Vic blurted a response. "*Kung Fu*?"

"Strangled himself in a closet in Thailand." Payson nodded. "A lot of these guys think they can put together some kind of safety device, like slipknots, or a support in reach, but then die because they restrict the amount of oxygen in their blood, causing them to pass out before they can release the pressure."

She continued taking photos. "The danger is compounded by the fact that the practice is usually done in secret and there's nobody to actually save you if something goes wrong."

I turned to Vic, who appeared to be gesturing toward the door from where she'd entered. "What was that all about?"

"Gary and Lynn."

"You sent them away?"

"Double-Tough did."

I glanced at the forensic examiner. "How long do you need?"

She straightened and sighed. "A couple of hours, at least."

"You've got as much as you need."

"Thanks."

Taking one last sweep around the room, I moved toward the door, where Dog met me, and I caught sight of Double-Tough standing at the opening to my right with his back to me, his arms folded. Coming up behind him, I studied the all but empty parking area, its the only occupant the Division of Criminal Investigation van, or Mystery Machine, as we all tended to refer to it. "I don't want anyone seeing this."

"Got it."

I patted his shoulder and, accompanied by Dog, headed back the other way toward the indoor arena where I'd sent Henry.

The Cheyenne Nation was examining the center of the vast roping area.

"Anything?"

"There was a mule in here."

"How can you tell?"

He lip-pointed to the far end of the arena. "There is mule shit over there."

"Say, you are good. Anything else?"

"No."

I knelt beside him as Dog sat a few feet away. "Really?"

He reached down and held up a fist of the arena bedding, allowing it to filter through his fingers. "It is shavings and sawdust, which does not hold much of an imprint."

"I thought the Northern Cheyenne could track anybody over anything?"

"You watch too much TV."

"I haven't watched any TV since they canceled *Have Gun—Will Travel*."

"There are two trails, the one where we stand now, which gives the indication that you walked this way and then back with Dog."

"And the other?"

He gestured again, this time with a wave of his hand. "And another where it seems as if the individual ran across the arena at an arc, not sure of where he or she was going, and then spotting the door, ran through there as Dog may have been chasing him or her."

I glanced at Dog. "Anytime you want to join in the conversation, feel free."

Henry grunted.

"Then what?"

The Bear stood and began walking toward the doorway as Dog and I followed. "If they were running with Dog in pursuit, then they did not have time to close the door behind them."

When he got to the doorway, he motioned to where a chain link and clasp held the door on the left. "Especially because it was chained open on this side."

"So whoever it was kept running."

"Yes." He walked through the opening and looked at the concrete floor for a long time before examining the storage area. "There are two doors: one to the right down that short hallway and outside, and then the one leading to the bathroom."

"Why not go for the one leading outside?"

"If you were in a hurry, you might miss it, or were perhaps unaware of where it went."

"So, not somebody from the ranch?"

The Bear grabbed Dog's muzzle, roughhousing as the beast playfully gnawed at his hand. "Or the Hound of the Baskervilles here . . ." Turning, he walked over and closed the door to the bathroom, revealing a massive dent in the hollow-core interior door. "Was hot on their trail."

Moving leftward, I studied the bathroom, the scuff mark still on the plastic seat. "Can you get anything from that?"

"It is a scuff mark."

"What about on the other side of the window, outside?"

"Concrete."

"Well, you're a lot of help."

"You are welcome."

I looked through the arena. "So, why would someone be down here and over at Manx's place at that time of night, anyway?"

"That would require knowing if the suspect was male or female."

"You actually think it could've been one of the women?"

"Why not?"

I considered it. "You don't think Manx's death has anything to do with Pepper."

"I did not say that, but I think you should keep your suspicions open."

"So, nothing more?"

He shrugged. "Well, I am no forensic podiatrist, but the first question that comes to mind is why run?"

I watched the monster as he circled the outer perimeter of the arena, sniffing everything, including the mule shit. "He can be pretty intimidating when he wants to be."

"Not if you know him, and his tendencies." We both studied the beast now. "I am not saying he does not have an aggressive nature, but it is almost exclusively in response to a hostile act."

"So it's somebody who doesn't know Dog?"

"Possibly, but there is also the fight-or-flight response, and if somebody ran, one would think that Dog would likely chase them, even if he did not mean to do them harm."

"That would also explain why he didn't catch them—have you ever seen anybody outrun Dog, especially in an open space like this arena?"

"No."

"Puzzling."

"Yes." He studied the behemoth, finally gesturing for me to call him over. "Get him and let us test the theory."

I stared at him. "You're kidding?"

"You will concede the point that there is no one in the immediate vicinity who can run faster than me?"

"Possibly Manx in that he's younger and not as muscled-up as you."

"And he is dead."

"A definite disadvantage in a foot race."

Raising my voice, I called out. "Dog!"

He was with us in an instant and I glanced at Henry as we walked back in the general direction of the stalls and the crime scene. "You're sure you want to do this?"

He reached down and ruffled Dog's ears. "You will not hurt me, will you?"

Dog panted and smiled up at him, knowing the game was afoot.

Stopping at the opening, we all turned and gauged the distance of sixty yards. "You're going to want a lead."

"Yes, I was thinking that about halfway, you should release him."

I firmly grasped Dog's heavy leather collar. "He's still going to get you."

"Possibly, but we will at least know where." Bear crouched down and prepared for a competition our and Dog's ancestors had participated in for millennia. "Ready?"

I clutched Dog's collar even harder. "Set."

"Go!" I watched Bear spring out of his crouch, his panther-like muscles stretching and compacting in a supple movement that I'd always envied. I was slightly bigger and a bit stronger in limited actions, but I would never be the natural athlete the Cheyenne Nation was.

Dog leaped forward and it was like holding on to a Kodiak, but I was prepared and still held him, barely escaping being pulled out of my boots.

The Bear was a third of the way across the arena and Dog made another lurch, but I was still able to hold him, barely.

Henry, hitting his full stride at the halfway mark, carried all the grace and speed of a cheetah, but I was about to release an A-10 Warthog—and did.

The amount of wood shavings, sawdust, and underlayment that flew up in my face as I released the hound of war was blinding, and I found myself stumbling backward as Dog shot away as if from a cannon.

The Bear didn't look back, but I was sure he knew he'd hit the halfway mark and that Dog was coming. His smooth gait was gliding toward the door, but it's possible he wasn't as quick as when he'd been in the backfield at Berkeley, and Dog was indeed coming on.

It almost appeared as though he might make it when Dog hit another gear and, despite his weight and girth, accelerated like a sports car going into overdrive with the advantage of four legs versus two.

For a second Henry had a chance to get to the doorway, but it wasn't meant to be. Dog was gaining on him so fast that he actually slowed and nipped the Bear's ankle. The momentum sent one foot into the other as he tried to bring it forward, and I watched in horror as the Bear flipped forward like a poker chip and smashed into the lower section of protective plywood at the bottom of the wall with a crashing thud.

Dog peeled off like a fighter plane and circled back to glimpse the crumpled body at the base of the wall, even going so far as to lower his front in an attempt to get the Cheyenne Nation to play some more.

When Henry didn't move, the beast looked at me and whined, finally turning back to the Bear and moving forward to nose his shoulder.

I was running myself at this point (but nothing compared with the impressive speed of both species I'd just witnessed), when Henry reached out an arm, wrapping it around Dog's startled head and pulling him in with a playful growl.

Slowing, I walked up and then sat, worn out from my minuscule efforts. "Okay, I concede the point that if you couldn't get away from him, then nobody could."

Tussling with Dog, he pushed the monster away; Dog sat beside him, tongue lolling. "Which supports the thought that it was either someone Dog here knew, or someone he really did not consider a physical threat."

"What about the dent in the bathroom door?"

Pushing up on one arm, he leaned against the plywood, banging it with a fist. "I am not saying the situation did not escalate."

"Okay, if that's the case, then I'm trying to think if there's anybody down here who could overpower Manx?"

He thought about it. "David?"

"Possibly."

"Gary?"

"Maybe, but there were no signs of a struggle or altercation."

"What about the handcuffs?"

"No ligature markings or signs that he'd struggled." I thought about it, picking at some of the sawdust and letting it fall from my hand. "All right, next two lines of thought—why kill Manx, and where is that S and W semiautomatic he was always carrying?"

"She's dusting the entire room."

"So, more than a couple of hours?"

Vic yawned and leaned against the gate. Double-Tough stood across the lot, talking to the television crew from Casper. "I guess so."

"What's going on out here?"

"They wanted to come in and talk with you, but we told 'em no." She turned her head. "I think you're going to have to do an interview unless you want me or DT to do it?"

"No, I don't think I want that."

Pushing the gate open, I watched as another vehicle pulled up behind the television crew, a black Suburban with tinted windows and Laramie County tags that read GOV. I crossed the parking lot to where a silver-haired individual was standing with a mic and held out a hand. "Hey, Sheriff, Mike Benning of KWWY Channel 12. We're here covering the fire, but heard that there had been a number of murders?"

Another younger, bearded man was standing to the right, focusing on us and I motioned for him to lower the camera. "You need to stop filming until I can see your credentials."

Benning produced a lanyard with a number of IDs, dangling them out to me. "Here you go." He gestured toward the bearded man. "This is Tad Willens, our cameraman."

"Uh-huh." Dropping the credentials, I glanced around as two very recognizable figures climbed out of the black Suburban and stood there watching me being interviewed. "Well, right now it's a singular murder, and an additional death, but I can't give you any details. Both are ongoing investigations."

He smiled with perfect teeth. "We just need thirty seconds at most, Sheriff."

"All right, ask your questions, but if you get out of line, I'm just going to clam up, which is going to make for really boring must-see TV, got me?"

He smiled some more, turning to the camera and urging me to do the same. "We're here with Absaroka County Sheriff Walt

Longmire at the historic O-Kay Dude Ranch where the owner was discovered dead in Crazy Woman Creek. Is that correct, Sheriff?"

"Pepper McKay was found in the Crazy Woman Creek, an apparent victim of blunt trauma."

"Mister McKay was struck in the head, was he not? In something of an execution-style killing?"

"No." I could see over his shoulder to where two very large men in suits approached. They stopped at a respectful distance to watch me. "It's possible he was struck, but it's also possible that he fell and struck his head while fishing."

"But there's also been another victim, hasn't there?" He shoved the mic in my face again.

"There is another victim, but there's no indication that the individual was assaulted in any way."

"So, there's nothing like a rampage, then?"

"No, in no way. I'm pretty sure the populace would be better served to be concerned about the fires up on the mountain that pose a much greater threat to the community."

"And do you have any news on that situation, Sheriff?"

"Not particularly, but the National Forest Service and the National Interagency Fire Center have constant updates on their websites and can give viewers a much more comprehensive idea of what's going on than I can."

He took the mic back, smiling at the camera. "Two dead with no answers here in Absaroka County. I'm Mike Benning, KWWY, Channel 12."

The lights went off on the camera as he lowered the device and Benning began rolling in the cord of his mic, but I noticed the cameraman was still furtively pointing the camera at me and the red recording light was still on.

"Nice tag."

"Just trying to spice it up a bit, Sheriff." Finishing rolling the cord and stuffing it under his arm but with the mic still near his mouth, he turned back to me. "Pepper McKay was kind of a big deal around here, wasn't he?"

I watched as the two large men came closer and stood behind the reporter. "He was a prominent citizen, yep."

"And he was killed, was he not?"

"Until DCI makes a formal statement, I'm afraid I can't comment on that." I pointed to the camera. "Do you mind switching that thing off?"

"Oh, sorry." He gestured to the cameraman and handed him the coiled cord and mic as the red light went out. "From what I'm to understand, McKay wasn't the most liked individual in the county?"

"I really can't answer to that. I'm a sheriff, not a social director." I gestured over his shoulder toward the Bobs. "What do you two want?"

Bob Delude smiled. "The boss wants to talk to you."

"I'm busy."

Bob Delozier was next. "Just take a second." He nodded toward the retreating news crew. "He's here for them, mostly."

I glanced back at the dark windows of the Suburban. "The fire?"

He shrugged. "We gotta look like we're doing something."

Walking past them, I approached the Suburban as the rear-passenger door opened and the Right Honorable Governor of the Great State of Wyoming, Robert Lang, took a last puff of his cigarette before rubbing the embers out on the sole of his boot. "Nasty habit, but I can't seem to give it up entirely." He stretched out a hand. "Congratulations."

I folded my arms. "For what?"

He let the hand drop, studying me as he adjusted his glasses. "Well, for being the father of the state attorney general."

"I don't think I had much to do with it. Besides, I guess we'll see if it turns out to be a blessing or a curse for her."

"She can always go back to private practice." He peered past me, toward the barn. "What's going on?"

"Routine investigation."

"I bet that's not what the TV folks wanted to hear."

"No, they wanted a little more red meat—but they're here mostly for the fire."

"Me too."

"I figured."

He studied me, smoothing his Teddy Roosevelt mustache with a forefinger. "You know, you may not like me, Walt, but I can do a lot of good for this state."

"I hope so."

He studied me some more. "Well, I've got an appointment with this fire management officer, J. R. Rose of the National Interagency Fire Center. Have you met him?"

"I have, and he seems quite capable."

"Good to know." Straightening the cuff of his pants, he lowered his boot from his knee and gestured for the Bobs. "Well, you don't seem to have a lot of answers for us—but it looks to me as if you've got another victim over there?"

I turned to see what he was talking about, only to find Vic sprawled on the ground with DT propping her up. With a quick nod to the governor, I started off. "Excuse me."

When I reached her, Double-Tough explained. "I don't know what happened. We were standing here talking and all of a sudden she just keeled over."

I heard some noise behind me and found that the TV crew had

switched the camera back on and were now, once again, filming us. Taking a step toward them, I lifted a finger and pointed. "Shut that thing off, now!"

They did as I said and I turned back to Vic, scooping her up.

I carried Vic into the breezeway and then over to a stack of bales in one of the stalls before carefully lowering her onto the flat surface. Double-Tough hovered as I checked her pulse, which seemed normal, and then peeled back an eyelid to see nothing but the white of her eye. "She passed out?"

"Kind of, but it was the slowest passing out I've ever seen." He considered her. "She said something about being tired and then held her hand out and I took it. She shook her head and then looked down at the ground and said she thought she might take a nap." His eyes came back to mine. "I laughed, but then her knees kind of went out from under her and she started to sag against the fence. I tried to catch her, but it was a bad angle, and before I knew it, she was lying on the ground."

I shot my eyes toward Manx's room. "Get Payson out here, she's the closest thing we've got to a med-tech in the immediate vicinity."

He disappeared and I felt Vic's pulse again, noticing it might have been a bit slow.

Payson appeared with DT and moved me aside, checking the pulse and eye reactions with a small flashlight. Carefully holding Vic's head, she gently slapped her face. "Her pulse is a little slow, but she's definitely out." She glanced at me. "Has she ever had anything like this happen before?"

"No."

"No heart condition, anything like that?"

"No."

"Hard to explain, it's not dehydration or anything like that . . ."

"The tea."

She looked at me. "Excuse me?"

"The Himalayan tea that Manx kept in that Kum & Go travel mug, he was bragging about it, and Vic tried some and said it was really good. She drank from it again when she came in Manx's room earlier today."

"You're sure?"

"I saw her do it." Moving past her, I walked quickly across the breezeway and stepped into the room, ignoring the body and picking up the travel mug from the side table. I carried it back out to the forensic pathologist and handed it to her. "Check this, but I'm betting that whatever it was that knocked Manx out so that somebody could do this to him was also what KO'd Vic here."

Payson took the travel mug, unscrewed the top, and sniffed its contents. "Nothing but black tea, as near as I can tell, but we'll know more after I give it a closer examination." She glanced at my second-in-command. "How much did she drink?"

"I saw her sip from the mug only once, but it's possible she was drinking from the thing the entire time Henry and I were gone." I turned to DT. "Speaking of, where's Henry?"

"He said he was going to check the area behind the arena for more tracks, and that's the last I heard of him and Dog."

Pivoting back to Payson, I gestured toward Vic. "What can we do for her?"

Putting the lid back on the travel mug, she shrugged. "Make her comfortable and let her sleep, but you might think of getting her to a hospital just to be sure. They can probably tell what she accidentally took and see if there are any other side effects we should be aware of."

Pulling my keys from my pocket, I tossed them to Double-

Tough. "Do you mind going and getting my truck and bringing it down here? I'll put her in there and run her to Durant Memorial."

He nodded, dragging the gate aside and heading outside.

"Also, gather everybody who was here last night and this morning and tell them that they are to stay here until I get back, no exceptions." I turned back to Payson. "So, Manx was drugged."

"I think so."

"It seems that either it was someone he knew or somebody who got into his place, drugged the tea while he wasn't there, and then came in, cuffed him, and strung him up."

"And then you and your dog happened on the scene."

"I'm guessing . . ." I thought about it. "How long would it take for him to suffocate?"

"Not long if it was damage to the vagus nerve that I mentioned."

"But you wouldn't need him to be completely knocked out to do this?"

"No, it would actually be easier if he had been only partially sedated and still compliant."

"Triazolam, flunitrazepam, Rohypnol, or, in the common parlance, roofies."

I stared at Dave Nickerson, who had replaced Doc Bloomfield. "The sex drug?"

"Well, the date-rape drug, yes." He studied the notes on his clipboard. "It came around in the seventies and was used for cases of extreme insomnia. It was actually pretty easy to identify, even with concentrations as low as four nanograms per milliliter. The elimination half-life of the drug is something like twelve hours. You can still identify it with urine tests and even hair samples after that, but I took a hunch and went with the most available drug." He clasped the clipboard and studied me. "Roche, the Swiss company, started lowering the doses per pill, made them less soluble, and even added blue dye to the stuff to make it easier to spot in somebody's drink."

"But not mixed with Himalayan loose-leaf black tea in a travel mug."

"No, probably not."

"Is it easy to get?"

"It's a drug, Walt. The only thing easier to get in the country than drugs is guns." Stepping over to a water dispenser, Dr. Nickerson plucked a paper cup from the dispenser on the side and poured himself a drink. "Thirsty?"

"No, thanks."

He took a gulp. "It's an illegal drug in the US. Schedule IV; possession is three years and a fine."

"But still readily available?"

"Yes." He crushed the paper cup and then, not seeing a trashcan, stuffed it in his pocket. "She's going in and out, but mostly out."

"There's no permanent damage, is there?"

"No." He laughed. "She was asking some pretty funny questions before you got here, but other than that, I think she'll be fine."

"What kind of questions?"

"I think . . . I think it might be best if you go talk to her yourself, just don't be upset if she falls asleep in the middle of a sentence." He continued to study me, smiling. "I'm sorry, but is he with you?"

"Excuse me?"

He chin pointed past my shoulder. "The odd bird over there?"

Maxim Sidorov was standing by the wall in his leather jacket, T-shirt with the holes in it, fingerless gloves, timing-belt belt, black jeans, and motorcycle boots, his hair doing its usual sideswiped stand-on-end. "What the hell are you doing out of jail?"

He shrugged. "I am not of officially arrested."

I turned back to the doctor. "How long will she be incapacitated?"

"Hard to say, but anywhere between four and twelve hours."

"Can I see her?"

"Of course, room 28."

"Thanks, Doc." He stared at me. "What?"

"That's the first time you've called me Doc with that emphasis, like Isaac."

I smiled back at him. "Get used to it."

I walked back to where Maxim stood against the wall like a heavy metal fan in line for tickets. "What do you want?"

"Nice of to see of you too."

"I'm kind of busy here."

"I have important information of case."

I glanced around. "Concerning Ruth?"

"No, of current case, here. Now."

I stared at him, more than a little incredulous. "About the Pepper McKay murder?"

"Da."

"You've got to be kidding."

He pushed off the wall. "You don't want information; I go back to jail and talk with nice lady at registration or play chess with deputy of impossible name."

I glanced around the hallway, figuring which way I needed to go. "All right, come with me." Moving past him, I crossed the hall and pushed open the door to room 28 and ushered him in.

The room was semi-dark and Vic lay in the bed in a hospital gown, the sheets pulled up with her arms over top. I placed a hand in hers and just stood there for a moment, forgetting everything and just feeling the warmth.

"Hi."

Startled, I discovered her eyes partially open. "Howdy."

"Mmmwhere am I?"

"You're in the hospital."

"Philadelphia?"

I sat on the edge of the bed, continuing to hold her hand so she wouldn't drift away. "No, Durant, Wyoming."

Her eyes closed. "Mmwhy?"

"You fainted or passed out."

"Passed out?"

"Yep."

"MmI pregnant?"

Even I could hear the small panic in my voice. "What?"

"Am I pregnant?"

"No. No, you're not pregnant. You can't get pregnant."

"Hmm . . . Tell my mother." Her eyes came back open. "You my boyfriend?"

"Actually, I think I'm your fiancé."

"Mmmy what?"

I squeezed her hand. "Your betrothed, your intended, groom-to-be, future husband."

"Oh, good. I like you."

I raised the hand and gave it a kiss. "And I like you too."

The eyes closed again. "Mmyou're sure I'm not pregnant?"

"Pretty sure."

"Mmtell my mother."

I watched as her head lolled a bit and then settled in the pillow and her breathing became regular. "I will . . ."

Slowly easing off the bed so as to not disturb her, I replaced her hand and crossed to where Sidorov now stood. "She is all right?"

"Drugged."

"How?"

"She drank from a mug that was used to sedate somebody else who's been killed."

He studied me for a long moment. "Native McKay son, Manx?"

I stared at him. "How do you know that?"

"And Manx has died of the type of hanging?"

I let out a breath of amazement. "And how do you know that?"

He glanced at Vic for a moment and then crossed toward the two visitor chairs in the corner of the room by the window. "Please to of sit down."

I did as he said, joining him as he sat on the arm of one of the chairs. "I'm asking how you know all this?"

Leaning forward, I watched as he laced his knotty fingers together, struggling to match words to his thoughts. "Do not be offended of next question, please."

"I'll try."

"You have read novels by Fyodor Dostoyevsky?"

"Excuse me for saying so, I'm not big on the Russians but some of them, yep."

"*The Brothers Karamazov*?"

I thought about it. "Yep, I studied it in a literary class at USC."

"Possibly most significant novel ever written, a literary inspiration that rival Shakespeare and Bible." He spread his hands. "Then you see."

"See what?"

"Someone is playing hideous joke on you—there is no way of

existence could reasonably let this happen, but caprice of criminal mastermind is at work."

Exhausted and annoyed, I snapped at him. "I still don't understand."

"Someone is committing crime in facsimile of Dostoyevsky novel *The Brothers Karamazov.*"

# 11

"How is she?"

I pushed the phone into the crook of my neck and answered the Cheyenne Nation, whom, along with my dog, I'd abandoned at the O-Kay Ranch in the south side of my county. "Groggy, but she'll be fine."

There was a long pause as he assembled the next question. "*The Brothers Karamazov*?"

"Yep, I know."

"That is crazy."

"I know, but he sure as hell has a point." I sighed. "Serves me right for slighting Russian literature in school."

He grunted. "Along with the murder of Manx, this puts a completely different complexion on the case."

"Yep, it does."

He breathed a chuckle and then elaborated. "The person you are after is insane or a literary major."

"Same thing—I should know." Taking my boots off my desk, I leaned forward as Ruby hung an arm in my office doorway holding up two fingers, the universal gesture indicating line two. I nodded and went back to my conversation with the Cheyenne Nation. "So, you want me to come get you?"

"We have a choice: If you are coming back down to do more interviews, we can stay here and wait for you. Besides, there is a very elderly gentleman here who is looking forward to your reacquaintance."

"Who?"

"An Elder Zebrowski, who you must have met in an earlier life."

"He's actually there?"

"In the one-hundred-year-old flesh, and I think he made the trip entirely to meet you—that, and pick up a wayward charge who needs to be returned to the monastery over in Meeteetse posthaste."

"That would be Alan's fellow novice Michael Rakin, whose Pinto broke down in Powder Junction."

"Well, Elder Zebrowski is here now and I am not sure for how much longer before he shuffles off this mortal coil, but Double-Tough says he can give us a ride."

I looked up at the old Seth Thomas on the wall, indicating that it was getting late in the afternoon. "No, I'm heading back down, but I don't want you to be stuck there."

"I do not mind—things are becoming interesting—and things are slow at the bar. Besides, Lynn has made us a late lunch, and you may need our help before this is all over."

"What about Dog, do you think he minds?"

"He is gnawing a week-old ham bone right now, so I do not think he cares if you ever come back."

"See you in a few." The phone went dead in my hand as I reached across and punched line two. "Longmire."

"Fancy that Longmire, I'm a Longmire too."

"What do you want, punk?"

"Attorney General Punk to you, mister. AGP for short."

"What's up, Cady?"

"So when did you decide to become a TV star?"

I sat back in my chair, listening to it groan almost as loud as me. "I beg your pardon?"

"KWWY, Channel 12, out of Casper, just aired a piece about a multiple murder so horrifying that the lead deputy upon witnessing the crime scene passed out?"

"Oh, good grief."

"Yeah, I was trying to imagine how bad a crime scene would have to be to cause the Terror to faint. Anyway, the gov called me yesterday, asking what was up. So, what's up?"

"He was just here."

"The governor, Bob Lang?"

"Yep, Pepper McKay was killed."

"That the asshole who tried to rape Mom?"

I stared at the phone. "How did you know that?"

"She told me."

I shook my head, staring at the little red light on the phone. "You know, nobody ever tells me anything."

"What, exactly, happened?"

"With the attempted rape?"

"No, with Vic conking out."

"She drank from a drugged cup of tea and took a powder, and the camera crew just happened to be in the vicinity and filmed it."

"Oh, good grief."

"My words exactly."

"But there are dead bodies involved?"

"Hey, do you remember Gary and Lynn Lyman?"

"I remember their son, Peter, the one who drowned out at Lake De Smet—he had the greenest eyes."

"Do you remember the Crow cook down at the O-Kay, Maya Noota, and her son, Manx?"

"No, I don't think so."

"Probably after your time, just another Pepper McKay sideshow . . . But I think he was a credible young man with a couple of issues. I think somebody strung him up to make it appear to be some kind of autoerotica thing . . ."

"Autoerotic asphyxia?"

I stared at the phone again. "And how do you know about that stuff?"

"It's a thing, not for me, but it's a thing—mostly guys from what I hear."

"Well, Manx was my lead suspect in the murder of his illegitimate father, Pepper, especially after he committed what we thought was suicide until we discovered he'd been drugged."

"Sheesh."

"Yep."

There was a long pause as I listened to her breathe. "You ever get tired of it all, Dad?"

"Every day, but Dog loves me."

"Well, Lola and I love you too. Especially now that you're a TV celebrity."

"Speaking of, how's my granddaughter?"

"Bossing everyone around in preschool."

I stared at the phone a third time. "Wait, she started school?"

"Hey, Pops, you wanna try to keep up?"

"Wait, she's old enough to go to school?"

"Preschool, but I've gotta go, the work of the Great General of All Attorneys is never done."

"Okay, but call me back about this preschool thing, okay?" The phone went dead in my hand for the second time in five minutes and I mumbled to myself. "What, no one says goodbye these days?"

I lumbered into the main office to find Ruby and Sancho in conference, so I leaned on my dispatcher's counter, making it a threesome. "Where's the Order of Lenin?"

Ruby adjusted her glasses. "Over at the library. Guess what the one book we don't have in the jail library happens to be?"

"*The Brothers Karamazov.*"

"You got it."

The Basquo leaned back, glancing between the two of us. "What do you think, Boss? What are the odds?"

"Life imitating art?" I shrugged. "Oscar Wilde says life imitates art far more than art imitates life, resulting not merely from life's imitative instinct, but from the fact that the self-conscious aim of life is to find expression, and that art offers it certain forms through which it may realize that energy."

Sancho glanced at Ruby. "What happened that made him like this?"

"No one really knows."

"Then there's the Aristotelian mimesis of art imitating life."

"Boss, can I get a syllabus for this class?"

The conversation was interrupted by Maxim Sidorov struggling up the stairs of the office like a Tibetan Sherpa with a stack of books a good two feet in height. Making the landing, he turned and sat on the bench, sliding the stack from his lap across the surface, the top one falling off the end and onto the floor.

I stepped in that direction to lift the tome. "The Pevear/Volokhonsky translation, 1990?"

He gasped. "I am to understand, as library woman tell me, it is of best one."

I straightened the stack, glancing at the titles. "And the rest?"

"Research."

"You honestly believe this?"

"It all fits of well." Catching his breath, he sat there for a moment. "I remember my father giving me of book for Christmas and reading of night and next day, none of the stop until I had finished it, knowing that through this book the world had changed of me."

"That still doesn't explain . . ."

"But there is problem."

Flipping the book open, I read a few words, realizing at once that I'd accidentally opened it to book five, or the "Pro and Contra" section, which is one of the more famous chapters in the book in which the Grand Inquisitor of the Spanish Inquisition interrogates Jesus when he returns to Earth. "And what is that?"

"It is horrible mystery novel."

"Really?"

"It is obvious that illegitimate son, Snegiryov, is killer of father, reassured in his suicide with guilt of having committed act of patricide."

"But our illegitimate son, Manx, was drugged and likely killed."

"Yes, and in book then suspicion is shifted to eldest son, Dmitri, through letter provided to court, which does not seem of possible, especially since portion of book in which he is condemned title is 'A Judicial Error.' This is Dostoyevsky providing clue that eldest son did not kill father." He slapped a hand on the stack of books. "*The Brothers Karamazov* was first portion of trilogy to be written, but Dostoyevsky died at end of writing this first part of book. I am certain that if given opportunity to write rest of book, real killer would have been of revealed."

Saizarbitoria came over and picked up one of the books. "Can I borrow this one?"

Sidorov peeked at the binding. "You may, but to bring back."

Sancho held it out to me. "This wasn't on the class reading list."

Ignoring him, I turned back to the Russian. "Well, give us a leg up and tell us who you think—What's the old man's name in the book?"

"Fyodor Pavlovich Karamazov."

"Doesn't everybody in this novel have twelve names?"

"No, is not as bad as *War and Peace*, but almost."

"Well, then who really kills the father in the novel?"

"I do not know."

I stared at the Russian, gave a glance to the others, and then came over and sat on the bench with him, the towering stack of books between us. "What?"

His face took on a ferocious expression of determination as he pulled at the soul patch beneath his lower lip. "I have every of intention to take books and sequester of cell and not come out until I have answer for you."

"You must be kidding."

"I wish I was, but you've got to admit that at least it keeps him in his cell and out of trouble."

Lynn brought over my sandwich and sat it down before me. "Here you go, Walt. I figured with all this going on you wouldn't havc timc to cat."

"Thank you." I reached out and took her hand, noticing the red around her eyes. "I'm so sorry about Manx."

She clamped her lips together, saying nothing.

"We're going to find out who's doing this, I promise you."

She gave another curt nod. "I'm just . . . I'm just hoping it's not someone else I care deeply about."

I glanced at Henry, sitting on the other side of the table petting Dog, and squeezed Lynn's hand. "Me too."

Letting her go, I ate and watched as she stacked dishes in the sink, put a few things away in the refrigerator, and then went through the swinging dining room door without saying anything more.

"She is very upset."

I took a drink of the iced tea she'd made for me. "I figured. Where's Gary?"

"I have not seen him."

"Anybody else?"

"David was on the porch but had to run into Powder Junction on errands. He said he would be back this evening."

"He better." I took another bite and chewed, reminding myself that every once in a while, it was good to eat. "And all his lady friends?"

"That, I do not know."

"And Ian?"

"He has established an operations center in the study where the internet works best and there is a large partner's desk where he can work yet be out of the way."

"Alan?"

"And his friend are out back with the abbot deputy and Elder Zebrowski, who, I am to infer, is something of a celebrity at Saint Benedict Monastery."

"Because he's what, a thousand years old?"

"I spoke with him, and he is quite amazing, actually."

Finishing my sandwich, I took another slug of tea to wash it down. "I think I recall that from our meeting all those years ago."

"He is eager to remake your acquaintance."

I leaned back in my chair, staring at the well-worn surface of the kitchen table that I was sure was never used by paying guests, thinking about what to do next in pursuit of a killer.

The Bear studied me. "This is a difficult one, yes?"

"Yep."

"Neither rhyme nor reason."

"At this point, no. I mean every reasonable suspect simply doesn't appear to have the required amount of motivation to murder not only one victim, but two. My money was on Manx, but now that he's been killed . . ."

"Two murderers?"

"I suppose, but that would require twice the impetus and make it doubly easy to find a culprit, and then that much easier to find the second."

"Jealousy, robbery, and vengeance."

I nodded. "That's the big three, yep."

"Assuming that Manx's death was a result of him seeing or finding something out concerning the murder of his illegitimate father, is there anyone we know who is jealous of Pepper?"

Picking up my plate, I carried it over to the sink and wiped my mouth, tossing the paper napkin into the trash. "He was rich."

"Perhaps, but with his demise, his three sons would inherit his considerable wealth."

"David, who has been siphoning off his share, wouldn't get as much."

The Cheyenne Nation drummed his fingers on the surface of the table. "Possibly, but Ian seems unconcerned as to how the money is divided, and Alan does not appear to care if he gets any at all."

I leaned against the counter, crossing my arms. "Vengeance?"

"Once again, David would appear to be the only one with an axe to grind but he just does not seem to be that easily provoked."

"Personal?"

"From what you have told me, this one is not so easily explained away."

I crossed over to the mudroom door and looked out the windows to where Elder Zebrowski and his handler held court with the two novices. "No, from what I'm to gather, Pepper was hitting on David's quasi-girlfriend and then so was Ian."

His dark eyes widened a bit. "This seems a richer vein in comparison with mine."

"Yep, but this once again points us back to David."

The Bear joined me at the door along with Dog. "And?"

"I can see David killing Pepper. Hell, I can see anybody murdering Pepper, but I just can't envision David killing Manx. He seemed to have had too much empathy for his half brother's plight—you know what I mean?"

"I do." Stepping into the mudroom, he glanced around. "You have spoken with the girlfriend, Paetra Agirra?"

"Yep, and I can see her killing anybody on the planet."

"Was she here last night?"

"I don't know, but I intend to find out. I don't think she could overpower Manx, but with the date-rape drug . . ."

He glanced back at me. "Does she seem the kind of young woman who would have a knowledge of such things?"

"Beyond any shadow of a doubt."

"And the fiancée?"

"Katherine Verkhov from over in Jackson. I guess David got her father out of some financially hot water over there."

"Was she here the night or morning that Pepper was killed?"

"Not that I'm aware of. We've got a call into her in Jackson, but she hasn't deigned to call us back. I'll have Teton County Sheriff's Office go over and knock on their gold-plated gate. In my experience, people are more likely to come across with answers when people with badges and guns show up at their front door."

He smiled. "Even rich people?"

"Even rich people."

"Elder Zebrowski."

The old man in the black robe and ornate headdress blessed his cataract eye upon me, the opaque white giving the appearance he was gazing at me from the caul of another world. "My son, it is so good to see you again. Please, sit."

I took the hand he held out and sat in the chair that Alan had pulled out for me.

Gesturing toward a very tall, older man in a black robe with oversized ears and nose, he introduced his assistant. "This is the abbot deputy, Brian Schiffer. You see, you are not the only one to have deputies . . ." He gestured toward the two young men, speaking in a low voice. "I was just telling these two about the fish that got away."

I nodded to the group and then returned my eyes to his. "And what fish was that?"

He laughed silently. "Why, you."

"You turned me away."

"Ah, but I did not give up on you, my son. I would never give up on anyone, ever. Anyone can change at any point in their life and look how your life has transformed." He released my hand and sat back in his chair. "We are all writing our own stories, our life story, and there really is no reason why we can't all pause for a moment to ask ourselves what it is we want in this life, what we really want." He reached out, touching my arm. "And begin rewriting the story of our lives, and isn't that what you did, my son?"

"I suppose so."

"And what a force of good you've become." He glanced at Alan and Michael, who both stood there in their cassocks a little away, smiling at the old man. "There are those of us who are meant for a contemplative life, a life of philosophical and theological thought." He examined me. "And then there are those who are meant for a life of action, facing the tumultuous challenges many of us are not willing to confront, setting their anxieties to one side for that greater good that benefits us all."

"I think I was just after a regular paycheck."

He shook his head. "Make light if you will, but it is a grand life of usefulness you have chosen."

"Still, I can't help but wonder how my life would've been if you'd allowed me entrance into the order."

He covered his mouth with his hand. "You would have been a miserable student, my son." He glanced back at the tall man behind him. "Something like my second-in-command and roundsman, Schiffer, here. All he does is read, and report to me the shortcomings of our novices."

"It is my duty to see that they remain on the true path, Elder."

I took a moment to study his extraordinary face. Each feature—eyes, ears, nose, and mouth—was larger than it should have been, and he might've been considered homely if not for the thin lips that compressed on his face, indicating a powerful control with which he witnessed the world around him.

"I simply wish you didn't pursue your duties with such zeal, my son."

"Amen." We all turned to look at Alan, who smiled, slightly embarrassed. "Sorry . . ."

Elder Zebrowski rested his hand on my arm again, his twinkling blue eyes peering out through his wrinkles. "And you, you cannot help yourself, there is an element of longing and yearning, a restless flame that will never stop moving—an ascetic life would have been a torture for you."

"You may be right."

He thought about it. "You were getting married when we first met."

"I was."

"And how is she?"

"I'm afraid my wife passed away a number of years ago, but we have a daughter who just became the attorney general of the state."

"She must be a great comfort to you."

"That and her daughter, my granddaughter. But enough about me, there must be some reason as to why you've come all this way besides reminiscing?"

Straightening, the old eyes peered at me. "You are a detective, aren't you, my son?"

"I try; now how can I assist you?"

He gestured a bony finger toward his two young charges. "I need to bring these two novitiates back to the monastery; the Great Schema has requested they resume their learning of monastic formation." He gestured toward Alan. "This one is preparing for his simple vows, and the feeling is that he must return." He nodded toward Michael Rakin. "And this one must come back for other reasons, which I am not allowed to divulge at this time."

"Now?"

He looked up at me. "I'm sorry?"

"You want to take them now?"

"Why, yes."

"I'm afraid that's not possible because they were both present during two murders."

His expression was puzzled for a moment. "Surely you don't think . . . ?"

"I'm not sure what to think, which means that everyone who was here must remain until I do know what to think."

The abbot deputy, Schiffer, spoke up. "But surely you could release them into our custody, Sheriff. It's not like you're turning them out into the wide world?"

"No, but I'm going to have to reinterview everyone who was here, and I don't intend to do that long-distance."

"How long do you suppose this will take?"

"I really can't say, but it's an ongoing murder investigation."

The tall man looked down at the Elder and then back to me. "That puts us in the clumsy position of either returning to the monastery empty-handed or waiting until you finish the investigation to your satisfaction."

"I'm afraid so."

He stepped forward and gazed at the old man with a sour face. "Elder, would you prefer going back to Saint Benedict, or remaining here?"

The old man laughed and then smiled at me. "Why, we must stay here and witness the investigation."

"You realize we only have a small amount of your equipment and medications with us?"

The Elder patted the arm of his second-in-command. "You worry too much, Brian, I will be fine." He turned to me. "Is there a motel nearby, somewhere we may stay?"

"Considering the circumstances, I'm sure they can make arrangements for you to stay here at the lodge." I glanced at the youngest McKay. "Alan, do you suppose you could speak with Lynn and Gary about getting these two a room for the night?"

He smiled. "I'm sure that won't be a problem."

"I want to thank you for receiving my call, Ms. Verkhov."

"Well, there wasn't much choice, was there?" She adjusted the phone, and we both sat there in long-distance silence. "We were on our way out to the airport and were met by two of your storm troopers at our gate."

Sitting at the gossip bench near the entryway, I held the receiver of the massive Belgian phone to my ear, feeling like I was lounging at the Ritz Paris. "I apologize for that, but you didn't seem to be getting back to me."

"We're leading very busy lives, Sheriff."

"Busy enough to keep you from responding to inquiries concerning a murder investigation?"

There was a long pause. "So, Pepper's death, it's been determined it was murder?"

"I thought you would've known by now?"

"No."

"David didn't tell you?"

"No, David and I don't speak as much as we used to, and things have become strained between Ian and me. I knew that Pepper was dead, obviously, from the newspapers, but they didn't say anything about it being a murder."

"I see. Well, I'm beginning to think I need a player card so that I can keep everybody's, uh, connections straight. I hope you'll forgive me asking a few somewhat personal questions?"

"Certainly."

"You were engaged to David, am I correct?"

"Yes, he was kind enough to assist my father and me in our business dealings and I fell in love with him, and we were engaged. It was only later that I came to the conclusion that he had only asked me to marry him as an obligation."

"I see."

"He thought it was something he had to do."

"And so, the two of you separated?"

"We did."

"And then how did you and Ian . . ."

She was quick to interrupt. "To be clear, Ian and I were never together in the greater sense."

"I see."

"We both made a few half-hearted efforts, but the specter of David was always there between us, and we finally ended it."

Henry and Dog appeared in the entryway but, seeing I was busy on the phone, abandoned me for the porch. "Well, that certainly clears the air on the relationships. I'm assuming you're not involved with either David or Ian at this time?"

"No."

"But I'm to understand that you were here at the lodge a few nights ago, the night before the morning that Pepper was killed?"

"I was."

"Do you mind if I ask why?"

"I was attempting to see if there was anything worth salvaging in the wreckage of either relationship."

"And was there?"

"No."

"Do you mind if I ask when you left the lodge?"

"I'm not sure, but sometime in the middle of that night I drove down to Casper and got a room at the Riverside Hotel."

"I'm assuming you were heading back to Jackson and went through Casper to avoid the fire."

"Yes." There was a pause. "I slept in the next morning and then drove the rest of the way back."

"And haven't been here since?"

"No." There was a pause, and then she laughed. "Are you seriously considering me as a murder suspect?"

"In all honesty, no, but I'm at the point in this investigation where I'm not sure what it is I'm looking for, so I'm looking at everything and everyone, hoping that something will lead to something else and start revealing what it was that happened."

"That seems sensible."

"Some might call it grasping at straws."

"In the small amount of time we've been conversing, you don't strike me as a grasper of straws." I listened as she readjusted the phone. "So, who are you suspecting?"

"I'm not sure if I can have that conversation with you concerning an ongoing homicide investigation, Ms. Verkhov."

"Oh, come on, you know I'm not involved and I'm even more curious than you are—besides, I'm never going to have any contact with the Brothers McKay ever again."

I stared out the window, squeezing the phone a little tighter to my ear. "Excuse me, but what did you just say?"

"I said I'm probably never coming back there . . ."

"No, about the brothers?"

"Oh, the Brothers McKay? It's an old joke between Alan and me about the family resembling the characters in the Dostoyevsky novel *The Brothers Karamazov.*"

"With the most recent events, very much so now."

"Yes, it's most horrifying." She paused. "If I was you, I'd make a close examination of Manx. If anybody has a motive to kill Pepper, he's the one."

"I'll, um . . . take that under advisement."

"What about Alan?"

"I'm not sure, but he has an alibi and just doesn't seem like a killer."

"Does whodunit, in your experience, seem like a killer?"

"No, but . . . Excuse me, are you insinuating Alan as a suspect?"

She laughed, wholeheartedly. "Of course not, but I do find it thought-provoking that his dissertation for his doctorate was on Dostoyevsky's *The Brothers Karamazov.*"

"Excuse me?"

She was quiet for a moment. "You didn't know?"

"Alan has a doctorate?"

"Yes, before he gave it all up for God."

Pinching the bridge of my nose, I sighed. "I actually have an individual working from *The Brothers Karamazov* angle."

"You're kidding."

"Nope."

"Maybe you are grasping at straws after all."

I blew through my lips at the truth of that statement. "Perhaps."

"Well, everybody on the North American continent despised Pepper, so that's not going to thin the herd, is it?"

"Probably not."

"But some people hated him more than others."

"What, exactly, are you saying?"

"I'd rather not, but there are some interesting letters in the partners desk in the study that were written to me, and since I wasn't planning on ever returning, I left them in the center drawer facing the door. They might make for some interesting reading for you."

"I'll have a look."

"Do, and if you have any other questions just call me at this number."

"Thank you, Ms. Verkhov."

"As a matter of fact, please do call me back because I'm dying to know how this all turns out."

"So, you haven't given up on the brothers as a whole, just yet?"

"In the romantic sense, yes—but who doesn't love a good mystery, especially one with literary underpinnings. Goodbye, Sheriff."

I lowered the receiver back onto the cradle. I stood and stretched, walking out the main door, and peered into the darkness to my left, where the Cheyenne Nation and Dog sat studying the faint glow in the sky toward the mountains. "That the fire?"

"Yes."

Walking across the wraparound porch, I joined them in their observation point at the corner. "Worse than before."

"Yes."

"Do you want to go home?"

"No."

"Okay."

I started to walk off as he called after me. "Elder Zebrowski and his abbot deputy are ensconced in the maids' quarters on the first floor. Lynn decided that it might not be best for a hundred-year-old man to be climbing the stairs."

"Boy howdy." I turned and started for the main doors again.

"Where are you going?"

I called over my shoulder. "To go riffle through drawers."

He and Dog went back to watching the sky. "Let us know if you find anything."

Going through the front doors, I headed toward the main stairway and then the study, where the lights glowed.

Ian McKay was seated in the chair at the partners desk, typing away on his computer.

"Are you going to make your deadline?"

His head rose and he peered at me through his thick glasses. "Maybe."

I leaned against the doorjamb, folding my arms. "Your brother Alan has been hiding his light under a bush?"

He pushed the glasses back on his head and regarded me. "Meaning?"

I glanced around as I entered the room. "I'm to understand that he's something of an expert on *The Brothers Karamazov*?"

He sat back in his chair with a bemused expression. "You've been talking to Katherine Verkhov."

"She finally returned my calls, yes."

He studied my face. "You're serious?"

"Don't you find it odd?"

Realizing the severity of our conversation, he reached out and closed the lid on the laptop. "I found it damned odd, but now, with the most recent developments, I find it terribly disconcerting and more than a little threatening."

"Why didn't you say anything?"

He stood, plucking a pencil from behind his ear and tossing it onto the surface of the desk. "Because I thought it was ridiculous."

Pulling out the center drawer facing me, I stared at the handwritten letters that lay there. "And now?"

"To be honest, Walt. I'm scared to death and fearing for my life."

I flipped through the letters. "Why, now?"

"It just seems so random." He stood and came around the desk, sitting on the corner and loosening his bow tie. "I mean, if someone had a genuine motive for killing both Pepper and Manx, I guess I could understand it. Not approve of it, but at least it would make some kind of sense."

I glanced at him. "But you said you feared for your life?"

"Anyone who could devise something like this would have to be insane, and that's what worries me—but that doesn't describe Alan."

"Excuse me being a little rusty on my Russian literature, but in our version of the story, you would be Ivan, the second brother?"

"Yes." He suddenly smiled.

"What?"

"I'm just wondering how strongly our antagonist will play by the rules?"

Looking back at the pages, I flipped another and read some more. "Meaning?"

"Ivan isn't killed in the book."

"Relieved, are you?"

"Not really, it means that I have to deliver the *If there is no God, all things are lawful* monologue in court or explain my *Grand Inquisitor* dream, and I'm not sure I can do either."

"Maybe the killer will let you write them down." I handed him the pages.

Giving them a cursory glance, he shook his head. "What are these?"

I reached out and tapped the sheets of paper. "Letters from your brother David to Katherine Verkhov, explaining in detail how he's going to kill your father."

# 12

"So this means I killed him?" David clutched the letters in his hand and stared at me, a one-iron tucked under his arm.

"I didn't say that."

I sat at the foot of the grand staircase, looking up at the young man as he paced back and forth on the Turkish rugs of the main hall. He put the letters down and began practicing his chip shot with an orange golf ball. "Then what are you saying?"

"Those are some pretty strong words."

He paused his shot, grabbed the sheets of paper, and crumpled them in his closed hand. "But that's all they are, words."

"Especially the part about hitting him in the head with a rock."

David made a face. "The very first murder was Cain hitting Abel in the head with a stone, Sheriff. It's a metaphor."

"A two-page metaphor?"

"What do you want from me? I was angry, okay?" He recommenced pacing. "If I was going to kill the old man, do you think I'm stupid enough to write it all down and even worse send it off to my ex-fiancée?"

"You tell me."

"I was simply expressing some of the vitriol that had built up with him." He held the crumpled paper out to me. "This is how murders don't happen."

Taking the letters, I smoothed them out on my knee and studied them. "Why do you suppose Katherine told me about these?"

"Hell hath no fury . . ."

"Like a woman scorned?" I studied him as he swung the golf club. "I thought she was the one who ended the relationship?"

"She was, but evidently I didn't try hard enough to get her back."

"And where does your brother Ian fit into all this?"

A moment passed before he responded, easing into a putting stance. "Why don't you ask him."

"I did."

"And what did he say?"

"He said that he'd discussed the situation with you, and you said that as far as you were concerned he had an open field with Katherine."

"That's right."

"He also said the relationship was doomed in that he didn't think that she was over you."

He spread his hands. "And I'm supposed to be responsible for that?"

"Well, she was here the night before Pepper was killed."

"And I'm the one who told her to go home." He glanced around. "Hey, is there any reason why Ian isn't here to answer some of these questions?"

"He already did, and I prefer to speak with the two of you alone."

He came forward, sticking the club in my face and raising his voice. "See if you can trip us up, huh?"

I dropped my head in resignation and then stood to my full height, my gun belt creaking like a tomb door. "I think you need to calm down, David."

He glared at me, defiant. "I don't like being accused of things I didn't do."

"Well, we're going to do everything we can to make sure we catch the person who killed not only your father but your half-brother. You understand that to do that we might have to ask some uncomfortable questions of a lot of people, including you."

He thumped the head of the club into my chest. "Well, I think I'm through answering your questions until I can get a lawyer."

I stuffed my hands in my jeans. "You have that right, and I have the power to arrest you and inform you that your constitutional rights allow you to remain silent, the right to an attorney, and that if you can't afford one that one will be appointed to you."

His expression immediately changed. "Did you just arrest me?"

"Excuse me." David turned to find both the Cheyenne Nation and Dog standing in the open doorway. "Is there something going on in here?"

"I'm not sure." I tapped his shoulder and he looked at me as I took the golf club from him, laying it across my shoulder. "Is there something going on here, David?"

He swallowed a little more than some spit and scanned the carpet, his Adams apple bobbing. "It's . . . it's been a long day."

"And you've been under a lot of stress."

"I'm thinking that maybe I should go to bed."

"Maybe so." I patted his shoulder, just to let him know there were no hard feelings, and handed him back the one-iron. "You know what they say if you are out on the green in a storm and worried about getting struck by lightning?"

"No."

"Hold up your one-iron, because even God can't hit a one-iron."

The three of us watched him climb the stairs to the bedrooms before the Bear turned back to me. "You do not know anything about golf."

"No, but I know a good quote from Lee Trevino when I hear one."

Taking a step after David, he stopped. "So?"

"I don't think he did it."

He glanced toward the study, where the late-night light still burned. "Ian?"

"I don't think he did it either."

"Alan?"

"Of all of them, I'm certain he didn't do it, but did you know he wrote his dissertation on *The Brothers Karamazov*?"

"Hmm . . ." He grunted. "Who else was here?"

"I think Paetra Agirra, who is my next person of interest."

He stepped back down, facing me. "And Michael Rakin?"

"I talked with him out back when I spoke with Alan, but there's just nothing there to indicate why it is he would kill either of the victims, let alone both."

"So we are back to the neighbors?"

"For lack of anybody else."

There was a knock on the door, and we all turned to find a highway patrolman standing in the open doorway. "Trooper Wilson, it's a little late for you, isn't it?"

Tipping his hat back, he approached. "I'm afraid I'm here on official business with the Forest Service . . ."

"Stage one of the evacuation: *Get ready*?"

"You got it but *get set* isn't far behind."

"What's the status?"

"Two of the fires co-joined, Sisters Hill and Pole Creek."

"That is not good."

The trooper frowned at Henry. "No, it's this damned wind. It's pushing the fire right into this canyon, and if that happens, then it's going to be like a flamethrower by the time it gets here."

"And when's that?"

"If the third fire joins them, it could be as early as tomorrow."

"So, the next notice we get will be *go*?

"Yes, then you're on your own; neither us nor the Forest Service guys will be back after that."

"But we get one more notice?"

"Hopefully, if I can make it."

"Just call the lodge?"

"I'm amazed you guys still have phone service now."

I walked past him and to the phone bench at our right, picking up the receiver and hearing nothing. "We don't."

Wilson glanced at Henry, my reputation with technology preceding me. "You got a cell phone?"

He pulled the thing from his jacket pocket. "I do . . ." He stared at it. "Uh-oh."

"What?"

"I have eight messages from your undersheriff." He handed it to me as if it were a bomb. "I switched off the notifications, since it was getting late."

I stared at the device. "I'm not listening to those."

"Sleeping Beauty must have awakened."

I handed him back the phone. "With a vengeance."

Wilson's voice took on a bit of panic. "You need to answer those or the next thing that'll happen is she'll run the roadblock and drive through the grass fire to get here."

The Bear handed me back the phone. "Take your medicine."

I took the phone and walked out onto the porch, figuring it was better to be yelled at alone than with an audience. Moving toward the turret porch corner to the left, I could see that the orange glow from the fire on the mountain had assuredly grown.

Hitting the button, I waited.

"Where the fuck is he?"

I cleared my throat. "Speaking."

"What. The. Fuck."

"Sorry, we were involved, and I hadn't heard that you'd woken up."

"Thanks for the concern."

"Whoa now, I was there for a good, long time before they told me to get out."

"Where's my Whitman's Sampler?"

"I'm working on that."

"Yeah, well, I'm working too. Did you know the whole mountainside is on fire?"

"So I've been told by Trooper Wilson, and I'm looking at it as we speak."

"We've been evacuating everybody off Route 16 from Muddy Guard north all the way to Durant."

"Call Sheridan County."

"We did, along with J. R. Rose, Campbell County SD, and policc dcpartments from both. They flew in firefighters from all over the country, along with dumper planes from Canada that have been picking up water from Lake De Smet that we saw."

"Well, Wilson's here and just gave us the *get ready.*"

"Fuck that, you're at *get the fuck out of there before you're a walking talking weenie roast.*"

I had to smile. "I wasn't aware that was an official evacuation stage."

"You will when your weenie is roasting."

"I'll try not to let that happen."

There was a pause. "Walt, I'm not kidding, you need to get out of there."

"Problem being, I'm not the only one."

"Then get all of them out of there."

"Easier said than done."

"So is getting your weenie roasted."

"All right, I'll get on it."

"Call me back when you're on the move."

"I will."

"And watch your weenie."

I hit the button and carried the thing back inside to where Wilson and Henry were still talking, Dog lying on the carpet with his head resting on the first step of the grand stairway. "Vic says we need to get out of here."

Henry cocked his head, peering at me through the hair curtain. "I am betting it was stronger language than that."

"There was a lot of weenie talk." They both glanced at each other and then back at me. "She says we should get everybody out of here, now."

"She might know a little more than I do." The trooper shrugged. "It's totally possible that I'll get back to the south roadblock and they'll send me right back here to lead you guys out."

"Well, I guess the neighboring investigation is going to be put on hold." I looked up the steps. "You want upstairs or downstairs?"

He started onward and upward. "I will take the high road."

"Meet back here?"

He called over his shoulder. "Agreed."

Starting with the dining room and kitchen just to make sure no one was left behind, I pushed open the swinging door and found Lynn. "I've got some bad news."

She placed some plates in the cabinet and turned to me. "We're being evacuated?"

"How did you know?"

"I've been listening to the scanner in the mudroom."

"Where's Gary?"

"Gathering as much stuff as he can and throwing it in the back of the ranch trucks." She glanced around at the grand hundred-year-old kitchen. "My God, Walt, where do you start?"

"I have no idea . . ." I stepped toward her. "Look, my priority is going to be the people, and possibly the livestock, and since Manx is gone, who can I get to help with that?"

"Probably Gary."

"That's going to take him off the personal-property assignment."

She shrugged. "So be it."

"He's out the side?"

"Yes."

"We have less than an hour, got me?"

"I do."

I started to go on and through the back but then stopped. "Papers, passports and birth certificates, prescriptions for both humans and animals, a change of clothes, credit cards and cash, photos and other personal irreplaceable items . . ."

"Cell phones and chargers along with hard drives from the computers?"

I smiled. "Um, yep, those too."

Ducking through the mudroom, I looked back up Crazy Woman Canyon where the fire, even from this distance, was even more dread inspiring as it spread its flaming waves across the range.

Turning the corner, I could see Gary throwing things into the back of an assortment of trucks. "Need help?"

His eyes were wet with tears. "My God, Walt, I can't believe this place is going to burn to the ground."

"Maybe not, but we better respond like it is." Helping him lift a large painting into the bed, I glanced down the main road and at the cutoff to the barn. "You want me to just run the animals out?"

He wiped his eyes. "Yeah, yeah. Manx already moved them to the paddocks in Powder Junction, so I think there's only the eight you made him bring back when he started for Arizona, and Borax, of course."

"Just cut 'em loose and run 'em on down the road?"

"All I can think of. They'll go in the opposite direction of the fire, I'm guessing."

I'd just started to go when he called after me. "Walt?"

I stopped and turned. "Yep?"

"I haven't been completely honest with you."

"Concerning?"

He began to speak, but the words caught in his throat. "There might actually be a reason I might've wanted . . . I might've, um, wanted Pepper dead."

I paused a moment and then walked back toward him. "And what would that be?"

"He raped Lynn."

"I stood there for a few seconds, just to make sure I'd understood him correctly. "Pepper raped your wife?"

"Yes." His eyes were cast down at the ground and then slowly returned to mine as if wanting to say more but unable to make the effort.

"Oh God, no . . . Peter."

"Yes."

I placed a hand on his shoulder. "I was just talking to Cady, and she mentioned Peter's green eyes."

He nodded his head uncontrollably. "I've got Peyronie's disease and have always been impotent, so when Lynn got pregnant, I thought it was a miracle. I guess she felt like she had to tell me. It's funny, but I was never angry, and after Peter was born . . . He was just such a blessing in our lives."

"It's okay, Gary, it's okay. I don't think you killed Pepper. You're not that kind of man, and if you were you would've done it a long time ago." I squeezed the older man's shoulder and started to go.

"Like you?"

"Yep, like me." Smiling back at him, I started trotting in the direction of the barn, hoping I could find all of the animals, but when the dusk to dawn light sprang to life as I ran across the parking lot, I could see eight horses standing by the gates in the center corral.

Unhooking the chain, I flung the things open and then rushed into the corral, pushing the animals to the left and toward the open gateway.

I needn't have worried because they busted through in a group as if this were the opportunity of a lifetime. They shot out of the gates, ran down the hill, and into the darkness with thundering hooves and volumes of dust.

I scanned the immediate vicinity but could see the big mule nowhere.

"Great." Raising my hands to the sides of my mouth, I bellowed, "Borax!"

Shaking my head, I made for the barn breezeway. "Well, at least it's not the entire twenty-mule team."

Swinging the next gate aside and propping it open in case I didn't find the mule later and he could still find his own way out, I peered down the area, noticing that the door to Manx's living quarters was open but partially blocked with crime scene tape.

Moving in that direction, I drew my sidearm and pulled up to one side of the door, pointing the Colt inside and sweeping the room with it as I switched to the other side of the doorway, revealing nothing.

I reached in to flip the light on, but the room appeared as it had when DCI had been scouring it. There were a few items missing, but they were just the things that the forensics team might've needed to test in their labs to reaffirm their suspicions.

I re-holstered my 1911 and moved toward the indoor arena where Henry had raced Dog. Trotting that way, I pushed open the barn doors and entered, pausing only to turn toward one of the loading chutes in the darkness, sure that I'd seen some movement there.

"Borax?"

There was no response, even after I pulled the Maglite from my belt and shined it in that direction. Sighing, I continued toward the arena and slid the large door aside, wondering if I wasn't wasting my time in that livestock generally don't close doors and gates behind them no matter how clever they are.

Hitting the switch, I watched the numerous lights in the open area flicker to life, revealing sawdust and not much else.

Even going so far as to look into the cluster of rooms and stalls at the far end, I cast my eyes in all directions before finally giving up. "Well, I did everything I can, and if all the gates are open, then he can find his own way out of here."

I'd just cut through the paddock between the barn and the arena when I heard a noise again, in the direction of one of the loading chutes. Shining the flashlight that way, I saw something large and dark on the other side where there was a smaller corral between the holding areas.

Walking through the chutes, I entered the area to find the massive mule pawing at the ground with a great hoof as large as a coffee can. "Borax, what are you doing?"

The big elongated head swung around toward me, and he just stood there, his enormous dark eyes blinking.

I walked over to pat his withers and made reassuring noises. "C'mon, you. There's a fire coming, and you don't want anything to do with it, read me? C'mon."

Starting off, I paused after a moment to turn back and see that he hadn't moved.

"Oh, this is not good." Holstering my flashlight, I clapped my hands. "C'mon you reject from a glue factory. I don't have time for this."

He blinked again.

"Oh, come on."

He stared at me for a moment more and then gazed at the ground where he'd been pawing, finally raising the same hoof to dig at the ground with a few more swipes.

Swinging an arm around, I gestured toward the area where I'd comc in. "Thc gatcs arc all opcn, so you don't havc to dig your way out of here."

Blink.

"All right, you leave me little choice." Walking around behind him, I unholstered my .45 and punched off the safety. "Last chance."

An ear turned my way, but little else.

Stepping back to avoid the impending rodeo, I lifted the big semiautomatic and pulled the trigger. In the quiet of the night, the thing sounded like a bomb going off, and that's what I fully expected, even placing a hand on the top rail just in case I had to climb the fence to safety to keep from being run down.

I needn't have bothered, in that Borax didn't move a singular muscle.

In the most dismissive way, he nonchalantly swiveled his head and gazed at me again.

Blink.

Glancing at the sidearm in my hand, I holstered it, figuring another shot probably wasn't going to have a different result. "Damn, I guess you are bulletproof."

Walking back around him, I stood there. "Am I going to have to go get a halter? And if I do, are you going to come along or just stand here until we both burn to death?"

Blink.

"I don't suppose slapping you in the ass is going to have any effect?"

He blinked again but then dropped his head and began pawing at the same spot.

Pulling the flashlight back out, I directed it at the hole he was digging in the loose earth by a pole. "Did somebody drop an apple, or what?"

Lowering myself, I reached past his hoof and dug at the ground, finally seeing a small wrist-sized loop of rawhide.

Digging deeper, I got a finger under the loop and pulled. Fully expecting the thing to break off in my hand, I was surprised to pull out a little-worse-for-wear vintage Southern Cheyenne war club with a large, round stone at the head.

"You are sure this is it?"

"I'm sure this is the one we found in the mudroom out back

and it certainly fits the bill for DCI's description of a murder weapon."

The Cheyenne Nation held the thing lightly in his hands, gently pounding the stone head into the palm of his hand as if breaking in a ball glove. "Hmm . . ."

"What?"

"Do you think we should be handling this?"

"In the greater forensic science sense, no, but I figure we can't do much more damage than burying it in a corral filled with horseshit and having a twelve-hundred-pound mule dig it up."

"You should deputize Borax."

"I'm thinking about it."

The Bear lifted the war club to peer at the beaded rawhide strap that held the stone. "I am not a forensic detective but there appears to be dark stains under the edge of the leather."

"Blood?"

"Most likely."

"So, they tried to clean it but then gave up?"

"Most likely." He handed it back to me as the electrical lights in the lodge flickered overhead. "I think your chances of getting prints from the porous leather material of the handle are relatively limited."

"But at least we have a murder weapon."

We stood there once more at the base of the great stairs, waiting for the occupants to come down, the lights flickering again. We both looked around, a little more than uneasy. "The grass fire?"

"Possibly, and if it blocks us, there really isn't any other way out of here." My eyes went back up the stairs. "Is there anyone else?"

"The brothers are on their way down, and I spoke with Schiffer, the abbot deputy, but he wanted to leave the Elder to sleep as long as he could before disturbing him." Moving over to the front door,

I watched as Gary brought out the final load of personal items, piling them into the bed of the last truck. "Gary and Lynn can drive two of the trucks and you can drive the third with the brothers in the Suburban down to Powder Junction."

"Yes."

"The abbot deputy has the monastery's van and the novice Michael was able to get his Pinto from the substation in Powder Junction after the Elder paid the bill to Boris. Where's Dog?"

"In your truck."

"No, take him with you."

"Why?"

"Because I'm going to be the last one going through this place, and on the outside chance that something happens, I want him out of here."

He smiled. "And that includes me?"

"I can't be everywhere and if something happens on the way out—you're it."

He patted my shoulder. "Have I ever let you down?"

"Only that one time in Tijuana, college senior year, or that time we golfed."

"You are never going to forgive me for either of those, are you?"

"No." Hearing some noises, we looked up the stairs to see David, Ian, Alan, and Michael coming down and carrying suitcases. "Is that everybody?"

David was the first to speak. "Yeah, it's just us."

"No one else?"

Ian was next. "No."

I glanced at Alan and Michael. "You're sure?"

They both nodded as I indicated Michael, the unrelated novice. "You're in the Pinto. You're sure it runs?"

"Yes."

"The rest of you are in the Suburban." I glanced at the brothers. "There's Gary, Lynn, the abbot deputy, and the Elder and that's it, right?"

They all agreed.

"In the rush, I don't want to forget anybody." They had nothing more to say, so I turned to Henry. "Get them all out of here and in the vehicles. You don't have to wait for me, I'll be right behind you."

"As you wish."

"And don't forget my dog."

"Never."

I watched as he led the others through the doorway and started to walk past me and onto the porch, but then stopped. "Did the mule, Borax, finally go?"

"No."

I could see he was disappointed. "After we dug up the war club he followed me through the chute and into the barn, but stopped at the door of Manx's apartment and then wouldn't budge."

"They are not like horses; you have to explain things to them so that they understand."

"Well, I'll stop and have a conversation with him when I drive out of here, okay?"

He paused for a moment and then looked at me.

"What?"

"I was talking with Alan."

"Yep?"

"We were discussing his doctoral thesis on *The Brothers Karamazov* and he brought up the reading habits of the abbot deputies, including Asa of Judah, Johann Tetzel, Rasputin, Roger Norreys, the Monks of Combermere Abbey, the Sōhei Monks of Japan, and Simon of Saint Osyth."

Flipping through my knowledge of religious history, I couldn't help but laugh. "That's a rogue's gallery of holy men, but it doesn't necessarily mean he's a murderer."

"I simply thought it was something you should know."

I raised an eyebrow. "This case is doing nothing if not becoming more interesting."

Lifting an eyebrow, he continued out the door to go help the group into their vehicles as the highway patrolman, Wilson, slid past him and came in. The lights flickered again, and I raised a hand toward the strobe effect. "What's the story on all this?"

"The grass fire got five of the power poles and they're getting ready to fall over, and when they do . . ."

"No electricity to the mouth of the canyon?"

"None at all."

"Well, we're gathering everybody as fast as we can, including a hundred-year-old monk, but as you might well imagine, it's taking some time."

He nodded, but I could see he wasn't happy with the situation. "Well, your status has just been officially elevated to *go*."

"So, this is it and nobody's coming back?"

"I'm afraid so, I've got other residences I have to check, but I'm the last one from the outside world you're going to see."

"You don't have to make it sound so dramatic."

"Yeah, I do."

I glanced around at the grand old lodge where luminaries like Buffalo Bill and Teddy Roosevelt had stayed. "Get out of here and don't worry, we're right behind you."

He gave out with a curt response and then I watched as our last link to the outside world slipped through the front door and was gone.

I went through the dining room and into the kitchen where Lynn stood in the middle of the room, crying. "We've got to go."

Taking off an apron and using it to wipe her face, she threw it into the sink and then picked up a cardboard box from the table. "Okay, I guess we've got as much as we're able to carry."

"Where's Gary?"

"By the trucks, waiting for me."

"Henry will drive one too, and they're out there ready to go."

"What about you?"

"I'll help the abbot deputy get the Elder into their van and then drive my truck out last." I gestured toward the front. "Where are the maids' quarters, where you put Elder Zebrowski?"

"Directly behind the main stairwell, there's a small door that opens into the servant-quarters hallway. I put them in the largest room, the last door at the end."

"Got it." Moving toward the dining room, I called back. "You and Gary get the heck out of here now, you got me?"

She nodded and I pushed through the door and trotted across the dining room and into the main hall where I made my way around the stairs before stopping. Staring toward the landing, I was sure I'd seen something move. I fought with myself, thinking it was just something out of the corner of my eye. I gave up and climbed the stairs, calling out. "Anybody here?"

There was no response, but at the far end of the hallway to the right, I could've sworn that I heard a door clicking shut. Moving in that direction, I rested my hand on my sidearm and called out again. "This is Sheriff Walt Longmire, is there anybody here?"

There was no response, and I didn't have much choice other than to begin turning knobs and pushing doors open. "The HPs just came through and gave us the *go* to evacuate, so if there is anybody up here, you're about to get left behind and possibly burn to death."

The first door I threw open must've been Alan's room—austere with a neatly made bed and nothing on the walls except a simple cross. I opened the closet door and found it completely empty.

I went back into the hallway and crossed to the next door across the hall. I snatched it open, and seeing a poster of George Orwell and bookshelves crammed to the gill, I figured this was Ian's room. In the closet, all I found was musty clothes and old shoes jumbled on the floor.

Coming out, I went to the next to last door on the same side and tried the knob, which was locked. I thought about kicking the thing open but decided to first check the last door across the hall.

The door opened easily, and it looked like the kind of bachelor pad that had to be David's, with what appeared to be an actual waterbed and racks of clothing hanging inside the closet, whose door had been removed. I glanced around the room, but there was no one there. "Anybody?"

Giving up, I returned to the hallway and walked back to the locked door and knocked. "Okay, I've cased every other room up here and haven't found anybody, which leads me to believe that you're in here, whoever you are." I waited a moment and then knocked again. "Look, I'm getting ready to kick this door in, and if it's a linen closet there isn't much room in there, so I'm liable to put my boot right through your chest, whoever you are."

Hearing nothing, I took a step back and prepared to splinter the thing when I suddenly saw the knob turn and the door slowly push out to reveal the linen closet and none other than Paetra Agirra. "Hi."

"What in the hell . . . ?"

"I spent the night with David. I left, but then I came back."

"Does he know you're here now?"

"No, I left my truck down by the bridge."

I shook my head. "Come out of there."

She did as I said as I held her arm and ushered her toward the stairs. "Do you know if there's anybody else here?"

"No. I mean there isn't anybody, but . . ."

I stopped her at the landing. "But what?"

"When I was hiding in the closet being quiet, I swear I could hear somebody sobbing."

"Sobbing?"

"Yes."

I thought about it. "Well, Lynn was crying in the kitchen."

"No, this was a man."

Pulling out my pocket watch, I took a peek to see how long it had been since I'd sent Trooper Wilson and Henry on their way. "Any idea which direction the sobbing might've been coming from?"

She glanced around. "Maybe downstairs?"

Walking her down the steps, I took her to the front door and pushed her on her way. "Check in with Henry out there in the parking lot if he's still there and hitch a ride down to your truck, and get out of here before the whole place goes up in flames, would you?"

Not waiting for a response, I started around the staircase and spotted the nearly hidden doorway that Lynn had indicated. Pulling open the hinged handle, I opened the door and swung it wide. There was a series of doors that probably led to at least a half dozen servants' quarters and a door at the end, which must've been the one Lynn had meant.

In the quiet, as I stood there, I thought I could hear something and quickly came to the conclusion that it must have been the sobbing that Paetra Agirra had said she'd heard.

Rushing forward, I got to the door and snatched it open to find the abbot deputy, Brian Schiffer, beside the bed of the Elder, his face in his hands.

The ancient holy man lying on the bed didn't move.

The tall man's face rose as he looked at me, the tears cascading down as his mouth twisted. "Elder Zebrowski is dead."

# 13

Of all the things I was thinking, the one that immediately came to mind as I checked the body was that Elder Zebrowski couldn't have picked a more inconvenient time to die.

Schiffer stood to the side, crumpling against the wall, covering his face with his hands. "You're sure?"

Moving Elder's head to the side, I could see deviation of the nose, eversion of the upper lip, and potential intraoral bruising.

Figuring we had no time for forensic sensibilities, I straightened the body, examining the old man's wrists, and then stood, sighing deeply. "To be honest, Abbot Deputy Schiffer, I can't be sure of the cause without an autopsy."

Schiffer nodded his head solemnly, his hands now folded at his groin in a fig-leaf posture. "A life such as his . . ." He choked a bit. "I would've hoped for something more epic."

"As someone well acquainted with these things, you'll have to take my word that an epic death is not to be desired. He deserved better but I'd imagine his passing was swift." Crossing the Elder's arms, I positioned him on the sheet. "Were you here all night?"

"No, I always sleep in the van."

The lights flickered again, going out for a moment before

stuttering on again. "Well, if we don't get him out of here pretty quick, we're going to be working in the dark and things could get epic whether we want them to or not." Scooping up the sheet at the foot of the bed, I made a homemade sling and gestured for Schiffer to fold and gather the other end. "We can carry him out with the sheet and get him in your van and then you can take the long way out to the highway and run him to the hospital in Durant, where they can do a more thorough analysis."

I thanked the stars that Elder Zebrowski was a small man and hardly weighed a hundred forty pounds as we carried him down the hallway, where I was able to sustain his weight with only one hand and turn the knob, opening the door to the main room. Then I again took the sheet in two hands and backed around the stairwell.

After opening the front door, I rested my end of the body on the wood planking of the porch and glanced at Schiffer as he lowered to do the same. "Do you have anything you need from your room?"

"Just a small valet case and a book the Elder was reading, both on the chair beside the bed."

"I'll get those, and you go get your van and back it in here so that we don't have to carry him so far."

He gazed down at the body. "And just leave him here?"

I thought about saying something along the lines that he wasn't going anywhere but then thought better of it. "I'm sure he'll be fine for a moment."

Watching him reluctantly move to get the van, I reentered the lodge and hurried back into the servant quarters just as the lights blinked one last time and then went completely out. "Great . . ."

I stepped into the room and fumbled around in the dark until I found the few items from the chair. Next I felt my way along the walls to the door and made my way down the hallway toward the half-light of the open doorway at the other end.

I stepped outside and went around the stairwell, listening and hunting for anybody else who might've been left. "Hello! This is Sheriff Longmire and I'm the last person who should be here! We're evacuating and this is your last chance to get out!"

Predictably, there was no response.

"Nobody here but us chickens, huh?" I saw Schiffer backing the van toward the edge of the parking lot, the haze of the fire causing me to blink through my watering eyes.

As I waited, I looked down at the covered body of Elder Zebrowski and then to the items in my hand, rubbing my eyes and then tipping the valet case to one side to reveal the cover of the thick, battered, and worn paperback underneath.

The abbot deputy stopped the van and then got out, opening the sliding doors on the side before approaching me. "The easiest way to load him will be in the passenger section through the side."

I held the book up. "Who was reading this?"

He studied the cover. "Why, the Elder."

Flipping through the pages, I stopped at the spot where a bookmark was lodged about halfway through. "Any idea why?"

"It was one of his favorites, he re-read it every couple of years, as I recall." He gestured toward the book. "That's the third edition I've seen him wear out alone."

Flipping the pages back, I studied the inside cover of *The Brothers Karamazov* and the initials written in the upper corner: MR. "Did he now?"

Still holding the book, I watched as Schiffer drove down the main road at a slow pace.

The abbot deputy had wanted to take the paperback for sentimental reasons, I supposed, but I'd kept it as evidence, staring at the nine hundred eighty-five-page tome and wondering at how the book seemed to be popping up an awful lot lately.

Stuffing it inside my jacket, I walked down to my truck, opened the door, and found my newfangled two-way handheld radio lying on the seat, likely from Vic by way of Henry. I had been known to forget that I had the thing, let alone how use it.

Setting it on the center console along with the paperback, I climbed in and started the big three-quarter-ton, flipped on the lights, and shifted her into gear before glancing back at the shadowy great lodge one last time.

There was a glow on the horizon above the treetops behind the structure, and unless the sun had suddenly decided to rise in the west, I knew what that glow was.

I drove down the road and had just passed the cutoff to the barn when I locked the brakes and sat there as the cloud of dust caught and enveloped me.

Borax stood in the circular glow of the overhead light, as if he were going to deliver a soliloquy.

Throwing the truck into reverse, I backed up and then drove down the short distance across the bridge and came to a stop a little distance away so as to not spook him, but I needn't have bothered. The mule simply stood there as if waiting for a bus.

Getting out, I walked toward him, raising my hands to show him I didn't mean any harm. "Borax, you've got to get out of here, buddy." I gestured upward and into the funnel-like canyon that, from our angle, looked like a perfect potential conflagration. "That fire is coming, and it means business."

Blink.

"I can't believe I'm having this conversation with a mule." Muttering to myself, I took another step toward him. "I'm not kidding, once I'm gone that's it, you're on your own."

His head turned back toward the row of stalls and Manx's living quarters.

I sighed, taking a step closer to him as the big head swung around and regarded me. "Listen, your buddy isn't coming back. I don't know how much of this you understand but Manx is dead, and the last thing he'd want is for you to stand here and be burned to death."

Blink.

"Borax, I'm not monkeying around, and I've only got so much time for this stubborn shit."

Blink.

"All right, I did everything I could do." Back at my truck, I stopped to look at the great-eared creature over the hood. "You know, I could tie you to the back of this truck."

Blink.

"I'm not kidding."

Blink.

I climbed in the truck and sat there staring at him, thinking that if I had an animal spirit, I was probably looking at it.

Getting out once again, I walked past him without a glance and entered the breezeway, finally locating a halter and an extended lead for corral work, taking them both and walking back toward the immovable object.

Holding the halter out to him, I fully expected him to move away, but he just stood there, quietly resolute. Slipping the thing over his nose, I buckled it at the side of his head and then clipped the lead to the metal ring underneath. "Be ye not as the horse, or as the mule, which have no understanding—psalm 32:9." I stroked his nose. "I have it from an expert on such subjects that you need to have things explained to you before you'll cooperate."

I turned his head and directed it toward the growing glow of the mountainside. "With the dry summer we had and the amount of standing beetle-kill, we're dealing with a fire the magnitude of which we've never seen in this part of the country. And if it starts down that canyon, it's going to be coming like a blazing freight train. Now, I have no intention of being here when it arrives, and my advice to you is the same—let's get the hell out of here, and I mean now."

I dropped the lead a loop or two and walked toward my truck like I meant business, but to very little avail.

I might as well have tied off the barn itself.

Yanking my arm back and almost losing my footing, I stood there for a moment before bringing my face up to look at him. Borax hadn't balked or even made an effort to move back but had just stood there, like a statue, extolling the virtues of obstinacy.

Blink.

Shaking my head, I dropped the lead and once again climbed in my truck, and then swung it in a circle before backing toward the mule before stopping about fifteen feet away.

Leaving it idling, I got out and picked up the lead, carrying it toward the bed, where I dropped the tailgate and then threaded the nylon rope through a clasp mounted inside of it. I turned to study him as I threw a thumb back toward the three-quarter ton. "That's about four hundred horsepower and four hundred twenty-five foot-pounds of torque, which means that if you don't want to come along, it will make you come along."

Blink.

Glancing back at the glow on the mountain, I marched over to the truck, got in, and pulled the V-8 into gear. Easing onto the accelerator, I moved forward, figuring that he might balk at first but then would likely give in and trail after the truck.

Slowly edging forward, I watched as the rope took up slack, but then saw the big guy pull back. He wasn't panicking as a horse would but just set his big hooves and refused to move. Giving it a little more gas, I watched as he was nudged a little but still held his ground, and I was amazed at the strength of the beast.

The mule finally heaved his head back, and there was a loud crack as the rope fell to the ground and I lurched to a stop. Getting out yet again, I expected to see the braided nylon rope broken but instead was confronted with the clasp having been pulled from the sheet metal of the bed, the bent screws still hanging from it.

Gathering my end of the rope, I started coiling it and walked toward him.

Blink.

Unbuckling the harness, I tossed it toward the corral fence where, the same as me, he swiveled his head in that direction.

It was then, in the first glimmers of the dawning sun, that I noticed a car parked on the road headed into the canyon and up the mountain, just past the corral fence.

I didn't remember there being a car parked there earlier in the evening and moved in to get a better view of the gold '74 Pinto sitting in the middle of the road, the Saint Benedict Monastery bumper sticker in the rear window on full display.

Quickly, I trotted over to where the thing sat with the key still in its ignition and the driver's-side door hanging open, a weak and herniated buzzing noise coming from inside.

Looking up and down the road, I could see no sign of the novice, Rakin, but saw the wool prayer shawl he'd wrapped himself in, lying on the road about ten yards from the front of the car. Raising my hands to the sides of my mouth, I hollered. "Rakin? Michael Rakin, are you here?!"

There was no response as I started back for my truck, yelling toward the barn. "Michael Rakin?!"

Arriving at my truck, I reached in and grabbed the two-way radio and, with a fumbling effort, switched it on, adjusting the squelch and keying the mic. "Hello, anybody out there?" There was no response, and I pressed the toggle again. "Anybody out there?"

Trooper Wilson's voice rang back. Static. "Copy. Is that you, Walt? Over."

"It sure is. Hey are you guys missing anybody?"

Static. "Not that I know of. Where are you? Over."

"Still at the ranch, near the lodge."

Static. "Walt, you need to get the hell out of there and I mean right now. Over."

"I'm trying, but I was waylaid by a mule and just found a gold '74 Pinto sitting in the main road leading up Crazy Woman Canyon."

Static. "I'm sorry, you're breaking up. You found a mule and a pony? Over."

"No, Michael Rakin's Ford Pinto is sitting here. Is he with you guys?"

Static. "I'm not sure, let me check with Henry. Over."

"Did Schiffer with the abbey van get down there, maybe he's with them?"

Static. "No, the van is here and he's not with them. Over."

Standing there, I glanced over at Borax. "I don't suppose you've seen him?"

Blink.

"Gotcha." I grabbed my bug-out backpack from behind the seat, closed the door to my truck, and looked around again, seeing no one. "Hello?!"

Static. "Walt, are you there? Over."

Holding the walkie-talkie to my mouth, I replied. "I'm here, talk to me."

Static. "Henry says Rakin was with them in that car but then left to go back to the abbey in Meeteetse. Over."

I keyed the mic. "In the Pinto?"

Static. "That's what he said. Over."

"Do you think he was stupid enough to follow his phone and try to go over the mountain through the canyon?"

Static. "I've been a Wyoming highway patrolman for three years; don't ask me about how stupid the average motorist can be. Over."

"Well, there can't be that many 1974 gold Pintos roaming around here, so it has to be him."

Static. "What are you going to do? Over."

"I guess try to find him."

Static. "Walt, you don't have that kind of time. Over."

"If the car broke down again, don't you think he would've gone to the lodge to see if anyone was still there?"

Static. "I told you not to ask me about how stupid the average motorist can be. Over."

"I'm going to head back in that direction to see if I can find him."

Static. "Don't take too long. Like I said, you don't have that much time. The wind is picking up topside and the Forest Service people and hotshot crews have already pulled back; it's a spectator sport at this point. Over."

"Roger that. I'll just take one more quick swing around and then head out."

Static. "How's the battle of wills between you and Borax going? Over."

I looked at the mule, still standing in the same spot. "Don't ask."

Static. "Keep us in the know. Over."

"You got it. Over and out." Hooking the walkie-talkie to my belt, I plucked the paperback from the center console and stuffed it in my pack and then started off toward the abandoned vehicle with one last glance at Borax. "Will you please get out of here?"

To my amazement, he took a step toward me.

Stopping, I held out both hands. "No! No, go the other way. Whatever you do, don't come with me." Satisfied, I turned and went around the corral to the main road and stepped to the Pinto, slamming the door to stop the annoying buzz.

I spotted the shawl ahead and walked up there, examining the footprints in the dry dust of the road where the blanket had been discarded. Picking the thing from the ground, I allowed my eyes to trace the prints as they roamed up the road. "Oh, hell . . ."

I thought about getting in my truck and pushing the Pinto into the ditch. I could certainly cover more ground in a vehicle, but surely he hadn't gotten that far in the early dark?

Looking toward the canyon, the sky was like a gray and flat ceiling, and I wasn't sure if it was low-lying clouds or just smoke. It certainly smelled like smoke.

I gave one last look at Borax to make sure he wasn't following, and was rewarded with him first gazing at me, then back at the barn, then at my truck, and then back at me again. Relatively assured he wasn't going to accompany me, I started up the road, throwing the prayer shawl over one shoulder.

Why would Rakin come back this way? The only reason I could come up with would be that he was heeding the electronic advice of his phone, something that led a lot of motorists astray in the state. It had gotten so bad that a lot of ranchers, tired of impromptu tourists, had taken to constructing billboards: THIS ROAD DOES NOT GO THROUGH. WE DON'T GIVE A DAMN WHAT GOOGLE SAYS!

But why drop the shawl?

Continuing to track the prints, I walked along the gravel road, watching the waving treetops for the first signs of fire, aware that if I didn't, it might be too late. Generally, people don't know how quickly a big fire can move, enveloping a vast area in a short amount of time. There are yearly stories of hotshot crews that would get in too far and have to hunker down and try to wait a fire out. Some made it, and some didn't.

The acrid smell of the fire was growing stronger, enough so that I brought the tail end of the shawl up and covered my face to breathe through it.

I tried to think of a worse geography than Crazy Woman Canyon for a forest fire but couldn't. It wasn't the first time tragedy had struck the area. The name alone had been credited to two different but still saddening stories. One where a Crow woman had been abandoned in the canyon after a tribal attack on her camp, leaving her insane and bereft, leaping from rock to rock in the moonlight; in another, the survivor of an Indian attack who tended the graves of her dead family, left alone by the Natives because she had lost her mind and was protected by the Crow Killer Jeremiah "Liver-Eating" Johnson.

Only thirteen miles long, the narrow and rugged road had a pretty steep grade farther up, but here it was gentle, with tall lodgepole pines swaying with the wind that was channeled by the solid stone cliffs that bordered the canyon.

Ahead, the canyon walls bulged and curved inward, guaranteeing that if the fire ever came down, the only refuge would be among the boulders, big as houses, or in the stream, which poured down at an impressive rate from the glaciers above.

The water looked cold, but if things got hot, it might be the only place to go.

Static. "Walt, are you there?"

I unclipped the radio from my belt and stopped, catching my breath and tripping the toggle in response to the Cheyenne Nation. "I'm here."

Static. "Where, exactly?"

"I don't know, about a quarter mile into the canyon."

Static. "No sign of Michael Rakin?"

"Nope, but his car was sitting there blocking the road, and his prayer shawl was just up from the vehicle, his tracks heading into the canyon and west."

Static. "Toward the fire."

"Yep."

Static. "Walt, you need to get out of there."

"Where's the fire?"

Static. "About a mile into the canyon, but it is moving fast."

I keyed the mic again as I shifted the pack on my shoulder. "Anybody down there have any idea why he might've headed back this way?"

Static. "I was speaking with Schiffer, and he said that the young man had been going through something of a crisis of faith and was emotionally upset."

"Upset enough to try driving through a forest fire?"

Static. "Evidently."

"Well, I'm just going to go a mile or so and if I don't see him, I'll turn around and skedaddle."

Static. "Skedaddle?"

"That's white man talk for haul ass." I keyed the toggle again. "So, no chance of them getting it under control?"

Static. "No, not with the pervasive wind." There was a pause. Static. "Walt, do not fool around with this fire. It is unlike anything we have ever seen before."

"Another half mile and I come about and head back."

Static. "Remember what the old-timers used to say about the hotshot crews we were on in our youth?"

"Once you see it, it's too late." I couldn't help but smile. "Roger that. You might not hear from me here in the next leg. The walls are getting tall and the two-way probably won't get through."

Static. "Is this the point where I should remind you that having a cell phone would be handy?"

"Nope."

Static. "Roger and out."

Figuring I'd save the battery, I started to turn the thing off but then decided that I wasn't going to be here that long and just clipped it back to my belt before continuing up the winding road. The gravel and stones had gotten larger and thicker in the more isolated areas of the canyon and the prints had vanished.

Looking toward the mountain I could see small flakes suddenly appearing out of the gray sky as if fragile pieces were breaking loose and falling from the heavens.

Snow, of all things.

Unable to help myself, I stuck out a tongue and allowed a flake to float there, but immediately regretted my decision as the acrid taste of ash filled my mouth.

Spitting, I wiped a sleeve across my lips and wished I'd brought a canteen. It would be easy enough to go down the bank and scoop a handful from the creek, but for now I needed to make time. Then I remembered the pack on my shoulder. I unbuckled the top, pulled out one of the two water bottles, and took a sip.

"A lot of good it does to have a bug-out bag if you don't remember you have it when you're bugging out."

The ash fell, and along with the frantic limb movement of the trees, it was almost as if the entire canyon was telling me to abandon all hope as I stuffed the water bottle back in the pack.

The ash wasn't a good sign, but at least I hadn't seen any flames yet.

The glow on the horizon to the north had disappeared, but I wasn't sure whether the light of day had masked it, or if the smoke had settled so low in the canyon that the flames were just above, and on a scale I didn't want to imagine.

With the constant winding of the road, the creek stayed close, and visibility was even further hampered, but I could hear a rushing, roaring sound that seemed to be coming from the west, approaching fast.

All I could think was that if that was the fire, I was done for.

I started running as fast as I could back down the road but knew in my heart of hearts that I wasn't going to make it as the sound grew so loud that there was nothing but it and the pounding of my boots.

It was then that the heavens opened up and I was suddenly flying through the air, only to hit the hard surface of the road and bounce a good half dozen times before sliding to a stop, with I don't know how many thousands of gallons of water crashing down on me like a tidal wave.

Dragging myself from the muddy deluge, I rolled over and gazed upward into the sky, looking for the Canadian dumpers that had just tried to wash me away.

Lying there, I started to laugh, thinking about drowning in the middle of a forest fire.

I sat up, took off my hat, and slung the water from it and my arms. I still couldn't see anything, but I listened the big engines of the firefighter circled away, probably gathering another load of water.

I waved my hat as if they could see me and croaked. "Thanks."

Static. "Walt, are you there? Over."

Feeling at my hip, I couldn't find the walkie-talkie and turned to see it lying in one of the puddles along with my pack, covered in mud.

Slowly pushing myself into a standing position, I walked back up the road and picked the thing up and shook it off.

Trooper Wilson's voice sounded again. Static. "Walt? Do you copy? Over."

Hitting the toggle, I held the muddy thing to my mouth. "I'm here."

Static. "Hey, the Royal Canadian Firefighter CL-415s are about to make it rain roughly on your position. Over."

Pulling my sopping hat back on my head, I laughed. "No, I'd say the Super Scoopers just got my *exact* position."

Static. "They get you? Over."

I glanced around. "And a surrounding area of about a hundred yards."

Static. "They were afraid that the fire was getting a little close, but with all the ground smoke it's kind of hard to tell. Over."

"Well, no need to worry about that now." Shaking a little more water off, I laughed again, noticing the water drop had at least knocked all the ash out of the air. "Thank 'em for me, would you?"

Static. "Thank 'em yourself, they're on our tactical fire frequency, two notches up—call sign Big Goose kilo two-six. Over."

"I'll do that."

Static. "Hey, we've all been giving some thought to this situation here and we think you should just turn around and get out of there before the place turns into Pompeii. Over."

"I'm just going to go a little farther around the next bend where it flattens out, and if I don't see him by then, I'll call it quits and head back."

Static. "Walt, this kid is screwy and the abbot deputy seems to think he might even be suicidal, and if he is, there's nothing to be gained by him taking you with him. Over."

I keyed the mic. "Just a little farther."

Static. "Roger that, but let's make sure that's not the last thing I hear you say. Over."

"Roger that. Out."

Clipping the thing back on my belt, I wrung out the wool shawl that hung to me like a second skin and watched the water dripping from the trees. I even spotted a middling-sized cutthroat that must've been scooped up along with the lake water, flapping around in one of the puddles.

Slipping the waterlogged pack onto my shoulder, I headed over, gently lifting the trout and tossing him into a wide tub section of Crazy Woman Creek. "Here, see if you can make it back to the lake." Watching the fish disappear, I looked back up the road, thinking about the prepackaged food in my pack. "If you were any bigger, I might save you for dinner."

Thank goodness it wasn't too cold, and even if it was, the fire was close enough to warm things up as I trudged along on the road.

If Rakin kept going in the direction he was heading, he would most certainly die, and maybe that was what he was planning . . . This seemed like the only obvious motivation.

Clomping around the next corner, I finally got to where the water hadn't hit, and the footing was a little better. There was a pretty good straightaway lined with aspens on one side, some of the few in the canyon road, and I glanced up and down the hillsides in hopes of seeing the novice sitting on a boulder, waiting for me.

No such luck.

The smoke was getting heavier, and a dark ceiling of it was hovering nearer, almost to where it was touching the high granite walls of the canyon, reminding me again that there was only one way out.

I inclined my head and could see that same orange glow at the precipice, indicating that the fire couldn't be too far from the edge. I studied the area where the rock walls grew less steep and the pines crowded in to gather the moisture the creek relayed from the high country, a lot of them brown from beetle-kill.

If the fire on the edge of the cliffs to my right worked its way east and came down that incline, there was only going to be a break of about thirty yards for that fire to jump and then this end of the canyon was going to be bottled like the cork in a magnum of champagne, and just as volatile.

A little voice in the back of my head again reminded me that if that happened, there really wasn't going to be anywhere to go.

Even if you attempted the impossible and tried to scale the cliffs to the left, you'd likely be met with another forest fire to the south, determined to team up with its partner to the north—the two of them joining in the eastern tail end of the canyon to conflagrate the entire east face of the Bighorn Mountain Range.

Then the other little voice kicked in, telling me I could go just a little bit farther.

Taking a deep breath, I coughed some of the bitter taste from my throat and noticed the ash flakes had returned, perhaps not quite as many as before but they were growing, filling the sky like a delicate, floating warning.

I took the water bottle from the backpack and sipped, then began walking again, trying to make time in the straightaway. But with my soaked clothes and boots, the going was a little slow and soggy.

I figured if I got to the end of the straight and still didn't see Raskin, then I'd done everything I could to save him. I tried to suspend the thought that the young monk was unaware he'd dropped the shawl and had instead gone back to the O-Kay Lodge, where he was sitting on the porch enjoying a Coke and a ham and cheese sandwich.

I was halfway down the straight when I heard the noise again—the rushing roaring sound coming from the west—and stared up at the sky. "You have got to be kidding . . ."

Glancing around as quick as I could, I spotted a jagged overhang to my left and ran in that direction as fast as I could, but evidently not fast enough as the sound of the big plane surrounded me, thundering through the canyon and dropping the tsunami.

Figuring my chances were better if I just hit the ground now, rather than being blown from my feet, I dove for cover but came up short and caught my foot between two rocks, which sent me slamming onto the roadway and sliding to a stop just in time to see the torrent that again poured out of the sky.

Ignoring the pain in my ankle, I grabbed the brim of my hat, covering my head, and felt like a truck was running over me multiple times. The noise of the engines was tremendous, and I had the urge to yell at the top of my lungs to release the pressure in my ears, but decided to hold my breath instead because I wasn't sure when I'd get my next one.

It felt like I was underwater as I lay there with the smothering weight pushing me into the rocky earth, and then a few seconds later, it was gone.

Listening to the big twin engines bank and circle away, I winced as my ankle informed me that I was more hurt than I thought. Rolling over again to pluck at the two-way still attached to my belt, I peered at the dial and switched the frequency up two clicks before raising it to my face.

Keying the toggle, I croaked, "Big Goose kilo two-six, this is Sheriff Walt Longmire. Over."

Static. "This is Big Goose kilo five-two, Sheriff Longmire. Two-six is refueling. How can I help you? Over."

"You could start by not drowning me." Holding the radio close, I sat and watched as the water ran off the brim of my hat. "Is that you, Rose?"

Static. "Roger that by any other name, Sheriff. I hitched a ride with our Canadian friends. Are you the one in the canyon? Over."

"Unless you guys flush me out the east end."

Static. "Sorry about that. We were told to divert to the center/east and keep the fire off you. Over."

I keyed the mic, staring at my ankle, encased in my mud-covered boot. "I appreciate that, but you guys have been a little too on-target and gotten me twice."

Static. "Well, at least you're fireproof for the moment." There was a brief pause and then he went on. "Just so you know, we've been diverted again to the north canyon east where the fire is going downslope and might cut you off. Over."

"I saw the glow on the rim, how close is it?"

Static. "I'd say the door is going to close in a couple of hours if the wind doesn't alter course. Over."

"Then what?"

Static. "You're on your own. The winds are about to knock us out of the sky and we're going to have to refuel—but they're going to ground us, I just know it. Over."

"So, get out of here now or never?"

Static. "You got it, we . . ."

I listened some more but his signal cut out and I could hear nothing. "Big Goose kilo five-two, do you copy? Over."

Nothing.

"Rose? Big Goose kilo five-two, do you copy?" Clicking back down two notches, I hit the mic again. "Trooper Wilson, are you there? Copy?"

Nothing.

I hit the button once more. "Anybody?"

Setting the radio down, I stared at my boot and wasn't sure if I wanted to see what was inside. Finally giving up, I reached down and pulled the slippery thing off and stared at my swollen ankle. "Oh, hell."

Running my fingers around the wet sock, I could tell the thing was already sprained and could feel a clicking when I tried to move it, as if something were loose in there, somewhere.

Knowing that if I didn't get the boot back on quick, I wasn't likely to get it back on at all, I positioned the thing and gritted my teeth as I pointed my toes forward and slipped it on.

With a growl, I pulled, immediately regretting it as it felt like my foot was going to twist off. Slamming backward, I lay there trying not to yell until the waves of pain subsided enough for me to sit up and see that at least I'd gotten the boot fully back on.

Still hearing nothing but silence and the ever-present dripping, I clipped the radio to my belt and shrugged the pack onto my shoulder, lumbering to a standing position.

The stabbing pain in my ankle sat me back down quickly, however, and I threw the pack to the ground before looking up and beholding a miracle standing in a puddle and staring at me from the middle of the rocky road—a very saturated sixteen-hand mule.

Blink.

# 14

He didn't move but just stood there as I struggled to stand and approach him, limping. The water dripped off him as if it were just another day to endure.

"Well, we got our Saturday night shower early, didn't we?" Reaching out, I patted his muscled withers, wiping some of the water away as he turned his great head to examine me. "Why didn't you listen and get the hell out of here?"

His head raised and gazed up the canyon, the gigantic ears twitching and facing that way as he ignored me.

"You do know there's a fire, don't you?"

Blink.

"Well, I know you can be ridden." Retrieving the pack, I opened it and fished inside until I found what I was hunting for—a couple coils of nylon rope, which I began fashioning into a halter. "I'm starting to think I should've left the harness from the corral on you . . ."

After a few false starts, I was able to put the thing together and then readjust it to fit him before slipping it around his neck and placing the forward end over his nose as he stood there patiently.

"I have to admit that I'm not unhappy to see you, and not only as a conveyance." Leading him toward the overhang as best I could, I flipped the wool shawl over his back to serve as a saddle blanket, even if I didn't have a saddle. I then got him in position and carefully stepped on the rock, my bad ankle throbbing in pain as I threw my right leg over his wide back, feeling like my hips were going to dislocate.

Circling him toward the road, I angled left, and we both stood there looking up the canyon as the ash began falling again. "Well, are you game?"

Almost in response, he began clomping up the road, and I was just as glad to not be putting any weight on my ankle.

"Like my father used to say—when in doubt, let your horse do the thinking, and I guess that goes doubly with mules."

As we clopped along, I gazed at the north rim and could see the ghostly etchings of flames at the precipice, the gusts there pushing the fire over the edge. "All right, that's it. We'll go to the end of this straight, but then we turn and hightail it out of here."

Giving him a little gig with my left heel, he accelerated his pace but not enough to break into a trot, and I wasn't sure if my makeshift harness would hold up to any equine misadventures.

We crossed a bridge, and the aspen canopy began to thin, revealing otherworldly rock formations, massive boulders that had fallen from the epic cliffs above, standing upright like sentinels.

In all honesty and in other conditions, it was probably one of the most beautiful places in the world, but I had to think hard about when the last time I'd been here was, and finally came up with it. There had been a missing child whom we'd found sitting on top of one of the great boulders, ignoring the plaintive cries of her family as they'd been wandering around below searching for her.

I remembered climbing the rock and asking her if she wanted to come down with me and rejoin her family, to which she had responded, "I'd rather not."

Assuring her I'd felt that same way about my family sometimes, I had scooped her up and carried her down.

Reaching the far end of the straight, I reined Borax in and just sat there, realizing I'd gone as far as I safely could and that I really didn't have any choice at this point but to head back.

Static. "Walt, are you there? Over."

I'd obviously gained enough altitude or clearance to enable me to once again pick up the trooper's frequency. Plucking the radio from my belt, I keyed the mic. "Wilson, is that you?"

Static. "Roger that. Hey Walt, you've got to get out of there and I mean right now. Over."

"What's up?"

Static. "The door is closing, and we've got a full-blown flaming front rolling down the north incline that's about to slam shut—those damn beetle-kill trees are exploding all over the place and this fire is using them like an expressway. Over."

Keying the mic, I leaned forward to pet Borax. "Well, I've got an advantage in that I'm no longer afoot, which is good, because I'm pretty sure I've sprained the hell out of my ankle."

Static. "Excuse me? Copy?"

"I've got the mule, and if I can just find some way to hang on, the two of us will be out of here in no time."

Static. "Good, then do it now. Over."

I smiled to myself. "With bells on. Over and out."

Clipping the radio back on my belt and then slipping my arms through both shoulder straps, I buckled the pack's chest strap to keep the thing on me no matter what and wheeled the big mule around. "All right, you heard the man . . ." Spinning the remainder of the rope, I twirled it and glanced it off Borax's hindquarter and dug in with my heels.

I'm not sure what I was expecting, if anything at all, but the single-mule team was set to surprise, as all that muscle contracted and we were off—perhaps not at a smooth gait but a powerful one.

Trying to stay seated, but not wanting him to back off, I held the single rein in one hand and twisted my fingers into his mane with the other. My ass was bouncing pretty good as we loped down the straight, and to be honest, I never would've thought that he could make time like he was, but his gait smoothed out and soon we were galloping down the dirt road at a pretty good canter.

We'd just made the first turn into the aspen canopy when I saw a figure standing in the road. Pulling on the one rein, I felt Borax slow as we came upon the novice, and Michael Rakin dove to one side, throwing himself over the embankment in an attempt to not be trampled.

Finally hauling Borax to a halt, I spun him around and trotted back to where the young man had raised himself to a sitting position and gazed at me through the falling ash.

"Where the hell have you been?"

Confused, he glanced around. "I've been here."

"Where? I came straight up this road and didn't see you." I patted the mule. "And evidently Borax here didn't see you either."

Rising as well as he could, I watched as he slipped off his cap, ashamed. "I . . . I was asleep."

"You were what?"

He pointed across the way, near the creek. "I was over on one of those boulders, asleep. I'm sorry, but I was tired and I . . ."

I started to get off the mule but then thought better of it. "My ankle is sprained and there may or may not be some bone chips in it floating around." Looking down at him, I noticed he was missing a shoe. "Where's your other shoe?"

He appeared even more ashamed. "I lost it in the stream."

I shook my head. "Well, we're a pair, aren't we?"

"I've been having a hard time as of late."

"So I've heard." I reached down to pick up the coiled rope attached to the mule. "Fortunately for both of us, we've got a ride." I extended a hand to him as he slung his small sling pack over his head and onto his shoulder.

I waited for a moment and then tipped my hat back, looking down at him.

He stared at me. "What?"

I shook my hand so that he'd notice it. "I'm trying to get you up on Borax here, so you can ride?"

"Oh." He stared at my hand.

"You're going to climb and then throw your other leg over his back when I lift you up."

"Right."

I studied him. "We don't have a lot of time here."

He nodded and then did as I asked, and we accomplished the clumsiest mount ever seen in the ancient annals of horsemanship.

The young novice sighed and his head dropped.

Nudging his thigh, I watched as his face rose, and I could see he was crying. "Listen, we've got to get out of here." I held out a hand to indicate the falling ash that danced in the air with the increasing and heat-broiled wind blowing up the canyon. "You know there's a fire, right? A full-blown end of the world forest fire going on, here, now?"

He wiped his eyes with a sleeve, and I noticed the smear of ash on his face, figuring I was probably wearing my share too. "I know there was one on the mountain."

I raised my voice to call back to him. "And where do you think this road we're on leads?"

Unbuckling the backpack's chest strap so I could breathe more freely, I listened to the emotion in his voice. "Back over to Meeteetse, at least that's what my phone told me."

Shaking my head, I guided the big mule toward the middle of the road and quickened my pace. "And did you tell anybody what route you were taking when you left Powder Junction?"

"No, I didn't."

"You just went where the phone told you?"

"Yes."

"And then your car broke down."

"Yes."

Even though I was feeling sorry for him, I couldn't help but ask. "At that point did you at least think about turning around and heading back down?"

"No, I can't say that I did."

"Do you mind if I ask why?"

"I thought it was a sign."

"A sign?"

"Yes."

I was quick to ask. "Of what?"

"From God."

I couldn't help but stop the mule for an instant to look back at him. "Like, here's a forest fire, my son, go the other way?"

He didn't laugh. "No, more like a forging of fire that I needed to surrender myself to."

I started us off again. "And why would you feel compelled to do something idiotic like that?"

There was no answer, so he either was lost in thought, or prayer, or hadn't heard me. Either way, I let it go, figuring we'd have plenty of time to talk once we got out of the canyon.

I had an uneasy feeling as I urged Borax forward at a brisk pace, the hot wind pushing back at us like it was coming from a convection oven. Even the ash swept up and rushed against us as I tilted my head back and studied the rimrock, now seeing nothing but a gray cast, looking more and more like the inside lid of a vintage pressure cooker.

There was a noise now, similar to the rushing reverberation of the Canadian CL-415s but different. Whereas the engines of the Super Scoopers had juddered the ground as they'd approached, this was more like the howling of superheated banshees whistling by and through my ears.

Clutching my hat, I cranked it down and pressed on, having an inordinately bad feeling about where we were heading.

I'd ducked in an attempt to keep my hat on my head, and with the increasing wind, it felt as if I were stumbling forward even though I was falling backward.

I'd almost fallen when the rope in my hand went taut, and all I could think was that Borax had felt me slip a bit and had pulled up short to keep from losing me.

Taking a deep breath, I coughed it back out and started off again, only to nearly be launched from his back as he stopped again.

I wondered what was up. I could see Rakin was huddled under the prayer shawl, which was now draped over his head and shoulders. He must've pulled it out from underneath us as we were bouncing along at a brisk pace. But that wasn't what riveted my gaze.

Snorting through his wide nostrils, Borax's head was swiveled around as he peered past me, and I'd never before seen the whites of his gigantic eyes, but I was seeing them now. His head was raised but he didn't strain against the rope—though he wasn't moving either.

Entranced by the image, my gaze was locked in his, the wet reflection of his eye like it was on fire, the flames licking the inside of his skull with plumes of red, orange, and yellow.

I squinted my eyes in the blowing ash and could feel the muscles in my neck straining as I lifted my face, looking up, up, and up at an absolute fortification of inferno. It wasn't motionless or static, this wall of flames, it was very much alive, and very, very ravenous.

Blazing tendrils coiled and uncoiled in pocketed hellholes, lunging for the oxygen between us.

"Sweet Jesus."

I turned to find Rakin, who had uncovered his face and was sitting there awestruck.

Swiveling back, I tried to gauge the size of the fire, but it was an impossible scale, like a curtained conflagration stretching from one canyon rim to the other no more than a quarter of a mile away.

I felt the rope in my hands give a tug, not strong enough to pull away, but certainly intended to get my attention. Turning to Borax, I nodded and reined him in. "Yep, if we're getting out of this canyon, it's not going to be that way."

Pivoting him completely, we hustled up the road, beating a hasty retreat.

I looked one last time before committing to getting away and snatched the radio from my belt, keying the mic. "Wilson, come in, are you there?" I listened, but there was no response. "Wilson, come in?"

I clipped the radio on my belt and held my hand back toward Rakin. "Gimme your phone."

He shook his head. "I don't have it."

"What?"

"I dropped it in the stream too."

"Maybe we can dry it out."

"No, I mean I lost it just like my shoe."

I started off again with one more quick look down the canyon and could see the fire approaching about as fast as we were traveling. "Well, hell."

The kid was panicking, having the same thought as me. "Can . . . can we outrun it?"

"I don't know, but the canyon is more sheltered from the wind, and with the rock faces and water it might slow it down some, but . . ."

"But what?"

I picked up Borax's pace once again. "But we're in the center of the biggest forest fire I've ever seen and that means this canyon is going to burn; it's just a question of how fast."

"But isn't there anybody here to rescue us—the Forest Service, firefighters . . . ?"

"Not at this point and not from the inside, which is where we are. Those Canadians were dropping water here in the canyon to help us, but now the same wind that's feeding the fire has them grounded."

He seemed to finally realize our predicament. The fire was no longer abstract, but a living and pursuing monster. "We're on our own?"

"Pretty much."

I glanced up and could see the ash was being pushed past us and then upward to the rim where the gray sky had descended even more, closing us in from all sides. "There are some large rock formations about a third of the way up the canyon . . . the ones that are half submerged in the creek. There's more rock and not as much vegetation, so it might slow the fire down. If things get bad enough that might be the only place to hide."

"For how long?"

"As long as the fire lasts."

"Overnight?"

"I'd say yes, at least that long." As we got to the spot where I'd been dumped on by the Royal Canadian Air Force the first time, I looked up the canyon at the straightaway and kept the big mule moving through the smaller areas of rocks. I could see some of the bigger boulders that had fallen above, which you could hardly call boulders, considering the size of the things, some of them as big as four-story buildings.

As we trotted on, I became aware of a series of glows flashing at different points on the cliffs above, knowing full well that the fire had found its way over the edge. Like a living thing, it was creeping its elongated fingers through the cracks and crevices of the granite, finding the combustibles and threading its way into the only place left for it to feed, the canyon.

With the scale of the fire, I was sure that there wasn't going to be anyone coming to our rescue and hoped we'd make it at least to the great rocky area with the bulk of Crazy Woman Creek flowing underneath.

It wasn't going to be comfortable, but at least we had a chance of surviving.

"I'm sorry."

Turning my head a bit, I glanced back at Rakin and raised my voice. "Excuse me?"

"I'm so sorry that I did this, causing you to have to come after me." He leaned in closer. "I can't help but think that I've killed both of us."

I raised the single rein, indicating the mule. "Don't forget about Borax, you might've killed him too." There was no response, so I gave out with a grim chuckle. "That was a joke, kid."

"I guess I'm not in a very humorous mood."

"Understandable, but we're going to make it out of this, trust me. This is a big canyon. As long as this damn fire doesn't suck the very last lungful of air out of it, we're in for a long night but a cooler morning. Heck, who knows? It's possible the weather might change, and those big water scoopers could come flying back in to put this thing out."

"Do you really think so?"

I didn't, but I didn't need him to know that.

We'd arrived at the narrower but rockier portion of the canyon after we crossed another short bridge, and I pulled Borax to a halt.

Carefully easing off, I tried to put weight on my ankle, but it was a no-go with a lightning strike of pain that almost brought me to my knees.

"Are you all right?"

I looked up to find Rakin squinting down at me.

"Yep." Trying to not limp too badly, I made my way to the right where there was an overhang much larger than the others, which had been a colossal section of rock that had fallen away, probably from the crevasse filling with water and then expanding when frozen.

The ground was sandy with some smaller rocks where you could sit about as comfortably as you would in a moldy dungeon.

It was large, though, and could even accommodate Borax. Conversation would be held to a minimum given that Crazy Woman Creek rushed through the makeshift cave, pounding the rocks with a crashing regularity.

Slowly coming back out, I found that Rakin had scooted forward on Borax, gathered the single rein, and had moved the mule farther up the road.

"What are you doing?"

He didn't look at me but directed his gaze through the canyon.

"Michael?"

He didn't speak for a bit, and then mostly mumbled to himself. "I'm going on ahead."

"You're what?"

"I did this, and I'm just going to go on ahead into whatever is up the road."

Climbing the bank, I limped toward him. "No, you're not."

He finally turned to me. "And why is that?"

"Well, even if I didn't give a hoot about you, I need a ride and I'm not going to let you kill Borax here."

His face twisted, he kicked the mule, but the great beast just stood.

"It appears he has a vote."

His face screwed up again and he began openly weeping as he kicked the mule again and again, with the same response. "C'mon!" He gigged Borax and at that point even raised a fist as if to strike his mount.

"Don't."

He stared at me between the falling ash, tears flowing freely as he wiped them away with a dirty sleeve, his face blackened.

I took a few more agonizing steps toward him as Borax stretched his elongated face to me, and I reached up and scrubbed his velvety nose with my fingertips. "He's a good boy, and he deserves to live, even if you don't think you do." Taking the rein from him, I held out a hand. "Here, get down, and let's get under cover before the fire starts falling from the sky."

Raising a hand, I supported Rakin under one arm and lifted

him down as best I could. "C'mon, I found a great little spot for us and Borax to wait this situation out." Allowing him to help me, we got down to the rocks and past the creek and I ushered him into the cave, and sat on a rock.

"Why do you call him that?"

"That's his name."

"But what does it mean?"

"I'll tell you sometime, but right now I'm going to have to go get Borax."

"I can do that."

I struggled to a standing position. "No. In case you haven't noticed, he doesn't care for you."

The big mule was still standing in the exact spot where we'd left him, staring up the road through the ash and low ceiling of smoke, not even turning to look at me this time. Gradually joining him, I gazed in the same direction and wondered if he could see more than me. I had to admit that I was just as glad that I couldn't see it, if it was what I thought it was.

"You know what's coming, huh?"

Blink.

Gathering the single rein, I accidentally grazed his chin and the huge right rear hoof shot out as the beast pivoted and glimpsed down at me. "Easy, easy . . ." I gently led him hobbling in my direction and then waited as he made up his mind to follow me. Leading him down to the creek, he surprised me by dipping his head and taking in about a cubic foot of the frigid water. "That's probably a good idea."

"Is there a problem?"

I looked over to find that Rakin had come out to the mouth of the cave.

"No, I just forgot that if you touch his chin, he fires that right rear hoof like a bazooka. Besides, he needs a drink, something we need to think about if we don't want to get stuck in there with nothing for ourselves."

He gestured toward the creek. "There's plenty of water."

Easing my boot in the stream to hopefully decrease the swelling, I glanced at the glimmering surface. "Not for long. This stuff is going to start getting pretty dirty with the runoff from the fire above. Search around in there and see if you can find any old beer bottles; high school kids used to come up here and drink."

He disappeared and I turned back to Borax, watching the torrents of water and slobber drain from his loose-lipped mouth. "You feeling better?"

In response, he dipped his head and took on a few more gallons like a derrick pump.

"I found four, and two that still have beer in them, along with most of a pint of Jägermeister." Rakin was standing at the opening again, this time holding the booty.

"Ugh. Wash the empties out and fill them. I'm going to soak my ankle for a minute more and then I'll bring Borax in."

He stood there looking at me. "You're going to bring him in here?"

"Yep." He went back in, and I spoke to the mule. "Not very accommodating, is he?"

Careful to lead where there was good footing, I brought the mule between the rocks and watched as he leaped over the creek with more alacrity than I would've thought possible. Catching up with him as well as my numb ankle would allow, I led him into the relative gloom where Rakin sat on a boulder, watching the dashing stream.

"I hadn't thought about that, with the water."

Having a glimpse at the collection of bottles at his feet, I dropped the single rein and moved toward the rushing stream, where I sat on another rock and reintroduced my ankle.

"Kind of damp in here."

"Thank your lucky stars it is." I paused as the frozen water removed all feeling from it. "You want me to make a fire?"

His eyes cast about. "That'd be nice."

I stared at the stream. "Don't worry, there'll be one here in no time."

Despite my protests, he did drag some branches in and broke them up, and I figured there wasn't any harm in starting a small fire to help keep us warm as we waited for the real inferno to arrive. There was a small fire-starter brick in my bug-out bag, and I used it to get the feeble flames going.

Borax had made a home for himself over against the back wall, and in the semidarkness, I couldn't be sure he wasn't asleep.

"Is it day or night?"

I glanced at Rakin, who was eating one of the granola bars from the pack and studying the side of one of the beer bottles he'd held to the light, gauging its hygiene. "When I checked the two-way the last time out on the road, I took a gander at my pocket watch. It was creeping up on two p.m."

"I assume there wasn't anything on the radio?"

"Some static, but that's about it."

Throwing caution to the wind, he took a sip. "Think they know where we are?"

"Yep, I think they know where we are approximately, but that certainly doesn't mean they can get to us." Tossing on a few more pieces of kindling, I watched as they smoldered. "Just our luck we'd find the only unburnable wood in the entire Bighorn National Forest."

"Why can't they just drop more water and work their way in here?"

"I think you're underestimating the magnitude of this fire."

Taking a stick, I drew a rough outline of the forest and wilderness area in the sand at my boots. "This area at the top is heavily forested, but the slopes in the canyons are even more dense with beetle-kill."

"And what's that?"

"Mountain pine beetles, which are a regular part of the ecosystem, but a lot of these forests are reaching a terminal age and start sending out pheromone-like signals that they're reaching the end of their lifespan, and then the beetles move in. A number of years ago, I guess a lot of the trees got to that point and that led to a catastrophic amount of forest loss, which left a lot of dead trees standing." I looked at him. "You've seen them?"

"No."

"Well, when there's drought and wind factors, pretty soon you've got all the makings of the fire of the century." Stirring my minuscule campfire with the same stick, I got a few flames to lick at the soggy wood. "I'm no expert, but they say that the beetles emerge in the spring, mate, and then bore into the bark to lay their eggs and once they hatch, they start eating the pulp of the aged trees. Now, from what I'm to understand, the larvae purge their guts before settling in for the winter, but if a cold snap comes in early enough, it can freeze the pulp in their bodies and kill them."

"Charming."

"Yep, we just haven't been lucky in the timing, and if the winter is more gradual, the beetles develop a kind of chemical antifreeze and it takes a sustained period of forty-below-zero temperatures to overcome that and kill the things." I poked at the fire a bit more, still not satisfied with the progress. "Between northern Colorado and southern Wyoming, they've killed a million and a half hectares of lodgepole pine. We've been lucky on our mountain range, but there was still a lot of damage just waiting for a spark to set it off."

"And what was that spark?"

"Lightning."

He chewed on his granola bar. "Act of God?"

"I'd rather he not have to take credit for it."

There was a long pause, and then he cleared his throat, and I felt his eyes on me. "Do you believe in him, Sheriff?"

I stared at the fire. "I think the bigger question is whether you do."

"And why is that?"

"That's twice I've seen you try to kill yourself in twenty-four hours and I can't help but wonder why?"

He stared at the ground. "I used to believe, but now I'm not so sure."

"So, you figure you'll test the theory and go meet him?"

"Something like that." He continued to study me. "Have you ever thought about it?"

"Suicide?" The fire-starter brick smoldered but refused to burst and I wondered how old it was. "Once."

"And when was that?"

"When my wife died." Giving up on the fire, I tossed the stick in and stood, trying to ignore the ghostly pain that fought through the numbness. Limping over to the opening with my frozen foot, I gazed at the gradual darkening of the sky and the increasing scent of the smoke. "I was pretty mad at something for taking my wife from me, and I was actively trying to have it out with someone."

"What stopped you?"

"My daughter, more than anything—that, and I knew it wasn't what my wife would've wanted."

"I don't have that luxury."

I turned. "Luxury?"

"Somebody to live for."

"What about your friend Alan McKay?"

"Oh, I'm his friend but I'm not so sure he's mine."

"Why would you say something like that? He appears to be a genuine individual in the extreme."

"I'm not saying anything bad about him, it's just that I don't think he really *needs* me as a friend." He paused and then laughed.

"Don't you have any family?"

He snorted. "No."

"No one?"

"One person." He yawned and then stared at the ground between us, probably thinking about the old man. "Someone who put up with all my idiosyncrasies, even made me feel like they were assets."

"Like what?"

"Oh, I've got a tendency to get fixated on things and they were very good at indulging me." I watched as he settled on the ground using his sling bag as a pillow, sliding to the side and pulling the shawl up over him. "I'm suddenly tired, isn't that strange?"

"Not really. It's a symptom of depression—your mind deals with the emotions involved by shutting your body down to conserve energy."

"Aren't you tired?"

"I am, but my ankle hurts and besides, when that fire shows from either direction, I want to be awake and ready." Stirring the tinder with the end of another piece of wood, I got a few more sparks going, and the fire was finally looking hopeful. "You're fatigued and upset, so get some rest and I'll keep watch."

He took a deep breath. "So do you think we'll make it?"

"Sure, why not?"

"I'm not sure that wording's very comforting."

"Well, there are no guarantees." I glanced around the open-ended cave. "But we've got a much better chance in here. "The problem will be associative heat and oxygen."

"Meaning?"

"If the air temperature on either side of this cave of ours gets too hot, it'll heat this place into a crematorium, then the lack of oxygen will smother us, and the heat will cook us like a flank steak."

He mumbled. "Great."

"But we have the advantage of the insulation of rock over forty feet thick and the glacial runoff of the stream; the big question being how hot and how long the fire can burn. These fires burn very hot, but once they lose fuel, they either move on or die." Standing and limping over to the opening, I scanned the canyon, but between the smoke and falling ash could only see about a hundred yards. "There's a lot of fuel down here, but it should burn quick."

"Good. I hate flank steak."

"Get some rest. There really isn't anything left to do except wait."

He relaxed the rest of the way and soon was softly snoring.

Heading back over to the campfire, I sat, feeding it some more kindling, fighting to get it going but still with middling success. I settled my eyes on my ankle, once again thinking about pulling off my boot and getting some relief from what felt like a leather vise.

If I took it off again, it was unlikely I'd get it back on and then there I'd be—"My son John . . . One shoe off, and one shoe on."

Rustling around in the bug-out bag, I found some over-the-counter pain pills and popped a few in my mouth, picking up one of the repurposed beer bottles and washing them down with what tasted like relatively clean water.

Raising the bottle, I toasted. "Giardia, the gift that keeps on giving."

I sat there in the semidarkness, thinking about what to do next, and had just started to set the bottle back down when I became aware of a strange chirping sound, but not something I'd ever heard in nature.

It sounded electronic, so I plucked the radio from my belt and looked at it, but it was turned off and silent. Reaching into the bag again, I sorted through but couldn't find anything that could be making the noise.

Finally, I raised my head and could see something illuminated in the opening of the sling bag positioned underneath Rakin's head, ringing, as he lay there.

His cell phone.

# 15

He stared at me.

"It's your phone."

Sitting up, he glanced around and then plucked the thing from the partially unzipped opening, hitting the screen and holding it to his ear. "Hello?" He held it for a moment and then touched the screen again. "There was no one there."

"I thought you lost it?"

"Excuse me?"

"The phone, I thought you said you lost it?"

Gripping it in his hand, he studied the thing. "I thought I did too. I guess it fell into my bag."

"You should check in there for your shoe."

He made a face. "Right."

"What kind of signal have you got?"

"Not much, and there isn't a great deal of battery power left."

"Try calling 911."

He glanced at his phone. "There's hardly any service."

"Wireless phones with no active service can still reach 911, as long as they have battery power."

"Well, there isn't much . . ."

"What are you saving it for?"

"An emergency?"

I widened my eyes in response to the ridiculousness of the remark. "I think our current situation qualifies as an emergency." I reached my hand out. "Can I see it?"

Reluctantly, he stood and walked over, handing it to me, and I studied the screen saver, a vintage-looking photo of a man and a boy who I assumed was him, standing in front of one of those pay-to-fish lakes, holding a diminutive trout on the end of the line.

"Is this you?"

"Yes."

I glanced at the photo again. "Your father?"

"Yes." He stood there studying the photo. "That was the year he left."

"Left?"

"Yeah, he just disappeared."

"Did you ever try to find him?"

"No."

"Why not?"

"He was a bad man." I glanced up at him and he walked toward the opening. "Sorry, but he's not my favorite subject and brings out the worst in me." He turned back. "He was abusive to both me and my mother, drank and used drugs . . . He used to lock me in a closet. He was a real piece of work."

"I'm sorry to hear that."

He waved it off. "Ancient history."

I looked down at the phone, but the screen had gone black.

He saw me staring at it. "Something wrong?"

"I don't know how to operate this thing."

He came over and took it from me, touching the screen a few times, then handing it back. "There, I already dialed the number."

Holding it to my ear, I listened as it rang only once. "Absaroka County Sheriff's Department, this is 911. What is your emergency?"

"Well, I'll tell you I've got twin forest fires coming at me from both directions and the only thing I've got to fortify myself with is a pint of Jägermeister . . ."

"Walt!" She screeched. "Where are you?"

"Hey Ruby. I just told you, between a hot rock and a flaming hard place."

"Are you all right?"

"I told you that too."

"Will you quit clowning around and tell me what's going on?"

"We're in a pretty safe spot here in Crazy Woman Canyon, but I think we're boxed in."

"You are! The hotshot crews call it a donut hole, and all the flame fronts are converging on you."

"So when is the cavalry coming?"

There was a brief silence. "They're not, with the wind they've got the planes grounded and the crews can't do anything but shadow the fires as they converge on you."

"How big and how hot?"

"The biggest and hottest they've ever seen."

"Doesn't sound hopeful."

"It's not."

"How's everybody else?"

"They're all down in Powder Junction evacuating people, and everybody seems to have escaped for now, except for that Agirra family."

"Boris?"

She sighed. "He's bound and determined to stick it out and save his place. The HPs went in one last time and brought the rest of his family out, but he stayed."

"Can't say I'm surprised." I glanced up at Rakin as he went back to his rock and sat, glancing around as if the fire might suddenly appear. "Vic and Henry are in PJ?"

"Yes."

"Whatever you do, tell them to stay out there and don't try anything stupid . . ."

"Walt."

"I've got the novice from Saint Benedict Monastery with me, Michael Rakin, and even Manx's mule, Borax from the O-Kay, here in that spot about a third of the way up the canyon, that really big boulder that makes that open-ended overhang in the stream?"

"Yes, I know the one."

"We'll be fine. We'll just hunker down and stay put here in the rocks, with the stream, and there's no way the fire can get at us."

There was a pause. "Walter, I don't think you understand the extent of this fire."

I let out a long, slow breath. "Well Ruby, it's been a long time coming."

"Walter?"

"I'm going to sign off and try to keep a little power in Michael's phone. I doubt you'll be able to call me back, but I'll call you again as things develop."

"Walter . . ."

"Talk to you soon." Touching the red button on the screen, I studied the electronic hieroglyphics at the right corner and then held it out to Rakin. "You've got more power than you thought."

Standing, he took a step around the fire and then looked at the screen and returned to his spot. "Huh, I guess it came back up."

The campfire was catching pretty good now and the smoke appeared to be drawing toward the lower opening to the east, which meant that the predominant wind and fire might be coming from the west and down the elevation of the canyon, but I wasn't willing to bet on it.

"It doesn't sound hopeful."

I glanced at him. "You heard the phone?"

"Yes."

"No, it isn't like we've got anywhere to go to outrun it, if that's what you're asking."

"So the same plan?"

"Yep. You start getting nervous and decide to make a run for it out there in the open and that's how you die. We're in a good spot, one that affords us the best chance of survival, and the trick is just being patient."

"I'm not good at that."

I smiled at him. "Well, maybe you'll get better."

"My mother tried to take care of me back in Oakland, where I'm from, but it was a bad neighborhood, and she just couldn't seem to get ahead." He sat up, sipping from one of the water bottles. "I think when my father abandoned us it was the last straw. She started drinking heavily and developed liver disease and died. I was put up for adoption and the people who took me were kind of odd; the man worked on the road and his wife was there alone with me."

I waited for him to go on.

"She cheated on him and told me that if I ever said anything that she'd send me off to a very bad place. I never said anything, but he found out and things started falling apart, and one day Family Services showed and took me away."

"To a very bad place?"

"Yes, it was a group home that had kind of descended into a

*Lord of the Flies* kind of deal out in the central valley, where there were tribes, and the only adult was this woman who came by once a day to drop off groceries and see if we were still alive." He stared at the campfire and was quiet for a moment. "I ran away and lived on the road for a few years. I got dropped off on I-80 by this truck driver and the van from Saint Benedict stopped and picked me up. It was Brian Schiffer who offered to take me to the abbey and feed me and give me a bed for the night."

"And you stayed?"

"I did."

"But then you tried to leave?"

"A couple of times." He stood and walked over to the fire, crouching on the other side. "I've struggled with my faith."

"That's understandable. You've been through an awful lot for a young man."

"I don't think I was aware of that until I met Alan."

"McKay?"

"Yes." He smiled. "He never talks about his family, but then very few people do at Saint Benedict's. One weekend he was going home for a visit and asked me to join him. I think he knew I didn't have any family, and I never left the abbey."

"The O-Kay Ranch was quite a bit different from what you were used to?"

"Yes." He laughed and then cut it off. "But it led to one of the worst arguments Alan and I ever had."

"Over?"

"Faith."

"In what sense?"

"The proposition that without faith, in an immoral world, there is no virtue and therefore no God—everything is permitted."

"Including murder?"

He stared at me for a long time and then finally spoke. "Everything. I mean, seriously, if you don't believe in the immorality of your own soul, then what use is God as divine savior. You need no saving, and so what use is God?"

"Those are some big theological steps."

"They're not steps I want to take, but the torture of doubt that my soul is immoral suggests a martydom that diverts me to nonbelief."

"So, you consider your soul to be completely moral?"

"No, I know it's immoral, but in an immoral world what else can it be?"

I sat back on my boulder. "So let me get this straight. You're saying God is immoral?"

"Or that he doesn't exist at all."

"That's a somewhat odd position for a novice of Saint Benedict's Monastery to be taking, isn't it?"

He raised his voice. "It's what tortures me."

I leveraged myself to a standing position and then limped over to get a few more pieces of wood. "So, your soul is by nature immoral?"

He seemed distracted but answered. "I would question that, yes."

"Doesn't the Bible have something to say about original sin?"

"It does, but I'm talking about acquired sin."

"We're born in sin, and through our very existence we do nothing but acquire even more?"

"Yes."

I smiled at the fire, shaking my head at the ridiculousness of our situation and how we were going to spend the last hours of our lives arguing theology. "But don't we also accumulate a certain amount of grace in those travels?"

"Not without God."

I tossed a few pieces of wood onto the fire, the sparks rising and then shooting east and through the tunnel. "No God, no grace, huh?"

"No."

"No redemption at all?"

"No, none."

I looked at him, his eyes glowing in the fire. "Seems to me you're putting yourself out of business—there's no hope in your sense of theology: no courage, no promise, no aspiration, no trust—only despair."

"There's freedom."

"Freedom to do what, immoral acts?" I shook my head again. "Now you're in my ballpark and I can tell you that that's a one-way road to chaos."

"Maybe that's the natural order of things: the way the world should be."

"Have you ever been in chaos, kid? Real chaos?" Limping back over to the opening, I stood there looking into the darkness, smelling the thick smoke and listening. "I have and believe you me it's nothing to be desired."

He started to speak again, but Borax suddenly decided to join the conversation with an ear-splitting bray that echoed off the stone walls and ceiling, threatening to deafen us both. The sound practically scared Rakin to death as he backed against the rock wall to get out of the way of the big mule as Borax moved from the shadows and around the fire to join me outside, gazing west at the limited view of the canyon road.

He was skittish, the second time I'd seen him like that, his ears forward, eyes wide, and still rumbling a squeal in his throat.

Rakin started to speak again, but I held up a hand to silence him as Borax moved past me and across the stream, scrambling across the rocks and finally positioning himself at the center of the road, looking up the canyon.

Stepping outside to escape the echoing rush of Crazy Woman Creek, I limped through the stream and around the boulders, finally getting to the side of the road, where I stopped and listened again as the big mule brayed once more, the sound vibrating my own lungs.

Rakin crossed the stream and joined us. "What . . . ?"

"He hears something, the same as me."

The kid peered into the darkness. "What is it?"

It was a rhythmic vibration, but unlike the engines of the Canadian planes. It was a rattling sound thundering the surface of the road, an earthly clattering.

I watched as Borax dipped his head, his heavily muscled body crouching down a bit as if expecting an impact, and it was about then that I heard the first call, a multitone bugling that began impossibly low and then ran through the scale into a full-blown scream—a lot of them.

Reaching over, I grabbed ahold of Rakin and pulled him in behind Borax, since that seemed to be the only place to take cover as the clattering and bellowing filled our ears.

Yelling, he tried to pull away, but I held on to him. "What is it?"

"Elk!"

Blowing through the smoke and ash, there must have been at least a hundred of them.

Borax stood his ground and didn't move, like a boulder in a stream, as big bulls and cows flowed around him like a river of ungulates.

Rakin tried to run again, but I knocked him off his feet and planted him against my leg, my ankle reminding me of its painful peculiarities.

The stampeding elk were steering around the mule but cutting back in as soon as they got past him, one of them stamping on Rakin's leg as I dragged him in closer.

He screamed and then yelled. "What do they want?"

"To get away from the fire!"

The numbers were increasing, and in all honesty, I'd never seen this many elk in my life. Peering over Borax's rump, I watched as they leaped out of the gray like dark ghosts, the swirling ash chasing them as if hoping to catch a ride.

A bull ducked in a bit too close and caught the sleeve of my jacket, instantly ripping it and knocking me off balance as I began to fall backward and on top of Rakin. Landing to the side, I tried to get up but was hit by a glancing blow from a hoof and fell again to the ground.

I could feel Rakin's hands grabbing at me as I tried to get back behind the mule, but then another fleeing elk stamped on my arm as I drug myself back. I saw the young man roll into a ball and scream.

Trying to reach him, I grabbed one of his arms, but he must've thought it was something else and wrenched away, struggling to his feet and turning toward the middle of the road as the large, dark shapes shot around us.

"No!"

He hesitated for a moment, then stepped out at the beginning of a run, only to be knocked back by the next elk that leaped by, causing him to spin into the far ditch as if hit by a car. Then another elk shot between us and blocked my view.

There were hundreds of them now, bellowing and blowing

down the road in a terrified stampede to escape the fires above, but Borax stood there as if it was nothing to him. I made a silent promise to never badmouth mules ever again.

I could see Rakin's prayer shawl flapping after him for an instant, the novice trying to get up at the far side of the road, but I couldn't tell if he'd actually made it. For a moment, I thought about following him, but with my ankle and bruised arm, I was likely to get plowed into and end up out there on the surface of the road, providing traction for the maddened herd's cloven hooves.

The clattering thunder was nerve-racking, and the squealing cries couldn't help but send shivers through your spine, but I pulled myself onto to all fours and looked between Borax's legs, watching the overcrowded roadway as the elk were now glancing off the mule's fore shoulders and point of hip.

I couldn't see Rakin and hoped he'd made it to the berm at the other side of the roadway where there was another jumble of boulders big enough to divert the elk back into the road and possibly the hillside behind it. My only hope was that he stayed where he was and waited until the bulk of the herd had passed so that I could get to him.

My arm was numb, but I was still able to move my fingers. Pulling my hat down tighter, I reached up and took ahold of Borax's tail, pulling myself to a partial standing position.

I could see there were still a number of elk dodging down the roadway, but fewer than there had been.

Peering over the mule's rump, I could now make out the individual animals rather than the mad rush that had been, a few cows slipping past as I straightened the rest of the way upright.

I stood there for a moment, still holding on to Borax's tail, as he swiveled his great head and regarded me. "Hey, thanks."

He said nothing in return, but I think he appreciated the sentiment.

Stepping to the left, I saw another, younger bull shoot by, causing me to stop.

Flexing my fingers, I inspected my forearm but couldn't see any blood and figured it was staved.

The next elk was another cow, so I checked the road to make sure there weren't any others making an immediate pass. One blew past on the other side of Borax, and I figured I could take my chances. I took a step in that direction when another bolted right in front of me.

Stepping back, I waited a moment and then took another try at it, this time not seeing any elk at all. Staring in the distance through the wisps of smoke and ash, I thought I could still see shadows in the darkness, but wasn't sure.

Pulling the flashlight from my belt, I took the next step on the darkened road and saw Rakin's stockinged foot sticking up from the rocks, twitching.

I sat on one of the boulders, pulled him out by his feet, and moved him to the roadside, lifting his body so that his head was more elevated before resting him on the ground. He was unconscious and bleeding from his abdomen.

I carefully lifted the shawl away and shined the beam, staring at the embedded material of his shirt trapped in the wound. Peeling the folds of the fabric away revealed a puncture at the lower right, where a portion of a broken antler protruded.

"Well, hell."

It was an antler point, and from the diameter, I was pretty sure it was a good four inches into his lower abdomen on the left side, which meant it hadn't gotten the ascending colon, and I hoped not the intestines—but it was still a pretty sizable puncture to a human body.

Trying to get a clear idea of our predicament, I glanced down the canyon to where the herd of elk had disappeared and then back up and to the west, from where I was pretty sure the fire was coming. Peering down at the unconscious young man, I thought about how far I'd be able to carry him with my busted ankle and then looked at the mule, still standing in the middle of the road, but having dipped his great head to gaze at me.

He didn't have a mark on him. "Hey, boy."

Blink.

"How 'bout you come over here?" To my surprise, he slowly turned and began ambling toward us, stopping at the edge of the rocks and lowering his head to sniff at Rakin's head. Reaching out, I picked up the single rein dragging on the ground and lifted myself into a standing position.

Patting the mule just to steady him, I kept the rope in one hand and reached down with the other and lifted the young man by the collar of his sweatshirt, trying to keep from brushing against the broken antler that stuck out from the trunk of his body like a pump handle.

Borax didn't move and I slipped Rakin on, positioning his body toward the rear so that he lay on his back. I headed toward the cave-like overhang, leading the mule across the road and holding Rakin steady so that he didn't fall off.

Making our way through the rocks, we got to the stream, where I could see the water was covered with black ash, some of it still steaming. I immediately looked up the canyon but could see nothing, the low-hanging smoke still obscuring the view. The smell of the fire was stronger, much stronger than it had been, and I had a suspicion that it would likely be here well before nightfall.

The elk.

Did they know something I didn't, such as a way out, or were they just running blindly from one fire into the next?

I could grab my pack and his and just start off down the canyon in hopes that there was a path through that part of "the donut," as the hotshot crews referred to it, but it was also possible that I'd just be leading Rakin, Borax, and me to our deaths out in the open.

*Deploy*, that's what we used to call it back in the day, and I was pretty sure that's what they still called it these days—bed down and let it pass through. We were in a good spot, the best we could hope for, and now here I was, like a rookie, second-guessing myself.

Leading the mule across the stream, I guided him into the overhang and turned him around near the wall where he'd been and where he was comfortable. I wanted him oriented in that direction so he could alert me if anything came down the canyon, including the fire.

Slipping Rakin carefully off the mule, I carried him long enough to get him close to the dying fire and the spot where he'd been lying.

Ignoring the pain in my ankle, I lowered him down and propped him against the rock. Then I drew the shawl back again to examine his wound. His shirt was saturated with blood, and I could only imagine the infection that was in there. But if I pulled the antler tip from his body it would introduce a number of other problems I probably wasn't prepared to deal with. Namely, the amount of blood that was likely to exit the wound.

I had a rudimentary first-aid kit in my rucksack, but nothing that was going to stanch a wound of that size any better than the foreign object that occupied the space now.

Like it or not, the fabric and whatever else I could get from the first-aid kit to help stop the bleeding would be all I could do until I could get him to some proper medical attention, which was hours and miles away—if we ever got there.

I took the time to poke at the fire with my stick, finally getting it to show some signs of life and shed a little light to work by. I tossed another piece of wood on the fire with an abundance of sparks and then dragged the kit over, digging through it and finding four rolls of gauze. I took them out and made a patch big enough to cover around the entire wound.

There was plenty of medical adhesive tape, which I used to seal the thing off before noticing his eyelids twitching. "Hey, you in there?"

He blinked a few more times and then groaned.

Reaching up, I took his chin in my hand. "Hey, you awake?"

His hand started to reach for mine but then dipped and started toward his wound.

Catching his hand, I took it away and rested it in his lap as one eye opened. "No, let's not touch that for now."

"What . . . what happened?"

"You had a fencing duel with a bull elk, and you lost."

He started to move, but winced.

"You're hurt, so stop moving."

He did as I said but then studied all the blood. "Ahh . . ."

"Yep." I then lied. "It's not as bad as it looks."

"It looks really, really bad."

"Yep, it's just really bad—not really, really bad." His hand tried to probe the wound, and I once again pulled it away. "No, don't touch it."

"What is it?"

"A piece of antler, stuck in you."

The one eye widened. "Well, shouldn't we get it out?"

"No."

"Why?"

"Because you'll bleed to death." Securing the rest of the tape, I sat back to examine my work. "I once watched a rookie deputy pull a piece of glass from a woman's arm after she'd fallen through a plate glass window, only to witness blood shoot across the room and cause the deputy to pass out."

"But shouldn't we . . . ?"

"I'm telling you, no. We're not going anywhere and the best thing to plug the wound is what made it, so sit back, relax, and concentrate on not bleeding."

"How do you do that?"

"I don't know, and I've had numerous opportunities." I moved back to my own rock and sat. "But if you come up with something, you let me know, would you?"

He started to reach for the wound again but then stopped himself. "What happened?"

"You panicked. When that herd bolted through out there on the road, you tried to make a run for it, and I guess one of them ran an antler into you and broke it off. You're lucky you got away with as little as you did."

"Am I going to make it?"

"Probably, if you lie there and don't poke at it. It's a good sign that you're conscious and talking, which leads me to believe you haven't pierced any important internal organs and the only thing we have to do is try to make sure you don't bleed to death."

"It hurts . . . Don't we have to get out of here, eventually?"

"No, once the fire burns through we can just wait it out till the temperature drops back to normal. I told my dispatcher where we are, and they'll come in here once the fire's done with us." Pulling two emergency fire-retardant blankets from my bug-out bag, I unfolded them and stuffed them into the stream, piling a few rocks on top to keep them in place.

"Done with us?"

I smiled. "I guess I could've picked a better turn of phrase, but there it is. Now we just do the hard part and wait."

He nodded, and I noticed he was shivering.

"Are you cold?"

"Yes." He studied his wound and then his eyes came back to mine. "Why, does that mean anything?"

"Yep, it means you're cold." Breaking up some of the smaller pieces of kindling, I could still feel the moisture in them. "This stuff is still damp, but I'll see if I can get it going."

I fussed with the fire some more, but all I was able to produce was more smoke. Frustrated, I looked over to find him smiling at the fire, or the lack thereof. "What's so funny?"

"Just an argument that Alan and I used to have."

"About?"

"About whether a faith that is tested is of more worth than one that isn't."

I shrugged. "Interesting argument, but . . ."

"But what?"

I leaned back on my less than comfortable rock and stared at him. "I think first you have to define your use of the word *faith*; how do you ascertain a degree in something like belief?"

"The scale would be determined by the amount of difficulty you're able to overcome and yet still believe."

"And let me guess: You feel as if Alan hasn't overcome enough hardship to truly believe?"

He studied me. "No, I don't."

"But you think you have?"

He choked a laugh, gesturing toward his wound. "If I didn't before, I certainly do now."

"But maybe Alan hasn't reached his true test of faith just yet." I stirred the fire again, seeing a bit of hope in the couple of embers that glowed back at me. "But who are we to judge?"

"Judge not lest ye be judged?" He smiled some more, reaching over and placing his sling bag in his lap before rustling through it with his one hand. "Elder Zebrowski used to warn me about condemning others . . . that I should practice self-reflection and humility, choosing compassion over condemnation."

"He was a very wise man."

"Yes." His eyes came back to mine for a second too long. Pulling out a thick paperback from the satchel, he viciously tore off a few pages, wadding and tossing them at me one by one. "Here, see if you can get the fire started with these—I don't think I'll be needing them anymore."

I sat there for a moment and then picked one up. I flattened and stared at the wrinkled page on my knee, reading in the flickering and dying light.

**Fyodor Dostoyevsky**

**THE BROTHERS KARAMAZOV**

*A Novel in Four Parts and an Epilogue*

# 16

When I looked back from the wrinkled page with his initials on it, he was pointing a semiautomatic pistol at my face. "I assume you took the book from my pack, and that's Manx's S&W M&P .45?"

"It's a gun, if that's what you're asking." With some effort, he picked up one of the bottles leaning against the rock with his other hand, bringing it to his lips and taking a swallow. "You knew?"

Folding the title page and stuffing it into the inside pocket of my jacket, I gathered the rest of the abused pages and tossed them in the fire, watching with satisfaction as they caught, the flames licking at the kindling. "Let's say I had my suspicions." I pointed toward the remains of the book in his hand. "The Elder's copy, but it's got your initials on the inside cover. Besides, you're not going to kill me, anyway."

He stared at the book. "And why is that?"

"Because with that antler sticking out of your gut, you're dead without me, and—even after all your big talk about suicide—you still want to live."

"What makes you think that?"

"You're still holding a gun on me, even though the thumb safety is on."

His eyes flickered with panic for a moment and then he gestured with the secured pistol. "Maybe I just don't want to be killed by you."

I poked the fire one last time before tossing the stick in with the burning pages and kindling, the fire-starter block finally giving out with a few sizzling licks of flame. "In case it's slipped your notice, I'm a sheriff, not an assassin, and I don't kill people unless it's an absolute last resort."

He gestured around us. "This doesn't constitute an absolute last resort?"

"Not till the fire gets here."

"But if I killed Pepper McKay . . ."

"You didn't kill him or Manx."

He stared at me. "What makes you say that?"

"You're not a killer."

"You're sure of that?"

"Pretty sure. With more than a quarter century on the job, I pride myself on reading people—it helps if you've got a knack for it, but years of experience don't hurt, and I can say with a certain amount of certainty that you're no killer."

"A certain amount of certainty?"

I stared back at him for a long while. "Okay, let's pass the time with a board game, shall we?"

"Excuse me?"

"If you killed Pepper, what'd you kill him with?" I shook my head. "I mean, was it Professor Plum in the ballroom with the dagger or what?"

He broke eye contact and turned toward the fire, now having fully caught and warming the place up just a bit. "A rock, I killed him with a rock."

"You're sure you want to open the envelope on that one, because you're wrong."

"You yourself said it was a rock. David told us."

"Us, huh?" Still leaning back, I stretched out my leg, wiggling my ankle to see if it felt better, which it did not. "I said it could've been, but there have been further revelations since then—but you're actually attempting to get me to believe you did it when you didn't, which leads me to another conclusion."

"And what's that?"

"That you're protecting someone." He had nothing to say to that, but I did. "Alan would be the most obvious guess because he's the expert on *The Brothers Karamazov*, but he's no killer either."

"So, you're an expert on killers?"

"Unfortunately."

"Are you one?"

"Again, unfortunately." I stood with some effort, moving toward the opening to the west and up the canyon, listening. "With the absurd literary bent that this case has taken, you could also make an argument for Ian, since he's the writer, but I can only see him committing such a crime under extreme circumstances and he doesn't seem to hold much of a grudge against Pepper."

"What are you doing?"

I edged a little farther out, hearing something in the distance but not sure what it was. "Then there's David with his military training and the fact that he had an open and aggressive grudge concerning his father, along with the fact that he and his father were both involved with the same woman."

"Do you hear something?"

"But I can't help but think that this situation is more nuanced than that." There was something I was hearing for sure, and I was having trouble differentiating it from the sound of the big tankers that had been dumping water on us—but this was different. "It was interesting because you picked up on my reference to Elder Zebrowski and the word *was*, but you didn't say anything." I turned to him. "Which does mean you already knew he was dead."

He sat there, silent.

"Which, in the very least, makes you a co-conspirator or accessory to murder." The sound was growing now, and there was no doubt that nothing man-made could make a noise of that breadth and Vesuvius-like magnitude. "Possibly three murders."

I could feel the air moving at my back, pulling in the opposite direction from which it had been blowing. I had to catch my hat to keep it from being pulled from my head.

"What did Elder Zebrowski find out?"

The campfire, finally having caught, was trying to pull itself from its flaming roots and shoot past me to join what we both knew was coming.

"He never would've been party to something like this, or is that what it was? Did he figure out what you were up to and that was the reason he stayed?"

Even the loose sand at my feet was vibrating, some of the grains lifting and being carried away, and I had to raise my voice to be heard above the din.

"That's what he wanted to talk to me about, wasn't it?"

I could again see the panic in his eyes as they cast about. He clutched his abdomen and searched for some avenue of escape. "We . . . we've got to get out of here!"

"There's nowhere to go, Rakin."

The sparks from our pitiful fire leaped from the flames like lightning bugs, swirling in the open area between us and then zipping away as the vacuum of stolen oxygen pulled at the bulk of my body like a riptide, and I fought it, taking a step toward him. "Old Testament stuff, huh? Biblical in nature, I'd say!"

His face twisted as he glanced about, now in full panic. "Aren't you afraid?"

I took another step toward him as he raised the pistol, aiming it at my chest. "No, I'm not—my conscience is clear."

There was a series of explosions and the air around us was suddenly darkened with smoke rushing by so thick it made it hard to breathe. Something out there was alive and devouring everything in its path and leaving only desolation in its wake. The wind was feeding a machine that was bound and determined to devour us too.

Maybe it was just a stagger, but Rakin moved to the far opening with a few steps before realizing that he couldn't see anything in that direction either.

The waves of heat felt like a gigantic oven, multiplying the fire's strength in the limited space of the canyon and forcing its way in the only direction where it could find fuel—toward us. Stumbling a bit farther toward the opening, I stood there only an arm's length away.

It was the only chance I was going to have to see what we were up against before we took cover back near where Borax still stood, silent as the grave.

I slowly turned, and even with the limited view of my stinging eyes, I almost immediately wished that I hadn't.

The canyon was loaded with low-grass fuel, but the canopy of trees made the flames actually move faster. The explosions we were hearing were the trees detonating from the tremendous heat that the fire was pushing before it, causing the vegetation to erupt like hand grenades, echoing off the granite walls of the canyon loud enough to deafen. The undulation of flames and the lack of oxygen made it feel as if we were underwater and could only wish that we were.

Stepping to the side, I pulled the two wet blankets from under the rocks in the dead stream where no water now flowed, and lumbered toward Rakin. "We've got to get under cover!"

He aimed the pistol toward me again. "No, we've got to run!"

I shook my head in disbelief. "Where?"

He swiped at his eyes, looking past me toward the wall of flames that were reaching out for us. "Away from it!" He lifted the S&W toward my face, and I saw that the safety was still on.

Acting as if I were turning away, I swung back around and slapped him with one of the wet blankets, watching as the pistol skittered away without firing. He fell backward over one of the boulders where he'd been sitting and I reached down, grabbing him by the collar and dragging him back toward the big mule.

Piling him against the rocks, I went to Borax and slid one of the blankets onto his withers, speaking in a low voice I wasn't sure if he could really hear, but satisfied that my tone was more of what he needed. "You're not going to like this, but it's the only way I can assure that you won't bolt on me."

His ears twitched and the eye nearest me widened as I gripped the single rein and pulled the end of the sopping blanket up over his head. "I'm not going anywhere and as a matter of fact I'm going to be right here at your big feet, and I'd appreciate it if you didn't do much dancing in the near future."

Like a statue, he stood there, but I could feel the tension in his body as all those massive muscles flexed, the rivulets of water streaming down his legs as he breathed heavily under the sodden wool.

Crouching, I dragged the sobbing Rakin toward me and took

the remaining blanket and lay flat in the wet sand, pulling him in beside me. I couldn't help but give one last glance toward the western opening, and once again wished that I hadn't.

Similar to fireworks, the blooms of fire erupted throughout the canyon like a flaming garden with seed heads of yellow, orange, and red growing with each burst. With the swirling drafts of the narrow throat of the canyon, it was as if the gigantic flames were dancing, playing with us just before the end, where it would cook us alive, or deprive us of the one thing we needed to survive, by ripping the superheated breath from our lungs.

"There's no way we're going to survive this."

Startled by my own voice, I couldn't help but choke out a laugh before pulling the blanket up and over Rakin and me. He was still crying, and I wasn't sure as to what to say to comfort him in that I wasn't feeling very comforted myself. Even under the wet blanket the sound of the fire was growing as if we were buried under a train station, but his words still reached me. "What are our chances?"

In the darkness, I turned my face toward his and raised my voice, calculating our odds but deciding to just give him the factors in our favor and leave it at that. "We're in the best spot we could hope for, surrounded by millions of tons of solid rock, which is the one thing this high-intensity fire can't destroy. We're in the wettest and narrowest part of the canyon, which means it'll likely burn right over us quickly, fully consuming fuels, and then race on down the canyon, barring any major shifts in wind patterns!"

"What happens if the wind patterns change?"

I was hoping he wouldn't ask, but there it was. "There's always a chance that if the wind becomes strong enough coming up the canyon that it could feed the fire onto itself and then it'll have nowhere to go!"

"What happens then?"

"Then the last vestiges of oxygen are going to be in this open-ended cave, where we are now . . ."

"And?"

"We cook." He started to push off from the ground, but I slapped him back down and held him there. "You go out there now, and you're dead!"

He screamed this time. "What can we do?!"

"The hardest thing in the world: We wait!" Borax moved a hoof, bumping into my shoulder and then settling. "We've got a very large canary in the coal mine with Borax, here. He's going to sense what's going on a lot sooner than we are, and as long as he stays calm and doesn't move, we don't have anything to be worried about!"

Rakin stopped scrambling and I let my mind wander for a moment, picking up the odds and ends that would distract him. "So you never heard of the Twenty Mule Team?"

He didn't answer but the fire did, pulling air through the tunnel like a scorching windpipe searching for words but finding only burned sound.

"There was this mineral they found in Nevada back in the 1880s, which was kind of rare, and until that point had to be imported from Tibet and Italy and was worth a lot of money. It was used for all kinds of applications from forging to pottery, fake teeth, glass, and medicine. But where it really gained popularity was as a laundry additive. The problem was getting it out of Death Valley and to the rail lines that were near Reno in one of the most dangerous and godforsaken broiling areas on the globe!"

He still said nothing, but I got the feeling he was listening as the wind shrieked through the living stone. I shifted my weight and pulled my arm from him.

"To make the venture worthwhile they had to haul a lot of this mineral. And at that time, this meant wagons, the largest wagons ever made. But then you had to have something that would haul that kind of weight over the mountains in temperatures over a hundred and thirty degrees."

Reaching a hand out, I patted the mule's great hoof and could feel the heat hanging in the air like a shroud. He shifted his weight, perhaps thinking my hand was something to eat, but then lifted the hoof, and all I could think was that it'd be just my luck to get trampled to death in the middle of a forest fire.

Figuring my voice might settle him a bit, I kept talking. "Mules were the only animal that could survive those types of conditions and pull that kind of weight, nearly ten tons."

To my great relief, the hoof dropped back down and settled, and I remembered a story my father had told me about the difference between a horse and a mule: A horse tangled in barbed wire will struggle and do damage to himself while a mule will calmly wait until someone comes along and releases it.

It was then that I felt the heated air lift the drying blanket and flap it on the back of my legs. Reaching behind me, I grabbed a fistful of the wool and pulled it back down, my hand thumping on the empty sand to my left where Michael Rakin had been.

Grasping around, I could feel nothing in the area where he had lain. Thinking that maybe he'd gotten confused and had crawled only a short distance, I sat up, pulling the damp blanket around my shoulders as I strained my stinging eyes to squint around in my limited view of swirling ash and smoke.

Nothing.

Borax exhaled a twin lungful of air, shuddering the blanket that covered his head.

"Easy, easy boy." Struggling to my feet, I tried to look around, but bits of flaming ash swooped in and out of the smoke-filled cavern like barn swallows from hell. I stood there like that, finally having to turn my face away and to the east for relief from the constant barrage of wind and fire, knowing what I was going to do but arguing with myself nonetheless. "If he's out there, he's dead."

Borax shifted, hearing my voice, but he still didn't move.

Now pulling the blanket over my face, I used it as a filter as I tried to breathe. "There's nothing you can do but go out there and die too."

A gust pushed me forward a step, almost in answer. "My prisoner, my responsibility."

I steadied myself with Borax's mass, pausing there a moment to reassure him before taking a step and looking down to where I could barely make out the prints from the novice's single hiking boot. They led to the left and east.

At least he'd gone away from the approaching flames, but to me it sure appeared as if, in all directions, the whole world was on fire.

Moving away from the flames, I pulled the blanket up as high as I could, glad for what moisture remained in the material. I thought about what the old firefighters used to say—how fire is dangerous but it's the smoke that gets you. At this moment I would've given anything for a P2 dust mask, a respirator, or a self-contained breathing apparatus—none of which appeared to be handy. So I did what cowboys have done for centuries and reached into my back pocket and yanked out my threadbare bandanna and began tying it closer to my face.

Finishing, I slung the pack onto my shoulder and surveyed the burning landscape and then back at Borax, slowly coming to the conclusion that if I did make it out of here alive, I wasn't coming back . . . and where did that leave the hapless animal, other than burned to death in some nameless section of Crazy Woman Canyon?

He trusted me, and he deserved better than that.

Better to die trying than abandoned and alone.

Walking back, I took the single rein in my hand and resecured the blanket, making sure it wouldn't slip from his head—no sense in both of us being scared to death.

Shuffling him toward the east entrance of our makeshift cave, I clutched the blanket with my other hand and then guided us out and into perdition.

My eyesight was limited, but I could see a thick lodgepole pine by the opening, with waves of vapor pouring from the bark. It's an old fallacy that trees explode because the sap reaches a boiling point. It's actually the humidity content of the tree that finally gets to the point at which the water has to escape and the whole thing becomes a bark-covered fragmentation grenade.

Quickly moving away from the thing as fast as I could, I stumbled through the dry streambed and brought us back onto the road, where I just stood, squinting in all directions for some way out but seeing none.

"Where would he have been stupid enough to go?" Borax whiffled and I turned to look at him, shouting to be heard over the grinding roar of the fire. "Honest, I tried putting a blanket over his head too, but obviously that didn't work."

There were flaming trees lying across the road leading east and down the canyon, with more of them slamming to the ground on the slopes around us. But fortunately the vegetation closest to the road was slighter—burning, but still small enough to avoid.

Where else could the novice have gone but in that direction? Maybe he hadn't been listening when I'd told him about the donut hole and the fact that we were completely surrounded by the fires. If he'd gone west in the canyon, then he was most certainly dead. But how far could he have gotten if he went east? I'd only turned away from him for a moment, and he wasn't in any condition to make time with an elk antler hanging out of his guts.

I was overcome with a coughing fit and figured I'd better make up my mind before I collapsed on the roadway or the heat became so unbearable that I just passed out, leaving poor Borax here to his own devices. Patting the big john mule's back, I tried to reassure him. "Just a walk in the park, ol' buddy."

He didn't respond and I moved forward at a pathetic stagger, the flat ground of the obstructed gravel road something of a relief.

The first fallen tree covered most of the roadway, but I could see where the bulk of the trunk trailed off, away from the flaming branches at the other end. It was at least something of an advantage that the lodgepoles grew to exorbitant heights, but with the bulk of their vegetation near the top of their relatively smooth and long trunks, hence the name.

The visibility remained limited to about twenty feet out, and it was continually unnerving to hear the unseen trees crashing to the ground around us. I didn't know how long it was till dusk and wasn't sure if with the amount of smoke that hung in the air that it would make any difference at all. But like anyone trapped in a continual night, I was just hoping for morning.

The ash that my blackened boots and Borax's big hooves kicked up on the roadway drifted and sullied the available air even more. Trapped under his blanketed hood, the mule blew out with a powerful sneeze, which did nothing to clear the air other than what occupied his flared nostrils.

I could've almost laughed, but there was another explosion to the right and the thundering crack and swish of two thousand pounds of burning wood that might, at any second, come crashing down upon us.

I stopped and listened as the weight of the thing dropped behind, hitting the ground with enough impact to shake the earth where we stood and pretty much finalizing the direction we were destined to go.

The heat was so airless, I was tempted to drop the oppressive blanket, but with all the flying spark and ash, it was doubtful we'd make it very far.

I almost toppled into the next obstruction, a two-way fall that crossed slightly to the left of the center of the road, its burning branches blocking the ditches on either side. "Well, hell . . ."

There were two choices: Pick a direction and commit to walking up the burning slopes and raging fire or . . . I recalled what Manx had said about the big boy, about how he would lay his jacket over a four-pole fence and that Borax would, after getting the gist, simply leap over it.

I wondered if a blanket would do the trick and certainly hoped that was the case because we were running out of options. It meant unmasking the beast, and I could only guess what he might do when confronted with the hellscape surrounding us. It was possible he'd balk and just freeze or that he'd go berserk and head for the burning hills.

Either way, I was about to find out.

Shifting my pack to my other shoulder, I slowly slid the other blanket from Borax's head.

Blink.

That was all he did. But then he cast his great chestnut eyes toward me as if to ask, What's next?

Still holding the rein with one hand, I slipped the blanket from his back and then moved toward the smoldering trunks and flipped it up to cover them. Turning back to him, I wondered what else I could do to reinforce the request, finally leading him in one direction where the branches burned and then orienting him in the other direction to let him see the conflagration on that end.

Glancing back at the bulk of the fire, still behind us but gaining on the hillsides, I stretched my collar and felt like throwing off the blanket again but knew better.

Bringing him back to the middle, I first looked at the crossed logs, which appeared to be about five feet tall at the lowest point, and then gazed at him, explaining in a reasonable voice. "That's the deal, the only way around is over, and Manx said you could jump higher than that and you won't even have me on your back."

Blink.

"I'll take that as a yes."

Stepping to his side, it was all I could do to clamber over the damp blanket and hope that his efforts in clearing the logs would be better than those I'd just exhibited.

Feeling the heat approaching, I stood there with the single rein in my hand, studying the mule as trees continued to explode and fall around us, the overpowering heat and clouds of smoke almost forcing me to retch.

Blink.

"Listen, you've got to do this or we're dead."

Blink.

Sighing, I started to climb back over the logs when he gathered his immense muscles and leaped into the air from a dead stand, slipping the rein from my hand and launching his weighty girth over the logs and almost on top of me as I did my best to scramble out of the way.

Leaning against the damp blanket and then sliding to the ground on top of my pack, I watched as he took another step, glanced around, and then pivoted, poking his big nose down in my face as if to ask, Anything else?

Blink.

"Good boy." I pet his velvety muzzle. "I won't underestimate you again, I promise."

I pushed off the ground and stood, slinging the pack onto my shoulder again and then pulling the blanket from the logs, folding it, and placing it on his back, figuring he'd seen it all now and no longer needed to have his head covered, but I most certainly was going to need a saddle blanket for want of a saddle.

Lifting my good foot up and into a cleft in the bark, I moved him sideways and clumsily threw my bad foot over his back and slid on. I could see a little better, but not much, and gigged him into a slow walk toward the next log, which must've fallen and rolled parallel to the road.

Looping to the left, we circled the blazing hulk and moved on at an estimated two miles an hour, which gave me time to think. If Rakin had headed this way, which was the only direction that made sense unless he was making good on his threats of suicide, then I was bound to find him. It was possible that he'd been crushed by a falling tree or had sidetracked into the brush and been cooked alive, but I was hoping that wasn't the case if for no other reason than I wanted answers.

Another tree fell behind us and I half turned on Borax's back to get a look at what was happening, but the only thing I could see was another bloom of yellow, separating itself from the orangey-red glow with more pursuing sparks that floated toward us like fireworks.

The road ahead was clear for as far as I could see, but the force of air currents was pushing against my back, and I began wondering if two miles an hour was going to be enough, and more important, when were we going to run into that fierce wall of flames we'd tried to outrun to the east.

At the base of the canyon were grass meadows where the streams widened into a quasi swamp, and I couldn't help but think that if the pincers of the fire on either side of the canyon ran out of fuel, they'd peter out until the one behind us met up with them—that is, if they had died down. If not, we were on our way into the angry maw of a fiery storm curtain and there would no longer be anywhere to escape to.

Hearing a strange noise ahead, I craned my neck to see, but all I could make out was more blackening smoke and stinging cinder. Borax kept his head down, avoiding the majority of the flying hindrance and perhaps keeping an eye to his feet.

I heard the noise again and reined him in to a stop. It was a low moaning coming from ahead and to the right. Gigging Borax off again, I glanced around but couldn't see anything other than another smoldering log that was blocking our way. This one was lying across the road at a 45-degree angle—and with a single hiking boot–clad foot sticking out from under it.

The trunk had gotten Rakin from behind and he lay there on his side, the mass of the log resting on the back of his obviously broken legs.

Using the blanket trick, I climbed over the trunk, figuring another two hundred and fifty pounds wasn't going to make that much difference. Nonetheless, Rakin groaned again as I landed on the other side, dropping my pack and kneeling down to get a look at him, catching a glimpse of a sobering old cross and grave monument that I recognized on the hillside.

He was burned, and it was possible that this portion of the tree had still been on fire when it landed on him. The whole left side of his face was a weeping mass of third-degree burns, his hair gone, and one ear mostly scraped away, possibly from the rough bark.

He had dug furrows in the gravel road with his burned hands, finally leaving blood trails in the earth where he had tried to drag himself out from under the log.

"Rakin?" He turned his face to me as best he could, and I would've been surprised if with the swollen eye he could make me out at all. "Can you move?"

His face fell back to the roadway, answering my question. He moaned again, trying to lift his head, and I put a hand on his shoulder to settle him. "Lie still. There isn't anything you can do."

I studied the tree trunk, every bit as big as the others, and wondered if there was anything I was going to be able to accomplish—it had to be close to two thousand pounds.

Pulling the two-way radio from my pack, I switched the thing on, adjusted the channel, and hit the toggle. "Big Goose kilo two-six, this is Sheriff Walt Longmire. Over."

Static.

"Big Goose kilo two-six, this is Sheriff Walt Longmire. Do you copy?"

Static.

"Rose, are you there?"

Static.

"Anybody? Hey, listen, if somebody can read me, I'm near the Doyle Irvan Cross Gravesite."

I gave a go at another exercise in futility, leaning my shoulder against the giant log and trying to move it. It didn't budge one bit, and what I wouldn't have given for a chainsaw with a thirty-six-inch bar or even a good double-bit ax.

Borax stuck his head over the log and studied me, probably curious as to what I was up to, and in all honesty so was I. "Think you can dead-drag two thousand pounds?" He continued to stare, his two elongated ears pivoting like an old television aerial seeking frequency. "Yeah, me neither."

Peering down the length of the fallen tree, I spotted a thick limb that had broken off into a snag on the near side, still sticking upward at a 30-degree angle—he couldn't drag it but maybe he could roll it.

The brushy top of the lodgepole had mostly burned away, but I couldn't see the base and just hoped there was an opening on the other side.

Pulling myself up, I stuffed the radio back in the rucksack and stepped over the novice, limping to the left and feeling my way along the rough trunk of the tree until I got to the ditch and could see the shattered end where the thing had exploded, still steaming, but loose.

Shuffling back, I reached down and lifted the pack, resting it on the trunk between me and my curious partner as more thunderous crashes sounded behind him, and flares of explosive fire merrily danced, reminding me that I had only so much time.

Rustling through the rucksack, I finally felt the tightly coiled length of synthetic rope and took it out, studying the orange kernmantle surface and wondering how much there was and to what kind of weight it was rated.

I stooped down again and tried to explain what I was going to try to do. "We've got to get this tree off you if we're going to get you out of here. Borax here is strong as hell but there's no way he can either lift or drag this tree, so we're going to have to try to roll it." The swollen eye looked up at me again. "There's just no other way."

His hand swiped my arm and I retrieved one of the water bottles, holding it to his face and letting him drink what he could, the majority dribbling from his mouth and onto the ground.

I sat on the trunk and swiveled my legs over, uncoiling the rope and fashioning a harness that would hopefully accommodate Borax's girth, thinking of the conversation I'd had with Manx. "Will is to grace as the horse is to the rider . . ." I studied the big animal as he listened intently. "Or mule, as it were."

We both turned our heads as another roar of consumed oxygen tugged at us as the channels of air fed the fire like a vacuum in the narrow canyon, and I fully expected the tree trunk to lift off the ground and wished it had. Instead, we were treated to an enveloping bloom of flames that reached out through the dark smoke, signaling to us that the fire was picking up speed and coming for us, and quick.

Quickly patting Borax's withers, I stood again, looping the makeshift harness over his head and across his massive chest, picking the blanket up off the trunk and stuffing it under the rope for a little cushion. "You ready? Because we've got to get going."

Blink.

"Let's go." Leading him toward the brushy end, I scrutinized the stub I was betting on and was happy to see it might've been even stouter than I'd first thought. The agonizing worry was that there might be another one down below that was lodged in the opposite direction and that this was all a great waste of much needed time.

Forming a quick ring, I wrapped it around the stub and then ran out the remainder of the rope, positioning Borax a good twelve feet from the tree—not as much as I wanted, but as much as I was going to get and as close as he wanted to be to the approaching landscape of flames.

Patting the john mule on the enormous shoulder again, I turned to have one more quick word with Rakin before we gave it the only chance we were going to get.

When I got to the spot where I'd crossed, I leaned over and was surprised to see the Smith & Wesson in Rakin's shaking hand, the thumb safety now off and the barrel aimed straight at my face. "You've got to be kidding."

"Le—" His voice broke and I watched the tears stream from his eyes, even the swollen one, cutting clean streaks onto his soot-blackened face. "Leave me."

"I can't do that."

He breathed, shoving the semiautomatic toward my face. "Shoot me, then?"

"Nope. I'm not going to lie to you. This log is going to crush your lower legs, ankles, and feet into pulp, but then I'll throw you up on Borax's back and we'll get out of here and you'll live." I leaned in, the barrel of the .45 only inches from the end of my nose. "Do you hear me? You'll live." I glanced over my shoulder and stared at the encroaching fire, threading its way toward us like destructive fingers, ripping everything in its grip and then blowing it to the wind.

"And if that's not enough to change your mind, then you better know this . . ." I faced him. "It's the worst way to die there is. The pain in the beginning is excruciating because your nerves are still alive and burning. After that—and I mean a long time after that, because those nerves don't stop sending their terrible messages easily—if you're lucky you'll die of suffocation because the blaze burns the respiratory tract, especially your lungs. You might die fast and that's best, but you might last longer than you want to, and in that case, the alveoli in your lungs—those little sacs that exchange the oxygen? Well, they're going to start filling up with the water that's being broiled out of your body and then the same thing will happen to you that happened to this tree, you'll explode from the inside out."

He stared at me with the one weeping eye from over the sights of the pistol.

"Make your choice because in a minute or two me and that mule are going to be heading out, and we won't be coming back."

The Smith & Wesson wavered for an instant and then went limp in his hand, swinging on the trigger guard around his finger as he held the thing out to me.

I took it, lowering the hammer and stuffing it in my belt. With one last look at him before turning toward Borax, I limped over to where the big mule stood, stoic as hell as he faced the fire.

I pulled at one of his elongated ears, scratching at the base. "I'll make you a deal; if you go in this direction for about four feet, I'll spin you around and we'll get the hell out of here in the other direction as fast as we can go. Deal?"

He swiveled his head and gazed at me soulfully, in what I could only perceive as complete understanding.

Urging him forward with the rein, I looked back at the rigid rope and kept the slightest pressure on the single rein before moving forward quickly to give him his head. "Haaaaaaaaaaah!"

I watched as nothing happened, except a quick prancing of position in those colossal front hooves—and then, boy, did it ever.

I played offense in a Rose Bowl back in the dark ages, and if you took every overly muscled young man on that front line and included every member of the defensive line we faced, and put all of us on one end of a rope attached to Borax, I'm pretty sure that big, beautiful boy would have dragged all of us to kingdom come.

His considerable chest expanded, and those haunches flexed, and like the unstoppable force he was, the unmovable object started to shift. I could hear the twanging strain on the rope as the trunk thumped, groaned, and slowly, agonizingly, began to roll.

I tried to ignore the screaming from where Rakin lay and exhorted Borax to keep at it. "C'mon boy, c'mon!" Lunging forward again, he dug his hooves in and the front of him came off the ground as his rear legs found purchase, rolling the log forward and off Rakin's legs and feet as the loop slipped from the limb and fell to the ground.

With the slightest pull of the rein, the big mule stopped in an instant and gave a great snort, blowing streams of mucus as he lifted his head and brayed in a lung-vibrating chorus.

Somewhat awestruck, I patted Borax, yanking the rope harness from him and over his head, still holding the one rein and leading him over to where Rakin lay unconscious.

With no other choice, I lifted him up, dangling his broken legs as I climbed over the log and carried him, draping him across Borax's waiting back. Not sure of what was ahead of us, I coiled the rope and stuffed it in the rucksack, slipping the straps over my shoulders. Taking the single rein again, I limped Borax to the broken end of the log and navigated us through the dry ditch before leading the big mule back onto the road.

Taking one last look back up the canyon, I froze for a moment, thinking the smoke must've been getting to my eyes and that my perspective was getting a little confused. The flames seemed to be a lot closer than the last time I'd checked—a lot closer.

"Oh, hell . . ."

Feeling the superheated gust in my face, I had my answer—the wind currents had changed, or the force of the fire had altered them itself. Either way, the thing was moving down the canyon like a blowtorch and would be on us in minutes.

I tried to speak to Borax in the most reassuring voice I could muster. "I know you're not built for speed, and neither am I, but I know for a fact that you're going to be able to get us out of this canyon faster than I ever could."

Leading him over to the log we'd just gone around, I sidled him to the fallen trunk and turned to study the fire, the base only about forty feet away with towering flames that leaned out and over us like a tsunami. He saw it too, and for the first time pulled up and away as I reined him in and stood eye to eye with him, peering into those big soulful eyes. "I need one more miracle today, old buddy, and you're the only one that can do it. I'm going to climb on your back and then it's all up to you."

He pulled again but I was able to convert it into moving his weighty rear toward the log, or maybe he did understand and was willing to go along with anything that went in any direction away from the all-encompassing hellhole.

Throwing a leg over the broad back just behind where I'd placed Rakin, I hoisted the young man up onto my lap as best I could and just hoped that whatever happened next I'd be able to keep us in the saddle or lack thereof.

Borax pivoted again, and this time I was certain he was getting a better look at that fire behind and above us as I loosened the rein the way I had when I'd urged him to roll the tree trunk and yelled at the top, middle, and bottom of my hoarse voice, "Haaaaaaa!"

It was only a four-hundred-pound load he was carting rather than the two thousand pounds of the lodgepole pine, and did he ever put the difference on display. His haunches bunched like they had before, but there was no instant of stillness this time, only a 30-degree launch, like a Saturn V rocket, and for a moment I thought we were literally going to fly out of that canyon like winged Pegasus.

Trying to not flip off his back, I wasn't prepared for what happened next: Rakin and I whiplashed forward, crashing onto his neck as the giant's front hooves hit the hard surface of the graveled road and added their own momentum.

I never would've thought that the big guy could settle into any kind of comfortable gallop approaching steady, but he did. It wasn't the smoothest ride I'd ever had, but considering his and our collective girth, it was nothing short of astounding.

I risked a glance behind and could see the tides of fire that were still gaining on us and then quickly circled back to the road ahead, where the smoke still limited our sight. I figured that under any circumstance Borax could probably see better than I could and as it turned out, I was right.

Another log lay across the road, but the big mule didn't hesitate, simply elevating over the still flaming wood in an elongated lope that carried us clear before encountering another and doing the same thing over again.

We hit the ground a little harder this time and I struggled to keep Rakin centered on my lap, but that appeared to be the least of our problems, in that, with the prevailing wind at our back, the smoke was clearing ahead of us, and I had to admit that I didn't like what I was seeing—nothing but fire.

Even Borax balked at this one, skidding to a stop and pivoting to the right before skittering wild-eyed and back up the road for a view that he liked even less.

Drawing hard on the rein, I circled him around in the direction I knew we had to go and then sat there looking over his head at the distance, thinking about how we'd almost made it and feeling heartsick.

We couldn't have been any more than a mile from the eastern entrance of the canyon, but it might as well have been a million as we sat with one forest fire blocking our way and another gaining on us like a wind-powered battering ram.

I wheeled Borax around again in a hopeless shot at seeing some kind of escape, but there was nothing in any direction. Through the vapored smoke you could see flames like hellacious apparitions reaching for us, ready to carry us into those lakes of sulfurous fire.

Swallowing, I choked and wasn't sure if it was from the smoke and soot or the realization that this was it, and for all my efforts we were about to die.

Urging enough voice I prepared to apologize to Borax for what I'd done to us when I became aware of a chattering noise. Looking down, I could see that Rakin was still out and that it wasn't him.

The noise was at it again, strange sounding.

Sliding a strap off, I reached into my rucksack and pulled out the two-way as J. R. Rose's voice spoke. Static. "Sheriff Walt Longmire, this is Big Goose kilo two-six. Over."

"Oh, Canada . . . Am I happy to hear you!"

Static. "Happy to be of service, Sheriff! There are a lot of people out here worried about you!"

Struggling to hold Borax back, I let him circle to the left. "Hey, I don't mean to be rude, but you wouldn't be anywhere in the vicinity with a couple thousand gallons of water, would you?"

Static. "We're winging our way over from Lake De Smet as we speak. What's your location?"

"About a mile up from the east entrance."

Static. "Can you be more exact?"

"Not really."

Static. "It'll be on the LED of your radio."

"I'll be damned." Holding the thing out, I gazed at the small screen. "Have you been talking to my undersheriff, Rose? We're at 44 18.4974, -106 84.9588, and if you could drop to the east on the fiery front just ahead of us?"

Static. "You watch us, but we'll be coming in low and coming in hot, and then we're going to drop down to 85 knots to pinpoint this drop. The water we're carrying is going to open only a narrow corridor, but then you've got to get through it fast before it closes on you, so be ready."

Borax reared just enough to get his front hooves off the ground as I pulled him back and circled to glimpse behind us where the constant roar of the fire continued to gain ground, but below it I could hear a low thrumming noise from the northeast.

Placing my hand down on Borax's neck, I patted him as he finally submitted to standing still. "Stay put, we're liable to get wet but I'd rather take a quick shower than be quick-fried to a crackly crunch."

The drone of the engines grew as the CL-415 changed direction and now sounded as if it were flying directly toward us and coming fast.

Straightening Rakin in my lap in preparation, I patted the big mule again. "Easy, easy boy."

He heard it now and began backing away with his head raised, but I gigged him with my heels, and he stood steadfast.

There are moments in your life when things just seem to happen in slow motion, like a scene in a movie, when your mind is moving so fast that reality simply can't keep up, and that's what happened next. One instant there was nothing but the blackened sky and the wisping strands of flame that were cresting and readying to crash down upon us like a breaker and all I could think was—We're done.

Then it happened, darkness suddenly swirling like twin drain holes in a skyward sink, pulling the smoke and boring through it with two turboprop engines having a combined 4,600 horsepower. The pointed yellow-and-red nose piercing the darkness as the whirling, serrated black gave way to a mechanized phoenix carrying six metric tons of water.

Everything was happening so slowly that I could count the

props on the engines and thought I could even see the reflective sunglasses on the pilot's and J. R. Rose's faces in the cockpit.

The plane discharged the water like a full-blown waterfall, and it was as if the thing simply hung there in the air, delivering the deluge. The cloudburst expanded in the air, seeming to occupy the entirety of the canyon, but the thundering impact was reserved for the road ahead, and when the water hit, it was like a liquid bomb going off.

Ducking my head, I held Borax tight as he brayed loud enough to challenge the engines of the firefighting plane.

And like that, it was gone.

Raising my head, I looked down the canyon as a perfectly rainbowed mist hung in the air, creating a tunnel in the flames, and I knew what we had to do next.

"Haaaaaaaa!"

He'd been waiting, maybe his whole life for this moment, and now that it was here, Borax blew out of the gates like Man o' War at the bell and shot through that tunnel of settling mist and water. Spraying mud and gravel, he didn't slip once and, in an instant, we blew through that encompassing fire like it had never even been there.

Keeping my head tucked in close to Borax's neck, I clutched Rakin, and we thundered into a parchment of blackness where the fire had charred the landscape like a charcoal sketch, and we were the sharpened pencil streaking out and beyond the margins.

Galloping along, I raised my head to see the landscape beginning to change as living color returned to the terrain and the smoke dissipated, enabling me for the first time in a long while to breathe relatively clean air.

Turning just enough to see the curtain of flames closing between the canyon walls like the end of a tragic five-act play, I leaned in and patted Borax's neck as he slowed to a lope, still carrying us at a good rate of speed until the S curve, cantering past the abandoned Pinto and depositing us back at the O-Kay Ranch and the remarkably undamaged lodge.

I veered the mule into the corral. He slowed to a stop as we entered the breezeway, and I couldn't for the life of me summon the energy to slide off, so I just sat there breathing, the effort lifting my shoulders and then settling them again.

Standing there in the dying light, he swiveled his great elongated head and eyed me as if to say—We made it.

"Yep, we did." Pushing Rakin off my lap and onto the mule's back, I slid off and rested my boots on the ground, placing the pack down near the stall partition and my head on Borax's shoulder, just standing there for a very long while. I'd just started to push off when I felt a tug and turned to find a tall, gaunt man in a robe pointing Manx's S&W .45 firearm at my midriff. "Imagine meeting you here."

Brian Schiffer, the abbot deputy, had a smile on his narrow face beneath his prodigious nose. "You knew?"

"I figured." I took a breath. "How did you know we'd be here?"

"They've been listening to you on the radio, even when you couldn't hear them, and I took a chance that you'd make it out." He gestured toward Rakin. "With him."

Taking a step forward, I placed a hand on Rakin's leg. "I knew he didn't have it in him, but you do, don't you?"

Schiffer stepped back past Borax's substantial hindquarters, keeping the distance between us. "Years ago I wanted the role of prior, but Elder Zebrowski made me the Master of Novices and then the roundsman. It's the most despised position at the monastery but I had the opportunity to pick a cohort in my experiments. It began as a joke, but then the more Michael and I talked about it, the more we thought it'd be fun to see if we could get away with it—punishing Alan with the very book in which he'd made a lifelong study."

"So, you talked him into it?"

"It suited my purposes."

"So, you killed Pepper McKay, figuring that no one could connect you to the act?" I moved a little to the right, forcing him to step away. "And then you drugged Manx and killed him because he was figuring things out."

He smiled, extending the gun toward my face. "It began as an intellectual exercise, but I soon reasoned that it might be an excellent end to my means. Like most things, killing gets easier the more you do it."

"So they tell me."

"I thought about running, but with Michael gone, there really wasn't anyone to connect me to all of this."

"Except me."

"Yes."

"Do you mind if I pull your partner off here? He's got an antler stuck in him."

Gesturing with the compact .45, he motioned me toward Rakin. "As you wish, but I'm going to kill both of you and then set fire to the barn."

Sliding the young man off, I placed him on the ground and then stood to face Schiffer, who took another step back, placing the big mule's rear between us. "But Elder Zebrowski also discovered what you were up to, and you killed him?"

His face was still. "When I saw you'd noticed the smothering marks on the Elder's face I thought you knew." He adjusted his wire-rimmed glasses and studied me. "It was inevitable, but it also suited my purposes of becoming the abbot. Eventually Elder Zebrowski was going to exile me, at best. He was over a hundred years old and it was time."

"How does someone rise to your level of theological pursuit and yet remain completely morally bankrupt?"

"Does it seem that way?"

"Yes, it does."

"I suppose that after a lifetime of contemplation, the acts didn't seem so horrible." He re-aimed the pistol, again training it on my face. "I have to admit that I thought you'd done me an inordinate favor by going after my young cohort in the fire."

"Two birds with one stone?"

"Exactly."

"Sorry to disappoint you." I reached over, petting Borax's nose. "This big guy had a lot to do with it."

"Stupid animal." He pointed with his pistol toward my sidearm, still safely holstered at my hip. "Your gun, please. There's no sense in making this any more unpleasant than it's already become."

"Oh, I don't think it can get much worse—but then again, maybe it can." I reached up under Borax's great chin and scratched.

Just as it had in this exact spot before, the john mule's massive right rear hoof kicked out with the speed of lightning and about as much force, catching Schiffer square in the chest as he and the pistol went flying in opposite directions.

I watched as he hit the ground, landing flat on his back before sliding to a stop in the sawdust and just lying there motionless, staring at the rafters of the old barn, where the morning light crept through the cracks in the board-and-batten like God appearing in a Cecil B. DeMille motion picture.

Walking over, I retrieved the pistol and then knelt by him as his eyes bugged out, the wire-rimmed glasses comically crooked on his face. Gasping, he choked, trying to catch something of his breath and failing miserably.

I adopted a casual and conversational manner, lowering my voice as if we were in a confessional. "A wise young man once told me, don't ever insult a mule—because they never forget."

# EPILOGUE

"Cracked him like a lobster and split his sternum in half, but he'll make it." Vic opened our office door and held it for me as I continued at a slower pace. "That HP Wilson is over at the hospital keeping guard on him as we speak."

Still covered in grime, I followed her, limping up the office stairwell and trying to keep the weight off my sprained ankle. "Couldn't have happened to a nicer guy."

She stopped two steps ahead of me to turn and look me in the eye. "You do realize that without the timely intervention of J. R. Rose and the Canadians, you'd be dead?"

"Yep."

She examined me from under the brim of my hat. "And you're not going to do stupid shit like that ever again, right?"

"Yep."

Straightening, she cocked her hips to one side, resting her fists at her gun belt. "Why don't I believe you?"

"Um . . . Previous experience?"

"Hmm . . ." She continued up and into the main office where Dog waited at the top of the stairs, tail wagging, and Henry sat on Ruby's stool talking to Maxim Sidorov.

The Russian was the first to study me with his one eye, rubbing his wayward mop as if he had to stimulate all the hair on his head before speaking. "So, it was all power grab by abbot deputy to take Elder's place?"

Vic crossed to the counter as I sat on the bench by the stairs, scratching Dog's noggin as he rested the full weight of his head on my knee. "No, I think it started out as an outrageous literary exercise but then transmogrified into punishment for Alan and an opportunity for Schiffer." I sighed. "That's the usual progression: thinking about a crime, talking about a crime, and then committing said crime."

Vic interrupted. "But the kid, Rakin, he didn't kill anybody."

I looked at all of them. "He was complicit by abetting and assisting, and he lied, which makes him an accessory, but no, he didn't physically kill anyone." I studied my ankle and asked about the young monk. "What did Doc Nickerson say about the kid's legs?"

"He said he couldn't be sure but that he'd probably never walk again."

I said nothing.

"Walt, you got him out and he's alive."

Sidorov, realizing the subject needed changing, held up some papers. "I have read extended essay by Boris Reitman who wrote that 'convincing interpretation' of *The Brothers Karamazov* was put forth in short book by Russian author Alexander Razumov. In Reitman essay, he summarizes Razumov's theory that novice friend of third Karamazov son is mastermind of killing old man for money in house, but that he has accomplice."

"As it turns out he did, if not for the money."

Sidorov held extended a single finger in the air like a baton. "Yes, but not the accomplice I would assume from book."

"There's no character version of Brian Schiffer in the novel?"

"There is, but I do not believe Dostoyevsky meant for him to be killer."

Leaning back against the wall with a thump, I stared at him. "Then who?"

"It is my believe that if Dostoyevsky had been able to finish second and third part of the trilogy, that would have been revealed that murderer was not illegitimate son Smerdyakov or friend of novice, but was Captain Snegiryov, who Dmitri pummels in street."

"The father of the crippled child, Ilyusha."

"You remember character?"

I shook my head. "I remember wondering why the two characters were in the novel."

"Exactly! There is no reason for characters unless comes to fruition later in story. Here is potential narrative: After Dmitri beats old staff captain, Snegiryov, in streets after pulling him from bar by beard, Snegiryov kills the old man, Fyodor, and acquires money from house. Snegiryov then puts blame of murder on Dmitri, which satisfies Snegiryov for his earlier public humiliation and desire to support of his impoverished family."

I looked at the Cheyenne Nation, Vic, and then the Russian. "That's pretty good detective work."

He shrugged. "Meh . . . Is all hypothesis since Dostoyevsky carried secrets of finished plot to grave."

"Okay, so for those of us who didn't get the syllabus on nineteenth-century Russian literature or just don't particularly give a shit?" Vic leaned against the dispatcher's counter. "What happens to the O-Kay Ranch at this point?"

I wondered absently if I was going to be able to stay awake long enough to take a shower. "I would imagine Con and Kat Ryan will end up buying it."

"And they'll keep Lynn and Gary on?"

"I'm sure."

She studied me. "What's the matter?"

I slumped back on the bench, taking off my hat and staring up at the delicate design of the pressed-tin ceiling. "It's all just so abstract, stupid, and petty."

Vic glanced at Henry and Sidorov, and then back at me before making her way over to the mini fridge and pulling out four cans of Rainier. Sauntering over, she popped the top of one and handed it to me. "How long have you been in law enforcement?"

"Most of my life, but I keep hoping that our species will evolve."

"Yeah, good luck with that."

Continuing to almost suffocate from the smell of smoke still emanating from my clothes, I took a sip of the beer as she delivered the others. "Where are we on the fire?"

The Cheyenne Nation picked up the conversation. "Your friend, the national commander of the Interagency Fire Center, says they have got it about eighty percent under control. Once it blew itself down into the canyon, it burned out all the available fuel and then started dying down."

"And the area where we were trying to dig in?"

"Completely burned out."

"So, we would've died?"

"Quite possibly."

I raised my beer in salute. "Thank goodness for Borax."

"Yes." The Cheyenne Nation stood, swallowing his beer in one gulp, and then walked over to me. "You should get that ankle looked at."

"I figure they've got enough to do over at the hospital tonight, so I'll just limp over there tomorrow morning and get it x-rayed."

He patted my shoulder and then started down the stairs. "Take a shower and then get some rest. We've got a celebratory dinner with the state's new attorney general at the end of the week."

Vic took another swig of her beer and walked over, sitting on the bench beside me. "C'mon, let's go home."

"I can't."

"Why the hell not?"

I indicated Sidorov, still seated on Ruby's stool, drinking his beer. "Him."

"Fuck him."

I sighed. The exertion—it was far more than I was prepared for. "I've barely got enough energy to make it downstairs and take a shower and then get back up here and collapse in one of the holding cells." I turned to gaze at her, thinking how lovely she was. "Take Dog and go home. I'll be fine, just bring me breakfast in the morning—not doughnuts."

She leaned in and kissed me on my soot-covered lips and I thought about changing my mind. "No doughnuts, cross my fucking heart."

She stood, patting her leg as Dog studied me questioningly.

"Go."

He did with a parting glimpse, and I listened as the two of them made their way down the steps and exited through the front door, the soft hiss of the hydraulics sealing the building as Sidorov and I sat there looking at each other. "You know, I'm starting to soften to the idea of you living in that apartment above Ruby's garage."

He smiled, the soul patch under his lower lip kicking sideways. "Perhaps you are beginning to trust of me?"

"No, I don't think that's it."

He studied me for a longer while and then stood, coming around the counter and standing before me, sipping his beer. "I was waiting for others to go."

The silence between us was more than palpable. "You've got information for me concerning Ruth One Heart?"

"Yes."

I stared back at him. "Well, I've got one more chore before I settle in for the night. Do you want to come along with me, it'll only take a minute." I reached a hand out. "Help me up?"

Setting his beer on the bench, he grabbed my hand with both of his and then slowly pulled me to a standing position. Shaking his head, he patted my shoulder. "You are very big man, perhaps what it takes to surround a heart such as yours."

Turning, I tossed my empty beer can in the trash and tromped down the stairs, pushing open the heavy glass door as a resounding hammering rang from the horse trailer attached to my truck.

Stopping, he stood there in the center of the parking lot, looking at the trailer with a great deal of alarm. "You have grizzly bear in trailer?"

"Something like that."

The pounding increased in volume and rapidity as I unlatched the back and swung the door wide. Stepping inside, I untied the extended lead from the tie-off and wheeled the big beast around, walking him out of the trailer, his giant steel shoes striking the surface of the concrete and causing sparks.

Sidorov backed away, obviously not used to being around animals like Borax. "He is friendly?"

Pulling a picket stake and a six-pound sledgehammer from the trailer, I led the john mule over to the grass lawn of the county courthouse. "Overly. Just don't scratch under his chin."

Sidorov trailed along and I handed him the lead before driving the heavy stake into the ground, then taking the end and clipping it to the swivel at the top. "There you go, big guy, a full twenty-four-foot circle of beautifully irrigated grazing."

Sidorov watched as Borax dropped his head and began ripping the grass by heaving mouthfuls. "Body politic will be happy with tearing up of lawn?"

I retrieved a bucket from the trailer, filling it from a spigot at the side of the courthouse and setting it where Borax could reach it easily. "They can bill me."

We stood there watching him eat, the munching noise very soothing in the late-night darkness. "So what's the word?"

He hugged himself in a bid to get warm as the temperature plummeted. "You remember name Anatoly Mogilevich?"

I thought about it but came up with nothing. "Is this another character from *The Brothers Karamazov*, because I'm beginning to lose track."

"No." He shook his head, continuing to watch the mule eat. "No, was man who I forced to shoot his murderer son after sending me to prison."

"Oh right, the oligarch, billionaire, crime lord." I turned to him. "So, he's working with the Regis family?"

"They have mutual of interests." He shoved his tattooed hands into his jeans. "They say that if I am to produce you, that all is forgiven."

"Produce me, how?"

I joined him in looking at the blinking streetlights of Main and thought for a second I might've even seen a few flurries of snow in the repetitious yellow light; a minuet of circling warnings within a warning. "We must prepare."

"For what?"

He stepped forward, and I was sure he could see the snowflakes dancing in the light, whether they were really there or not, and his voice sounded hollow and flat. "We are going to ends of earth."